# THE SILVER SCAR

# THE SILVER SCAR

## BETSY DORNBUSCH

Talos Press books may be purchased in bulk at special discounts for sales promotion, corporate gifts, fund-raising, or educational purposes. Special editions can also be created to specifications. For details, contact the Special Sales Department, Talos Press, 307 West 36th Street, 11th Floor, New York, NY 10018 or info@skyhorsepublishing.com.

Talos Press is a trademark of Skyhorse Publishing, Inc. ®, a Delaware corporation.

Visit our website at www.talospress.com.

10 9 8 7 6 5 4 3 2 1

Library of Congress Cataloging-in-Publication Data is available on file.

Cover design by Claudia Noble
Cover illustration by Chris McGrath

Print ISBN: 978-1-940456-78-2
Ebook ISBN 978-1-940456-79-9

Printed in the United States of America

Deus vult! God wills it!

# ONE

A sh blackened the pentacle graven in the tombstone, but all the angels and crosses in the churchyard cemetery had been scrubbed clean recently. To Trinidad, whose family lay under the Wiccan marker, this reminder of Christian hatred for his abandoned religion twisted his typical low-grade anxiety into a coil of pain in his gut. He tightened the magnetic latches on his armor, wishing he'd drawn any duty this morning but pulpit guard.

Bells rang a strident call to mass, pulling his attention away from the cemetery nestled near the door of the church barracks. Trinidad glanced at the twin towers fronting the sanctuary. Two centuries before, architects had used crenels as decoration to enhance the gothic look of the church buildings. They'd since been reinforced with composite shielding to protect the marksmen positioned there.

Icy wind tugged at his black woolen archwarden's cloak and stung his face as he strode across the churchyard from the barracks to the sanctuary. Overhead, a thick bank of clouds threatened snow. To his left, parish archwardens flanked the gates to the street, looking like black-draped statues as they greeted congregants with unsmiling courtesy. Adults muttered in tense knots under the shelter of the cloister. He paused his trek at the meditation labyrinth in the center of the yard. Children giggled along the winding paths of flagstone laid into gravel.

"Trinidad!" They surged toward him, little hands pulling on his legs and sword belt.

He ignored their parents' frowns and tossed a handful of coins. They flashed like shrapnel against the gray light as they scattered over the labyrinth. The children scrambled on the ground, grabbing and squealing. But one coin landed on the low wall topped with memorial bricks.

Trinidad moved toward the wall, his lips framing the name carved into the brick beneath the coin. Israel. The world conspired to keep his family in his thoughts this day. He bent and pocketed the coin. The boy who had claimed it was dead.

The bells ceased. Incense and cavernous organ music wafted through the churchyard. The kids ran to their parents and he hurried to the sanctuary, checking his weaponry with numb fingers: sword secure in its scabbard, knives in wrist bracers, pistol snug at the small of his back. Inside the narthex, he had to struggle to make his way through the gathering processional. Two women in the center aisle stepped aside at his approach. He inclined his head politely. They nodded back but whispered in his wake. Even though he'd been inparish a dozen years, they never ceased gossiping about Trinidad, the son of ecoterrorist suicide bombers who had taken sixteen Christian souls, the Wiccan orphan turned Christian archwarden.

The air in the stone church felt cold and damp, but Trinidad's skin prickled with sweat beneath his armor and the cloak draping his shoulders. Congregants crowded into the pews and quieted. Feeling eyes on his back, Trinidad genuflected to the altar, drew his sword, and kissed the blade before raising it in offering to Christ. Then he took his place before the pulpit. He realized he was holding his breath and exhaled.

A change in organ music cued the procession to begin. Led by an acolyte carrying the golden cross, it centered on the visiting bishop. Her Grace had graying hair and rigid posture. But it was the silver scar that captured Trinidad's attention. It slashed her forehead like a lopsided crown, glowing in the dim sanctuary. Candlelight rippled through it, turning it into a molten sterling stream.

The rumors had proved true. Trinidad, his blood roaring, struggled to remain still. There was only one way she could have such a scar: someone had roved Bishop Marius to the Barren. But that was impossible. As far as he knew, the only person alive with the magic to rove her there was himself.

B ishop Marius' voice boomed from the pulpit at Trinidad's back. "The angel ordered crusade against the heretics. I, in my pride, dared to argue. It smote me with its sword, leaving me scarred, and bent me to God's will."

She paused, every eye in the sanctuary locked on her. Trinidad felt a frown forming and schooled his face back to blank as she continued.

"And so, I argue today as Saint Bernard argued for crusade centuries ago: The enemies of the cross have raised blaspheming heads, ravaging with the edge of the sword the land of promise. Alas! they rage against the very shrine of the Christian faith with blasphemous mouths." She launched into lengthy accountings of

Indigo raids, ecoterr attacks, the recent church bombing in Denver, slave raids, and the heresy of Wiccan magic.

The very magic she had used to get to the Barren and earn that scar.

She made the case that if they had the crusade well underway before Lent they could expect to make an official end on Palm Sunday. She asked them to imagine celebrating Easter with such purity and triumph.

At last she stepped down from the pulpit to lay her hand on Trinidad's armored shoulder. His fingers tightened on the hilt of his sword, but he stared unblinking down the center aisle as she quoted from the ancient call to crusade:

"But now, O brave knight, now, O warlike hero, here is a battle you may fight without danger, where it is glory to conquer and gain to die. Take the cross and you shall gain pardon for every sin."

She released him and turned back to the altar to prepare for communion.

Trinidad eased a breath from his chest. Pardon for every sin. Tempting thought, but he would find no salvation in lies and violence. Those days were long past.

Never mind. His vows to Christ bound him to protect and obey the clergy. He had to have faith that God would see the truth out. In the meantime, he would take the cross alongside the rest of his order. He would kill who they required him to kill. And he would say nothing as the heretical witchcraft from his past became a weapon in the bishop's crusade.

Father Troy and the bishop joined the final procession and disappeared amid the crowd. Their archwardens followed, the long white crosses on the backs of their cloaks glowing in the candlelight. When the last of the parishioners filed through into the narthex, Trinidad slid his sword into its scabbard and rolled the stiffness from his shoulders.

Dressed in homespun acolyte robes, his foster brother Wolf tended the altar, folding the cloths and collecting the melted candles. No one knew quite how old he was, but he'd grown tall enough to look Trinidad in the eye and his shoulders filled Trinidad's old practice armor. His shaggy hair mostly hid the red burn scars that mottled the right side of his face and neck.

"Wolfie," Trinidad said. "Go rest. You look like death."

Wolf had been fighting a fever for two days. His good cheek flamed as crimson as his scars and he coughed constantly. He picked up another candle-nub and scrunched his runny nose. "Practice. Roman'll kill me if I skip."

Trinidad frowned and nodded as Father Troy, his white beard stretching around a smile, came down to join them. He gave Wolf a one-armed hug. "Quick work, lad. Well done. Go on, now. I need to speak with your brother."

Wolf looked at Trinidad. "About what?"

"You heard him," Trinidad said.

"Yes, Father." Wolf sighed and went out the side door.

"I know what you're thinking," Father Troy. "But it's not ashrot. Wolf is too young. Besides, Roman will send him to the infirmary if he gets bad."

Trinidad suppressed a snort. A novice had to be practically bleeding to death before Roman would let him out of practice.

The priest gave him a close look. "Tired this morning?"

"Wolf's coughing kept me up." Wolf woke screaming from

bad dreams almost nightly now. But Father Troy had enough on his mind these days—the crusade and his cancer—and Wolf had begged Trinidad not to say anything to anyone.

"Come. Sit," Father Troy said.

Trinidad eased down onto the steps leading up to the altar, elbows on his knees, facing Father Troy, who levered himself onto a pew.

"We're not going to Denver today," Father Troy said.

"But you have to, you—" He pressed on despite the priest's frown. "—you need your treatment."

"I must stay here. Her Grace is auditing the parish prior to placing a new rector this week."

"This week?"

"She wants the new rector to take the cross right away, as she assembles the army. You realize Denver Parish is already gathering at the south wall."

For a crusade based on a lie. He hadn't dared a close look at the bishop's scar, but he knew where it came from. No angel, for sure. But who had learned the magic to rove? Everyone who knew it was dead, save Trinidad.

The truth rushed from his mouth without his planning it. "That scar isn't from an angel."

A beat. Another. Father Troy's eyes narrowed. "You're accusing Her Grace of lying?"

Trinidad lowered his gaze at his priest's sharp tone. Didn't he even wonder about the scar? It was all the talk in parish. "No, Father."

"Mystical meetings aside, she makes a good argument for war. Rumors have it the Indigos are out for blood since Roi d'Esprit went missing."

"Sounds like Indigos, blaming us with no proof." Trinidad knew the Indigo leader was dead. Roi d'Esprit had dared openly threaten Father Troy, and rumors of an assassination plot had become too prevalent to ignore. Trinidad had killed Roi and hidden the body far in the mountains in a deep cave. Indigos never strayed past the front range and the cave was too well concealed even if they did.

Troy leaned forward with a weary frown. "It makes an old man worry for his son, Trin."

Trinidad hoped his dark skin, part of his Mexican heritage, hid the flush warming his cheeks. "I've had a price on my head since I took vows, Father, like all archwardens. Indigo attacks are no reason to worry." Or crusade. Not now Roi was dead. His daughter seemed much more restrained, so far.

"How about ecoterrs setting bombs at the power plant last night? Is that reason enough to worry?"

Trinidad couldn't help raising his brows. "They were Wiccan?"

Father Troy nodded. "Most of them were captured."

"Even so, it's no reason to go to war."

Wind whistled around the metal plating protecting the stained-glass windows as Father Troy fixed Trinidad with the steely glare that used to root him to the floor as a kid. "If you don't want war, son, you should have left it alone."

Trinidad reminded himself he was no longer that kid. But still, chills prickled his spine. "Left what alone, sir?"

Father Troy leaned forward and rubbed at his arthritic knee, bunching his vestments and then letting them fall smooth. "Wiccan magic."

The prickles turned to a wire brush.

Father Troy searched his face. "There've been disturbing rumors. Accusations. Concerning you."

Suspicion of heresy was far, far worse than Father Troy learning he had killed Roi d'Esprit. "You can't believe that."

"The diocese claims to have a witness."

Trinidad shook his head. "Not true or I'd be in chains right now."

Father Troy lowered his gaze to his folded hands. "It might be meant more as a warning. Your adamancy against crusade has not gone unnoticed among your order."

"They have to know I'll fight as I always have, as I've sworn to do."

"Will you?" The astute, watery gaze lifted to hold Trinidad's. "It is, after all, your people who will die. I could hardly blame you for refusing to take the cross."

Trinidad had already taken the cross, tattooed on head and hands for all to see. He saw no use in pinning another one to his cloak. "My people, yes. Christians will die in the crusade. Archwardens will die."

Father Troy's face softened. "It's perfectly understandable that you might succumb to the temptation of your old ways. Maybe you thought you could prove something, maybe you thought you could help your coven survive. I am sure your intention was pure, but witchcraft, Trin? I fear for your soul."

"Father! I didn't do anything! I haven't worked the craft, not since—" Trinidad broke off at a movement in the shadowy narthex. He realized too late how his voice echoed against the stone walls of the sanctuary.

"Since we don't have to go to Denver, you can help Roman

with fight practice. That way you can keep an eye on Wolf." Father Troy rose and headed back to the narthex, his quick gait belying the arthritic cant to his body and weakness from the disease that would soon take his life.

Trinidad rubbed his hand over his mouth and clenched his fingers into a fist. The day had dredged up long-buried memories. When he and his childhood friend Castile had been kids, roving through other peoples' dreams seemed a game. The otherworldly silver graveyard they called the Barren was their private play-ground, until one of the older kids heard them talking about their secret place and tried to beat the truth of it from Castile. Trinidad had put the kid's curiosity to bed with his first real violence. But it tarnished the Barren's allure. He looked at the silver scar on his left palm—so small and darkened with age no one had ever noticed it. He thought of it rarely—he and Castile panting from pain as they stabbed their palms, smeared their blood together, and swore never to tell anyone about the Barren. The graveyard sand had burned as it seared their wounds closed.

That blood vow had made it strangely simple to forget the Barren ever existed once he'd come inparish. Forgetting and the grace of Christ were the only ways a boy witch could shed the craft for his new faith. But Trinidad was no longer that boy, and Bishop Marius, too, now bore a scar healed by the silver sand.

The bishop. She made no secret of her hatred for witches, hav-ing lost her husband and child to a Wiccan ecoterrorist's bomb. She'd never admit to engaging in magic. No wonder she'd made up the story about the angel.

And Trinidad could say nothing. Accusing a bishop of lying or other sin without proof was high treason against the Church, and the only proof he had on offer required him to draft spells, heresy punishable by death.

Bishop Marius obviously didn't expect his archwarden vows to bind his tongue. She had already taken the offensive, dishonoring him with rumor and innuendo. If the bishop was willing to use private lies to destroy him and public lies to start a war, she was more than willing to condemn Trinidad for heresy. The bones of deception had already been laid.

# TWO

R eine d'Esprit climbed the ladder of the guard tower near the gates of her Indigo freehold. The Wiccan called Castile sat on his horse outside, gazing upward, steadying a big, awkward bundle tied across the horse's rump with one hand. His fringed scarf hung loose around his neck, accommodating her tribe's custom of baring faces to indicate respect.

Her spearguards muttered among themselves.

"Fuckin brought us a body."

"Knowin Castile, it's a bomb."

That was just a joke, really, even with the Wiccan's hard-won reputation as an ecoterr assassin.

Reine sighed. "That's no bomb. Let him in."

One of the spearguards signed a salute in her direction. "Will do, Reine d'Esprit."

Hinges squealed as the gates swung open. Reine climbed down the ladder to greet him. Castile rode through, slung a leg over his horse's hindquarters, and slipped to the ground. He heaved the bundle, stiff, man-shaped, and bigger than him, over his shoulder.

"We might want to do this in private," he said to her.

She turned and led him to her house.

Castile followed, unsteady under his heavy load. He didn't ask for help and no one offered, but all eyes followed their progress. She opened the door for him and let him pass into the cold front room. No fire burned, not even in Reine d'Esprit's hearth. They saved their scavenged combustibles for the common house where the children slept.

Castile laid the body on her table with a thud and rubbed the cold from his bare hands.

A knife of fear twisted in Reine's middle. She caught her breath as Castile undid the rope and pulled the fabric free. Face waxy in death, Roi d'Esprit's blue eyes peeked between half-open lids. Castile kept ripping the fabric, baring her father's naked body from his stiff face to his little worm of a prick. She barely noticed any of that, though, for the Christian cross carved into his chest and stomach.

Reine stumbled forward, but Castile caught her arm. "I'm sorry, Reine. I thought you would want him back."

She closed her eyes too late. The profane symbol defacing her father's body had already branded itself on the inside of her lids. The Ancestors would never let him pass through the Veil marked like a Christian, not until his murderer had paid a steep toll in blood. And it was up to their tribe's spirit queen, Reine d'Esprit, to claim it.

She jerked free of his grip and crossed to her liquor cabinet. Grabbed the old brown bottle, her papa's. Couldn't pull the cork with her shaking hands.

Castile moved to her, soft as a shadow. He gently took the bottle and pulled the cork, handed it back. "You know who did this."

She waited until her voice firmed up. "Rumor says Trinidad."

"It's a deal more than just rumor. It's the truth."

"Fuck you know?"

Castile's lips twitched. "We were friends as kids. I heard the rumors and went to look for the body on a hunch. I found Roi d'Esprit in a place only Trinidad and I know."

"He won't come after you for this? Givin him to us and all." Reine let the liquor sear her throat and offered the bottle to him.

"Trinidad thinks I'm dead." He drank and coughed. "Shit. This would rip the red out of flagstone."

Castile hadn't run his horse through the freezing wind for free. He was here to savvy over something needing doing. The notion made her itchy. "Why'd you come, Castile?"

Castile nodded, half a shrug. "I got a job for you. Earn food, meds. Maybe some livestock."

"No." She let her gaze rest on the ragged cross slashed into her papa's skin. She had better things to do, an archwarden to hunt.

"What if you never found your Papa Roi, never knew about that?" He stabbed a finger close to the ripped flesh. "He'd haunt you the rest of your life."

Reine scowled at him but he pressed her.

"I can smell your hunger," he said. "The freehold stinks of disease. Been a rough winter and it's not half over yet. How many have you buried already?"

His words burned holes through her shock. "What of it? Fuckin whole county's starvin."

But as she spoke she realized Castile looked good, healthy. He'd shaved and washed before he made the run from his foothills cave to her county freehold. His worn armor was scrubbed of ash stains, mesh blade-stop sleeves free of debris. Knives on each hip. Chin-length hair shining and clean. An old Savage rifle hung on his back amid the folds of his cloak.

None of it fitted with what the archwarden Paul had reported: that two weeks ago Castile had been screaming to his gods, sliced shoulder to ass, bleeding to die. Paul had no reason to lie to her about that. On the face of it, she was tempted to kill Castile where he stood. She and Paul had discussed the usefulness of having him dead. But her tribe considered Castile a friendly so it would take some explaining around the freehold. He was blessed to them, already a warrior spirit even though he was Wiccan. The delivery of their dead Papa Roi would only solidify his good reputation.

Castile did have magic, proved it by standing here after that death blow. But her tribe didn't know about that. They didn't know what she knew, not about the Barren, not about the crusade, and not about Castile. They only knew Castile should have died in Folsom Prison or come out a whipped slave. Instead he'd come out stronger than ever.

Meanwhile, her tribe's weapons rusted and their kids starved. Reine fingered the hilt of her knife, drawing it a bit and then letting it slide back into its sheath.

Castile raised his thick-lashed eyes to hers. Ancestors knew, that face could charm the rattles off a snake. "I know you want to go after Trinidad, and I'll pay you to do it without killing him. You bring him to me alive, and I'll make his wrongs come right. Your Papa Roi can rest, and you can feed your people."

"I don't get you. Wiccans don't do revenge. Why do you want Trinidad?"

Castile bit his lip for a moment before answering, leaving white marks in the plump, pink flesh. "He owes me blood. We have history, him and me. I can hurt him in ways you could never dream up."

The alcohol stung her chapped lips. She ran her arm over her mouth. None of this made sense, not coming from a Wiccan. Particularly this Wiccan. "What about the crusade they're talkin inparish? Trinidad disappeared will make it worse."

"Not much can make that worse. Bishop's turned up with this scar on her face. Damnedest thing. I hear it looks pure silver, right in her skin." He tipped his head at her, stormcloud eyes locked on hers.

She swallowed hard, craving more liquor. "Silver."

"She says an angel of their god cut her and it told her to crusade. And now she's all about killing the unclean. The unbelievers, yeah? That's you and me, if you missed it." He signed Wiccan Horns with his fingers, aiming back west, inparish.

She made her face stay calm, like they hadn't just broached the kind of mutual lies that bring angry Ancestors into play. The small smile on Castile's lips made it seem this was all merely a joke between friends. Good one on the superstitious Christians. But Paul had described the man who gave the bishop that scar and fuckin it wasn't no angel. That was the last thing Castile was.

She bit down the temptation to throw the truth at him. "So?"

"So I'm willing to pay good bounty if you bring me him alive."

"I want him dead."

"He will be. Eventually." He shrugged. "Look. I'm going to get

him, one way or another. I know ecoterrs, even slavers, from inside
Folsom. Someone else will be happy to take his bounty. But you're
good at this sort of thing. And it looks like you could use that
bounty more than anybody I know."

That didn't go down easy on an empty stomach. They'd just
had another body burn last night. Half the tribe's kids were down
with flu. And now the crusade ... Oh, she knew. She knew Marius
wanted to control that silver dreamland. Why else would the high
and mighty bishop savvy with dirt-scrabblers? But Reine could
swallow her anger and frustration over that for a while yet. Paul
had sworn to her he'd protect her people from the crusade. Paul
had never once lied to her.

But Paul couldn't feed them. If she didn't get food and meds
into her people soon, they'd all end up bones rotting in the county
dirt without the Christians swinging a single sword. If feeding her
people cost her properly avenging Papa Roi, then Ancestors plague
her and have done. She had people counting on her.

"I'll do it. But why you riskin a fuck-all inparish? Didn't you get
it up the ass enough in prison?"

She expected anger, a flinch at least. Castile left her disappointed. "Trinidad will be on Highway 93 tonight."

"How do you know?"

"He'll be there."

"Where do we meet? Your cave?"

"Don't push it, Reine. South end of Dragonspine. Come after
nightfall. It might be a wait."

"I still don't get what's in it for you."

"Not your problem. I'll pay for him and he'll pay for his wrongs.
That's good for both of us, yeah?"

She gritted her teeth and nodded.

"May your hearth keep ever warm." He bowed to her, palms pressed together before his lips. Then he spun and strode out the door.

It didn't quite close behind him. Her sister Javelot pushed through without knocking. Reine rushed to cover their papa but couldn't get there in time. Javelot reached for the bloody corpse before Reine could stop her. She touched the skin split over bone on her father's chest and sank to the floor, staring up at Reine with big, tearless eyes, gulping air.

Reine couldn't meet that stare. She headed back for more liquor, wishing instead for the sting from her knife.

"Castile just put a bounty on Trinidad," she said. "We're pickin him up, but the Wiccan wants him. Alive."

Javelot's notched eyebrows dropped over narrowed eyes. "Fuckin we kill him. We kill him dead and cut him into bits and eat his heart. The Ancestors—"

"The Ancestors don't feed us, Jav, and Trinidad's heart won't feed us neither. Don't you get it? Castile has food. Meds." Reine swallowed down another gulp and corked the bottle. "Send me every spare spearguard. You stay here, watch things."

Javelot gritted her teeth in a snarl.

Reine sighed. "We don't raid together. Tribe Rule."

She resented having to call out Tribe Rule so often on her sister. Sometimes she just wanted to scream: *Fuckin you want to be queen so bad, you take it!* Javelot had no idea what it took to run the tribe. Reine had trained for it her whole life. But with their papa's rotting corpse here in the same room, it fresh hit her what a shitty job she'd inherited.

Javelot stuck her hip out to one side, her bottom lip quivering. "You going tell Castile you're fuckin an archwarden? Huh?"

"This has nothing to do with Paul," Reine said.

Javelot ducked her head. A sob broke through. She'd always loved Papa more than Reine had. But their mama had pushed Reine out first. She was queen, whether Javelot or Papa liked it or not.

Reine sighed. "Go pray to Papa, tell him we got his body. He's probably lonely."

Javelot climbed to her feet and went. Cold swept in as she shut the door behind her.

It would take a few minutes for her spearguards to weapon up. Reine took another gulp of liquor and raised the bottle in salute. "Cheers, you old fuck, and good riddance."

She drew her knife, pressed the razor edge against the back of her hand and sliced. Blood ran over her skin, taking with it her grief and fear, making room for Trinidad and revenge.

# THREE

Marius escaped the afternoon reception filled with parishioners hungry for reassurance, and most of them just plain hungry. She went to her austere basement guest room and shed her bishop's robes for warmer civilian clothes. She'd finished with Father Troy. The old man seemed distracted, but his energy had surprised her. Being eaten alive by an ugly disease hadn't erased his astuteness. Still, it was only a few days before she placed her own priest inparish, and sooner suited her plans. Father Troy seemed prepared to stand aside, though he expressed worry for his archwardens. They had good reputations, surely they'd be easy to place.

Paul arrived at her door a few minutes later. She smiled at him but he only nodded in response. He wore the blank expression and tense readiness of a man who guards his bishop and keeps her secrets without ever expressing his opinion.

"Why are you so apprehensive?" she asked.

"They are more sympathetic to Wiccans than is healthy."

"Boulder has always been lenient. It's part of its provincial charm."

"Leniency gets people killed. Particularly bishops."

"And here you are fooling me into thinking you care."

That made him blink. He tipped his head, some of the stony façade dropping. He looked more handsome with the strong lines of his face softened by surprise. "I care," he said.

His soft voice almost made her apologize for her little joke. She touched his cheek, smoothed her thumb over his thick brow. "Come. I should make the rounds again."

As they climbed the stairs, she heard boyish laughter and the clatter of composite swords. The parish hall at the top of the stairs had been turned into a large fight practice room, with mats for hand-to-hand training and every manner of weapon hanging on the walls. Adolescent sweat clouded the air, sour and thick.

"Let's see what the latest crop has to offer, shall we?" she said.

Paul nodded. "There's Trinidad. I've always wanted to see him fight."

Trinidad, the tall archwarden who had guarded her at service, and the armsmaster Roman, a veteran whose grayed hair and heavyset build belied his skill and speed, sparred in a violent dance of skills. They both wore the steel-reinforced arm bracers from their armor harness but sparred bare-chested in the manner of high-ranked fighters. Apparently, Roman subscribed to the "Real fear and real blood equals a real fight" philosophy of training. Bright welts from Roman's hits webbed the archwarden's ribs. Roman's darker skin showed none, a testament to his defensive skill.

Teenaged boys ranged in a loose, shifting circle around them, shoving each other and playing with their swords instead of paying attention to the demonstration. Only one novice, the severe burn scars on his face mottled by waxy, incompetent grafts, ignored the others and focused intently on the two fighters.

Trinidad and Roman ran through blocks and challenges so quickly she could barely tell where one started and the next ended. She narrowed her eyes at Trinidad. Excellent form, efficient technique, calculated power behind each blow. And yet Roman blocked his hits and scored his own, landing the occasional blow to Trinidad's midsection, drawing hard grunts.

"What do you think?" she asked Paul.

"Roman trained Trinidad from a pup and I hear he's a favorite. I can see why." He narrowed his eyes and gestured. "Roman scored first blood though."

Trinidad bled from a cut high on his chest, where his shoulder plate would overlap his breastplate had he been wearing his full kit. It was a tough kill, but doable.

"I lost an archwarden that way once," she said. "An Indigo slipped a spear under his plate and it got infected—"

A cheer and rhythmic clatter of swords cut her off. Trinidad had Roman pinned in a lethal blade-lock, his sword resting against the side of the armsmaster's meaty neck, his left hand gripping the older man's sword arm and trapping it to one side. Roman had his blade up under Trinidad's sword, but Trinidad could easily press and draw blood.

"Well done, Trinidad," she said over the excited chatter.

The circle parted and quieted. The polite novices bowed their heads. The more brazen stared at the scar on her forehead. Roman nodded and smiled, a courteous quirk of the lips that didn't touch his eyes.

Trinidad turned to face them and took a knee. Maybe it wasn't all courtesy; his bare chest heaved and sweat slicked his skin despite the drafty hall. His gaze passed over her to spend more time on Paul.

"Carry on, armsmaster," she said to Roman. "I don't mean to interrupt."

"Get on, slackers," Roman said, striding toward the hushed novices and scattering them with his sword slashing the air. "Fighters to ready!"

Trinidad got to his feet and approached them as the novices found their places. His voice was deep and so soft she had to lean in to hear him over Roman's shouts.

"Your Grace." He bowed his head to her but offered his hand to Paul. "Seth talks about you all the time. He says you're the best shot he ever saw."

"Seth and I trained together," Paul said for Marius' benefit, and added to Trinidad, "He bragged on you, too. Always thought it was just talk, until today."

"Thanks. Care for a round?"

Paul shook his head and gave Trinidad a rare grin. "Love to, but I'm on duty."

"Disengage, fighters!" Roman shouted, and thunked one of the boys on his helmet with the flat of his blade. "Wolf! Get over here and show them how to not die the first time someone swings a blade at them."

"Another time, maybe." Trinidad glanced over his shoulder. Marius wondered if it was the refusal to spar or that one of the boys hadn't done well.

"I'll spar with you," she said.

The cross tattooed on Trinidad's forehead wrinkled but cleared as quickly.

"Colorado Army," Marius said. "I enlisted as a chaplain, but everyone trained to fight then."

Decades before, after the federal government had collapsed, state armies and religious militias had sprung up across the country. Battles over dwindling natural resources had torn the United States into warring political regions, hindering the manufacture and distribution of munitions. The price of bullets skyrocketed, explosives were made in kitchens rather than factories, and hand-forged weaponry—spears, bows, and swords—became common-place, even in the hands of priests.

"Don't worry about hurting Her Grace," Paul chimed in. "She's very good."

Marius walked to the sword rack and lifted a practice blade, testing it for heft. "This will do."

Trinidad undid the full-length hinged bracer on his left arm and offered it to her. "The boys are wearing the others, Your Grace."

She held out her arm, forcing him to step closer to latch it on. It felt damp and warm against her skin. Up close, he smelled of ash and sweat. His dark close-shorn hair glistened. He frowned down at the bracer as he snapped the magnetic latches.

"I haven't heard of anyone with your name before," she said.

He stepped back, the bracer in place. "I was raised Wiccan until I was twelve. They don't use traditional names, but animals, places. Things like that."

"A charming custom," she said, offering him a smile he didn't return. "I wonder why?"

"In my ..." He paused. "In the coven I came from, it was a way to venerate the world."

She wondered if his ignorant Wiccan parents had realized they'd given their heathen child a Christian name. Probably not.

After a glance at Roman, who was busy scolding another novice, Trinidad raised his sword.

He let her attack first and then his reserve evaporated. He parried her blow and counter-attacked, driving her back a step and forcing her to use her blade in defense. She had to block two provoking feints and then missed his quick attack beneath her guard. She had the sense he was holding back, but the flat of his blade still hurt enough to drive the air from her lungs. He adjusted his footing for balance; she attacked. He blocked with his hilt. There was the tiniest lag as he shifted his guard and she pressed his low line, forcing him to protect his midsection. Faster than even she anticipated, she swept her bracer against his sword blade, knocked it aside, and jabbed the point of her practice sword up into the cut on his chest.

Blood spilled over the tip of her composite blade and she yanked it back. "Kill," she gasped.

His body stilled as quickly as it had flown into motion. The wound wasn't deep, but fresh blood ran down his chest in a sweaty rivulet. "You fight well, Your Grace."

She drew in a deep breath to steady her heart. "Shall we go again?"

"I'm sorry," he said. "I've duty in a quarter hour. Best get into my kit."

"Of course," she said, undoing the bracer and stepping closer to give it to him. "A question before you go?"

"Your Grace?"

"Have you taken the cross?"

He dropped his gaze. "No, Your Grace."

"Well, I'm asking. Will you join the crusade?"

"I ..." He blinked rapidly, then his face calmed. "I should speak with my priest, Your Grace. My first duty is to him."

"And if he releases you to me?"

He lifted his dark eyes to meet hers. "Then I will speak with God."

Most of the novices had stopped to watch their round and their gazes followed Trinidad as he left the room. A couple frowned at her, especially the scarred boy.

Roman bellowed, "Show's over, children. Fall back to ready." His commands followed Paul and Marius down the corridor as they left the practice hall.

"The novices didn't look too pleased with me for besting their pet," she said to Paul, amused. Trinidad was a pretty thing, despite his stiff manner and intense stare, and a Wiccan convert to boot. "He does seem popular. It might be worthwhile for him to take the cross publicly."

Paul shook his head. "Colin heard Trinidad and Father Troy talking after the service. Trinidad is against the crusade."

"Trinidad doesn't know about the Barren," she answered. "If he did, he would take the cross right away."

"You really believe that? He's ex-Wiccan."

She waited until they were in the privacy of her quarters to continue. "Is Trinidad's loyalty under question?"

"Apparently he is a model archwarden, but some inparish don't trust him because of his background. His parents were ecoterrs, suicide bombers." Paul shrugged his armored shoulders. "Old prejudice dies hard. Boulder Parish has a long memory."

A long memory, and Folsom Prison looming over the town to remind them of the ecoterrs held within. And yet the parish remained stubbornly tolerant of outsiders. "What news from Reine? Is she onto you yet?"

"She trusts me and thinks I'll see her through the war. That much is clear." Paul hesitated. "I honestly believe she doesn't know where Hawk's coven lives."

"Threaten her or charm her, but we need Hawk in the flesh," she said.

Paul said nothing, just lowered his chin and clasped his hands behind his back. The tattoo on his forehead was fading to a mottled blue; he'd need to see to getting it refreshed when they finished the crusade.

"What will convince her to find them for us, then? Food? Medicine?"

Paul took his time answering. "I've already offered her all that, Your Grace. Indigos are starving and dying this winter. She's desperate. Trust me, she'd turn Hawk and his coven over to me if she could."

Marius paced the short length of her quarters, frowning at the concrete floor. Securing the Barren wasn't happening nearly fast enough. Soon Hawk would realize Denver Parish crusaders were canvassing the mountains, searching him out. He would cut them out of the Barren entirely. And how would she keep the Barren and its healing powers for God then?

"It appears we're to go to war, then. I only pray we're able to find the Wiccans with a minimal loss of life." She crossed herself.

Paul mirrored the motion. "With God's grace, His own should not come to much harm."

Not to mention the Christian army outnumbered the heretics five-to-one. She rubbed at her sore ribs absently. The archwarden's hit had left her bruised. "What if Trinidad can rove us to the Barren as well as Hawk can? Evidently, at least one other Wiccan can rove." She brushed her fingers over the scar on her forehead. It was so oddly warm and pliant.

"Even if Trinidad can, he took vows against practicing his old religion, Your Grace."

"I'll give him special dispensation," she said, waving a hand. "It would solve a deal of our difficulty. If he can rove, having him in our service would make all the difference."

Trinidad seemed as pious and disciplined as any archwarden she'd met. She realized with a start that Trinidad reminded her of her hopes for another beautiful, broken boy. Had her son survived, would he have become half the man Trinidad was? Or Paul?

She nearly winced before refocusing back on the matters at hand. Crusade wasn't pretty or glorious, but it appeared to be the only way to keep the Barren in Christian hands. If Hawk had his way, anyone could go to the Barren. Foolish man.

"Do you think Trinidad let me win?" she asked, letting her jacket fall to the threadbare rug.

Paul swept forward to pick it up. "'Be patient and you will finally win, for a soft tongue can break hard bones.' That, to my mind, is Trinidad."

"Point taken," she said.

Paul dipped his chin and turned to go, but she stopped him with a hand on his armored shoulder.

"There is time before evensong. Stay," she murmured and kissed him. Her hardened nipples rubbed against his armor as he took her in his arms.

# FOUR

Sweat coated Trinidad's bruised skin, stinging the welts and scrapes from practice. He wasn't fit to put on his armor harness before he accompanied Father Troy to evensong, so he indulged in a rare warm shower at the rectory. Besides, he figured feeding the priest supper early, as well as a proper show of devotion at chapel, would temper Father Troy's worries and the bishop's suspicion. But he didn't have to face Father quite yet. The rectory was empty.

Trinidad scrubbed soap into his skin, ignoring the blazing cut on his chest. After, while he laced up his shirt, he glanced through the kitchen window across the churchyard. Candlelight flickered through the windows of Father Troy's office, evidently the only one currently occupied at the administrative building. Most of the barracks was still dark, including the window to the basement room he shared with Wolf. Best if Wolf was getting some sleep.

He made a meal of goat cheese, bread, canned applesauce, and warm broth, hoping to tempt the priest's failing appetite with some favorites. But the food chilled on the table as Trinidad waited.

The faint glow from the study windows still smoldered against the night. A few people made their way toward the chapel.

They were going to be late—not good with the bishop inparish. Father Troy would have to reheat his supper after prayers.

Thinking the priest had lost track of time or fallen asleep at his desk, Trinidad stored the food and walked across the open ground to the administrative building. The offices inside were dark but for the slice of light beneath Father Troy's door. No archwarden stood guard outside, as usual.

Frowning, Trinidad knocked, but Father Troy didn't answer. "Father? Time for prayers, sir."

Cold air leaked from the gap at the threshold. He pressed his ear to the wood and, after a hesitation, tried the latch. The door swung open to reveal the priest's dimly lit, book-lined office. Candles dripped into saucers and guttered in candlesticks, but no Father Troy. Several had blown out from a cold wind whipping through the open door to his little walled garden.

It was empty except for the frosted bones of plants. Boots had scuffed the snow. He shut the door and frowned. Only then did Trinidad realize the priest's desk chair was shoved back, tipped against the wall behind the desk. The blanket Father Troy often wrapped over his knees had fallen to the floor. Trinidad lifted it and Troy's favorite cross tumbled from the folds. He didn't wear it outside of service, but he often worried it as he worked at his desk.

Fear snatched at Trinidad as his fingers closed around the cross. He placed it on the desk and went back the way he'd come, reaching for the gun on his belt. All seemed quiet and well outside, but he chambered a bullet as he strode for the barracks to wake Daniel.

He knew. He didn't need to check the sanctuary or search the basement. He knew.

Someone had taken Father Troy.

# FIVE

The low all-clear call—familiar from Castile's days in the movement—should have been comforting. But after seven years in prison it sounded more like a baying hound from the Great Hunt, and he couldn't shake the feeling he was the Hunter's prey. He stretched his back as much as he could under his armor, seeking the calm that had eluded him ever since he'd left the Indigo freehold six hours before. Even the lack of pain from his injury unnerved him, the ghost of agony still haunting his every movement. He took a deep breath and emerged from the protection of the rock outcropping.

The ecoterr from the inparish cell was a large man clad in typical homemade clothing. A tatty cloak hung from his shoulders. Not a pentacle in sight. Instead, he wore a cross and several loops of prayer beads around his neck. Castile had never seen any real Christian hang themselves with so much religious swag, but maybe things had changed since he'd been in prison. The ecoterr showed no armor or weapons. It didn't mean they weren't there, and it didn't mean he wouldn't use them.

The ecoterr had Father Troy by the arm, more supporting him as they walked over the rocky ground than to keep hold of him. The old priest looked bent and sleepy, raising watery eyes to Castile's face and beyond. No reaction from him. The drugs maybe. Or a half a century of shepherding Christians had trained him to be as impassive as an archwarden.

Still, Castile felt nervous, watched. The notion came, no doubt, from yesterday's scouting trip to check out the gathering troops in Denver Parish. Small companies of Christian soldiers from Denver already scoured the foothills, searching out pockets of heretics.

"Castile? I'm Bear. You look all right for all you been through." Bear grinned. His teeth were yellowed but all there, making him younger than Castile would have thought. Hard telling these days. Hunger aged everyone.

"Surviving, yeah?" Castile said with a forced smile. "Hello, Father Troy."

Troy carried on looking past him.

"None the worse for wear, daresay." Bear had a gruff voice, strained from smoking too much shitty Alteration. Had the look, too, a gaze that slid too often to the middle distance. The movement wasn't what it had been in Castile's day.

"Let's get you out of the wind, Father." Castile offered his arm but Father Troy paid him no heed, pulled loose of Bear's gentle grip, and shuffled obediently to the coven's dray. It was a beat-up beast with an armored cab from Castile's childhood, but it did the job. Hawk hadn't been thrilled about lending the vehicle to Castile, but he hadn't been able to come up with a valid reason why he shouldn't.

Castile's heart seized at the hardship he'd caused the frail old man. "I really appreciate it, Bear."

"Anything. You know that. You done your time like a man. And Marius, you really outdid yourself with her—"

Castile hissed for silence. The Bear's gravelly voice cut off like Castile had slit out his tongue. Seven years of bending over in prison and now he could silence a man with a whisper.

Bear coughed and cleared his throat. "But this? Stealing a priest? That's some heavy lifting, Castile."

Castile scanned the area again, still feeling eyes on his back. The scraggy ground and rough black road stretching far in either direction was still empty. No one rode over the top of Dragonspine this afternoon. Only a fool would be out in this wind.

A desperate fool.

"Didn't go so well at the coal plant, huh?" he asked.

Bear cursed softly and spat. "Three of us got caught. One talked. Had to up-end all manner of shit with the cell. Marshals confiscated the last of our blast, too."

Castile rubbed his hand over his gritty brows. Bear was coming at it sideways, but he knew what he was being asked just the same. "Gray house with red trim at the west wall. You know it?"

Bear nodded, face set, all business now.

"My blast store is on the outside of the wall, ten paces north-west, buried knee-deep at least. Bring a spade to dig, something heavy and sharp. The ground is rocky." He ignored the cold disapproving breath on the back of his neck, chalked it up to the wind.

"Goddess keep you," Bear said.

Castile turned away without answering.

In the dray, Father Troy spoke. His voice sounded sure and strong, same as always. "You could have asked and I would have come."

Castile shook his head, startled. "Not with the crusade. Not with the bishop inparish."

"You've forced the archwardens to come after me."

He put the dray in gear. "I'm counting on it, Father."

"After you sent the message about the Barren and the bishop, I questioned Trin. He denied using magic. He was genuinely shocked I brought it up."

Castile ignored the thought that Trinidad had never had it in him to lie. What did he know of the man after twelve years anyhow? "He saw the bishop's scar? Did he mention the Barren? Did he question you?"

Father Troy hesitated, ran his gnarled hand along the inside of the armor bolted under the window, touched the gun port where the wind whipped through the hole in the meshed glass. "He only said her angel story was a lie and defended himself against your accusations."

Sharply. "You told him about me?"

"He still thinks you are dead." A pause. "He's always been against crusading. I linked the accusations to that."

"What did he make of it?"

"Hard to say. He doesn't show much."

"He's learned archwarding well." Castile had never seen an archwarden indicate anything at all by expression. They wore their stoicism like their armor, black and impenetrable.

"You need to understand," Father Troy said, "the order saved his life. He dedicated himself to the Church. It was his salvation. I'm sure he felt the accusation quite deeply."

They'd had this conversation before. "Is he dedicated enough to lead the Church to the Barren?"

"Dedicated does not mean blind or stupid," Father Troy said. "This is a mistake, accusing him, taking me. I only hope Trinidad doesn't pay a steep price for it."

He would. Curse him, he would.

They fell silent. As he drove, dread crept over Castile again. He drew in a breath of cold air, trying to wash away the ugliness of the past few hours: cutting up that dead body to savvy with the Indigos, putting high grade blast in the hands of people with the will and means to use it, abducting a sick old man who had only ever shown him kindness, who had kept his secrets even when it meant denying his own loyalty to his bishop and church. But this was war and fighting dirty was the only way Castile knew.

# SIX

Daniel frowned as Trinidad reported Father Troy's disappearance: the open door, the guttered candles, the obvious abduction despite the lack of evidence. He thought a moment before telling the novice on duty to say nothing to anyone else but to fetch Wolf to help him guard the gate. When the kid trotted off, he turned to Trinidad. "Easy. I think you and I should go alone."

"What?" Trinidad bounced on his toes, fists clenched. "No. We need to alert everyone. This is my fault. Besides, the bishop is here—"

"Trin, think. This isn't Indigo work. They aren't this smooth. Roi d'Esprit couldn't manage to think about trying to kill Father Troy without spouting off so loud it got back to us, right? This smells different. Professional."

Trinidad stared at him. "Wiccans."

Daniel nodded and lowered his voice. "I don't like the bishop any more than you do. She'll twist this somehow. Use it to rile people up. Maybe keep us from searching. Father Troy abducted, maybe dead, is powerful motivation to take the cross for a lot of people. It'll just goes to prove what she's been saying all along, that we'd be better off without the Wiccans."

"You're no friend to the Wiccans."

"Especially if they did this. But I am sworn, as you are, to protect God's people. They are His people whether they know it or not. Asking us to kill them for their beliefs is flirting with evil."

More than flirting. Trinidad nodded. "What do you want to do?"

"I just want to do a little looking on our own first. Maybe we can keep this quiet. Maybe whoever took him will talk to us, but they won't if dozens of us start hunting them down, right?" He eyed Trinidad, laid his hand on Trinidad's shoulder and said gently, "Do you remember how to get to your coven's home?"

Trinidad blinked. It made sense. His old coven was the closest one with the most ties inparish, and as such, was an important target of the crusade. It was known to foster ecoterrs. He nodded, not meeting Daniel's eyes, and told him the way.

T rinidad tucked the toe of his boot under a bar welded to the bed of the dray and steadied the belt-fed rifle mounted on the armored cab as they rolled over a pothole. A bishop's ransom in bullets rattled in a crate by his feet. The full, red moon cast cold light and frigid wind swept over his bare head, promising more of the bitter cold snap that gripped the front range. In his hurry, he hadn't taken time to replace his cloak with a coat. He tied a black scarf around his nose and mouth against the blowing ash clogging each breath.

Old commercial buildings squatted on either side of the street, some gutted by ecoterr bombs, some salvaged into residences by resourceful parishioners. More metal than glass covered windows; few cracks of light shone through. How many ecoterr cells hid behind those windows? Most citizens who lived along the wall were loyal to the parish and confrontational over breaches. Bullet casings and dead souls littered their yards from the attempts. But someone had smuggled ecoterrs and bombs into the power plant just yesterday. Maybe the same cell had taken Father Troy.

He scanned the windows and crevices between buildings as they passed by, searching for the glint of a rifle barrel, discarded packages that might hold bombs, ecoterrs posing as citizens breaking curfew. But only trash scuttled along the snowy gutters.

Folsom Prison rose into the darkness as they rounded it on their way to the town gate. The red stone walls had long ago blackened from pollution, turning it into more shadow than building. Impossible to imagine it had once been a university stadium, built for games. Thank God Father Troy had given up making his monthly visits there.

Father Troy . . . Trinidad swallowed the sick rising in his throat and steadied himself on the mounted gun as the dray rolled to a stop at the town gate. Spotlights and lanterns burned against the gloom, lighting the road immediately inside the gate and some distance outside. Constructed of cinderblock and red stone salvaged from dismantled university buildings, the walls flanking the gate were thick enough for two marshals to walk abreast. Heavy artillery jutted from the top like thorns. Since the wealthy Church funded the protection of the parish, marshals usually played nice with the black-cloaked, tattooed men who bore the Church's sword. Still, archwardens never knew when they'd run into a marshal who had something to prove.

One of the marshals strolled their way. "Evening, archwardens."

Trinidad took the opportunity to crouch down, out of the wind. "You see anything odd pass through here? Any Wiccan traders or the like?"

The marshal took a step closer and leaned his arm against the side of the dray, next to Daniel's open window. His gray-and-black camo smelled of gunpowder and stale sweat. "Quiet day so far. Weather's driving them all inside, I guess."

"Gate cleared?" Daniel asked him.

He reached up and tugged on Trinidad's blue scarf. "Depends. Hunting Indigos tonight?"

Trinidad felt a muscle in his jaw twitch. If gate guards knew about him killing the Indigo king, then how high up had the rumors climbed? To the mayor? The bishop?

Daniel coughed. "Nothing like that. Just a little parish business."

"Well, be careful for crissake." The marshal waved at the gate operator and the thick sheets of riveted plate metal slid open on creaking wheels.

A poor settlement lay in the remains of a mid-twentieth-century neighborhood beyond the south gate. It crept up the foothills toward bombed-out shells of old government buildings, dissolving from houses into shanties. Moonlight glinted on occasional patches of snow and the protective white sigils painted on doors. As they passed beyond the neighborhood, they saw no one and nothing but copses of dead trees and the black ribbon of unkempt highway stretching through the no-man's-land between the Golden and Boulder Parishes.

The air chilled Trinidad's lungs, seeped through the heavy cloak, and crept beneath his armor. He gritted his teeth against chattering and tried to focus on facts rather than his fears. Most hostages were kept safe enough, held for ransom. It'd be that way with Father Troy, too. Indigos might want revenge against Trinidad, but if parishioners were hungry enough to take the cross, surely Indigos could be bargained with as well. The Church would offer food, medical care, livestock. Whatever it took to get Father Troy back.

Ahead, the long ridge called Leyden on old maps but Dragonspine by the locals cut into the opalescent smoggy sky like a monstrous backbone. It used to be a playground when he was a kid, but no one lingered there anymore. It was too dangerous in this era of Indigo and slaver raids.

Trinidad stomped a boot to reawaken a numb foot. He forced himself to stretch his body, exposing his wind-burned cheeks to the cold air—accepting it, becoming one with it, as Roman had taught them. But he muttered into the wind, "You're riding in back on the way home, Danny."

An oblong, boxy shadow blocked the road a half-klick ahead. He squinted, but the moon snuck behind clouds before he could get a better look. Still, it could only be another dray, and this close to Boulder Parish, it could mean hostiles. He thumped his fist on the roof, but Daniel had seen it. He slowed as shots clipped the cab, and Trinidad dropped to his knees to take cover, wishing he was at the wheel, wishing for control.

No room for a full bootlegger's turn, the road was too narrow. Daniel steered the dray to one side anyway, and Trinidad had to cling to his gun to not be thrown out as they bumped and tilted into the ditch at the side of the road.

Inside the cab, Daniel fought the wheel as the tires caught in a rut. He slammed against the rut a couple of times but couldn't climb back out of the steep ice-slicked mud in the gully next to the road. He settled for running the dray alongside the road. The ditch was deep enough to give them a little protection, but even as Trinidad swung the gun around and fired, he knew it would all be over in a few minutes.

He couldn't see well and he couldn't steady his shots from the bouncing gun. Return fire pinged off the dray's armor. Trinidad decided to let go, to throw all the firepower he had at them. If he was going to die here—in the cold, in the dark—he wasn't going to leave his enemies any binary aerosol ammo to kill Christians with. The rifle barrel heated and steamed in the cold but Trinidad kept the belt running through. No time to change it. No time to think. Nothing to do but keep his finger on the trigger and sweep the area with binaries as best he could. What the bullets didn't kill, the binary gases would.

He couldn't hear anything past the rip of his gun. Daniel slowed, trapped by the noose of Indigos. Fleet figures surrounded them. As the dray jolted from return hits, Trinidad struggled to keep his balance and fire at the same time, working his way through the heavy coil of rounds. The mesh-reinforced glass of the windshield and side windows cracked and buckled under the blizzard of return fire. Trinidad could only answer with long sweeps of his rifle, peppering the air with binaries and wondering how in God's name he hadn't been hit yet.

The moon, stained crimson by pollution, emerged from the clouds like a bloody sore on the sky casting a reddish light on the scene. Indigos spidered forward, covering their progress with return fire, more Indigos than Trinidad could ever recall seeing in a raid. Fifty. A hundred.

*Me,* Trinidad thought. *They're after me. Not Daniel—*

A spray of blood splashed the inside of the cab and the rear window exploded. A bullet punched Trinidad's breastplate and knocked him onto his back. He scrambled for purchase on the flatbed as the dray lurched. It thudded to a halt against a boulder, throwing Trinidad to the ground. He hit hard. Empty of air, his lungs seized in his chest. Icy wind swept over him. The last of the warmth sieved from his body. A beat. Two. Four. He sucked air, clinging to consciousness. The taste of copper and ash coated his tongue. His head rang.

The world reeled beneath him but training drove him to stir, even if he didn't know why it was important to move. Nor did he know why the ground shuddered under him or why so many people shouted and screeched or who they all were. Blood poured from his nose and clogged his throat. He coughed, trying to breathe. Sweat glued his Flextek to his skin, ripping free painfully when he shifted to look at the dray.

The door creaked open and Daniel fell out. He left a trail of blood as he crawled across the dirt on his belly—one arm dragging from a shoulder wound.

It all came back to Trinidad with startling clarity. Screeching battle cries. Indigos.

A subfrag boomed. Blood-soaked memories of his parent's explosion bombarded Trinidad. But Roman had spent years conditioning him to a single response. The explosion drove him to his feet like the hand of God lifted him, sword in one hand, pistol in the other.

Daniel released a broken cry, piercing the Indigo voices. He writhed, clawing at his chest, trying to get at the binary aerosol burning holes in his lungs. Trinidad felt a wave of panic, waiting for the first sting, for the bubbling of blood in his airways. But the gale at his back scoured the air around him of the murderous aerosols. Thick, heavy silence lay behind the echo of the subfrag.

A nearby Indigo, face obscured by a gasmask and scarf, stared at him. Trinidad ran at him and leapt, sheathing his sword in the Indigo's shoulder.

The copper scent of death filled his lungs. The world flipped and came back screaming. Indigo war cries grew to a cacophony; feet pounded the earth. It was all silenced with a clanging shout and an answering rattle of spears banging metal breastplates.

Two Indigos, heavily armored and filter-masked, dragged the gasping Daniel into the broken light shed by the headlight of the dray. One of them pressed his pistol to Daniel's good shoulder. A woman's hard voice, hollowed by a gasmask: "Fuckin throw down or I blow him apart, limb by limb."

Daniel's hoarse voice snagged on his failing lungs. He writhed in the Indigo's grip, gasping for air. She didn't let go.

"He's gonna die tonight," the Indigo said. "It's up to you how long it takes."

Trinidad let his gun and sword clatter to the stony ground.

The Indigo shifted her pistol to Daniel's forehead and fired. Blood splattered the dray and rocks. She reached up and pulled down her gasmask and hood. The light sparked on chains woven into her blonde dreadlocks. "Consider that my last act of mercy."

Trinidad ran at her, screaming incoherent rage, but they flocked to him, driving him to the ground with boots and fists. He choked on unshed tears and blood, trying to suck air into unwilling lungs, struggling until someone kicked his groin. The sharp spike of pain obliterated his air and fight. Rough hands hauled him to his knees, gasping and coughing. They unsnapped his armor, tearing the plates from his body and flinging them aside. Someone grabbed his arm and yanked it behind his back, pulling until he groaned in pain. The woman who shot Daniel hit him with her fists several times in the stomach and face, leaving him breathless and stunned. She stepped away, shaking out her hand and cursing.

"Do you know who I am?" she asked.

Trinidad's head hung low, he could barely lift it to look at her. Still gagging on his own blood, he shook his head.

Hands cut Trinidad's shirt from his chest with a knife and held the blade out to the woman, hilt first. She took it.

"Reine d'Esprit. You must know the name. You killed my Papa Roi."

"He tried to kill my—priest." A coughing fit broke through his words and he spit out a mouth full of blood. "So help me, if you've done anything to him, I'll kill you too." He fought them, nearly got free until a fist slammed his head back and lights sparked behind closed eyelids.. He sagged in the Indigos' grip. Laughter filtered through a blackening haze.

Reine's voice knifed through it. "Fuckin wake him up."

Someone waved an acidic scent under his nose and he twitched back, abruptly clear-headed. She punched him again. Pain flared so hot in his ribcage he choked on stinging bile.

"Get him on the ground," she commanded.

Rocks and roots dug into his back as they forced him down. They spread his arms out, a man on each, two on his legs, pulling each limb uncomfortably straight. He thrashed his body, but his strength failed under the unrelenting strain on his joints.

Reine knelt next to him. She tickled the blade along his cheek, gently, not cutting. He cringed away, unable to help himself. He tried to drag Roman's torture training back into his mind, his will to hold firm, to resist succumbing. It wouldn't come. There were too many Indigos, too much oppressive hatred.

"The Wiccans want you. Castile's payin good for your bounty. You're gonna feed us for months."

Trinidad twitched violently at the name. Castile . . . Castile was dead. He is supposed to be dead.

"Can't let him have all the fun though." She gestured with the knife. "Hold his head up so he can watch. And get that torch over him so I can see what I'm doin."

They shoved Trinidad's head up until his chin locked against his chest. He groaned as his neck and shoulder cramped, but the vicelike hands didn't relent, fingers digging into his skull. Someone lowered an oil torch low over his bare chest. A spark fell and stung him, struggle again, snarling wordlessly, but their grip held him firm. She flicked the knife along his chest, caught the skin there. He felt the sting of cold air on severed nerves as she lifted the blade to her mouth and licked it. She flicked her tongue across her lip, leaving a crimson smear.

"I'm gonna to do to you what you did to my papa. Remember that, bitch? What you did to him?"

His sword had caught on the old man's spinal column. She was going to cut his throat. He threw his body into a futile struggle again. The one who held his head slipped fingers around his throat and squeezed. He couldn't get air and he couldn't move. A shroud fell over his eyes and the Indigos spun away.

The acrid scent assaulted him again. He startled back to

consciousness, gulping air. They'd reset their grip on him while he'd been unconscious, paralyzing his limbs under their weight. He tried but couldn't move. They shoved his head up again, chin-to-chest. Silence fell but for the light wind rustling the dried grasses and the heavy breath around him.

"Stop strugglin or it'll go too deep. You're worth nothin to me dead." Reine lowered her knife to his skin. He couldn't close his eyes, couldn't twist away. The blade sliced through with a slight pop, blood welling over the edges. Deep stinging followed, burning like she'd set his chest on fire. Satan's Kiss, archwardens called such cuts with a sword because the wound blazed like the devil had licked it.

Trinidad tried not to scream and failed. Blood sheeted from the gash in his chest, steaming in the cold. He clenched his eyes shut but callused fingers pried them open, forcing him to watch as she carved another agonizing gorge into his skin. She ignored his screams, her tongue in the corner of her mouth, eyes on her task.

His whole world narrowed to the wet sound his skin made as the knife scored it, the searing pain, the metallic scent of blood so thick he could taste it, the soft grunts of his tormenter between his screams. Voices wavered like the torch flickering over him, harsh laughter and jeers seeping through the agony. But it all seemed far away in comparison to the knife. The night started to close in, but someone waved the foul-smelling stuff under his nose in time for him to realize fresh anguish. The acrid scent blended with the salt scent of his own blood, keeping him lucid. Trinidad destroyed his voice screaming, pain and horror leaving him breathless. Incessant tremors jarred him. His heart raced under the edge of her knife, pumping blood from his wounds.

Reine considered her handiwork. She tapped the tip of the bloody knife against her lips and pushed her dreadlocks from her sweating face before lowering the blade again. The final line, curving and cruel, took longer than the rest. It stole the last Trinidad's breath, sheared every nerve to the quick. His heart clenched and blackness closed over the pain.

# SEVEN

When Castile and Trinidad had been young, all the coven kids used to race along Dragonspine. Whoever kicked a stone woke the dragon and lost. As the firefight raged below on the road and then dwindled into silence, Castile stared down the length of the moonlit stone ridge to where it disappeared into darkness. He suppressed a shudder. He fancied the dragon stirring beneath his feet as if it scented prey.

This is a mistake. This is a mistake. An echoing mantra driven by uncertainty. "Hunter's great balls," he said aloud, more to break the silence swathing the six coven warriors he'd brought with him. "What's taking so long?"

One of the soldiers with him, Sage, flicked a sign against the night sky. "Herne, bestow upon us strength and resolve."

The others answered in low voices. "So mote it be."

But Castile took no comfort from the words. This was really it. Their last chance at stopping the Christians' crusade. And stopping them had gone so well in the last one—

"They're coming." Magpie's voice, loud against the wind, made Castile hiss at her for silence, but she held her ground. She was right. No need to hide their presence anymore; this was a scheduled meeting.

The rest of his soldiers—holding bows, arrows nocked—turned their faces toward Castile. He twitched his chin and they started the trek down the rocky path off the north end of Dragonspine. He tightened his grip on the one shotgun spared for the mission, then on second thought handed it over to Magpie. He might need his hands free to handle Trinidad.

His warriors followed silently, barely moving scree under their boots. All that running and racing and play had trained them to ghost through the night.

"This is all wrong," Magpie muttered to him. "We shouldn't be doing this."

"There are things you don't know, Mags."

"Only because you won't tell me."

Castile's words came out sharp. "Take point."

"Yes, sir." She pushed ahead of him, shoving at his shoulder and knocking him off balance. He gritted his teeth and held back a sharp retort.

The wind whipped up as they'd waited, tugging on cloaks and jackets, stirring doubts. Everyone's faces were white and pinched; the group stiffened collectively as they neared the Indigos' flatbed dray. Indigos hopped off the back, adjusting their scarves and pushing dreadlocks back from their faces. More followed on foot. Confused by their numbers, Castile stepped forward, seeking Reine. She appeared around the dray, her arms loaded with an awkward bundle, her dirty blonde dreadlocks looking black in the dark. She didn't acknowledge Castile as a couple of Indigos dragged a limp body off the flatbed and dumped it on the ground.

Castile stepped forward, squinting. He hadn't expected things to go easy for his old friend. But Trinidad's tattooed head lolled without resistance, his bare chest a ruin of blood and torn flesh. Castile tensed.

Reine dropped her bundle, a pile of armor and weapons, next to the archwarden. "Your new toy comes with accessories."

Castile dropped to his knees next to Trinidad and pressed his fingers to his jugular. A pulse, skittering far beneath the surface. "What have you done to him?"

"Same he did to my father," Reine said.

Air sieved from Castile's chest. "Go," he said to Reine. "Get the fuck out of my sight now."

"No. Fuckin you owe me. I brought him to you. That was our savvy."

"Our savvy . . ." Castile choked on mirthless laughter. "He's no good to me dead, you stupid bitch. He's no good to any of us dead."

"He's not. I made sure of it. Now. The bounty."

Bows behind Castile creaked as fingers drew back strings. Castile looked at the Indigos, most of their faces still covered with scarves. The half-dozen Indigo spearguards lifted their spears to their shoulders.

"Cas?" Magpie, her shotgun pointed at Reine. Her hand was steady, but she'd never seen how red blood ran, not up close. He couldn't count on her to hold her shot, much less duck one of those spears.

Trinidad stirred against Castile's knees. No matter what Reine said about "making sure," the cuts were still bleeding steady. He didn't know what else they'd done to him, though bruising shadowed his cheeks and arms. Castile bit his lip deep enough it hurt. If they took the time to fight over this, Trinidad could bleed out. Bargaining could cost his life. And the Indigos outnumbered them.

"Half now," he said. "Half in a week. If he survives."

Reine lifted her chin. "Fair enough for the fun I had."

Castile spat at her feet. "If this is your idea of fun, I should just let the crusaders kill you and good riddance."

"You should show me respect after what I done for you. But maybe I should I have a little talk of my own with the Christians. Tell 'em where Trinidad really ended up."

Castile rose and gathered up Trinidad's things. "I still have all my old connections, Reine. I can get my hands on enough blast to erase your tribe."

Reine took a step forward. "Don't threaten me without backin that shit up."

Castile forced a smile, stretching his lips in a hungry grin. "Tempting." He thrust Trinidad's things into one of his soldier's arms and barked commands to the rest. "Take him. Gently. Sage, signal the dray."

A match flared and Sage held it aloft, cupped against the wind. It blew out almost immediately, but their dray had been waiting. It bumped toward them and the driver stopped, the engine running rough and fast. Castile climbed in the tarp-covered back and helped guide his old friend in. He cradled Trinidad's head in his lap, studying the stark, black cross on his brow in lieu of the damage on his chest. Words wouldn't come, just pictures to his mind: Trinidad breaking into a rare smile, rough boyhood wrestling, roving through each other's dreams ...

Magpie climbed in next to them. "It's not as deep as you think," she said. "She knew what she was doing. It'll leave bad scars. But it won't kill him unless it gets infected."

Magpie undid a roll of soft cloth and started binding Trinidad's wounds. It required Castile's help to lift him so they could wrap the cloth under his back. Trinidad rolled his head and moaned. Castile bent over him, whispering softly, not really knowing what he was saying. He laid his hand on the archwarden's cheek, cupped his fingers around his chin. Trinidad quieted as Castile's callused fingers scraped across his day-old beard.

The last time he'd seen Trinidad, they weren't even shaving yet.

M ismatched lanterns lit with elk grease and tallow candles shed just enough light to keep a body from tripping over the rough path between caverns. The strongest witch among them carried Trinidad's limp body in his arms. The cold had stemmed the tide of blood somewhat, as well as the makeshift wrapping Magpie had done. Trinidad remained mostly unconscious. Castile urged them along with sharp, low words. There was only one place to take him where the bleeding could be stopped quickly and the infection kept at bay, and he had no idea if he could get Trinidad there in time.

Castile's home lay in a quiet offshoot off the main cave. "Gently. But quick, now. Take him to my bed."

Magpie had run ahead. She stood next to her brother Hawk, the coven high priest, and Father Troy. Castile hadn't had the guts to tie the old priest, not one who had prayed to his false god over him in prison. Their high priestess Lady Aspen, heavily pregnant, tended the common fire at their feet. Castile meant to avoid them, but Lord Hawk caught his arm.

"I have to go," Castile said. "He's hurt."

"I'll go," Magpie said, and jogged off before he could answer.

"What's this about, Castile?" Hawk asked. He ran a hand over his white-streaked beard. "Savvying with Indigos? Where'd you get the goods?"

Castile looked at Father Troy. "Ecoterrs raid for me. I still have connections with the movement. A lot of people owe me favors."

Hawk pursed his lips and lowered his voice. "You just pointed the crusade right at us."

"The Christians will think Indigos took Trinidad. That's why I used them to collect him." Castile knew Hawk couldn't argue with that logic.

"Why did you take him at all? He's not one of us anymore."

"Because he's roving them to the Barren," Castile said. "I have to find out why. And stop him."

A muscle twitched in Hawk's cheek, but he said nothing.

Castile wanted to walk on, but Father Troy was watching. Goddess knew, it always had been like Father Troy could see into his soul or something. Back at the prison, that sensation had compelled him to tell the priest all manner of things, of mistreatment and horrible abuse, of the ugliness he lived with every day. If Windigo had known everything Castile told Father Troy, he'd had the old priest murdered.

"Trinidad killed the Indigos' Roi d'Esprit. Reine's father." Castile focused on the old priest's beard rather than meet his eyes.

Troy's voice was sharp. "Are you certain, Castile?"

"Yeah."

The priest sighed and bowed his head.

"I'll fix this, Father. I swear it. I won't let him die."

In his cavern, the witches had laid Trinidad on his bed. Only Magpie was left, standing over Trinidad with her hand on the blade at her hip like she was about to draw and thrust it into his heart.

"How are you going to go to sleep? Do you need peyote?"

He'd learned efficient, meditative sleep in prison. Roving had been his only escape. "I can't do this with you here."

"Don't cut me out, Castile, not now—"

"Go." He refused to look at her even as she made a pained noise. She laid her hand on his arm; he pulled away and walked toward the bed.

As his curtain rustled with her departure, Castile grabbed Trinidad's sword. The low coals in the hearth flashed red on the silver blade, turning the engraving into a bloody cross. He sank back on the bed, stiff back resistant to stretching out, his fingers finding the grooves Trinidad's grip had worn into the leather-wrapped hilt. He had to spread his fingers apart to match the archwarden's hand span. As kids, Castile had been slightly taller, but Trinidad had shot past him in the twelve years since they'd last seen one another.

He took Trinidad's limp hand. It felt colder than the sword. Castile closed his eyes, shoved away all thoughts of injury and mislaid plans, willed his nose not to smell the blood, and sank into a trance. He and Trinidad shattered into a million tiny silver pieces.

# EIGHT

L ight behind us, Reine," Cur said.

Reine twisted in her seat to look, shoving her locks from her face as the wind blew them back. A single vehicle; motorcycle, most like, with a faint torch. No reason for anybody to ride the county alone at night unless they were following the Indigos home. Their old dray, rigged with armor, crept over the busted road. Motorcycles could move quickly on their solar engines. Whoever it was could catch them easily.

She sighed. "Stop."

Cur obeyed and the engine ground to a halt as the light gained on them. It was a motorcycle. She got out and stood her ground, rifle at the ready—Cur did, too—but they lowered their guns when they saw who it was.

"What do you want, Hawk?" Reine said.

Lord Hawk stared hard at the pockmarked rust-bucket dray painted with protective sigils and stacked with their munitions and Trinidad's bounty. His eyes were close-set in his heavy-cheeked face.

"A private word," he said.

Reine waved Cur back to the dray and walked with Hawk a distance. When they got out of earshot, Hawk turned on her, chipped teeth bared in his chubby face that didn't match his lean body.

"Castile is supposed to be back in prison," he said. "But I find out he visited you and still walks free. We had a deal."

"Castile made me a better offer."

"What's the bishop going to say?"

She shrugged. "My people are hungry and the bishop don't feed them."

Hawk threw up his hands. "She'll spare them. Isn't that enough?"

Another shrug. Reine thought of her papa's body on the dirt, waiting for burning, hopefully protecting them as a revered Ancestor rather than rotting in an unmarked grave and seeking the Fury of the Dead. Her lip turned up.

"You brought Trinidad to him." Hawk's whispered vehemence took Reine back to the moment.

*And got Papa revenged*, she thought.

Castile's offer of food was tough enough to turn down but getting back at Trinidad clinched it. The dead demanded revenge. But Hawk wouldn't care about all that. She'd heard Wiccans believed their ghosts came back to life in their babies. She dismissed the thought. The only way the dead came back was as ghouls, to finish what their children left undone.

"Castile took Trinidad to the Barren. They're there now," Hawk said.

"What if he shows Trinidad the way to get there?"

Hawk said, "Trinidad already knows the way."

Huh? Reine thought fast. "Then we need Trinidad dead. What

do you think happens when the bishop gets hold of somebody else who can rove, hmm? She doesn't need us any more, is what. And she starts the crusade, kills us all."

Hawk frowned and Reine knew she'd struck deep. "She's already got people looking for our coven," he admitted. "She heard about the Wiccan who survived Folsom, what he looks like. The bishop is not stupid. She suspects Castile is the man who attacked her in the Barren. She's more anxious than ever to capture him, and me too. She gets hold of one of us, this whole thing is done."

"Why'd you ever take her there anyway? Been better if you hadn't." He hissed, silencing her, but she stepped closer. "No. You dragged me into this fuckin mess and you're gonna to tell me why it started."

He stared a thousand steps past her, quiet long enough she thought she'd have to beat it out of him. "I savvied with Denver. Thought I'd bring the coven inparish, make a better life than living in caves. They wanted us to convert. I told them I couldn't; I had proof they were wrong."

"And you're surprised now she wants to take it from you?"

"Bide within the Law you must, in perfect love and perfect trust. Live you must and let to live, fairly take and fairly give. It's the Rede, and I can't ignore it. The Barren belongs to all of us. To hold it back is profane, an insult against the Goddess. Not to mention Threefold Bane. We might already be feeling that." He got in her face. She could smell the sour on his breath. "Castile and Trinidad held back on the Barren and look what happened to them. Trin's family blown up and him a slave to the Church. Castile seven years gone in Folsom."

She didn't believe in this Wiccan nonsense, that the world got back at you when you didn't do right. She didn't believe but an unmistakable chill ran through her nevertheless.

"You're right about wiping us off their shoe. Bishop Marius has ten thousand soldiers at Boulder Parish," Hawk said. "Another thirty thousand at Denver. Can you stand up to that? At least we're hidden and out of the way. Your freehold, though, is right in their path. Your farmlands must be looking pretty good about now. They're hungry inparish too." He laughed, caustic and cutting. "I bet you think Paul will save your fine little ass. No such luck. He might fuck you, and he might even like it, but he's using you."

Reine stared past Hawk at the blades from the old windfarm, pale knives against the dark mountains and black sky. She could ignore the jibe about Paul. They knew where they stood with each other. But forty thousand? She'd known there was a lot of manpower inparish, but an army that size could flick her freehold off its shoulder like a fly.

"Get Trinidad and Castile out of your cave and I'll kill them in a day or so," she said.

"No. Tonight. Now. I'll rove you and Paul to the Barren and we finish it. We needed them dead yesterday."

# NINE

Trinidad's chest burned like hot oil seared it. Something heavy lay over the rest of his skin, an apron of iron. He heard a thousand tiny bells ring in his ears. Familiar. Frightening. He thrashed but he found no purchase or light. Hands held him down, but the fingers didn't dig in like the Indigos' had.

Someone said his name. Not angry, not jeering like before. Just, "Trinidad."

He'd know the voice anywhere, even deepened by adulthood. But it couldn't be.

He opened his mouth to speak and it filled with silken grains. He choked. The hands slipped under his arms and pulled him from the darkness. He sat up, gasping and coughing and spitting sand. Tiny chimes rang as the grains fell away from his body. He caught sight of a veil of brown hair, an elfin chin, sharply defined lips curved into a wry smile.

"Cas—" He couldn't get the name out for coughing. When it was over, his raw throat could barely manage a whisper. "You're dead."

"No. I was in prison." Castile kept hold of his shoulders and ducked close to look into Trinidad's face, flint-colored eyes intent on his. "Steady. You've had a bad day."

Castile. The sting of his nearness assaulted Trinidad. He knew the voice, but most of all, he knew the face. Grown now, but Trinidad had memorized every facet of Castile's fine features when they were still softened by youth, imagined him as an adult a thousand times over. Now scars marred his arms; rough, misshapen knuckles showed his fists had met a face or ten. Bulky, hard muscles slid under his skin. Short, quick movements betrayed a life lived in tight quarters. Like a prison cell.

Trinidad's naked sword lay across Castile's lap, dull against the silver sand.

Silver. *God help me, the Barren . . .*

Trinidad focused beyond Castile at the sterling world around them. Overhead, the sunless sky died to black, as if the glow shed from the silver sand couldn't penetrate its depths. As always, reflected light closed around them like a fog, softening edges and blurring his distance vision. The silver glow soothed his eyes, too long strained by the harsh sun of day and pitch of starless nights.

Tombs and graves stretched to the tarnished horizon in every direction. Nearer, great tombs hewn of silver stone stood in pale relief against the dark sky. Every tomb and marker bore carvings. He knew them without squinting, had explored them all: crosses and suns and moons. Swastikas. Sunwheels and triskeles. Stars, five-points to eight. Pentacles and ankhs. New Orleans Voodoo and Hatian Voudoun and African Hoodoo warding symbols. Words in every language and every alphabet: from ancient Egyptian hieroglyphs to Old Craft lettering and newer Farsi and still newer Americano next to long forgotten runes.

And the statues, thousands of memento mori dissolving from stone to ghosts at a distance: angels and dancing children, piping fauns, Herne with a great rack of horns and a fierce visage, cats, horses, sharp rows of soldiers, six-armed women, chubby seated elephants and chubbier men with beatific smiles, draped gods and goddesses on pillars, the enormous lion with the stubbed tail. Stone doves perched on carved tree branches and eagles spread their wings on great engraved altars. A herd of cattle so realistic he used to imagine their lowing; some bedded down on the sand, others appearing to wander but never moving.

Nearby, a smooth boulder was graven with Herne's Horns and a triskele, maybe the marker of some Wiccan priest. Silver-veined marble books lay open on the ground, each page as thick as his finger, scattered by whatever gods had made this place. The stone slab of a door made a rough ramp into the doorway of a nearby crypt, still fallen from when Castile and Trinidad had broken into it out of childhood curiosity. Crumpled silver skeletons lay within, undisturbed since. A wall of tarnished bones barricaded a massive tomb marked with angular Greek; in other places knee-high bone hedges surrounded single graves as if protecting the final rest of someone important.

Everywhere, the silver sand heaped against it all.

The Wiccan's voice sounded faint in the enormity. "Still full of tombs and bones. A fuck lot of bones."

His eyes flicked down to Trinidad's chest and his lips parted. He reached out and brushed aside the sheet of sand glued to his skin.

Trinidad flinched at the memory of pain as the sand fell away. A winding river of smooth silver filled the gashes made by the Indigo. He touched the ragged lines dug into his skin. The scar flexed under his fingers, warm and silken. A five-point star in a circle that stretched from the top of his chest to below his ribcage. Realization left his heart racing.

The Indigo had carved a cursed pentacle in his skin.

*I'm just doing the same you did to my papa.*

Reine d'Esprit had not killed him, but perhaps she had done worse by mutilating him, marking him a heretic.

"Reine d'Esprit." Castile swallowed. "She tortured you. Do you remember?"

Trinidad twitched a nod.

"You were bleeding, in shock. Pulse faint, the works. I got scared. I roved you here and buried you in the sand. I." He drew a ragged breath. "I didn't know what else to do."

Trinidad blinked down at the silver glittering bright against his skin and clutched at his training. Roman's voice cut through his fugue: *You're alive aren't you? Buck up and do your job.*

But the agony and horror were too recent to ignore. He closed his eyes and felt himself sway as he saw a spray of blood and fragments of skull shattering across the snow in his mind's eye. *Godspeed, Daniel.*

"I know. It hurts. I got my own." Castile twisted around, tugged his shirt up, and showed his back. A gash of silver crossed his spine from his shoulder to his waist. Trinidad reached out for it but let his hand fall without touching him.

"I'm sorry," Castile said. "I'll make it right, Trin. I swear she'll pay for what she did, no matter how this whole thing turns out."

Archwardens had no business with revenge, but Trinidad couldn't bring himself to rebuke him. He lifted his head. This whole thing? What whole thing?

"Her Grace said an angel gave her that scar," Trinidad said, his voice low and rough. "She said it told her to crusade."

"I'm no angel and I sure as fuck didn't tell her to crusade."

That blew off the cobwebs. "You."

"She showed up in the Barren. I was trying to get her to leave. We fought. I cut her. She screamed and I tried to run, give myself space to rove. Her guard attacked me from behind, got me across the back. I couldn't move my legs, but I rolled over and roved out."

Trinidad closed his fingers around the warm sand and let run over his palm. It had been quick thinking on Castile's part. He'd always been sharp that way, escaping scrapes and eluding blame like Herne Himself led him by the hand.

"It's okay," Castile added. "I had a hood on. She didn't know it was me ... at least I don't think so."

Trinidad released a slow breath.

"Remember when it was just us? Remember we used to come here and run? Remember when we used to ..." Castile's voice faded as Trinidad pushed himself to his feet.

Trinidad held out his hand for his sword. "That's mine."

Castile got up and backed away, the sand chiming under his feet. "Maybe I should hang onto it for now."

Trinidad took a step forward, noted that Castile did not raise the blade against him. Castile was shorter than him by half a head, and not as bulky, either. "Give it to me."

"You going to kill me with it?"

"I'm not going to hurt you, Cas."

Castile stepped closer and pressed the hilt into his fingers. He closed his free hand around Trinidad's wrist. His fingers were callused. "The only reason I didn't finish what Reine started . . . well, fuck. We bled on keeping this place secret and we were friends then, so I think I owe you the chance to explain. But you owe me, too. Why are you bringing her here?"

Trinidad shook his head, bewildered. "I don't rove."

"Trin. Don't try and shit me—"

"I don't rove. It's against my vows. I haven't been here since we were kids."

"It's me, yeah? Tell the truth."

The fine line of Castile's curved nose warped slightly like it had been broken and his cheeks had hollowed in adulthood.

"You don't know me. Not anymore. Not if you think I'd go back on our blood and my vows." Trinidad dropped his gaze, focused on Castile's fingers clamped around his wrist. A tiny thrill crawled up his arm from his touch. "I swore to Christ I wouldn't rove again at all. And I haven't. No matter how many times you ask me, I still haven't."

Castile released him with a little shove. "You never could lie worth a shit anyway."

"No. Not like you."

They stood in silence, not meeting the other's eyes. Trinidad broke it. "I thought you were dead."

"It was better that way, yeah? Archwarden. Even your Father Troy thought so." A pause. "He was . . . very kind."

Trinidad forced his fists to relax. "He wasn't going to tell me, was he? You were never going to tell me."

"Hadn't meant to, no."

Trinidad held out his palm, marked with the little silver scar that matched the one inside Castile's fist. Foreheads touching, both hissing in pain. He swallowed the memory, forced it down. "So I'm here because you think I broke our blood."

Castile had a good game face, but even after all these years Trinidad recognized the signs of secrecy: the lowered brows, the lopsided hitch to his hips. Before he could call him on it, Castile talked.

"Someone is bringing the bishop here. And both our family lines ... and the ability to rove ... it ends with us, remember, unless you got a kid running around somewhere. Your dad—"

"My father was wrong."

"You ever know your dad to be wrong about anything in his life? He didn't get to be high priest by being stupid, Trin. He was wicked smart."

Trinidad frowned. "Wicked. That's about right."

Castile winced. "Yeah, that. Look, I'm sor—"

"No, Castile. No."

He didn't want to rehash his parents' crimes and death. Not with Castile. Not with anyone, but especially not Castile.

Castile cleared his throat. "It didn't occur to me that someone else could get here. I mean, I've been kind of preoccupied in prison. And it took us long enough for us to figure out the way here, yeah? What in fuck was I supposed to think? It's . . ." Castile's voice fell off as his gaze switched from Trinidad's face to beyond him. Soft chiming broke the Barren's underlying silence.

Trinidad spun. Twenty paces away, two figures ran at them, clad brow to boot in black. One brandished a knife, the other had a sword at the ready. Nearby, the Indigo Reine d'Esprit held a spear over her dreadlocked head.

"Souls take you!" Reine screeched as her spear took flight toward Castile.

# TEN

T rinidad had a flash of thought: Castile was unarmed. He knocked the spear aside with a thrust of muscle and a sharp clang and brought his blade back up to defend himself as a swordsman attacked. His hood fell back to reveal a face tattooed with a black cross.

The bishop's man, Paul.

Trinidad blinked in shock, defending from pure instinct as Paul's sword sought a weakness. He followed it with a try under Paul's sword, a small part of his mind noting the lack of catch in his muscles from the damage to his chest. Paul twisted his blade around Trinidad's to counter. It was all Trinidad could do to hold onto the hilt, his arms bowing as they absorbed the force of the blow. Their swords locked; their bodies pressed together. Trinidad felt Paul's breath on his face. As if in silent agreement, they disengaged and shoved apart.

Trinidad spat out, "Why are you attacking me?"

Paul came at him again. Trinidad tried to swing; Paul parried with his hilt. Then he pressed hard, putting Trinidad on the defensive, each blow crashing against his sword. Trinidad cringed inwardly at the damage to his blade, but he had no other defense, no bracers, no armor. Castile shouted his name; Trinidad was too busy using his crossguard to catch Paul's blade. He tried to disengage Paul's sword and knock it aside, a risky move that left him open. But Paul kept hold of his weapon, fists bunched on his two-handed hilt.

Trinidad shoved away. He had to adjust his balance, his bare feet churning the sand, and Paul took the opportunity to provoke him with a feint. Trinidad saw through it, knocking his blade aside, frustration building. They seemed a match. Trinidad might win first blood in sparring, but he had no doubt Paul meant to kill him.

They repeated their previous stances: both backed up a step, readied their blades, lungs sucking air. Hollow shouting penetrated Trinidad's concentration, causing him to glance to one side.

The Indigo who'd thrown the spear was attacking Castile, fists flailing, kicking, spitting like a cat. Castile seemed to realize that his salvaged spear worked for fending her off. But another hooded figure also circled him with a knife, dividing his attention.

Castile couldn't hold them off for long. Without thought, without planning, Trinidad swung hard at Paul. It left him open, but without armor to encumber him, he could put extra speed and power behind the blow. But he was out of range even with this lunge, and his blade caught more at Paul's clothing than his body; he barely spilled blood. It only served to anger Paul. He cursed and darted in close, attacking Trinidad's high line. The sharp blade nicked Trinidad's right shoulder. He shoved Paul away with his crossguard.

He'd gotten first blood, but Paul had answered it on the next swing. Paul was bigger, stronger, skilled. It was going to take timing and cunning to beat him. Meanwhile, Castile might die—

His shoulder stung deeply. Satan's Kiss. Trinidad grunted in pain and dropped his right hand from his hilt. He let his sword fall to guard low with his left, praying Paul wouldn't realize his feint. Paul attacked, aiming high again, for Trinidad's throat. Instead of parrying, Trinidad ducked, dropping to his knees and stabbing up with his left, his right hand guiding the sharp blade home. The blade slid under Paul's ribs without resistance.

Paul fell, jetting blood, screaming wetly as the blade sliced through his lung. Trinidad, propelled by the muscle memory of long training, followed him down, twisting his sword to increase the damage and driving it deeper into the wound. Brackish blood fountained across the silver sand and soaked his arm. Paul writhed violently around the blade in his chest, gasping and gagging on blood from his torn lung. Trinidad glanced up at their other opponents. Reine was still engaged with Castile; the one with the knife disappeared around a tomb.

Trinidad met the dying man's gaze as the light fled his eyes. "Why?" he husked out, desperate.

But his voice was overtaken by someone screaming Paul's name, a woman's agonized voice, and the sand chiming. Before Trinidad could turn around, Castile tackled him and the silver world spun away.

# ELEVEN

"P aul!" Reine d'Esprit came awake on her feet, mouth shaped around her lover's name. She stared wildly at her familiar surroundings: quilted cot, guttering candles, corners stained by shadows. Cold air iced her lungs. She hadn't been roving more than ten or fifteen minutes.

She yanked on boots with shaking hands, realized she'd never get her pants on over them. Cursed, jerked one boot off, and threw it. It thumped against the hair-plaster wall, probably cracked it.

A knock from Javelot. "Reine?"

"Go away."

She bowed over the stabbing fear in her stomach, talking her heart down. No future in it. He's an archwarden. He's never going to leave the Church, he as good as told you. But the man she knew, the Paul who had come to meet her in person on behalf of his bishop, had been as surprised at their attraction as she, had been tender in bed and out of it, had wanted to find a way to stay together. Memories of the past months surged through her mind. His arms around her. His voice. His calm brown eyes on hers, sharing a laugh and a bottle. The way his tattoos had shifted with his moods. She'd never seen an archwarden smile before Paul.

And now he was dead.

She reached for her clothes with a shaking hand.

Once dressed and armed, Reine stepped out into the night. Coals glowed in a pit between houses, a bloody smear against the dark. Javelot squatted by it, her furrowed brow aimed at her sister. She stood as Reine stomped down the steps.

"Somethin happened," Reine said. "I'm goin inparish."

"Orders from your new friend?" Javelot hadn't warmed to the idea of Reine allying with the bishop.

Reine shot her a glare.

"You can't, Reine. You get tracked or caught, you leave us with no queen."

"In your dreams."

Javelot held out a corked bottle. Part of Trinidad's bounty from the Wiccans.

Reine fought off a wince at the sting of the first swallow. "You're right, by the way. Fuckin should've killed Trinidad when we had the chance."

She swigged again, clenched her hands around the bottle. The sisters fell quiet for a full minute, listening by long habit for wrong sounds. Only soft, night noises filled the pervasive dark: cleared throats of the guards, a baby's cough, a child crying muted by the walls of the common house, the snuffle of a horse.

Javelot tapped her fingers on her wool-clad knees and nodded. "Ancestors talk some sense into you?"

"They killed Paul."

All trace of Javelot's disapproval vanished. "What? How—"

"Trinidad. Castile. Killed him."

"When?"

"Tonight." Reine lowered her gaze. "In that silver place."

Javelot sat back on her heels, lips twisted into wry frown. "Just a fool dream."

"Was no dream."

"Oh, so you got Wiccan mojo now?"

Nobody, least of all Reine, really believed Wiccan dreamwalking was real. And it wasn't, not really. Gods weren't real, not like the souls of people who had actually lived. The Barren had to be a trick. She barely believed enough to admit to Javelot she'd gone there. She sure as fuck didn't want to believe it now. But seeing Paul tumble to the silver sand . . .

Javelot tsked. "Fuckin dream and you're out here baitin bears? At this rate you'll get too soft to lead us—"

"Enough, Jav."

"Enough? Enough what? You're the one head-over-ass for a fuckin archwarden."

"Javelot—"

"I'm second-in-command and I'm your sister. You want me to lie to you?" She jabbed a finger at Reine. "Paul was a mistake from the start. Now you're soft over him and it'll cost Indigo lives. Fuckin sharpen up."

Reine felt a stillness wash over her, a blank calm. Her foot lashed out and she caught her sister in the solar plexus with her boot. Javelot sprawled on her back in the snowy mud. She lay there for a few seconds, mouth working, trying to gulp air. Finally, she rolled over. She started to coil into position to tackle Reine at the knees. Reine stepped over her, brandishing her drawn knife, and grabbed Javelot's locks. She yanked her chin up and held the knife close to Javelot's notched eyebrow.

Javelot spat a bloody curse. Her fingers scrabbled back, at Reine's thighs. Reine barely felt it.

"You want to be queen so bad, call me soft again and fuckin fight me for it."

Breathing rough, Javelot managed to shake her head.

Reine shoved her down but kept hold of her hair. "Lower."

Javelot dropped her chin almost to the ground.

"Got else to say?"

"No, Reine d'Esprit."

"What I thought." Reine cut two of Javelot's locks off the back of her head, scraping her scalp bloody, and threw them into the fire. "Let that show how you bow to me." She gave her sister a last shove and backed away.

Javelot scrambled to her feet, hatred smoldering in her eyes. But she said nothing.

Reine jerked her chin toward the common house and the crying baby. "Meds in the bounty. See what's for that kid before he wakes up the whole fuckin freehold."

Reine turned her back on her sister and mounted the steps to her house. Before going back in, she cast a last glance back at their fifty-family settlement, pale lanterns of light glowing behind what glass windows they could salvage, patrols moving like ancestral ghosts along the wall. Javelot had disappeared toward the bounty stores. A spearguard passed by, lit only by the glow of a pipe.

*Probably that Cur*, she thought. *Makes him a target.* But she didn't have the heart to go slap him around over it.

In the relative warmth of her house she snicked a match and

lit a candle. No sleep tonight with that kid hacking up a lung. She reached for her paper packet of toke—Alteration grew reliably even in their shitty dirt—and her own pipe. Used her knife to ground out the leaves. *Now you're soft over him and it'll cost lives.* The smoke in her lungs didn't slow her pounding heart.

She closed her eyes and sliced her knife across the back of her hand. Felt her body settle in and refocus as the sting broke through the worst of her worry. Javelot didn't know the first thing about queening Indigos, didn't know leading was about serving the tribe, about dying first, if it came to it.

She dragged the knife along the side of her thumb, tensing and then sighing.

But Javelot was right about one thing. Reine didn't know for sure Paul was dead and rushing inparish over it was a fool's run. Get herself caught, just to find it was all a dream. Not real. Not true. Just a dream, right?

"Fuckin you better be alive, Paul."

Reine drew the knife across the back of her hand again, criss-crossing the other cut and old white scars, watching the blood well as smoke blazed in her lungs.

# TWELVE

Castile smelled smoky candle-wax. Gun powder. Dust. He squinted but didn't recognize the room. Not his rooms, nowhere he'd been before. He'd just wanted to get Trinidad out of the Barren, away, not caring where. It was his dreamscape, all right, the edges faded into nothing like always. A hot, pungent scent slowly overtook the others. He heard his heart thudding. He was draped over Trinidad's back, a stretch of warm, taut skin. His dreamscape, but something was . . . different.

Trinidad knelt over the man he'd killed, gripping his sword with both hands. It stuck up from a cavernous wound. The dead man's tongue lolled like a pale slug. His eyes were fixed beneath the black cross tattooed on his forehead.

"By the Crone," Castile breathed. An archwarden.

He pushed away from Trinidad, rested on his heels, and looked around. A room with twin beds, a window high on the wall. They huddled before a tatty sofa. The room was dark and grim. And he'd never been here before. "This your place?" He didn't know why he was so surprised. It could happen; Trin was the strongest dreamer he knew. He'd overrun Castile's roves and dreamscapes before, like the first time they found the Barren.

Trinidad slid back, sank to the ground. The bloody sword slid free of the dead archwarden's chest and clattered to the floor. "His name is Paul," he said, his voice hollow in the silence between them. "He works for the bishop."

"Steady." Castile touched Trinidad's back, feeling the muscles contract under his hand. He kept his voice low. "Hey, is this your 'scape?"

"He's the head of my order."

"He attacked you," Castile said. "You couldn't help but kill him."

Trinidad's face twisted into an expression Castile couldn't label but didn't much like. "You don't understand what this means, Cas."

Castile cleared his throat and looked away from the gory leavings of Trinidad's kill to study the dreamscape anew. Everything felt more off-kilter as the seconds ticked by. The colors were off; yellowed and too sharp. The dreamscape felt too big, shelves higher than they ought to be, beds longer.

He swallowed hard. Had Trin brought them here? He shook his head. That didn't make sense. Trin was too shaken to overcome Castile's rove. They should be in Castile's dreamscape, but he had never been here before. So, someone else, someone who had some powerful mojo, had pulled them in.

Maybe the same someone who was roving the bishop to the Barren.

"I think we should go," Castile said. "I think we might be in someone else's head—"

A door slammed and the space morphed into another. A mean little room. A patch of harsh, hot sun. The shadow of a man loomed over a bed shoved against a wall. A teenager cowered against the mattress. Burn scars had wrecked one side of his face. Castile trembled. This wasn't in his head. Who's was it? Trin's?

Trinidad took a couple of steps forward, brow furrowed. "Wolfie?" Then louder: "Wolf. It's me. Trin."

Castile's heart began to thud. He knew this place. The cold room, rough hair-plaster walls. He'd been here the day before, at the Indigo's freehold. "We should go."

Trinidad raised his hand. "Shh."

"—accept that your family doesn't want you," the man was saying, but the voice was indistinct, unclear, like a half-remembered recording.

The teenager gave a soft plaintive cry, childlike compared to his long body. The shiny skin of his scarred cheek and rutted eye caught the light, revealing burns garishly fresh and angry.

Castile touched Trinidad and started to rove them away, but Trinidad caught his arm. "Not yet. I want to see what's going to happen."

Castile waited, heart pounding, feeling with distinct pressure each of Trinidad's fingers around his wrist, his own palm firm against Trinidad's bicep.

"You have a new purpose," the man went on.

*Maiden, Mother, and Crone,* Castile knew that voice. Roi d'Esprit. Reine's father, the old Indigo spirit lord. He squinted at the figure to confirm but couldn't make out the details of his face. That meant Trinidad wouldn't either. Would he know him? Maybe. They'd met at least once—the day Trinidad had killed him.

"I want to go home," the boy said.

"You are going home." Roi d'Esprit leaned down and laid his hand on the boy's chest. "And you'll be safe there, while you wait."

*Wait?* Castile thought as Trinidad's fingers gripped his wrist. *Wait for what?*

The boy shrank back from Roi d'Esprit and snuffled. "I want to go home. I want Trin."

Trinidad was about to crush his wrist. Castile pulled back, but Trinidad didn't let go.

Roi d'Esprit signaled to someone. "He needs more conditioning. He still knows Trinidad."

"No!" The boy threw his arms over his head.

Trinidad dropped Castile's wrist and strode forward. "Wolf."

"What are you doing? Stop it," Castile muttered, grabbing for him.

Roi d'Esprit blurred away. Wolf's forehead wrinkled as he sought Trinidad's face. "Trin?"

Castile tackled Trinidad.

"Wake up, Wolf, it's just a dream! It's all right, wake up!" Trinidad shouted as Castile dragged him back through the fading edges of the dreamscape.

Castile opened his eyes and the world spun slowly into stasis. Coals still glowed in his hearth, emitting the smoky scent he only noticed when he'd been away from it. His eyes felt sticky. He coughed and realized he was gripping Trinidad's arm. Trinidad was just stirring and Castile let go, hoping he didn't notice. He shoved back the covers and rolled from bed, cold sweeping his sweaty chest. He tried to talk but his dry throat only produced more coughing. He bent over the bucket and ladled water into his mouth, gulping. Shivers set in.

"Wolf has amnesia," Trinidad said, like they'd been mid-conversation. "Ever since he came to us. This is the first clue to where he came from."

"It's just a dream, a nightmare. Not a memory," Castile answered, though he didn't believe it. When would an archwarden novice have ever met Roi d'Esprit? Unless ... Castile eyed Trinidad, wondering if he knew the man had been Roi d'Esprit. The voice was the same but the body was different. Wolf had dreamed the spirit king when he was much younger, his skin smoother, his body harder. Castile reached for his cloak. He threw it over his shoulders, fixed the clasp, and flexed his fingers to stop their trembling. "You know better than to interfere in a dreamscape," he said.

"He's young," Trinidad gave him a dark look. "He's not going to have a heart attack."

*You don't know that*, Castile thought. The boy could stroke out. Horns, he might be waking all shocky and sick this very moment. Confused, at least. But Castile wasn't about to challenge that hard stare.

"He's chemwiped?" he asked instead.

"Yeah, we did blood tests."

"Escaped from slavers, then."

"That's the theory."

*Fucking Indigos*, Castile thought. *What have you done?* Whatever it was, he bet Reine was in on it. But telling Trinidad the man in Wolf's dream was Roi d'Esprit would only infuriate him. He might not know Trinidad too well anymore, but he knew he didn't want the archwarden angry.

"Maybe since he got hurt they didn't want him." Castile tapped his own cheek to indicate Wolf's burns. "Maybe that's why they sent him inparish. He wouldn't have been much use for the sex trade."

"Compassion? From slavers?" The words lashed the air like a whip. "They would have just killed him."

Castile shook his head. "I don't know. It was just a dream—"

"Just a dream? You're seriously saying that to me after this?" Trinidad let the covers fall away. The ragged pentacle glowed against the shadow of his skin.

Castile flared. "You know the difference between what happened in the Barren and Wolf's dreamscape as well as I do, so stop pretending you don't."

"The line has narrowed between the two since we used to rove as kids, apparently."

Castile gritted his teeth. "The Barren is real. Dreams are only in the mind. A dreamscape is a person's mind. Or did you discard the truth along with your faith and family?"

Trinidad gave a sharp shake of his head. He spoke through gritted teeth. "How could someone else enter your dreamscape? We brought Paul's body back with us, through the dreamscapes. How could I kill Paul if we were in your mind?"

"You were touching him and I was touching you. Maybe the guy was still alive right then and we carried him along, and then he died."

Trinidad rubbed his hand over his face and focused past Castile. "If Paul survived that long, we might have healed him with the sand."

"I'm more curious about how we ended up in Wolf's dreamscape without trying to rove there. Makes me wonder if Wolf was powerful enough to draw us in." Castile's joints felt soldered. He lifted his hand to touch his temple, still tender from the fight.

Reine had gotten a punch in past the spear. "If he can, it makes him another rover and there aren't supposed to be any more besides us."

Trinidad still stared past him, dark eyes hanging on the middle distance.

"Damn it, Trin. Pay attention." Castile snapped his fingers at him. "Your papa always said there were no other rovers, no one outside our coven that he'd ever heard of. But—"

Trinidad shook his head. "My father was wrong. God knows he was wrong about everything else."

Castile pursed his lips. That way lay fury and violence. But keeping Trinidad on the damn topic was like herding cats. He was still traumatized after everything that had gone on tonight, Castile decided. "If your boy Wolf is a good enough rover to draw us into his dreamscape, maybe he's good enough to bring other people to the Barren."

"I don't think so," Trinidad said. "And he'd have to find it first."

"Maybe he's Wiccan. You said you don't know where—"

"There was no sign of it at all. No pentacles. No totem marks or piercings. Nothing."

"Look. We were in his dreamscape, yeah?" When Trinidad didn't argue, Castile went on. "So maybe Wolf was there, in the Barren. With the bishop's man and Reine d'Esprit. One man wore a hood."

"Then how do you know it was a man?"

Castile pursed his lips. "He was bigger than me."

Trinidad flicked his gaze over Castile as if judging his size. "It wasn't Wolf. He's too young."

Castile sighed but relented with a nod.

"We didn't see Wolf until after you pulled us out. He acted as surprised to see us as we were to see him." Trinidad got to his feet and picked up his sword from the covers, held it up to show Castile the blade. It was black with blood. "And this isn't roving. Not like we knew it."

Castile had to admit Trinidad was probably right. They'd never carried blood through dreamscapes before. But then, they'd never killed anyone as kids, either. "You're injured."

Trinidad glanced at his arm. "It's already stopped bleeding."

"Still. I'll fix it up. Don't want an infection."

It was an ugly, jagged cut, but not deep. Trinidad let Castile smear on salve and tie a clean length of cloth around his arm. The muscle was hard under Castile's hands, flexed as if he could spring into violence at any second. Trinidad's shoulders had broadened from years of blade-work. His heavy chest and muscled abdomen had replaced all his preteen gawkiness. Tattoos of swords ran up each veined forearm.

He'd caught a glimmer of his old friend in the Barren, but this man seemed fabricated of secrecy, eyes shielded beneath the black cross on his brow. His voice was so controlled and soft Castile felt loud and bumbling by comparison. Trinidad didn't shiver despite the cold cave, too consumed with staring at his bloody sword.

Castile backed away, dipped a rag in his metal bucket of water, and tossed it to Trinidad before squatting down and poking up the fire, glad to put his back to the silver pentacle graven on Trinidad's chest. "I've never had a body follow me to another dreamscape before."

"You've killed in dreamscapes." Trinidad didn't sound the least surprised.

Castile grimaced at the fire to erase any expression of uncertainty, drew in a deep breath, and faced Trinidad. "Only when they attack me first."

Trinidad scrubbed at the blood with the cold rag as if he could wipe away Castile's foreboding. "You ever come back bloody?"

"I never had anything come back with me. Mama made me swear not to kill on roves when I went ecoterr. She was against the whole thing anyway, practically disowned me when I took up with the cell. Not that I much cared what she thought back then. And after your parents died—"

Trinidad stiffened.

Castile sighed. "I'm sorry about what happened. I am. But we can't avoid the topic forever."

"They're dead, then? Both your parents?"

Castile nodded. "While I was inside. A bad flu took out a third of the coven. Most of the kids died."

Trinidad sheathed his sword, shrugged out of the remains of his shirt, and tossed it into the fire. He picked up his armor harness, fixing his arm bracers over his bare skin. He wore better armor than Castile had ever seen up close, from the thick leather strapping to the ridges of steel in his bracers designed to stop a sword blow. He yanked his breast plate over his head, winking out the silver gleam of his pentacle. The magnetic catches snapped like gunfire in the silence.

But when he finished, his shoulders slumped. "What have I done? Paul was an archwarden. A brother."

Here he was, back again.

Castile fought the urge to reach out to him. Touch his shoulder or hug him or . . . *Horned One, save me from myself. He's a Christian now, for crying out loud. Doesn't mean he can't have a moment of doubt and he sure doesn't need to cry on my shoulder.* Still. It was gratifying to see Trinidad soften, however briefly.

"They attacked us, remember? You only did what you had to do. Even your god can't grudge you that. And if that archwarden dying helps stop the war, so much the better."

"But what if all Marius' archwardens know how to get there?" Trinidad said. "There'll be no stopping the crusade, not with sand that heals."

"Lord and Lady, it's a good thing you're here to work all this out for me," Castile said. "The notion hasn't been keeping me up nights or anything."

Trinidad blinked, slow. When he opened his eyes, the mask was back in place. "Let's count heads. There was Paul, the Indigo you fought off with her spear, and the man with the knife. He ran away through the graves."

"I know only five of us alive who've been there. You. Me. The bishop. Your man Paul."

"And the Indigo queen."

Castile held himself perfectly still. Reine d'Esprit. If his savvy with her came out, Trinidad would never get over it. Scratch that, he'd probably kill Castile where he stood. "The Indigo queen," he agreed reluctantly.

Trinidad nodded. "You said five."

"What?"

"You don't sound like you were counting the Indigo as a rover."

"She's not." At least he didn't think so.

"So? Without her that's four, not five. What aren't you telling me?"

Damn. "All right. I brought Hawk once," Castile admitted.

"Hawk? You broke our blood oath to bring him?"

"He's Lord Hawk now. And he already knew about it, yeah? Or guessed."

Trinidad just looked at him, leaving Castile wondering whether he recalled Hawk beating up Castile for not roving him when they were kids and Trinidad's violent revenge, or whether he was contemplating sticking Castile with that sword and having done with the whole affair. Castile leaned toward the latter when Trinidad said, "You were ready to kill me tonight for bringing the bishop there. We swore on our blood."

"Don't look at me like that. Hawk's a good man, Trin. Changed. He brought me back from prison, didn't he? And he's our high priest now. I thought we owed him after we lied—"

"After you lied."

Castile flared. "For somebody who wants to pretend his dad never existed, you sure sound like him."

"You're the one who threw our blood vow in my face after you broke it." Trinidad shook his head. "I can't believe it. Hawk . . . high priest? Impossible."

"It wasn't him," Castile said. "He can't rove on his own, and he wouldn't even if he could. He's got healthier respect for the spirit world than you and me. He made it clear he didn't want to go back. But maybe it's time I run all this by him, get his opinion on the bishop."

Trinidad arched an eyebrow. "You took him to the Barren, but you didn't tell him about the bishop going there? Even though he's so changed."

Castile's lip twitched. He cursed his lack of game face. "He seems a good man. Seems fair now. I've only been back a few weeks. I trust him as far as it goes."

Trinidad frowned, but he dropped the issue. Good thing, too. All Castile needed was Trinidad and Hawk at each other's throats like when they were kids.

"Who else, then?" Trinidad asked.

"What does it matter? Obviously, the bishop is the problem. Eliminate her, eliminate the crusade."

Trinidad shook his head, jaw clenched. "I want to stop the crusade as badly as you do. But I can't accuse Bishop Marius of all this, not without proof and serious backing. I'd have to get my order behind me, and Father Troy. I can't ask that of him—" His voice broke and he scrubbed a hand over his short hair. "If I ever see him again. Someone abducted him. I have to go find him, and let the Parish know."

Father Troy. Herne's balls. What would Trinidad do when he found out Father Troy had been sitting here at the cave the whole time, much less that Castile had been behind the priest's abduction? The plan had seemed sound, but that was before he'd realized Trinidad was so dangerous.

"Politics are against us," Castile said. "What else is new? We still have to stop the bishop. She's the one they've rallied around. Without her, the crusade dies."

Trinidad shook his head. "I don't know that we can stop her. She's been talking crusade for years, and now she's using that scar to her advantage. It's got people inparish riled up for war."

"We can't let people die over a fucking graveyard."

"It's a graveyard we can only reach through the craft and it has sand that heals."

"It's a pretty prize, you mean," Castile said, but Trinidad took on a pensive expression.

"No. The crusade is not about winning the Barren. She already has it or at least thinks she does. It's about keeping it secret. She's looking for you, for people who can rove, who might betray her lies.... She must think it could disprove Christianity."

"The Barren disproves Christianity as much as it disproves Wicca. Or the Indigo ghostfaith. Christians always think they're the downtrodden ones."

"I didn't say I agreed with her," Trinidad said, his voice quiet.

Castile drew a breath. Another. "I knew you didn't believe."

Trinidad's head snapped up. "Every single ecoterr in Boulder Parish is a witch. I know the signs, even if the Christian courts don't. You tell me, which is more evil? The ecoterr war or crusade?"

Horns, they stumbled over one prickly topic after another. Maybe it was time to bring up Father Troy after all. He sighed. "I just don't get how you could turn your back on the craft when you know it's real."

"I was twelve," Trinidad said. "I thought Christ was an aspect of The Horned One."

Castile bent to pick up Trinidad's black cloak. It smelled of him, and the outdoors. He held it out to Trinidad. "And now?"

A muscle twitched along Trinidad's jaw. "Now the bishop is killing to keep the Barren secret, and I'm falling in line."

Their fingers bumped amid the folds of the cloak. Blood pulsing in his throat, Castile gripped Trinidad's hand. "You think killing that man Paul shames you. But you also saved my life back there, yeah?"

Trinidad's eyes shadowed beneath his furrowed brow, but he didn't pull his hand back. "I won't be so careless with it again."

A cleared throat broke them apart. They turned to find Hawk pushing the curtain aside. His hair was smashed to one side and exhaustion hollowed his eye sockets.

"I'm glad you're back, Woodwose," he said.

Trinidad frowned, probably at the nickname. "Hawk."

"Lord Hawk now," Hawk said. Castile suppressed a sigh. Trinidad didn't answer.

"What's wrong?" Castile asked. "You look sick or something."

"No. Aspen just woke me." Hawk combed his beard with his fingers and eyed Trinidad. "There's something wrong with your priest."

Trinidad fell deadly still. He turned his head to look at Castile. "Father Troy? Here?"

Castile nodded, caught. "I didn't get a chance to—"

"You brought him here?" Flat. Lethal.

"He's a friend. I would never let anything happen to him. He's fine—"

Trinidad slid his sword into his scabbard with a sharp hiss. "He's not fine. He's sick. And you've probably just killed him."

# THIRTEEN

Trinidad knew the way without thinking. He fastened his cloak as he went, heart hammering his ribs. He made a cursory note of two Wiccan soldiers hanging about in the main part of the cave, bristling with knives and rifles. Awake at such a late hour and positioned where they'd do little good against external attack, they had to be due to his presence. A third soldier leaned against a cavern wall, rifle resting on her shoulder. She pushed herself off her wall and tagged along behind them.

Wooden structures leaned against the walls, doorways were covered by curtains made of various materials or real doors when the owner had salvaged one and hinges to hang it with; smoke tunneled up through chimneys to blend with the clouds and ash in the open air of the canyon.

In what must have been Hawk's house, Father Troy reclined against cushions, eyes closed and looking pale. His wrinkled hands were balled into fists. He looked old and frail. Trinidad felt like he hadn't seen him for weeks, not hours. This morning, he reminded himself. It had just been since this morning. A woman sat on her knees next to him, pregnant belly filling her lap. Trinidad recognized her freckles and sharp profile from childhood. Her name was Aspen.

Trinidad dropped to one knee next to Father Troy. "Father? I'm here."

"Thank God, Trinidad, you're all right." His voice was breathless and raspy, but he took Trinidad's hand in his weak one.

Pain obviously strained his dying body and struggling heart. The doctors had warned him not to go too long between treatments, and he was already a week late. "I told you not to put off your dose."

Father Troy squeezed his hand. "Don't nag, son." Just those few words left him breathless.

"I have to get him back inparish now," Trinidad said to Castile. "He needs to be in the hospital."

Castile shook his head. "You can't go back now. Not after you … not after everything that's happened."

"I'm not going to let him die in this cave."

"But we need you here—"

"Castile," Hawk said.

Castile spun. Though Hawk met his gaze with a mild expression, Castile lowered his chin. "My lord."

Trinidad's gaze flicked between the two and his lip curled. But he bit back a retort. Arguing wouldn't get Father Troy to the hospital any quicker.

"I'm going to get a litter and Castile, you will take them back," Hawk said. "I agreed to let you bring Trinidad and the priest here, but we can't let Father Troy lie here in pain when something can be done about it." Hawk turned to the woman who had followed them, muttering orders. "Magpie, run out and prepare the dray."

Magpie crossed her arms and balanced her weight evenly on both feet. Another fighter, Trinidad noted. She'd been really little when he'd left the coven. Beneath his notice.

"Go, Mags. I'm not asking," Hawk said.

Magpie raked them all with her glare, dropped a haughty chin to her brother, and shoved through the curtain. Hawk headed for the curtain as well.

"I'll take him inparish," Castile said to Trinidad. "You stay here."

Trinidad started to draw his sword. "Let me go or die trying to keep me here. Your choice."

Aspen laid her hand on Trinidad's arm. "No one is killing anyone today. We're all doing everything we can—" Her breath caught. She hunched over with a moan and reached out. Trinidad let his sword slide back into its scabbard in order to catch her by the hand. He lowered her to the ground, supporting her weight as best he could.

"My lady?" Castile took a step forward. "What's wrong?"

"Contraction," she hissed. She ground Trinidad's finger bones together and didn't say anything for several seconds. At last she released him. Her voice was strained, breathless.

"Let Trinidad go with his priest, Cas. But don't go inparish. Swear to me you won't go inside. It's too dangerous."

"Done. We take him only as far as the wall," Castile said. He narrowed his eyes at Trinidad. "And you're not going inparish with him either."

Trinidad frowned, but found no point in arguing it out now. He could better manage Castile away from the coven.

Father Troy rubbed Trinidad's knee. "Are you all right, son? I heard they almost . . . killed you."

Trinidad's shoulders stiffened. It wasn't all right. Nothing would be right again, not since he'd killed Paul. Castile was right. How could he go back inparish? They would imprison him, execute him. But he couldn't just run, either. He bowed his head. "Father. Paul and I—"

"Later," Castile said, sharp.

Hawk shoved the doorway curtain aside and dragged a litter inside. Aspen straightened and wrapped the blanket closer around her. A sheen of sweat slicked her pale face.

"Problem?" Hawk laid the litter down next to Father Troy but looked at Trinidad.

Trinidad thought fast. If he was surrounded by Wiccans, he'd never get away, he'd never get inside parish walls. And whatever Castile said, he would never trust Hawk.

He forced a polite tone. "Stay with your wife, my lord. She's in labor."

Hawk held for a moment, brows raised at Aspen. "Labor?"

"I'm fine." She wiped away a strand of hair stuck to her sweaty brow.

Trinidad cleared his throat. "When Israel was born, Papa said the baby was getting close when Mother about broke my hand during a contraction. Like you just did."

Castile glared at him. "We can't go with just the two of us."

"I'll go," Magpie said from the doorway.

Aspen grimaced as another contraction overtook her. She sank to her knees. They waited it out for several seconds in silence until she looked up. Trinidad's blood roared in his head. They didn't have time for this. They had to get Father Troy back.

"No. Not you, Magpie," Hawk said. "Someone else."

"You swore to me," Magpie said. "You swore you'd treat me like any other soldier."

Hawk frowned. Castile pressed his lips together in a scowl and shook his head.

"It's safe for me to go. I have no record. They have no reason to hold me. I can get in and out without any trouble. Not like the rest of the coven."

Castile's fingers tightened into fists. "You have no idea what you're talking about—"

"Ahh," Aspen moaned. "Goddess spare me, just go, the lot of you!"

"All right, Magpie. Go with him." Hawk cast another unreadable glance at Trinidad before turning to his wife.

Castile said, "You follow my orders. To the letter. Understand?"

Magpie gave a saucy salute and helped Trinidad arrange Father Troy on the litter. The priest didn't stir much. Trinidad felt his forehead. Clammy and cold.

Trinidad tried to focus on keeping the litter steady rather than on the shallow rise and fall of his priest's chest. He smelled the ash from outdoors and acrid sick-sweat from the priest combining with the sour scent of tallow burning. He realized the Barren might have been the only place he'd ever been where he could not scent ash and death on the air.

As they reached the grotto, Trinidad slowed without meaning to. The altar laid with sweet-smelling beeswax candles and holy items, the faint glow of oil torches, the scuffs on the cavern floor marking where three generations of Wiccans had laid Circles. It all was the same. His own father had once taken the Hunter Aspect, horned head menacing and thrilling as he danced . . .

Castile took the litter and sent Magpie scuttling ahead to ready the dray. He spoke low and hard to Trinidad, dragging him back from the memory. "Don't think I missed what you did back there, getting Hawk to stay behind. But I'm still holding you to our oath. No matter what happens, we hold the Barren and we stop the crusade. You're in it as deep as me now."

# FOURTEEN

Bishop Marius learned Father Troy was unexpectedly missing and that Trinidad and Daniel had disappeared as well, supposedly gone off with him. Seth had been nervous explaining it to her, but she did her best to ease his fears of foul play. That they hadn't alerted the rest of the archwardens as to their whereabouts caused her no particular worry. Surely it was a misunderstanding. Seth was silent and grim in response. She retreated to safety in her basement room and waited, praying and doing some planning.

But she had learned over the years that archwardens rarely fetched her in the night with good news. So, when someone knocked on her door, dread fell like a stone in her stomach. She rose from her desk and opened the door. Seth waited for her.

"Did you find them?"

"No. No news there." He paused. "We went to find Paul to ask him to help look, but . . ." Staring past her, at attention, the tattoo on Seth's pale brow creased, betraying his strain. "He's dead, Your Grace."

The rock in her stomach ruptured into a familiar void. She drew a breath to steady her voice. It came husky and rough. "What happened?"

"We knocked and tried his door. It was locked. We broke in and found him . . . stabbed."

"Stabbed," she whispered, stiffening her weak knees against toppling.

He held out a hand as if to catch her. She didn't take it.

"Yes, Your Grace." Seth shook his head. "I don't understand how this could have happened. The door was locked from the inside and the window is too small for anyone to fit through."

She understood, all too well. "Take me to him."

Seth turned and led the way down the cold basement corridor, the parish archwarden Malachi and a couple of her own men following her. An exorbitant guard detail, but they wouldn't take any chances with what they now considered was an abduction of their priest and two archwardens, and now a murder. Two veteran archwardens flanked Paul's door, in full armor kit complete with decorations of honor and black cloaks despite the hour. One opened the door and bowed his head, granting her entrance. The Order of Archwardens dealt with their dead with stoic conduct in public. Raw grief was for private, away from their priests—under cover of darkness with brothers and alcohol.

She took a step forward and then raised a hand as they made to follow.

"Alone." She paused. "A few moments. I must pray."

They bowed their way out and latched the door softly behind her.

Cold silence pervaded the air, as it did when a room held a life-less body. Paul had been sleeping on his side. Blood had pooled in his cheek and temple. They'd since turned him on his back and covered him with his crusader's cloak. His naked sword lay under his hands, aligned with the crimson cross embroidered on the black drape of fabric, blade pointed toward his feet. His face hung slack, lips slightly apart. His lashes lay quiet on his cheek.

She walked forward, careful to make no noise, and touched him, slid his hand between hers. The same long fingers, hardened from life as a fighter, as cold as the room. All the warmth had faded from his body. And his damned tattoos, also fading . . . he couldn't go on like that, couldn't go into the ground like that . . . she sucked in a hiss of breath.

She shifted the cloak and found the gash from a sword under his ribs, a savage stab wound, direct to the lung. He'd been laid on clean bedding and the blood was gone. Stark white sheeting under-scored the viciousness of the wound. The murderer had twisted the blade, ensuring death.

Wiccan ecoterrs had brought their war to Christ's doorstep when they'd murdered her child and the war was still on. Trembling overcame her and she leaned over Paul, pressed her cheek against the cold steel of his sword and his motionless hands. She tangled her fingers in the prayer beads wound around his wrist.

"What must I do to prove my faith to You, Lord?" she whis-pered. "Who else will You take?"

She twisted the prayer beads and the cord snapped. The wooden beads sounded like far-off gunfire as they hit the concrete floor. She scrambled for them but only caught a few before the rest rolled away into shadowed corners. Sometime later, she found herself kneeling on the floor, arms wrapped around her stomach, listening to the silence.

She rose and straightened her back, thinking, *For we walk by faith, not by sight.* Stupid to have expected an answer. She had to prove herself to God, not the other way around. With shaking hands, she straightened the cloak over Paul's still form, patting his stiff chest, not sure how to comfort a dead man. She jerked her hand away. Paul wasn't here any longer, just like her son hadn't been there as she'd cradled his limp little body. They were with God now. Her son sat at His left hand as a martyr, and now Paul had joined them. He would watch over her little boy in Heaven as he had always watched over her on Earth. That would please Paul, no doubt. Such service always had.

*Take up the shield of faith, with which you can extinguish all the flaming arrows of the evil one.* And with the shield, a blade.

Grief fell away into nothing and her mind stilled. God stole it away, as He always did. There was His answer and with it, her charge to prove herself yet again. Death was ever a challenge from Him, as it had been since those first deaths, since her son.

Her vision blurred, not with tears, but from a hard stare. The door had been locked. No one had entered and killed Paul in this room. Only one place he could have died. The Barren. Only one real suspect. The Wiccan, Castile. But why? And, most of all, how would she make him pay?

# FIFTEEN

Rust ate at every edge of the coven dray and its door hinges creaked like screaming banshees. The refitted meshed windows were pocked and cracked. Pebbled steel and polymer sheeting armored it, and it stunk from the burning trash it ran on. Solid, run-flat tires gave a ride that jolted the teeth from your head.

Trinidad sat in back next to Father Troy, who appeared mostly unconscious. Once they escaped the valley unseen and were nearing Dragonspine, Castile glanced back at him. Trinidad pulled the clip from an old Savage rifle to count bullets. He gave Castile a dark look.

"That's the best gun we've got," Castile said from the driver's seat. "If you have a problem with it, you can carry your priest home over your shoulder."

"I didn't say anything," Trinidad said.

"You didn't have to."

Magpie sat in the passenger seat next to Castile, eyes fixed forward. He ignored her. She'd managed to wrangle her way onto this little jaunt, to impress him or win his heart or some damn thing. She didn't know how risky going inparish would be for Castile, or she'd be arguing the whole way. Thank the Trine for small favors.

Castile pushed the old dray as fast as it could go. They drove in a stiff, heavy silence, enduring the cold and jolting without further comment, for nearly an hour. Ash floated on the clouds of their breath. Castile never thought he'd be relieved to see the glow from Boulder Parish, white spotlights looking like pearly clouds by the ash on the air.

"That's a roadblock up ahead," Magpie said as Castile squinted, seeing the same thing as she spoke. Old kegs and a lot of slavers, armed with rifles and torches, painted up for battle.

Trinidad crawled forward to lean over the seat. The archwarden's warm breath made Castile's neck tingle as Trinidad leaned close to peer through the windshield. "They can't be out this far with no transportation."

"Drays behind us, I'm sure," Castile said. "It's a trap."

Slavers drove slick armored drays and wielded heavy firepower financed by the trade in other American regions and Mexico. The skull sigils of Santa Muerte decorated their armor. Multi-hued paint distorted their faces. Slavers didn't usually bother with roadblocks. They had sophisticated infiltration techniques and people inparish to do their bidding. When those provisions failed, they used blunt force. Despite the parish's best efforts, little kids disappeared into the slave trade every day.

This was all wrong, all wrong, though. Castile cursed silently and then aloud. "Fuck. Why are they here, now?"

Trinidad shifted away, leaving a cold spot on Castile's skin.

He said it as Castile thought it: "Somebody tipped them we were coming."

More cursing, though he kept it to himself. Reine d'Esprit. That Indigo bitch had pulled favors with her slaver contacts to get them killed. He didn't know how or why Reine had embedded herself with the Christians, but he had no doubt she was at the bottom of this ambush.

"You're slowing down," Magpie said. Her voice broke and she cleared her throat.

Artemis, give her strength to shoot. "The barrels are weighted. Got to bully our way through. Brace yourselves and when I say go, make every shot count." He looked over his shoulder. "Steady back there?"

In answer, Trinidad chambered a bullet and slipped the barrel of the rifle through a hole drilled in the armored plating. His face hardened to stone. He looked like he'd forgotten all about the unconscious priest at his side.

Sickness ached deep in Castile's belly. From his first day in prison, he'd met a lifetime's worth of people who could kill without regret. For them, efficient brutality was a way of life. Very little of his childhood friend was left in this man who had become a Christian archwarden.

Trinidad held his gaze for a moment that seemed to stretch into minutes. "Just drive, Castile."

Castile turned back to the barrels. The slavers shouted and waved rifles. No shots yet. Only a matter of time.

Magpie rested her rifle on the dash, the barrel jammed in a drill-hole. The red moon slipped out from behind a cloud and cast a bloody hue over the scene.

"My job is to get through the barrels, Mags. Your job is to kill them," Castile said to her. "You wanted to come along, so make yourself useful."

She stared hard at the slavers, acknowledging that he'd spoken with the barest of nods. Not deferential enough to suit his rank as leader, but Castile decided to take Trinidad's advice and just drive. As he rolled forward without hesitation, the slavers started to fire on them. "Right on fucking cue," he muttered.

Bullets pinged off the armor and glass, putting fresh cracks in the meshed windows but not breaking through. Yet. Bullets kept peppering the dray. This was a hit, not a slave run. Trinidad and Magpie fired their weapons. He heard screams, saw slavers erased into crimson mist.

The dray shoved through the kegs, slowing dangerously. Only Trinidad's whip-crack aim held the enemy at bay, but they didn't have enough bullets to stop them for long. They were too many. Castile gunned the accelerator as he shoved against a barrel. The engine whined and the tires spun against the broken road. What was in these things? Lead? A slaver rushed the driver's door and pressed his gun to the glass. Castile raised his gun to the port by his elbow and fired. The slaver fell away.

"I'm out," Trinidad said, voice flat.

Castile gritted his teeth and concentrated on his acceleration, feeling their tires slip on the rough road. Slavers crawled on top of the dray, pounding on it with fists and rifle butts. Others did the same, trying to break through the window in the back. They unwittingly pushed the vehicle and helped it gain traction. It was enough to shove through the barrels, the dray reeling and creaking as the run-flats stuck to and then jerked free of the ground-spikes set behind the barricade. More slavers swamped the vehicle, painted faces looking like a nightmare's collection of evil gods, pressing their guns against the glass. Castile went cold. They weren't moving fast enough. There were too many.

A bullet punctured the meshed glass and Trinidad barked vague words, whether in pain or fury, Castile couldn't tell. Not knowing if Trinidad was hit, he risked stalling the engine by stomping on the accelerator. For a few heartbeats the engine revved and choked. A bullet cracked the windshield, and then another.

Magpie screamed. Castile wrenched on the wheel to change their angle, "Fight, Magpie!"

Wind whipped through the holes. Castile kept steady pressure, focusing on the Horns in his mind's eye, a wordless plea for passage through the flying bullets.

With a bone-jarring jolt, the engine bellowed back to life and the dray leapt free of the barrels, throwing Castile and his passengers from side to side. It was all he could do to hang onto the wheel and steer straight. The slavers scattered from his random path. As the immediate fire faded behind them, Father Troy moaned loudly; it choked off with a cough.

Trinidad spoke, his deep voice fatally calm. "Quickly, Cas. Father Troy is hit."

Bullets pelted the dray, but by then they were too far out of range to puncture the glass or metal. Castile glanced over his shoulder again, past Trinidad huddling over his priest, hands pressed to the old man's leg, blood thick on the air. A slaver dray barreled behind them, gaining.

Next to him, Magpie curled into a shaking ball, her breath deteriorating into whiny gasps. Realization aborted a lecture on bucking up. She'd screamed, back there— "Fuck me, you're hit." He reached out and laid his hand on her leg. "We're almost inparish."

Inparish. Marshals. Prison. He had no place to bail outside the gates now, not with slavers behind them. His voice shook. "They'll take care of you at the hospital."

"I don't want-t to g-go."

"You have to," he said. "It'll be all right. It'll be all right." He stopped talking, wondering who he was trying to convince.

A spotlight flashed behind them, glaring off the inside of his cracked windshield, nearly blinding him. He eased the pedal down a bit more, urging speed. The old dray shimmied in protest. They had reached the outlying houses of the old Martin Acres settlement, many gutted for scrap and the rest filled with desperate squatters. His jaw hurt from clenching his teeth against the jarring ride; his elbow hurt from banging into the door. Even this close to the parish the pavement wasn't any smoother than county roads.

Maybe the marshals came out and sledge-hammered it when they were bored, out of spite. Castile fought back panicked laughter.

"Stop. Please don't make me go in there." Magpie sounded breathy with pain. "I'll never c-come out."

*You and me both*, Castile thought. Bullets from the slaver dray raked the road behind them and pinged off the back window. He sharpened his voice to a command. "Strength, soldier. Just keep pressure on that wound. You'll be fine."

"Slow down for the gate," Trinidad said.

"I don't know if you've noticed," Castile retorted, "but bullets are still hitting the back of the dray."

"We'll get far worse if you rush the gate," Trinidad said. "Let the marshals deal with the slavers. Slow down."

Slaver bullets came hard and fast again, the clamor pounding rapid-fire in Castile's skull. Slaving must pay well to afford to throw away ammo like that. Either that, or someone very rich wanted them very dead. He squinted past his wind-strewn tears and focused on the gate. There was no way for the marshals to know they were friendlies, not with rabid slavers mauling his dray with bullets.

"Stop," Trinidad said.

"What?"

"I won't let them hurt you."

That low voice again, filling him with confidence when he should only feel alarm. Castile let the car roll to a gentle halt, mindful of his injured passengers and twisted around to look at Trinidad. "Now what?"

Trinidad still wore his impenetrable warrior face. "Now we wait."

The slaver dray careened toward them, still firing. Trinidad bent low over his priest, his face turned toward Castile, holding his gaze. Castile opened his mouth to ask for reassurance that they were doing the right thing, that the marshals wouldn't frag their dray, that the slaver dray wouldn't kill them on impact—

"Faith," Trinidad whispered.

The slaver dray exploded into a firebomb, raining chunks of metal and worse. Trinidad closed his eyes, pushing low over his bloody hands where they compressed the bullet wound in Father Troy's thigh. His lips moved, forming words Castile couldn't hear. Father Troy's trembling hand eased up to cradle the back of Trinidad's head.

The gate slid open and marshals ran toward them, brandishing rifles.

"Uh, Trin? I think you're up," Castile said.

Trinidad lifted up, blinking like he'd just woken. He looked at the burning hulk that had been the slaver dray. "Open your door."

"They'll—"

"I won't let them hurt you, Cas."

Castile opened his door. Marshals dragged him from the seat and slammed him up against the pockmarked dray, knocking the wind from him, bruising his cheek. Other marshals pounded on Magpie's door. He could hear Trinidad talking, calm and earnest. "Let him go. He's a friendly. We have injured. He needs to drive us. Father Troy is bleeding, and I can't take the pressure off."

A marshal leaned down and peered into the dray to speak to Trinidad. "We'll call an ambulance. Or I'll drive you."

"There's no time to wait for one to come. He'll bleed out. And you have more slavers to see to. There's a blockade a klick or two back."

"This one's wearing a pentacle." Someone kicked the back of Castile's knee and he winced against the dray, held up only by their grip.

Trinidad met Castile's eyes through the pocked glass. "He's under my protection."

Those seemed to be the magic words. They released Castile with a shove. He slid back into the driver's seat, resisting the urge to swagger. The gates swung open and he drove through, gaining speed. "I still feel like their guns are sighted on my back."

"That's because they are. Magpie really has no record?" Trinidad asked.

Magpie cringed against the seat, fear casting her wordless. Castile bit his lip, not even trying to school his face to play poker. No point in it, not with Trinidad. "No. She's clean."

"Then what's wrong?"

"I'm supposed to stay ten klicks from Boulder Parish, per my parole."

A beat. Two. "Why didn't you tell me before?"

"You didn't ask." Castile got the distinct feeling if Trinidad had a hand free, he'd have smacked him on the back of the head.

With terse directions, Trinidad got them to the hospital and they pulled under the torch-lit throughway at emergency. Orderlies were already coming to meet them, hauling a gurney. Two marshals flanked the door, holding rifles across their chests.

Castile eyed the marshals. Dank clouds swirled over their heads, gray against the night sky, warning of a storm. He hadn't noticed it with everything going on.

The orderlies climbed in next to Trinidad and exchanged terse words as Castile got out to help Magpie. The marshals watched with intent curiosity but didn't change position. Magpie was smeared in blood, but Castile breathed a sigh of relief; the wound was in her arm, not her body, like he'd feared. Maybe they'd just patch her up and he could take her home.

The first sleet from the storm pelted their faces. It smelled stale, of dirt and smoke. Trinidad started to follow Father Troy on his gurney and then stopped and looked back at Castile and Magpie.

Magpie started to resist again as soon as she saw the gurney. Castile hugged her close, trying to suppress her struggle. "You'll be all right. Magpie. They'll take care of you."

She clung to him. "Please don't leave me. Please."

After Castile had returned home from prison, Lord Hawk had suggested he marry his sister Magpie to secure his position in the coven. Castile had said it wasn't fair to Magpie if he didn't love her, if he could never love her. Hawk had retorted that there was a higher cause than love, one of procreation. Magpie had clung to him when he'd refused her, just as she did now, digging her fingers into his back, her tears soaking his chest as the orderlies tried to pull her away.

"Come along, miss," one of them said. "We're just going to see to that wound."

Her fight gained in viciousness. She swung wildly at the orderlies, and then Trinidad was there. He pried her off Castile with hands still bloody from Father Troy's wound and placed her on the gurney. She surrendered to his touch, but she gave Castile a bruised look.

"You'll be all right," Castile said, hands hanging at his sides, helpless as they rolled her away.

A marshal approached. Sleet glistened on his helmet and froze against Castile's scalp. "Archwarden? I'm Lieutenant Quinn."

"Trinidad," he answered, bowing his head with stiff courtesy.

"I have a few questions for my report," Quinn said.

"There's not much to tell. We were chased by slavers outside parish walls," Trinidad said. "Two of us were injured, as you see. The guards at the gate sent us on."

"And this Wiccan?"

Castile reached for the pentacle hanging at his throat, thought better of it, and let his hand fall back to his side.

Trinidad took hold of Castile's arm. He shoved Castile inside the back of the dray like he was a prisoner, pushing his head down with a firm hand to make sure he didn't bump it on the roof. "He's my business. My bishop is inparish. I'm certain she's been in contact with the mayor's office. They'll have more information for you."

"I'm here, now," the marshal said. "What's so secret?"

Trinidad slammed the door shut and spun to face the marshal so fast Castile thought he was going to hit him. Castile couldn't hear what he said. The marshal didn't look too happy, but he didn't protest further.

Castile scrubbed the wet from his head with his fingers as Trinidad pulled off from the curb. Sleet tap-danced across the windshield and slipped in through the bullet holes in the dray. He climbed over the seat into the front despite Magpie's bloodstains.

Trinidad clenched the steering wheel, but his gaze was steady, moving over the road ahead calmly. "You keep looking at me like you have a question."

Castile turned away from the hard, clean lines of Trinidad's profile and cleared his throat. "What was that about the bishop and the mayor?"

Trinidad shrugged. "Each fights for the upper hand. It's a distraction. Hopefully it lasts long enough to get you somewhere safe."

Castile grunted. "And Magpie?"

"They'll let her go if she's got a clean record. She's the least of our worries. Those marshals are curious about you. They'll message the gate. When they find out you're not expected, they'll detain you for a background check." He gestured to a street lamp, glowing faintly against the sleet. "Power's on. Comms are working. There's no way we can beat that call to the gate. Which means I can't get you out of town."

# SIXTEEN

The wind whipping through the bullet holes in the dray's windows tore at Trinidad's raw throat with every breath. He drove steadily toward the church. Hardly the best place to seek refuge but he didn't know where else to go. Roman would beat them both senseless if he took Castile to his apartment. Besides, the marshals were smart enough to make that connection, and Roman's place was under marshal jurisdiction. The church was not.

What would Father Troy advise? Father Troy . . . it took everything he had not to turn the dray back around.

"You're going to be in a lot of trouble over this, aren't you?" Castile crossed his arms over his chest, hands tucked in against the cold whistling through the bullet holes. "I'm surprised you didn't just leave me with the marshals."

Trinidad had performed a vast collection of nasty things during his archwarden training. One of these hardening exercises had been to throw executed convicts into the prison incinerator. Every single body bore torture marks. He glanced at Castile. "I wouldn't do that."

Castile blinked, drew an audible breath. "We have a safehouse against the west wall. If I can get there, I can get out of the parish. Just let me out here, yeah? We'll regroup later."

"It's after curfew."

"I'm good at ghosting."

No one was that good. "The church is the only place inparish that marshals don't have jurisdiction. You're safer there than anywhere."

"You're going to have to answer to the bishop, right?"

And maybe she'd have to answer some of his questions, too. *God forgive her for lying,* Trinidad thought. *God help me.* "The Church will give you asylum. My vows—"

A sharp pitch of tension corrupted Castile's voice. "Your vows blind you to the truth. You don't belong there. You are a witch. You can rove."

"No. I'm an archwarden who can rove. You probably hoped it would be an advantage, my having a foot in both worlds. But you don't get to use what I am and then insult me with it."

Castile rubbed his hand over his face. "We were friends, yeah? Like brothers. More, even. I just thought—"

"You thought you could control me. But I don't answer to you. I answer to my order, my Church, and to Christ."

The shining bell-tower emerged from the smoky darkness amid the hills and buildings of downtown, still a couple of blocks away. Lights flashed against the inside of the windshield from behind them. Trinidad twisted around to look. A marshal's street comber, gaining on them. He punched the accelerator as he turned a corner, the run-flat tires jarring his bones over every pothole and crack in the rutted street.

A siren sounded and more lights approached from a cross street as Trinidad rolled through the intersection. The bell tower beckoned, belying the snipers policing behind the merlons—snipers culled from marshal ranks.

The gates to the churchyard hung open. Against his archwardens' advisement, Father Troy had ordered them kept unlocked at all hours. All were welcome for worship or sanctuary, risks be damned. They needed quick sanctuary tonight, so Trinidad would never complain about the gates again.

A novice or archwarden would be manning the gate. Trinidad recalled the schedule and chilled; Wolf had duty tonight. Maybe he wasn't there, maybe he was still sick and sleeping . . . but his brother stood up in the little gatehouse and gaped at the Wiccan dray careening past him.

Trinidad hit the brake, but they slid on the frosted ash coating the pavement inside the gate and crashed against the low wall surrounding the labyrinth. They both slammed forward. Trinidad's armored chest hit the steering wheel and his knee banged the dash casing.

Castile tumbled into the dash. He righted himself and rubbed at his forehead gingerly, but he didn't seem hurt beyond blood welling from a small cut over his eyebrow.

Trinidad shoved the door open, but Castile caught his arm. Blood ran in a steady stream down his face. His breath made sharp little noises. "I remember what we had, even if you don't."

"I spent a dozen years trying to forget." Trinidad's words came out rough. Castile didn't move, just held his gaze. Trinidad reached up and rubbed his thumb over Castile's eyebrow, wiping the blood away from his eye. "Stay here, Cas, where it's safe."

He walked back toward the gate as the marshal's comber rolled to a more conservative stop, its front wheels resting where the churchyard gates would close.

A marshal got out of the front seat. Trinidad put himself in the comber's path but didn't draw his blade or a gun, not yet. That would be something he couldn't come back from. The comber's engine hummed almost silently, but it shifted slightly. Packed with marshals.

"Archwarden," the marshal said, spreading his hands wide. He gripped a pistol, ruining the portrayal of imploring reason. "Your Wiccan is a convicted terrorist."

Wolf peeked through the window of the gate tower and Trinidad twitched his chin at him, indicating retreat. Wolf glanced toward the dray and Castile before joining Trinidad, taking position to his left.

"Castile seeks asylum within the church," Trinidad said. "As an archwarden, I am bound by oath to provide it."

"Felons have no right to asylum. City marshals wish to question him about the altercation at the west gate."

"I was there," Trinidad said, eyeing the marshal's pistol. "Question me."

The marshal scowled and lowered his gun. "You would challenge me, your Christian brother, over a filthy Wiccan?"

"He helped our priest," Trinidad said, even as a voice inside protested that Castile had abducted him, had mixed him up in the Barren and the wrong side of the crusade.

"He may be a Wiccan, but he is a human being," a gentle voice said from the darkness. Trinidad turned his head. Bishop Marius strolled from the sanctuary, followed by two of her archwardens.

Trinidad took a step back and dipped his chin. "Your Grace."

"Stand down, archwarden." The bishop turned to the marshal. "What is your business here, sir?"

"Your Grace, that man," the marshal pointed at Castile, "is a Wiccan ecoterr and felon. He's broken parole by trespassing inparish. The archwarden brought him and—"

"No. He brought us," Trinidad said. "He was helping us. Father Troy is hurt—"

"I said stand down, Trinidad," the bishop said.

Trinidad closed his mouth and chanced another glance at Castile. He was starting to edge away from the dray. Trinidad shook his head slightly. Castile stopped.

"Your authority ends at these gates, does it not?" the bishop asked the marshal.

"Yes, Your Grace, but—"

"So you may be about your business, and God willing, we'll see you at matins tomorrow. Christ's peace be upon you."

Marius' pointed tone flayed Trinidad's nerves, but the marshal dipped his head in a cursory bow. "And you, Your Grace."

They all watched the comber back from the gateway and turn around. No one moved until its lights faded into the darkness.

"Come, Trinidad. Bring your guest and we'll sort this out." Bishop Marius turned back toward the sanctuary, taking the route beneath the cloister, but her archwardens waited. They met Trinidad's gaze with implacable stares.

"Trin?" Wolf asked lowly. "What's going on?"

"Back to position, Wolf," Trinidad said. He nodded to Castile, who emerged from behind the battered dray to follow, his body all stiff lines and taut movements.

Bishop Marius led the way into the sanctuary and climbed the steps to the altar, genuflecting before turning to face Trinidad and Castile. Two of her archwardens brought her a chair and then flanked her, hands clasped as if they'd been put at ease. Trinidad knew the deceit in their pose. They could have a gun trained in a half-second. Two more of the bishop's archwardens kept behind Trinidad and Castile, hands on their hilts.

Trinidad laid his sword at the bishop's feet and took a knee before her. He stripped his gauntlets and tucked them in his belt as an additional sign of respect. Ordinarily, he wouldn't have. This was no ordinary night.

"Explain, archwarden."

"Your Grace," he said. "This is Castile, a Wiccan from the mountains. He brought us back to the parish when Father Troy fell ill."

"And how did you meet?"

"We were attacked by Indigos and Castile . . . helped us." Simple was best. Still, he cringed inwardly at his omissions.

"And where did you find Father Troy?"

"I—I don't know, Your Grace. I was knocked out from the fire-fight." He indicated the damage the bullet had caused to his armor. "When I came to, Castile and his people were there. They'd run off the Indigos and found Father Troy in one of the drays."

"Indeed." Her thin eyebrows raised, creasing the silver scar. He tried not to look at it. Was she pretending not to know Castile or had he actually managed to conceal his identity from her in the Barren? Either way, he might as well climb in all the way into his own bed of lies. The truth would be sussed out later, but right now he needed to buy Castile some good will and time.

He heard Castile move behind him. The archwardens attending Bishop Marius shifted as well. Trinidad gestured with a flat hand behind his back. Castile quieted.

"Where are the other inparish archwardens?"

Trinidad blinked and forced himself to stare into her eyes. He realized he was letting the silence drag on too long. Curse him for using Daniel's death to prove a lie. "I partnered with Daniel in the search. He died in the attack."

The rest of the truth lay in the silver lines etching his chest and Paul's blood crusting the engraving on the naked sword at her feet. How would he keep all that from her? She would learn Paul was dead soon enough and figure out where it had happened. If she hadn't already. Paul had been dead for hours . . .

The bishop just looked at him, waiting.

"Seth and Malachi didn't come with us—they weren't here at the church."

"Their absence was unexpected?"

If his lies didn't collapse right away like a house of cards, Malachi and Seth would pay for it. He'd just accused them of desertion, if not in so many words. He nodded.

His knee throbbed where it had banged in the crash—kneeling on it wasn't helping—and his chest felt constricted by his armor. The more he tried not to focus on the pentacle in his chest, the horror of watching that knife carve a sacrilegious symbol into his skin and the searing sand as it healed his wounds, the shallower his breaths became. Heat rose from his collar. He lowered his head.

"Are you all right?" Marius sounded almost gentle.

He answered with absurd understatement. "It's been a long night, Your Grace."

Marius arched an eyebrow at Trinidad, gestured for him to stand. He watched the archwardens take note of his favoring his injured knee. Marius glanced at Castile. She folded her hands. "And all this is why you brought a convicted Wiccan eco-terrorist inparish, endangering the relationship between town and Church?"

Christ in Heaven, was she actually believing him? He nodded.

"Witch," Castile said.

The eyebrow climbed higher. "Sorry?"

"We are called witches, my lady," Castile said.

Trinidad's shoulders slumped. They had been so close to wrapping this up quickly.

Bishop Marius leaned back, her attention firmly on Castile now. "Come nearer. Let me have a look at you."

Castile stepped up and took his place next to Trinidad, who felt a cold draught sweep the back of his neck. He could have sworn the archwardens behind them drew nearer as well, but he didn't dare look back to check.

"You are unhurt?" Marius asked.

Castile sounded easy, friendly. "Just minor cuts and bruises, my lady. I'm fine."

"The proper address is 'Your Grace,'" one of the bishop's archwardens said.

"I'm sorry," Castile said, dipping his chin. "I mean no disrespect. I'm not familiar with your ways."

"Why do you seek asylum here?" Bishop Marius asked.

"It's as Trinidad said. My patrol came upon the Christians during the firefight and we helped them get the priest back inparish."

"But you're banished from the parish."

"I am, yeah. I meant to stay outside the gates, but someone had to drive the dray after slavers attacked us and shot your priest. My own soldier was also wounded, or I would have let her drive."

"It seems a particular cruelty for your lord to send someone in your position."

Castile shrugged. "Banishment is a position Christians imposed on me. To my coven, I am just another soldier."

Bishop Marius frowned and switched her attention back to Trinidad. "Many hours have passed since you left the parish."

Trinidad opened his mouth but Castile jumped ahead.

"We secured the area and went home," he said. "To get my lord's opinion on what to do next. We weren't quite sure how to proceed, Your Grace, having never captured a priest and an arch-warden before."

"You considered ransom?" she asked.

"No. My lord would not reap three ills upon my coven for such a wrong. He is a good man, Lord Hawk." Castile let the name hang there for a moment. "Perhaps you've heard of him."

The lines creasing Bishop Marius' thin lips deepened. "I'm not familiar with him, no."

Her Grace's prejudice against Wiccans and Indigos was well known, but she couldn't be insulted by Castile suggesting she simply knew a name, could she? Or maybe she did know Hawk. How could he find out? She'd lied more in one homily than Trinidad had since he'd taken vows—including those he had just told. It didn't make him feel any better about his lies tonight, though.

She sat back in her chair and drew in a deep sigh. "I accept that you acted in good faith, Castile."

Trinidad's spine relaxed a little.

"However," she went on, "I fail to see how or why we should keep the city from questioning you. We must maintain good relations with the mayor's office. We need their cooperation now more than ever." She cast a steely look at Trinidad. "This you surely understand."

Trinidad understood well enough. She needed the mayor to free up marshals to take the cross, to fight in the crusade. He also understood she wanted Castile somewhere private, where she could further question him. He hadn't forgotten that Castile had given her the scar, and whether she'd seen his face or not, she'd remember her attacker getting slashed across the back. If she found the silvered cut on his back, he would never escape.

He drew a breath and plunged in, vows for truth be damned. "I swore Castile safe conduct throughout the parish, Your Grace. My protection. In exchange for his help."

"You don't have that authority," Marius said. "And now I must ask you to stand aside in this matter."

"You're asking me to go against my word."

"Your vows to the Church surpass your word to outsiders. As far as you are concerned, I am the Church. And I am not asking."

"Father Troy would be dead if Castile hadn't brought us back here," Trinidad said.

The bishop dropped her chin, blinked her eyes. Sniffed. When she lifted her head, tears were rolling down her cheeks.

"I didn't want to get into this here, now," she said. "We received word that Father Troy is dead."

The world tilted and spiraled. Trinidad stared at her, knowing it was rude but unable to help himself. Castile leaned closer to him so their arms lightly touched. The warm brush of proximity served to ground him.

Her face grew stony beneath her tears. "As well, my archwarden Paul. Murdered in his bed. We have suffered great losses today. Three good men dead. I am not a believer in coincidence. So, you see we must have a full inquiry. I know you did all you could for Father Troy, but there are still many questions. Especially about Paul."

Trinidad felt as if she had butted him in the gut with a rifle. *She knows, Christ save me, she knows.* He glanced at her solemn, expressionless archwardens and clutched at his order's collective stoicism, beaten into him by years of training. He drew on it to lock down his grief and fear. Time for that later. This was about Castile now.

"Castile helped Father Troy too."

"I know. But Father Troy put you all in danger. He made a bad mistake," she said. "One we must forgive the dead."

The dead. He held himself against swaying.

"I appreciate your position, Trinidad," she went on. "But I'm not willing to risk the Church's relationship with the mayor for a promise you made to a convicted ecoterr."

Despite the bishop's tear-streaked face, her authority loomed over him. His gaze flicked over the soft targets on the bodies of the archwardens flanking her, the eyes, nasal cartilage, their Adam's apples. He saw them doing the same to him. He stiffened, drew up to his full height.

Marius leaned down and offered Trinidad his sword. He took it, slid it automatically back into its scabbard at his side. But he couldn't make his feet move away. As soon as he left this room, the world would come crashing down. It would be graven into reality. Father Troy was dead.

Marius gentled her tone. "Get some rest, son. Things will seem clearer in the morning."

The archwardens approached Castile. Chains clinked in the quiet, drawing his attention back to the Wiccan he'd promised to protect. He turned to them, hand on his hilt, but Castile met his gaze. Shook his head.

Castile was right. The archwardens were too many. Still, he held, unable to walk away.

Castile's voice was steady, soft. "Just go."

Trinidad turned for the door. This time as he passed the cross, he did not bow his head. He heard the shuffle of boots, the guards clicking metal bracelets on Castile's wrists. Castile made no sound. Trinidad glanced back at him. The Wiccan seemed smaller somehow, childishly thin, belying the strength Trinidad knew lay within his narrow frame.

"I'm sorry," Trinidad said.

"I know, my son. In time you'll come to see the rightness of my actions," Marius answered.

"I wasn't talking to you," Trinidad said, and he passed into the shadowed cloister.

# SEVENTEEN

B ishop Marius suppressed a shiver and averted her eyes. Slack-
jawed, bruised inmates stared from their chains at her and
the archwardens as they dragged Castile down the corridor of the
jail. He struggled but James, a hulking silent archwarden whose
muscles strained his armor, manhandled the smaller man inside.
Seth and Malachi followed, faces set into hard lines.

Once inside the interrogation cell, with its chains and bloodstains, Castile redoubled his fight. Before Malachi or Seth could
step forward to help, James punched Castile's chin, slamming him
back against the wall. The crack of fist against bone echoed against
the bloody concrete. Castile fell to the stained floor and stayed limp
for a few breathless seconds.

"Cooperate," James said when Castile came to. "It'll go easier
on you."

"I'm not telling you shit," Castile sputtered droplets of blood
from a split lip when he spoke. "And you're about to have a fuck lot
of questions."

But few that could be asked in front of James and the others.

Fortunately, Marius had found a public goal that fit neatly with her private ones of locating Lord Hawk and punishing Paul's murderer.

"I only have one," Marius said. "Where is your coven located?"

Castile shook his head and gave her a bloody grin.

"I will have it from you. Your people are a threat to parish security. Strip and chain him," she said to James, and gestured Seth and Malachi outside the cell.

"Your Grace?" Seth said once they were in the relative quiet of the corridor.

She studied them. Seth's pale face showed wisdom hard-won through scars, particularly a jagged red crease that ran along his jawline. At twenty-one, Malachi was the youngest archwarden inparish. He looked it with his plump cheeks and wide-eyed stare, but he already bore two ribbons of advancement on his chest. Two more than Trinidad had.

She drew a breath. "I understand how difficult this is for you, with Father Troy and all the questions around Trinidad's activities tonight. Did he speak to either of you before leaving the parish?"

Seth and Malachi looked at each other. Neither answered.

*Ah, and Trinidad's lies start to unravel.* "Because he said he couldn't find you."

Another exchange of glances. "Perhaps he said that to protect us," Seth said. "Trinidad was very upset by Father's illness and his actions tonight—I've never seen him so frantic."

"Trin is more devoted to Father than anyone," Malachi said, and dipped his chin. "Since he is Father Troy's adopted son."

"He hasn't advanced through his colors since he was invested in the order," she said.

"Trinidad isn't interested in advancement," Seth said. "He only wants to serve his priest and his Church. If he misspoke tonight, I'm sure he had good reason."

"His service is about to change, regardless of his interests," she said. "Two archwardens are dead. Father Troy disappeared under mysterious circumstances, only to be returned to us with a bullet wound. It also looks as if Trinidad has befriended a convicted ecoterrorist. There will be an inquiry. This night could reflect badly upon all the Boulder Parish archwardens. Do you take my meaning?"

Only Seth dared meet her eye, for an instant, before bowing his head. "Yes, Your Grace."

"I want you to publicly take the cross tomorrow, so there is no mistaking your commitment to stamping out Christ's enemies. This will reassure the people, which is our first concern. Otherwise I fear you two could be implicated in whatever rumors will surely plague the parish archwardens after the unfortunate events tonight."

"And Trinidad, Your Grace?" Seth asked. His eyes didn't flick upward to her scar like it did with so many others.

He was one to watch. "I intend to put the question of taking the cross to him tomorrow morning. If you get the opportunity, encourage him to do so. It could go some distance to clearing his name."

"Your Grace," James said from the cell door. "The Wiccan is secured."

"Leave us, but stay close," she told James. "I'll have need of you in a bit." She had no doubt Castile would fail to cooperate.

James glanced at the scar on her forehead. "As you wish, Your Grace."

Interrogation cells had solid doors rather than barred. She

shut it behind her. Inside the cell, James had chained Castile facing the wall, nude. He bore various scrapes and scars from prison life. But his narrow frame carried well-defined muscles, unmarred by major injury—all but the long silver scar that ran diagonally from shoulder to hip, confirming her suspicions: Castile was the man who had tried to kill her in the Barren. She knew from experience he was stronger than he looked.

Marius considered Castile. Obviously, he could rove. That meant he was one of only two people who could have killed Paul: Castile or Hawk. She doubted Hawk would do such a thing. He'd been respectful in their dealings. Castile, though, had attacked her in the Barren. He must have killed Paul at his earliest opportunity.

She laid a hand on Castile's back, ran her finger down the smooth grains of the silver scar. "Let's have a talk, you and I."

# EIGHTEEN

C astile reminded himself he'd had worse. Still, his back tensed at Marius' gentle touch. His chains rattled. They held his hands out to the side, stretching his arms. Cold shackles secured his ankles close to the wall. One of them had a metal burr inside that dug into his skin every time he moved. "I already told you. I'm not talking. Just do what you're going to do to me and get it over with."

Something cold and sharp pressed along the edge of his scar. "What about what you did to me?"

He forced a chuckle. "What about it? You should be dead. I'm out of practice."

The stinging edge of the knife dug in. Something hot ran down his skin. He hissed in pain.

"See now? You're much better at playing the victim," Marius said.

He grunted, tried to think of something to say to distract her. "And to think Trinidad defended you."

"He's sworn to me. Of course he defends me."

The knife came away. Air stung his new wound. Her hand caressed the smooth skin of his hip. He quivered at her touch and willed his body still. It didn't behave.

She leaned in close to whisper, "You were close once. Maybe you would like to be with him again? But Windigo might not approve."

He stiffened. Not from the name of his cellmate but because it was a short step from his prison file to the truth. Fuck. Fuck. "You studied up on me. I'm flattered."

"Yes, once we suspected you. Paul thought he'd killed you, but since my wound healed it was logical to assume yours had, too. We had no idea who you were. There were rumors, though, about a Wiccan who had emerged so strong and clever after years in prison. Your description fit what we'd seen of you in the Barren. So, I read your records, the damage you caused, the lives you took. Father Troy saw you often in prison because you'd been friends with Trinidad."

Castile tried for a disdainful snort and failed. His sorrow from the priest's death still resonated through his heart. "The sun and moon and stars don't revolve around Trinidad."

"I'm beginning to wonder. Every time I find a problem in Boulder Parish, there he is, standing at the heart of it."

He shook his head, scraping his cheek on the wall. "I dragged him into this. He doesn't know anything, not about roving or the Barren, none of it."

"No matter. He'll come to heel. Archwardens always do. I'm more interested in you at the moment. You attacked me. Now my archwarden Paul is dead. I find it difficult to believe it's all coincidence."

That he could deny calmly. "I didn't kill him."

"You're a convicted ecoterr. You've killed plenty. You all do."

"Convicted for possession of explosives, for my association with the movement. For arson. Not for murder."

"But you have, haven't you? Murdered." She pressed the sharp edge of the knife into his flesh again.

Castile cringed away from it, pressing hard against the course wall. Jagged bits of stone bit into his chest and scuffed his cheek. His breath came in short pants despite all efforts to slow it.

"You killed Paul in cold blood, a good man, a man of God," she said. "Admit it. Tell me the truth—"

"I didn't kill him. It's the truth!"

"Surely even a heathen can see God has brought you to me for justice."

He twisted his head around to squint at her. Her scar reflected the faint light, glinting in his eyes. "At least I never pretended my gods liked it when I was blowing your town up—" His words broke off with a scream as she stabbed the blade through the fleshy part of his hand, between the thumb and forefinger. Blood coursed down the wall, painting over countless other stains. Tears slicked his cheeks

"Where is your coven?" she asked.

Castile shook his head against the rough wall, tried to think of words for prayer. None came.

"I know there are more rovers," she said.

His breath came in pained gasps. She twisted the blade and he screamed again. Fragments of denial darted through the agony. He clung to them. "No! I'm the only one—"

"You're lying. You're lying about your coven, about the rovers.

You're lying about Paul. Just admit it. Tell me where your coven is. Tell me why you killed Paul."

He rolled his forehead against the cinderblock wall. A deep whine caught in his throat. "I didn't. I didn't kill him. I swear it—"

She yanked out the knife with a twist, drawing another sharp scream from him. "God brought you to me."

He shuddered at her breath against his ear.

"You'll realize that soon enough. But like Christ on the cross, sometimes the only path to peace is pain."

She pulled away from him and opened the door. It grated against the floor. The noise jolted through him and he scraped his chest as he startled. He drew a ragged breath, tried to marshal his wits and string her words into some kind of sense. She meant to torture him, but she had some sort of spiritual justification for it from her god. She was insane.

That explained a lot. A sick tremble started in his gut.

Marius spoke so he could hear: "James, I leave it to you to find out where his coven is."

The shaking spread out through his extremities, making his chains clink softly.

A hoarse, low voice: "Yes, Your Grace. How badly do you need the information?"

"Badly," Marius said. "But the Wiccan may still be of use to me alive."

She summoned the others from the hall. A pause as the arch-wardens stepped inside and shut the door. Someone hissed a breath.

"Surprise." Castile drew a breath, then another. It steadied his voice. "She's not the only one with a scar."

Boot steps.
Another breath.
And then pain.

# NINETEEN

T rinidad paced the streets outside the church for a miserable hour. Sleet stung his cheeks and ran down his back, but it did nothing to cleanse away his grief and anger. He might as well have tried to climb ice without a pickaxe.

At last some semblance of reasoned thought broke through. He knew he should be ashamed at how he'd spoken to the bishop, should go and beg her forgiveness. Castile had come inparish knowing the potential consequences and, of course, she had to take him into custody. Castile had broken his parole. It was law. Yet, he couldn't let go of the thought of what they would do to him, especially once they found the scar on his back. Bishop Marius had called her silver scar a wound from an angel. What would it mean when others discovered Castile had one, too? He rubbed his hand across his breast plate, remembering the sand searing the pentacle in his chest. What were they doing to him right now?

He clenched his hands into numb fists. What was he supposed to do? Stage a rescue for a convicted ecoterr, turn his back on all he believed for the sake of one good man in danger? Speak the whole truth, bare his own scar, and let the bishop deal with the fallout?

The truth about his killing Paul would surely come out. If he confessed to even some of what he'd done in the past twenty-four hours, he'd earn discipline from his order for lying, or worse, be imprisoned and executed for murder. What would become of Wolf then?

Wolf. He still had to tell Wolf about Father Troy.

H is younger brother sat cross-legged on his rumpled bed. He wore a pair of Trinidad's old sleeping pants and clutched a blanket around him. A few tapers illuminated the burn scars on his face, which reached down his neck to wrap around his shoulder. Trinidad had grown so used to them, he barely saw them anymore. This night the scars glared at him, red and unforgiving. If he'd been taken to the Barren in time, that side of his face would be silver, and the skin on his damaged shoulder wouldn't catch when he swung a sword.

"Trin?"

Trinidad stripped off his gauntlets to find his hands were shaking. *My God, please let it all be a dream.* When he spoke, it didn't even sound like his own voice. "Father Troy has ... died."

Wolf shook his head, an uneven, jerky gesture of denial.

Grief cinched Trinidad's words to a whisper. "After Father Troy was kidnapped ..."

"What? K-k-kidnapped?" Wolf stuttered in his confusion "You didn't know?"

"I've been asleep. After practice, Roman sent me ..."

"Yes, of course. We ... we found him and ... escaped." He

couldn't tell his brother the complete truth. "We were attacked by slavers on the way back here. He was shot. It was . . . sudden."

"He was fine. This morning he was—" Wolf's voice pitched and broke.

Trinidad pulled Wolf against his wet, armored chest, his heart tearing. "I'm sorry. We did everything we could. I'm sorry."

"No!"

"You don't understand. He was ill—he was dying anyway—"

Wolf's anguished wail drowned out the futile words. Trinidad hushed him with useless soothing noises. They stayed like that for a long time. At last Trinidad allowed Wolf to push him away. He dropped down on his bed.

Wolf scrubbed at his wet face with his bed sheet. "You don't care. You're not crying."

Trinidad rubbed his hand over his eyes. Blood flaked off his palm, from Father Troy. Or when the Indigos had taken him, had killed Daniel. Or maybe it was Paul's. He couldn't make himself say two archwardens had lost their lives as well.

"That's not it. I just . . . I'm used to it."

"Because of your brother?'

Trinidad shot Wolf an unintentional glare. "You are my brother."

Wolf rubbed his eyes with the back of his hand. "I'm sorry I cried."

Trinidad thought of what Father Troy had told him when he'd refused to cry over his parents. "We owe him our grief—we owe him that much."

A long silence before Wolf stirred again. "Can I ask you a question?"

"Anything."

"What did you do when you they died? Israel, I mean. Your parents."

After the explosion that had taken his family's lives, Trinidad had been too numb to feel. They brought him to the rectory and put him to bed. Father Troy found him in a screaming rage late in the night, destroying the bedroom. His soon-to-be trainer Roman tackled him and held him down—a ragged, infuriated twelve-year-old—until the tantrum subsided.

After that, against parish wishes and despite their Wiccan faith, Father Troy put his family's shared urn into a hole in the church graveyard. For Trinidad's sake, he said. A reminder to forgive. Trinidad never had the heart to tell Father Troy that he hated the marker with the pentacle amid all the crosses.

His father had been holding Israel when the bomb had gone off. Even at six, Israel still wanted to be carried sometimes.

"I don't really remember." Trinidad dropped his forehead to his palm. Exhaustion dragged at his muscles.

"Before. About finding Father. You said 'we.' Who went with you?" Wolf asked. His voice was steadier.

"Daniel . . ." Trinidad swallowed. "He was killed during the attack. We brought Father to the hospital, but it was too late."

Wolf was quiet for a few moments, and then: "I dreamed about you."

Trinidad lifted his head.

"I thought you woke me up for guard duty, but you weren't here. I slept some more but woke up again. Then I couldn't get back to sleep. I was hungry. I found something to eat. Paul died. They told me in the kitchen."

Trinidad stared at him, then nodded. "Yes. Bishop Marius is very upset."

"I don't know how he died."

Trinidad couldn't answer. He lowered his gaze.

"No one said anything about Father Troy or you missing, even when I was on duty."

"Maybe they didn't know." Or were so upset over Paul no one thought to tell him.

Wolf faltered and snuffled his nose. "When you crashed the dray I thought you must be hurt, but then you got out."

"You were bold, flanking me like that," Trinidad said.

The smooth half of Wolf's face flushed. "I thought that marshal was going to shoot you. I thought he might kill you."

"I'm all right, Wolfie."

"Who was that man in the dray?"

"He's a Wiccan. From the mountains."

"Did you know him? From before, I mean?"

Trinidad hesitated before nodding. "We were friends, as kids. He helped me tonight. He tried to get Father to the hospital in time."

"But he didn't."

Trinidad's shoulders sagged. "No."

Wolf rose. "Do you want me to help you get out of your armor? You must want to sleep."

Sleep. As if. But he could see Wolf wanted something ordinary to do. His shirt and armor were soaked. And Wolf was going to see the pentacle eventually. He got to his feet. "Thanks."

He handed over his sword belt and his bracers with their knives, and stood, wavering slightly, enduring the ache in his head and joints as Wolf unlatched his armor. Trinidad lifted his sore arms when he needed to, bent over to let Wolf pull his chest and back plates over his head. His shirt came off with it.

Wolf stopped and stared, the glow of the silver flashing in his eyes.

Sickness welled in Trinidad's gut. He crossed to his stash of his coveted whiskey, a birthday gift from Daniel, and swallowed two mouthfuls. His voice came out harsh. "I don't want to talk about it."

"But that's—"

"Not a word to anyone. You got me?"

Wolf opened his mouth and shut it with a nod.

Trinidad pulled a tunic over his head. The silver light winked out. Then he sat to remove his greaves and leg armor. He needed a shower, but he didn't have the energy to face the cold water in the basement of the archwarden barracks.

"Don't put my kit away. I'll be up in a few hours." He lay back and pulled the covers up and Wolf climbed into his bed.

Each aching vertebra rebelled against relaxing. The scar felt like a weight on his chest. He'd once worn a pentacle necklace, like all his fellow coveners did, like the one Castile still wore. He'd dropped it in his family's grave, trading his whole life for the cross. Now his old faith had chased him down and imprisoned him with the past as surely as the cross tattooed on his forehead marked him as an archwarden. But he couldn't be both. He was an archwarden, had sworn his life to Lord Christ. He would die an archwarden, no matter what was graven into his skin. But he'd been a witch, a heretic, something few parishioners ever forgot.

He almost envied Paul. Whatever he had done, whatever his

mislaid ideas and violence, he had died an archwarden. Paul had held fast to what he was through the end.

"Trin?"

"Yeah."

"What will happen to us?"

So much death. Paul's body rested in a room nearby. Daniel had been reduced to a stain in a gully. Father Troy? Probably in the hospital morgue. Alone. Cold. He sighed deeply, feeling the air fill his marked chest and yet feeling disconnected to his own breath and body. "I'm not leaving you, if that's what you're worried about."

"But what if the diocese reassigns you?"

That was the least of his worries. At best, the bishop would demand he take the cross to prove his loyalty. At worst, he'd be brought up on charges of heresy and murder. His throat tightened. What would he do without the old priest's guidance? How would he ever see Wolf to adulthood alone? He abruptly realized that some of Father Troy's wisdom had actually been stalling tactics.

"Let's worry about it as it comes, all right, Wolfie?"

He rolled over and stared at the ethereal dance of shadows cast by the guttering candle on the table between their beds. Before his eyes could well with tears, he squeezed them shut.

T rinidad?"

Trinidad recoiled from Castile's strained voice. A cold stone sank in his stomach, anchoring him. "Where are you?"

"Still in my dreamscape. I can't get to the Barren. I can't get deep enough. It still hurts."

Trinidad held for another moment, considering. He had Wolf

to think of, a priest to bury, a parish to defend. Mostly he didn't want to see what they'd done to the Wiccan.

Witch, came the memory of Castile's soft voice. We're called witches.

"They'll be back—soon—" The words came in stunted gasps. "Please, Trin."

Trinidad willed himself to drift, let himself shake free of his body, and he reformed at Castile's side.

Nude and soaking wet, the witch shuddered on a stained concrete floor. Someone had splashed water on Castile and the floor recently, but it hadn't cleared all the muck. One of his hands stretched out by a filthy drain, missing fingernails. Blood oozed from a wound in his palm. Bruises marred his face. One of his torturers must be left-handed.

Malachi was left-handed.

Trinidad crouched down next to Castile. "What did you tell them?"

"Do I look like I've told them anything?" Castile's swollen lips slurred his words.

I said I would protect you, and I will. Trinidad didn't repeat the promise again aloud, though. God might be listening. "I'll get you out of here."

Castile's voice strengthened. "You don't owe me anything. I'm the one who dragged you into this, took you back there—"

"Exactly. You took me back there. And it changed things. But not everything."

Castile stirred, met his gaze with the eye that wasn't swollen shut. "She keeps asking about the coven. She wants to know where it is."

Trinidad frowned. "She wants more rovers."

"I said there weren't any. Look, Hawk . . ." Castile stopped to cough and Trinidad waited. Even in his dreamscape, blood drops splattered the concrete in front of Castile's mouth.

"What about Hawk?"

"You have to warn him. He told me he'd come inparish if I didn't make it back. But it's too dangerous. He needs to stay with the coven, keep them safe."

Trinidad felt his lips draw back. Hawk. He was no friend. Never had been. "If he's stupid enough to come here, then he deserves it."

"It was a long time ago you hated him. You were kids. Please, Trin."

"Hawk doesn't trust you, Cas. And I don't trust him."

"He gave me soldiers to command, his own sister even—"

"Don't you get it? Magpie was sent to watch you, not take your orders."

"No, no. He—"

"He called you Woodwose."

Castile's nostrils flared and he focused on some spot beyond Trinidad. "So? He always called me that."

Woodwose was a Wild One. The life of the party. Fun, but foolish and dangerous. "It's an insult."

"Do it for the coven, then. He can protect them."

Trinidad shook his head.

"Please. Trin. House . . . against the west fence. Gray with red trim. He'll come. Warn him."

"I can't."

"Please. They took me in. Despite everything."

Exactly the way Father Troy had taken Trinidad in, a heathen kid with scars too deep to ever really heal. Trinidad closed his eyes and gritted his teeth. "All right. I'll go."

Castile paused to swallow. "I'll rove if I can. If not, I'm glad I saw you again."

Trinidad forgot himself and reached out for Castile again. "Stop talking like that."

"Like what? Like I'm going to die? I am going to die." The edges of Castile—his voice, his body—blurred as he struggled to finish: "By the Crone, man, at least let me say goodbye— Wait. Someone's here. Go!"

Trinidad came awake in a shaking panic, his feet on the cold, threadbare rug between their beds.

Wolf whimpered in his sleep and stirred. Trinidad reached for his brother's blanket-clad shoulder and shook gently. He startled and blinked up at Trinidad. Gray morning light made fresh shadows on the walls around them and brought out every ridge and valley of his scars. A spider had strung a web in the corner over Wolf's bed, just like in the dreamscape.

"He's hurt," Wolf said.

Trinidad stopped breathing, moving. "What?"

Wolf blinked, rubbed at his eyes and sat up. Trinidad watched realization darken his expression as he recalled Father Troy was dead.

"That Wiccan man," Wolf said.

Wolf never remembered his dreams. Except he remembered seeing Trinidad in them. And now Castile.

Trinidad drew in a sharp breath. "You were there with me," Trinidad said, incredulous. "You were the one Castile saw coming."

Wolf's lips parted. "It was just a dream—"

A knock on their door and it swung open. Seth stepped inside. "You're up. Good. May I have a word?"

"Of course." Trinidad glanced at Wolf. "Go back to sleep."

Seth led the way to his room. Three doors down, two archwardens in full kit stood guard outside Bishop Marius' door. Crimson crusader crosses shone like blood against their black cloaks. She was here, then. Not at the jail.

Malachi stood inside the room he shared with Seth, waiting. Trinidad passed through the door and waited while Seth closed it behind them. He couldn't look at Malachi without anger flaring, so he looked down instead.

Seth said, "Have a seat, bro."

He sat.

"What exactly went down last night?" Seth asked.

"Danny and I . . ." He faltered. Seth's knuckles were bruised and cut. You tortured Castile. "We were out looking for Father Troy. Indigos attacked us. They killed Daniel. Wiccans came and shut them down. They helped us bring Father Troy home—"

"Why was Father Troy out there?"

"He knows . . . knew Castile from visiting the prison. I think, though . . ." Father Troy was dead. Nothing could harm him now. "I think Father Troy had some problems thinking straight. He was saying crazy things. Castile was very kind to him. When we realized how bad Father was, Castile agreed to help us get back."

The words rushed from his lips like snowmelt down a canyon. Lying got easier, the more he did it. Not a comforting thought.

"The bishop suspects you met with the Wiccan on purpose," Seth said. "You and Father Troy. Makes us wonder what interest you and Father had with a convicted ecoterr."

"I told you. Father Troy—"

Malachi edged closer. "Enough lies."

Trinidad focused on Malachi's fists. Yes. Enough lies.

"He's an old friend, isn't he? Castile?" Seth asked.

Trinidad sighed. Who knew what Castile had said under torture? *Do I look like I've told them anything?*

"You never made any secret of it. You don't want crusade," Malachi said. "Admit it. You met with the Wiccan to make plans for treason."

Trinidad looked from one to the other. "You don't want war. Neither of you."

"I knew it." Malachi smacked his fist against his palm.

"The bishop is making us take the cross today," Seth said. "What choice do we have, with Father Troy gone?"

Trinidad shook his head. "The order will back you if you decline."

"All the high-ranking archwardens are diocese guards. They all wear crusaders' cloaks now." Seth cupped Trinidad's chin with his long fingers. His other fist hung at his side. "We're on shaky ground. No parish priest. Two dead archwardens. Bishop Marius out for blood over their murders."

"I don't want to take the cross," Trinidad said. "I can't. I won't. Father Troy—"

Malachi hissed at him for silence and glanced at the closed door. "It's your duty. Come with us today and take the vow."

Trinidad tried to twist free. Seth cupped the back of his head with his free hand, holding him in place. "If she suspects a whisper of protest, you'll end up dead, somehow. Friendly fire or an accident inparish. And we'll end up right there beside you. Guilt by association. See my point?"

Trinidad swallowed, his throat dry. "I see."

"So keep your mouth shut and do as the Bishop says. Even when it comes to the crusade."

Trinidad considered. Seth's eyes narrowed.

"I'll keep my mouth shut," Trinidad said.

Seth released him with a shove. "All right, then. I knew we could count on you. We'll see you later, at the service for Paul."

Trinidad nodded, lies cinching his heart, and escaped. Back in their room, Wolf rested in his covers, waiting.

"I told you to go back to sleep." Trinidad ignored his brother's curious eyes. The less Wolf knew the better.

He inched his sword from its scabbard. Paul's blood still caked the etching on the blade. A sudden wave of nausea caught hold of him. He leaned against the wall, shivering. What he wouldn't give for a hot drink. He remembered the smell of tea at the coven's cave. Trinidad pinched the bridge of his nose and tried not to think of his unsteady stomach. It subsided some, but a headache thudded behind his eyes.

"Are you taking your sword or should I clean it?"

"I'm taking it." Marshals wouldn't find this unusual if he had to pass through a checkpoint; archwardens rarely went about unarmed. Trinidad slid on his armor harness and buckled the straps to his shoulder pieces. Then he pulled the body plates over his head. Wolf got up to secure the latches for him and then looked into his face.

"Where are you going, Trin?"

"Wolf, don't."

Trinidad's body protested every step as he crossed to a cabinet and found their bottle of aspirin. It was running low but he chased three with a mouthful of whiskey, which bubbled on the aspirin and burned his throat. The acidic, foamy taste made him shiver. He took another mouthful of whiskey, letting it smolder on his tongue.

"You look sick," Wolf said, retreating back to his own bed.

"I'm just tired and sore." Not as sore as if he'd been tortured all night.

Wolf's voice broke through his thoughts as if he'd read them. "What are they going to do with the Wiccan?"

Trinidad scrubbed at his eyes with the heels of his hands. "They're questioning him."

"You mean marshals are torturing him," Wolf said in a small voice.

Not marshals. Not this time. Trinidad sat on the edge of Wolf's bed, considering how much to say. He lowered his head in a nod. "Yeah."

Wolf's eyes were big in his pale face. They rested on Trinidad's chest, where the pentacle lay hidden beneath his armor. "But how can you let that happen? He's your friend."

"We're not friends. Not exactly." Not anymore.

"But he's one of God's people. That's what Father would say."

"Castile is a convicted ecoterr. He's on parole. He knew what he would happen if he came here."

"Why did he come then?"

"Why do you care?"

Wolf closed his mouth and averted his gaze for long enough Trinidad thought that was the end of it.

"I guess ... because you said the Wiccan helped Father Troy," Wolf ventured again. "He must not be a bad man, if he would do that, risk torture to bring you both home. He deserves better, doesn't he?"

"And you're implying what? That I should break him out of jail?" Trinidad reminded himself that Wolf was older than he'd been when he had started his novitiate and hardened his tone. "I am an archwarden. I am sworn to the Church. If I tried to get Castile out, it would be treason against the Church."

"You're changed," Wolf said sullenly. "Something happened to you."

That stung. When Father Troy had been in the lead, defying the crusade had seemed more like a game of bravado. But one horrible night had dragged Trinidad down the path of treachery. His brothers-in-arms would have him take the cross to prove his faith, or the pentacle in his chest would clinch a trial against him. And now Wolf was looking at him like he'd completely lost respect for him, mirroring their father-priest's familiar reproving stare. Wolf had brought it up first: what would Father Troy advise?

Christ first, always.

"Fulfilling our vows means forfeiting our own opinions sometimes." Trinidad locked eyes with Wolf. "Sometimes. Not always. You get me?"

Wolf gave a stiff nod, his chin up. Trinidad caught the eerie image of the man living within the boy.

"Where are you going?" Wolf asked.

Trinidad glanced toward the door and lowered his voice. "To see a man about a Wiccan."

Wolf nodded.

Trinidad considered his brother and thought of Castile's dreamscape. Had he truly roved? Or maybe Trinidad somehow caught him up in his roving, because of their proximity. He had no idea.

"Wolf, another thing. Don't tell anyone what you dreamed last night, about Castile and me. All right? Not Seth or Malachi. Not the bishop. No one. And not a word about . . ." He tapped his breast plate to indicate his silver pentacle.

"Who did that to you? Why is this all happening?"

Not questions he knew the answers to, not entirely. "Do you trust me?"

"Yes."

"Then no more questions for now."

"You can trust me, too, Trin."

Trinidad cupped the back of Wolf's head and pulled him close for a brief hug. "I know I can. Good dog."

It was an old joke between them, but Wolf didn't smile.

# TWENTY

C astile lay on his side on the stained cell floor, watching the bishop watch him. Every inch of his body ached, stung, or burned. One eye was swollen shut. Splatters of blood fanned out from him. His swollen cheek scraped against the rough floor, damp with blood and urine.

Marius had yet to touch him; that was what the archwardens were for. They grunted as they removed Castile's fingernails with pliers and slammed their fists into his body. They listened with impassive faces as he screamed. The bishop did all the talking.

"God is here, with you, in this cell. You understand that to succumb to us is to succumb to Him, don't you?" She bent her head, closed her eyes, and clasped her hands together. "Heavenly Father, let your son Castile see the error of his ways. Pave a path to his heart as You show him the path to Yours."

As she droned on, he thought: *Are you hearing this, Horned One?* But he felt no presence of protection or thrill of anger from his patron. Nothing but a kick to the gut recapturing his attention.

"That's enough, James," Marius said. The archwarden backed off without a word.

"Let's start at the beginning, Castile, with what I know. You may fill in the rest."

Castile dropped his gaze to stare at the hem of her robe as the archwarden left the cell. She'd repeated this phrase in various forms at least five times in the past few hours. His inevitable silence left him with more pain and humiliation. Tears rolled down his cheeks. His throat was raw with screaming. But she didn't know enough to hurt the coven, that was clear.

He might let himself cry. He'd never let himself talk. "Kill me," he whispered. Just kill me. "I won't tell you anything."

"James?" Marius said.

"Your Grace?"

"Secure him to the table as we discussed."

The archwarden manhandled Castile up and shoved him face down on the table, bent him over at the waist. Castile fought a little, but weakness and pain kept him from doing much. James chained his ankles to the table legs, stretched his arms out, and secured them to the other legs so that his arms stretched over the edge uncomfortably. He caught a glimpse of the bishop's bony face, lips pursed in disgust. The light winked out as James shrouded him, waist to head, with a thick, rough blanket, covering his back—his scar—and his head.

With his backside exposed to the cold air, Castile could well imagine what this was about. Violent trembles seized him. He strained harder against the chains binding him to the table and screamed wordlessly, terror eating him from the inside. He fought until his wrists and ankles were slick with blood from the shackles, until he'd bruised his swollen cheek again by banging his head against the table.

No one touched him or spoke, just left him alone in his futile battle. Castile had no sense of time within the suffocating cloth, he only knew he'd sworn to himself he'd die before letting himself be used like this again. Bile rose from his gut and filled his mouth. But without the freedom of light and air, and with the press of pain from his injuries, his struggle started to wind down. The shame of past violations struck him anew, and he felt himself slip unwilling into the strange oblivion of submission. Hope for help flickered and died. Finally, exhausted, he sank against the cold steel.

*Herne? Herne, are you hearing me? Great Hunter, free me!*
"Mercy."

The Bishop's voice felt like a splash of cold water. "Did you give Paul mercy?"

"No, I—"

"Did you kill Paul?"

"I ..." He squeezed his eyes shut, willing himself to see the truth of it. He was lost. Trinidad was not. Trinidad had to remain free, to stop their hatred, their crusade. To stop it from happening to anyone else. "No."

"Then who did?" A gentle hand stroked the soft flesh of his buttock, patted him like a pet. Like Windigo had always done ...
*Maiden, Mother, and Crone, if you ever loved me ...*

Castile thought of the pentacle in Trinidad's chest, how the Indigos had ruined his flesh, had nearly killed him. "I don't know."

"Where is your coven?"

Didn't they see? He was already lost. He had nothing but his own life to offer. The coven wasn't his to give. He shook his head.

The chains slid along the table legs with a metallic scrape. The weight of dread grew in his chest.

Again, the bishop's voice assaulted him. "Your Lord Hawk takes me to the Barren. He has allied with me. Already forsaken you."

Castile's heart seized and blood roared through his veins. He sobbed quietly, writhing in his chains, his sore muscles rigid against the hard table beneath his chest, until something inside him fell away, leaving his middle a granite tomb. He was shaking, no longer from fear, but fury. *I'll never doubt your instincts again, Trin.* As if he'd ever get the chance.

"Fourth Street," he husked out. Someone leaned close to hear; he felt their breath warm the fabric over his head. "Gray house, red trim. Hurry or you'll miss him."

"Your coven is in the mountains." Marius laid her hand on the back of his neck, rubbed through the suffocating fabric.

"Hawk..." He coughed and barely swallowed before the words poured from him. "He'll be there. We were to meet."

"See? So simple." The bishop laughed softly, acidic against Castile's panting. She took her hand away. "All I had to do was tell you about Hawk and you give him to me."

Castile heard a scream in the distance and shut his eyes. He'd do Hawk one better than that. "Horned One, curse Hawk for a fool and a traitor." Curses worked best spoken aloud. "Slaughter him in your woods, let naught grow where his blood falls, and scatter his soul to the winds, never reborn. Curse him, curse him, curse him threefold. So mote it be."

He felt the chill of ethereal breath on the back of his neck, colder than the air on his bare buttocks and thighs. *Herne?* He let his head fall back to the table. Now, maybe they'd free him—

"This man killed one of your brothers, James. He is condemned. Fetch the guards."

Castile barely heard the words. Trinidad had been right about Hawk.

Marius was calling names. Seth and Mala . . . something. Telling them to find the house, find Hawk.

Castile imagined his lord brutalized and dead. Not a twinge of guilt crossed the chasm of his wrath and fear—

Trinidad!

Lady spare him, he'd sent Trinidad to meet Hawk. If the Christians caught Trinidad at the Wiccan safehouse they'd realize he was helping the coven. He had to stall, keep Trinidad alive. Marius would cut Trinidad down next. Fresh terror flooded the fires of his anger. But the archwardens were already murmuring assent to Marius' orders. Boots thumped away.

"Trinidad can rove." He focused on the pitiless lick of cold air over his bare thighs.

"You're lying. Now you take it too far."

Castile swallowed hard. "No. He can rove. I wasn't lying. Hardly any of us can. You won't want to hurt him." Please don't hurt him.

Castile listened to boot steps emerge from the coughs, bangs, and moans of the jail.

"Your Grace?" The archwardens were clearly waiting for decision based on this bombshell.

Marius cleared her throat. "He's talking nonsense, but at least he's talking. James, let the jail guards have the Wiccan for a bit. Maybe afterward we'll see if he comes up with some gems of actual truth. Hawk will fight us, but I will have it from one of them. We must find that coven. They're setting plans in motion as we speak, and we must stop them before more Christians lose their lives."

"Yes, Your Grace."

More footsteps. Castile realized they were leaving him to his fate. To the guards.

"No! You can't hurt him!" he cried out, panic setting in like a brush fire. He strained against his chains again. "No!" The word deteriorated to a guttural scream.

More boots on hard floor. Voices came down the hall. Rough laughter. Castile yanked on his chains, whimpering with the strain. Heavy footsteps, too many to count blindfolded. Someone ran their callused hand along his hip, ended with a sharp slap. "Be still, ecoterr."

Conversation and laughter. Fingers dug into his muscles. *Lady save me, how many are there?* Castile fought like the fly fights the spider, trying to writhe from the chains and their rough hands. Someone tore into him, deep, stabbing. He hissed and tried to kick free. They slammed fists into his thighs and back when he wasn't pliant enough. The world rocked and spun. Panic fully realized, Castile twisted his soul from the grip of the physical world, roving through prisoners' tortured dreamscapes, desperate to escape the screaming, until he realized it was his own.

# TWENTY-ONE

T rinidad took well over an hour to get to the Wiccan safehouse. He had no transportation and was forced to walk a roundabout route toward the western border of the town in order to avoid detection. As an archwarden, he was used to striding through Boulder without much care. Parishioners treated the men marked with the crosses and swords of the Order of Archwardens with respect and even awe. Now he wasn't sure who might be looking for him and what they might do to him when they found him. He certainly didn't want to be followed. He told himself that warning off Lord Hawk was a Christian act, even if it went against implied orders.

The house backed up close to the fencing, separated by a tiny square of a back yard. It was the same gray as the dingy morning sky, with chipped red trim. Trinidad had to wade through boot-high debris to see the fence. He kicked aside tumbleweeds to reveal a body-sized hole cut through the wire. All the poisoned barbs had been clipped well back. He scowled in habitual annoyance. But this hole confirmed this was the house Castile had meant him to find.

These houses on Fourth had been old a century ago, well before the wall had gone up. They had since fallen into decrepit piles of rubble that made another obstacle behind the lengths of fencing. The street was too far up the mountain for anyone but the most athletic of climbers to use as an entrance into town, especially with the roads bulldozed and trails piled with rubble. And there were the poisonous barbs interwoven into this stretch the fence. Even clipping through was a major risk, should a barb swing back and catch the skin of an intruder.

The wind rolled empty cans and bottles, clanging dully against the broken earth. Dried weeds, shingles, and bits of paper rustled in corners. The door squeaked on its hinges. His back to the wall, he eased his sword from its sheath and drew a breath to regain control of knotting muscles as he scented blood. He slipped around the corner, sword first. He swallowed. Blinked. The sword lowered to his side.

Hawk's armored body crumpled in a corner, legs and arms splayed. His head hung at a wrong angle, nearly separated from his body by the single, deep gash in his throat. Blood spilled like a gory apron over the Wiccan sigils painted on his old Flextek. Trinidad knelt and stared at the wound. Only a sword. A well-honed archwarden's sword could score flesh and bone with a single swing.

Hawk had fought back, been beaten nearly unrecognizable but for his beard, still scarred white where Trinidad had cut him deep so long ago. Pale lips, parted in horror. Dead eyes stared past him from bloody, swollen sockets. Most of his fingers scattered the floor like slugs.

He heard the noise of movement and the harsh whisper at the same time. "Ah, Hell, Trinidad."

The cold touch of steel above his armor's neckline made Trinidad raise his sword. "No. This is business, bro. The silent kind."

"Seth?"

"What do we do now?" An edge of panic. Malachi.

Trinidad shifted and the tip stung him under his ear. Seth hissed for silence.

"I told you," Seth said. "You've got to leave this, Trin. Leave it alone."

"Seth, just listen to me—"

"No. You listen to me. As soon as Marius finds out you knew Hawk, you're a dead man. We have to figure this out, get you out of here."

"It's too late for that," Malachi said. "He dug his own grave."

Seth's tone sharpened. "Malachi, no—"

Something solid met the back of Trinidad's head, ferrying him into darkness.

Trinidad landed on his feet in the silver sand, blinking at the faint echo of a scream.

"Castile?" he called.

No one answered. But he felt a thrill like Castile was near, like they'd brushed arms or Castile had whispered in his ear. The witch must have called him, pulled him from his unconscious dreamscape. He scanned the Barren, turning in a complete circle. A flesh-colored bump against the silver made him squint and break into a run, shouting the witch's name.

Castile was scrubbing himself with sand. His face was swollen on one side, blood running down his cheek. Bruises and welts still stained his body, not yet washed away by the sand. He gave

Trinidad a bleak smile and didn't bother to hide his nudity. "I'm glad you're here. We need to talk."

"Every time you say that, someone dies," Trinidad said. He edged closer to the Wiccan. "Castile, I have to tell you. Hawk . . . he's . . ."

"Dead, yeah. I figured as much." Castile ran his tongue over his bottom lip and spat the rest in a rush of words. "I shouldn't have come here, I know. But I couldn't think of anywhere else to go, and I don't think she can follow me. I shouldn't have said anything. But I couldn't help it. I just—"

"Wait, slow down. What happened?"

"I told Marius where to find Hawk."

Trinidad blinked at him. No wonder Seth and Malachi had been at the house. For a moment he was tempted to go back, try to wake up and fight. What were they doing to his unconscious body? Where were they taking him? The thought unnerved him, but Castile's face was pale. Silver flecked his skin where they'd cut into him.

"Why did you tell them?"

Castile busied himself with rubbing more sand over his bruises, leaving clear, pale skin behind. Some grains caught in the scrapes and more thickened over his bare nail-beds. Trinidad caught his hand. A jagged line of silver had filled a stab wound in the fleshy part of his palm.

Castile pulled his hand back. "I'm not like you, Trin. I can't hold up under this."

Trinidad wanted to tell Castile it was all right, that there was no disgrace in breaking under torture. But shame bound his tongue. Men from his own order had hurt Castile, men he counted as brothers. He'd questioned Indigos before, and he'd seen things get nasty. He'd done dozens of things he wasn't proud of since taking his vows, not the least killing Roi d'Esprit. But it was part of the unspoken archwarden creed. If he had to sell his soul to protect Christ's people and clergy, then so be it. He'd always wondered if simple regret and prayer could ever be enough. With his priest dead and archwardens torturing Castile, the bishop openly involved, maybe the order was lost, and he with them.

He ran his hand through the sand, watched it fall in a tiny storm of silver. If only it could fix more than physical ailments.

"Hawk betrayed the coven," Castile said. "He took Marius to the Barren."

Trinidad sank back, absorbing that. Pieces were falling into place, but he'd never have guessed how they'd land. "They probably would have found Hawk anyway," he said. "There's no shame in breaking."

"Forget Hawk. It's worse than that," Castile said. "I told her you could rove."

Trinidad's head lifted.

"Hear me out," Castile said, lifting his hands. Silver laced the deep wound between his thumb and finger. "I did it so they wouldn't kill you. Once I figured out they were going to keep me alive, at least for a while, I realized they needed a reason to keep you alive too."

The stillness of acceptance settled over Trinidad, that deep pause between realization and action. Castile meant well. He knew that. But he was unconscious, in Seth's custody now, probably being dragged to the jail.

Castile gave a derisive grunt, sounding slightly closer to his regular self. "I learned something else in there. Your bishop is one crazy woman. A good weapon, yeah?"

Weapon. As if they were in a war they could possibly win. Trinidad reeled for a moment, closed his eyes to get his bearings. Castile went on, not seeming to notice.

"Her anger blinds her. Marius is mistaken about a few things, the first being that Hawk is the one who showed me the Barren." He spat. "Traitor."

"Cas, they nearly beheaded him, they tortured—"

Castile stiffened. "Stop looking at me like I should be sorry. You suspected him right off and you were right. Our high priest, the most trusted member of our coven, betrayed us. If the gods let it get ugly, then who am I to argue?"

After a moment, Trinidad crossed himself, feeling ill. "It could have been me. Bishop Marius could have sent me to torture and murder him."

"If you were a good boy, which we know you're not. Look, with Hawk dead, she needs us. She's going to make me rove. At some point..." He looked away from Trinidad. "I could give in or pretend to. I could rove Marius here and you could kill her. Now. Tonight. Think of it. With Marius dead, there's no crusade. Problem solved."

Trinidad caught up a fistful of sand. If only it were so easy. "No. I can't kill her. I can't even harm her. I vowed to Christ to protect her." He'd already broken enough vows: killing Paul, roving, consorting with the enemy, resisting the crusade, lying to his superiors...

"We all betray our gods, Trin. Why not get a little good out of it?"

Trinidad shook his head. "I can't. I just can't."

Castile threw sand at him. It chimed over his stomach and

thighs like distant church bells. "The fuck? Don't you see? This Church, this order you signed into, it's all a lie—"

"Christ is not a lie." Before Castile could protest, he went on. "I vowed to Lord Christ, to Holy God, never to harm His believers. To protect them on pain of death."

"What kind of god expects you to protect one kind of person and not another? That doesn't even make sense."

It was a valid question, one he'd avoided until Castile voiced it. What kind of god expected him to fight and die? The only one he knew. The Church had given him a life, a family, and Father Troy . . . but his priest was dead and the archwardens were doing things he didn't understand, driven by a bishop who craved war. He'd thought it a noble cause: protecting Christians. Even crusade made a brutal kind of sense. With the unbelievers gone, there'd be no reason left to fight, no one left to die.

Except one of the unbelievers was sitting here, right in front of him. "Christ is peace," Trinidad said. "He never fought. He needs someone to protect His people."

A measured silence before Castile spoke. "God or not, it's not right that he asks it of you."

"He didn't ask. I offered." Trinidad lifted his eyes to meet Castile's. "It's all I have left, Cas."

"You have me."

Hot sweat stung his back. A muscle twitched irritatingly in his jaw.

Castile drew in a breath as if his lungs pained him. "Aspen always said I come on too strong. I don't have the best judgment just now. But our Lord lives, loves, and dies for his Lady every year, and so it goes. The least I can do is the same."

Unease cut a swath through Trinidad's chest. "What are you talking about?"

"Nothing. I'm just talking."

"No. You brought up the Lord and Lady. Loving and dying. Why?"

"Just, you know. I was in prison, yeah? Not the first time. I'll survive. I always do."

Realization sluiced through Trinidad. The Great Rite was the ultimate holy act, the earthly recreation of godly love between the Lord and Lady. Using sex as torture was a particularly profane thing to do to a witch. He closed his hands around Castile's wrists and pulled him closer. "I'll get you out. I swear by all that is holy, by Saint Michael and Lord Christ."

Castile kept his gaze down, didn't so much as twitch. "No. Get yourself somewhere safe. She'll come for you next."

Trinidad didn't have the heart to tell Castile that Marius already had him. "All right. I will. And I'll come for you."

He had to fight his way back into the pain from the quiet. It was a chaotic rove, fear and fury battling for control, tossing him between nightmarish dreamscapes. But at last the silver world faded away. Cold air swept Trinidad's face. He twitched violently at another noise, saw it was the open front door squeaking as the icy air moved it. He winced at the ache in his battered head. But he felt only emptiness inside.

He was alone. Seth and Malachi had left him.

By nature of what they had to do to serve the Church, most archwardens had done some evil to serve the common good. The Order of Archwardens worked for the Church and served Christ, but it was foremost a brotherhood of shared secrets. His brothers-in-arms had kept his secret about killing Roi d'Esprit. Likely, they hoped to keep who murdered Hawk secret, too. Now they knew he'd come here to meet him.

As soon as she found out he knew Hawk, Trinidad was a dead man. If his betrayal got out, it would reflect badly upon the entire order. They probably wanted to give Trinidad the chance to come back to the fold on his own, quietly. But Seth and Malachi didn't know the biggest secret of all: his roving. The bishop knew, and the first thing she'd do was use it against him.

He pushed to his hands and knees and caught sight of Hawk's bloody body sprawled in the corner. The scent of blood hit him anew and the world veered beneath him. The thought of what Castile was enduring charged through his gut. Trinidad huddled over, retching. At last he lifted his head and forced himself upright. He hated the thought of disappointing the order, his brothers. But they were no longer who he thought they were. Maybe they never had been.

He couldn't trust his Church or his order any longer, and he couldn't leave Castile to be tortured further, or killed. Trinidad had to get him out, and for that he needed help only the godless could give him.

# TWENTY-TWO

Reine d'Esprit walked along her freehold's fence, a rifle under her arm. It had been a year since she'd pulled a regular guard duty shift, but if—no, fuckin when—Paul showed, she wanted to meet him. Their conversation, the one that had dispelled the last of her doubts about allying with the bishop a couple of months back, replayed in her head.

"What if this all goes south?" she'd asked.

His skin rubbed hot against hers. He smelled of smoke, sweat, male. His heart thudded against her ear when she pressed her cheek to his chest.

"I will find a way to come to you," he said. "We'll stay together, always."

"Marius won't let you."

Paul's dark eyes drank in the candlelight. Vicious, his voice a low growl, "The bishop doesn't own me."

Reine wrapped an arm around her hollow middle. Paul was alive. He had to be.

But the night had passed without him coming to her in flesh

or dream. No one from their little alliance communicated with her since they'd fled the silver place after trying to kill Castile and Trinidad. No crusading army marched through the dawn or evening, seeking to bury her tribe. Even the slavers were quiet.

She stared out over the mountains, shadows waiting for the sun to light them. They looked like a jagged tear across the bottom of the sky. From this far back, she had a fresh appreciation of just how big they were. She swiped at ash floating on the air. *In a thousand years we'll be gone and the mountains will still be here*, she thought.

"Reine d'Esprit?"

She spun on her spearguard, who backed away from her rifle aimed at him. She lowered her gun and cleared her throat, humiliated at being caught in a contemplative moment, much less letting someone sneak up on her when she was walking guard duty. Shadows hollowed his cheeks and his clothes hung on him. "Scout back from inparish," he said. "I'll take over here—"

Before the words left his mouth, Reine was running toward the inner circle of huts and houses that made up the heart of camp. People gave her respectful greetings as she passed by, but she didn't turn her head.

The scout, Cur, sat by the fire, cross-legged on the ground. He pulled his blue scarf down as she approached, and gave her a nod, stayed sitting after his hard run from inparish, fifteen klicks west. Javelot pressed a bowl into his hand: precious rare stew.

"Bishop's mobilizin troops," Cur said, and shoveled stew into his mouth to talk around it. "Archwarden banners. Marshals. Drays, guns, swords, camp's spreadin out by the gates. Snuck in and heard two guards. Plan to march in two days."

Two days.

She met Javelot's gaze. Javelot broke first and rose to poke at the fire, coughing wetly and spitting into the flames. The flickering light revealed the grooves drawn into her face from three decades of living mostly outdoors. The scarred notches cut from her brows only hardened her looks. Five years of too little food and too much work and strain had aged her beyond her years.

Reine cursed inwardly but steeled herself to keep calm. "You sure?"

"It ain't Greek, Queen," Cur said around a bite of stew. "Fuckin were pretty crystal on it."

Javelot's eyes narrowed, but Reine waved off the impertinence.

"One more thing. Fresh word on Trinidad. Rumor says he lost it for good now, out for blood, I guess." Cur spat out a bite of gristle. "Shoulda killed him when we had the chance."

"That meal is from his bounty stores," Reine said coldly.

Cur shrugged, kept tucking in.

Reine turned her back on them and climbed the steps to her house but left the door open. After a low exchange outside, she heard boots on the steps behind her. She choked down a gulp from her jug and turned to offer it to Javelot.

Javelot swallowed without expression. "It's time for the Israel job, Reine."

Reine frowned. "We don't even know if it will work."

"When'd you ever know Papa Roi to fail?"

"Sure. The chemwipe'll work. Can't undo that. But we have to get to him, right? And the explosives could be dead, wet, found. Movin around inparish is a bitch at the best of times." It was a dangerous, desperate trick, blowing up buildings inparish.

Javelot punched her fist into her palm. "I knew it. You're goin soft."

Reine tightened a noose around her anger, her fingers instinctively finding the knife at her belt and slipping it far enough out of the sheath to press an already open cut on her fingertip to the sharp blade. "No. I'm thinkin things through. You pull that trigger, you can't get the bullet back."

Javelot shook her head. "You sound like Papa Roi."

Reine blinked slowly at her sister. "I'm runnin the tribe, like he did. Fuckin stands to reason I sound like him."

"You're never cutthroat enough. Not like Papa Roi. After Papa died, you said we'd go after Trinidad. Said he was mine. And then you sold him to Cave Coven—"

"You fuckin want us to starve to death over a grudge? Maybe Papa Roi would starve the tribe. Maybe you would, too. But it ain't your choice, is it? Or his."

"Because Trinidad killed him!"

"Trinidad won this round, Jav. Let it go. We have to look at the whole war."

"You said the crusaders would go around us. You said the Bishop told you—"

"I don't trust her. Not anymore."

Javelot lifted her chin. "Fuckin about time."

*I'm doin the best I know. Can't you see that?* Reine scowled, not hiding her anger this time. Javelot ducked her head. But she muttered, "We're goin to war. We need weapons. And Israel is the best we got."

Their father-king had planned years for this moment, strained his skills at chemwiping and explosives, even brought Reine in as a back-up trigger. But now that the time had arrived, it felt wrong. Like a trap. Like she'd missed a piece of a puzzle.

"You don't have to go alone," Javelot added. "I'll come, too."

Reine yanked her knife from its sheath and openly sliced it across another sensitive fingertip, letting the sting take over. Javelot shifted from foot to foot and frowned while the blood welled up but said nothing.

The sting pinpointed Reine's focus. They were out of options. She didn't like it, but Javelot was right. It was time.

"All right. Israel." She pointed her bloody knife at Javelot. "But I go alone."

# TWENTY-THREE

Malachi and Seth kept some distance between them while preparing to take the cross. Marius found that vaguely odd. Maybe it was the formality of the ritual. But they were compliant and obedient as they knelt and presented their swords to her and God.

Seth shifted on his knees as she laid the crusader's cloak over his back and kept his gaze cast down. Malachi raised up slightly, shoulders stiff, to receive his cloak. The crimson crosses glared against the shadow of black wool enfolding them.

The congregation had fallen still and silent, staring at the two kneeling archwardens bedecked with the raiment of their new rank. Some stood with hands spread, pale, rapt faces tilted to the darkness of the arched ceilings overhead. Several had knelt already, indicating their wish to take the cross. Her archwardens ghosted among them, laying red woolen crosses on their shoulders. At a distance, they looked like fresh wounds.

Marius lowered her head, considered a smile, and settled for solemn instead. She raised her voice to let it carry to the back of the sanctuary. It rang off the old polished paneling and stone pillars.

"Do you take this vow freely, in exchange for grace in life and the glory of Heaven in death?"

"I do." Seth spoke softly. But the crowd more than made up for it. Several dropped to their knees and spread their hands, seeking grace in crusade.

"Indeed, I do, Your Grace," Malachi said. More congregants took a knee.

"Will you freely and joyfully lay down your lives for Christ?" A renewal of their archwarden vow.

"I will." Louder, that.

She laid a hand on each of their heads. Their cropped hair was soft beneath her fingers. "None can overcome those who bear the mark of Christ. You wade in protected waters, you stride fields of grace, your swords shall not falter. As Jesus said: If anyone would come after Me, let him deny himself and take up his cross and follow Me. For whoever would save his life will lose it, but whoever loses his life for My sake will find it." She lifted her hand and signed the cross over them. "Rise, reborn, Christ's warriors."

The crowd clapped and a low, swelling cheer rose up, a few already wielding weapons, even more kneeling as passion for the crusade moved them.

Bishop Marius sank down on a chair in Father Troy's office. Books, guttered candles, scattered papers, and dust surrounded her. How could anyone live like this?

Seth stood at ease before her, hands clasped behind his back under his newly adorned cloak. Malachi kept to one side and back a little. She hadn't noticed his bruised cheek before, in the dim candlelight of the sanctuary.

"It becomes you, the cloak," she said.

Seth dipped his chin. Malachi didn't move.

She sighed. To business then. "You eliminated Hawk?"

Seth grunted. "We couldn't get him to tell us where the coven is, Your Grace."

"Then we must find another way."

The cross tattooed on his forehead distorted briefly as his brow furrowed. "Castile must tell us the location, lest his soldiers surprise us when we least expect it."

She sniffed. Scarcely an hour before hundreds of people had taken the cross. She itched to join her soldiers and launch the fight. "How many can they be?"

Seth shrugged. "Twenty? Forty? A hundred? But they could join with other covens. We just don't know and Castile has proved resistant to . . . persuasion."

"Trinidad grew up in the coven. He might have a sense of their numbers and the location of the cave."

Malachi's nostrils flared and a muscle twitched in his cheek. "We spoke this morning at the church. He agreed then to take the cross."

Indeed. "Then why wasn't he at the ceremony?"

Seth's gaze skittered and landed back on her face. "He is taking Father Troy's loss very hard. But he's always been devout, dedicated to the Church. Given some time ―"

"We don't have time." She smoothed her hands over her robes. "It was a powerful thing you did, taking the cross. But think what it would have meant if Trinidad had knelt with you. A Wiccan convert swearing to wipe out God's enemies, some of whom are his former friends, perhaps even his family."

"Trinidad came inparish when he was quite young, likely before he ever really embraced witchcraft. He never speaks of the coven, he severed all ties—"

"And yet he turns up with Castile, a known terrorist, a man from his coven. Pay attention, archwarden. They are conspiring to stop the crusade, to spare unbelievers even at the expense of the faithful. They wouldn't attempt it unless the coven had a significant fighting force." She paused. "I wouldn't be surprised if Trinidad was a spy all along."

Malachi lowered his eyes, his lips in a hard line.

Seth shook his head. "I can't believe that of him. I've known Trinidad for years, Your Grace. And what his parents did—"

"Perhaps you don't know him as well as you think. After all, Trinidad can—" She stopped, blinking at her near slip. Seth and Malachi knew nothing of the Barren, nothing of roving. "You have something to say, Malachi?"

Malachi glanced at Seth and drew in a breath. "It is my feeling Trinidad is unduly influenced by witchcraft. Maybe even worse. Maybe even demons or Satan have their claws in him."

She raised her brows. "Indeed. And what makes you think this?"

"Seth is right. He's usually loyal, steadfast. Suddenly he isn't."

Well. It was one theory. She left it to examine later. "Where is he now?"

Seth hesitated. "I don't know."

She let her gaze flick to Malachi. "You let him get away?"

Malachi glanced at Seth.

"We were not under orders to hold him, Your Grace," Seth said.

She should have locked Trinidad up in the cell next to the Wiccan, let him listen to the screams and confession. "I understand Trinidad is your friend. But surely you know God requires sacrifice."

Seth blinked at her. "Father Troy taught us faith is not only based in action, Your Grace. It is based in belief. In a true heart."

"God wills us to have faith in Him, but not in each other. Only by action can we know what a man believes. Trinidad let harm come to his priest, he broke his vows, he gave aid and comfort to our enemy. Do these seem the actions of a faithful man?" This she directed to Malachi.

Malachi cleared his throat. "No, Your Grace."

"I'll ask Wolf his opinion," Seth said. "He's closest to Trinidad—"

"Don't bother. He's too loyal to Trinidad, likely at the expense of his devotion to the Church." Wolf was a problem for another day. "You must know Trinidad's haunts. Find him. Bring him to heel. Make him understand he must take the cross publicly to prove his loyalty."

"Or?" Malachi asked.

She raised her brows. "Or he may join his Wiccan friend in jail to await trial for treason. Those are his choices. See he makes the right one."

# TWENTY-FOUR

R oman opened the door to his apartment and scowled at Trinidad before pulling him through the door by the scruff of his neck and yanking him close for a hug. The quick motion made Trinidad's head throb, and the sudden weight on his banged knee made him bite back a moan.

"Come in and tell me what you did to the other guy." Roman turned and led the way down a narrow hall lined with boxes— mostly old weapons and books, Trinidad knew—into the galley kitchen.

The apartment had been decent a half-century before. Now the walls were as battle-scarred as their owner. Boards covered all the windows but the small one at the end of the galley kitchen. Roman opened the window and pulled a bottle from a box bolted to the wall outside. After pouring, he turned to Trinidad with a chipped glass in his hand.

"Milk?" Trinidad took it. "Where'd you get milk?"

Roman shrugged, a motion made tight by an old bullet wound in his shoulder. "I know a girl with a goat."

Trinidad raised his brows. "Wiccan?"

"What do I care who the goat prays to. Hungry?"

Trinidad thought of Hawk's brutalized body and swallowed hard. "Starved," he lied.

Roman waved him out of the way with a spatula. Trinidad retreated to a hard metal stool in the corner while his armsmaster yanked items from a cabinet.

"You have enough food to feed the school for a week," Trinidad said. "You think we're in Revelations already?"

Roman threw him a red-eyed glare and bared his teeth. "Don't taunt me with that Bible bullshit. You know better, boy. Talk."

Before Trinidad could even wonder where to start, words spilled from his mouth. "Daniel is dead. Indigos. They captured me and sold my bounty to a Wiccan coven in the mountains. Except, when I got there, Father Troy . . ."

Roman didn't pause in his cooking as Trinidad told the whole story, even when he slipped up and told about the Barren and killing Paul, even when he told of the harrowing ride back to town. Roman didn't flinch when he heard Father Troy was dead; he just put out plates and filled them. He shoveled food into his mouth as Trinidad talked between bites, describing Wolf's grief, the Bishop's ire, archwardens torturing Castile, roving and dreamscapes and the Barren, and Seth and Malachi, who had caught him off guard.

"Why didn't they kill me?" he asked by way of conclusion. "Or take me back?"

"Maybe you still have some friends inparish," Roman said. "Seth has always been solid."

Trinidad pushed his plate back and stretched, wincing at his various bruises. He contemplated lying down on the floor, just for a minute. Soldiers never sleep in war, Roman liked to say. The ones who want to live, anyway. At this point, Trinidad thought a nap might be worth a trade on his life.

Roman stuck out his hand. Pale scars crisscrossed the skin on his forearm—cuts from years of practice and battle. "Sword."

Trinidad reached back for it, wincing at a bolt of pain in his shoulder, and handed it over. "Never got a chance to really clean it," he said in half-hearted apology.

Roman tsked as he ran his finger down the cross etched into the blade, scraping away dried blood—Paul's blood—with his fingernail. "Father Troy is not dead."

Trinidad had to battle the food in his stomach from coming back up. He met Roman's eyes and half-rose from his chair, ready to challenge the lie.

Battle wounds, cancer scars, and wrinkles marred Roman's face. His hair was shorn close to his head, a cap of graying fuzz. But hard muscles still bulged under his shirt. Roman could take him. Especially in this condition. Trinidad broke their stare first.

"Marius is a lying bitch," Roman said. "When are you going to get it through your thick skull that the cross doesn't protect anybody from what really they are?" *Even you.* He'd said it enough in the past that Trinidad filled in the words even though Roman didn't add them this time.

"But . . ." He paused, unaccustomed to questioning Roman. It was a hard habit to break. "How do you know?"

"Saw the old man this morning, didn't I? Contacts at the hospital told me he was there. Even so, it was a circus trick getting past security. All that hassle, and he just caws at me about keeping you out of trouble—too damned late for that—and that you'd be along, yapping about some Wiccy nonsense. About another world. I figured it was the drugs talking but turns out maybe I was wrong."

Trinidad shook his head. "You actually believe me?"

"The bishop has that weird scar." Roman drained the rest of the dark liquor in his glass. "And if your condition is any indication, some brand of serious shit is going down."

Trinidad leaned back, an arm across his middle as if to ward against another blow. His head ached and now that his belly was full, he felt tired and blurry. Between his sore body and the dim apartment, it felt like evening rather than midmorning. "Why would the bishop lie to me about Father Troy? She had to have known I'd find out."

"Obviously, she wanted you to keep away from Troy, even if it meant selling her soul to do it." Roman's lips twisted at his own joke. But his tongue flicked across his chipped tooth. His tell. The bishop's lie disturbed him more deeply than he was letting on.

Trinidad failed to see the humor. "I did kill Paul."

"So you said." Roman said. "But he came after you first, right? Nothing you could do about it. Marius can't prove anything. You weren't even in the church at the time."

"That's what Castile said." Trinidad shook his head and rubbed his face.

"He's one to avoid, the ecoterr."

"I can't, not now. I have to get him out somehow."

"The man is an ecoterr. It's like you want to be tried for treason."

"Castile is changed. He knew what would happen if he came back inparish. He seemed scared at first. Then he acted almost like he deliberately got caught so he could find out what the bishop knows."

"Torture in the screamwing is a hell of a price to pay for a little intel," Roman admitted. "Got to respect a man who'll put himself through that."

Trinidad flexed both hands and wished the meal had made his stomach feel better. He couldn't make himself tell Roman the worst of the price Castile was paying. But Roman was also wise to their ways.

"Can I have a whiskey?" he asked instead.

Roman picked up his plate and headed for the kitchen, returned with two bottles: whiskey and antiseptic. "Look, I don't get what all this is about or why you can't just take the cross like a good little archwarden, but they'll come after you again. You better be ready for it."

Trinidad nodded absently, his mind racing around what the bishop might do next. Castile seemed so certain she'd come after Trinidad, take him captive. Even Roman seemed worried. They were probably right. If Trinidad kept low, maybe the Bishop would just get on with her war. He swallowed the whiskey down but the burn didn't wash away his distaste at the crusade. A Church-funded army would crush every Indigo and witch in its path.

He'd never liked the idea of crusade. It held no romance for him, only the sickening scent of blood. He would have followed his order and fought, though, convinced that in the end, the Christians were in the right.

But now . . . after Castile . . . he had no idea who was right. The Indigos who carved the pentacle in his chest? Castile, who had been an ecoterr? Or his own order, who had tortured Castile and murdered Hawk? He had no idea where to turn next. He needed help. Advice.

He needed Father Troy.

Roman pressed a cloth to Trinidad's forehead and the sting of the antiseptic brought him back. "*Ow.*"

"Hold the fuck still." Roman grabbed the back of Trinidad's head and rubbed sealant glue into the cuts over his eye and on his cheekbone. "Now. Show me your knee. Don't give me that look, you're favoring it."

Trinidad rolled up the leg of his trousers. Roman undid the binding and shook his head at the swelling. "You never could wrap a joint worth a shit."

Trinidad grimaced as Roman probed his knee with his callused fingers. "You think Marius will tell anyone else the truth about all this? I mean, she already lied. She said an angel gave her the scar."

Roman considered as he positioned coldtape and buried it under a thin, neat wrap. He shook his head. "Mark my words, that woman wants something that has nothing to do with God."

"Melodrama aside," Trinidad said, relaxing a little as the cold-tape eased the ache in his knee. "The sand does heal."

"Don't back sass me, boy," Roman said as he finished abusing Trinidad's wounds. "You're the one gimping around like you went eight rounds with a sledgehammer. Where's your sand now?"

Stupid. He should have healed himself in the Barren. But he'd been too wrapped up in Castile.

"I have go talk to Father Troy," Trinidad answered, reaching for his jacket. "Make sure he's all right. Maybe he has an idea on how to stop the bishop. Now that she knows what the sand does, she can use it in the crusade to heal her soldiers."

"You're one of those soldiers, if you've forgotten. But you'd rather get yourself executed for treason."

"Marius is going to take us to war over a graveyard we can only reach through Wiccan magic. With an army that can be healed at will. Don't you understand what that means?" It was on the tip of his tongue to say he himself could rove, that Marius wouldn't kill him because she needed him.

But Roman shook his head. "That you're raving crazy, the whole lot of you, with your gods and angels and magical healing graveyard."

Trinidad considered, but didn't yank up his shirt. The silver pentacle shamed him. Or maybe it was admitting again that he'd let Indigos kill Daniel and capture him, that he'd been tortured, that he'd aligned himself with a Wiccan ecoterr, of all people. But he settled for a shrug. "Sometimes I forget you don't believe."

"Oh, I believe, boy, in what assholes people are to each other in the name of God. He's plenty real as far as that goes." The armsmaster peeled back his lips in a scowl and started digging in one of his boxes. He came up with a grappling hook and a line.

"You work for the Church," Trinidad said sullenly.

"I'm in it for money, and they're the only ones who got any."

# TWENTY-FIVE

Roman squinted at Bishop Marius. "What's this about?"
    She stared at him, taken back by his lack of manners.
He'd come to see her immediately when requested. But he didn't
take a knee or drop his chin or even address her properly as "Your
Grace." He just barked the question at her as if she worked for him.

"We got the idea Trinidad might come see you today," she said.

"He already did."

Her brows lifted before she could stop the surprise from regis-
tering on her face. "Where is he now?"

"He knows the priest is alive. He's gone to see him."

She leaned back in her chair, trying not to wince. Her back
ached. A storm must be building. "Why are you here? I thought
you were fond of the boy."

"Boy? You've seen him fight." Roman settled, feet spread like he
was about to swing a sword. "Trinidad is a good man. Always has
been. He's got himself into some trouble, apparently, if there's any
truth to the tale he told me today. But it's a rare thing for him."

"What did he tell you?"

"A lot of nonsense." He glanced at her forehead.

Damn. "Such as?"

"Wiccy magic. Walking in dreams. Killing an archwarden."

Killing an archwarden? Oh, God. Paul. . . . Hurt flared deep inside her breast, her heart clenching in agony until she wondered if the silence meant it had stopped.

Roman gave a sage nod. "Yeah. It's enough to make me think maybe some of it is true. Trinidad is solid. But he has always been . . . emotional. The sooner you take him to heel, the better."

"He seems quiet," she observed.

"Until he picks up a weapon."

She rose and stretched out her hand. "Thank you."

He took it in his rough fingers and gave her businesslike shake. "No thanks necessary. Just my pay."

She studied him. "Done. And more than we agreed upon, if I've more use for you."

Roman left the priest's office. Marius sat back down and crossed her arms. She could think of a half-dozen tasks for Roman that had nothing to do with Trinidad. Fortunately, he was motivated by something she had plenty of: money. She clapped her hands, a sharp crack in the still air.

Seth filled the doorway. "Your Grace?"

"Trinidad has gone to the hospital. It's time for him to come home, where he belongs."

The shadow of a frown crossed Seth's face. "Yes, Your Grace."

"Remember Trinidad is your brother. Also remember he has worked against me and is very dangerous."

Another nod and Seth disappeared.

Bishop Marius fingered the gold cross hanging between her

breasts. Seth didn't much like collecting his errant brother-in-arms, she could see. But he seemed smart enough to go along with her orders. And maybe it wasn't all coercion. After all, Seth bore the crimson cross. He was destined for crusade and that meant tearing down all barriers to Christ, including brothers-in-arms.

# TWENTY-SIX

E arly afternoon shadows were short, not giving Trinidad much cover. As he stood in the alley across the street from the hospital watching the carriageway leading to Emergency, he realized he was just assuming Father Troy was still there. But he had to be. Where else would they have taken him if they meant to keep him alive? He had been hurt, badly.

The hospital was a heavily marshaled area because of the defenselessness of the sick, and it had been hit by homemade mortars often, back when things were really ugly with the eco-terrs. Things had quieted in the past couple of years but Trinidad expected more patrols with the parish on the brink of crusade.

He circled the building, seeking the quieter service entrance. He'd come in that way once, after a dray had been blown to bits by a road bomb and the rest of the caravan's goods had been jacked by Indigos. Two civilians and an archwarden had died that day. Trinidad had taken an arrow in his calf. The raid had been demoralizing to the Order and devastating to the town. He hadn't wanted any parishioners to see him injured and bleeding. He figured he was in even worse shape tonight, as he limped along on his swollen knee, head still aching from getting knocked out, Roman's cheap whiskey gnawing on his stomach lining. If Castile hadn't so quickly distracted him, he'd have healed his sore knee in the Barren.

Castile. His own hurts were nothing in comparison.

He kept studying the hospital, but no one else clung to the shadows. He shuffled across the dark street, but as he reached the building, the door on the raised loading dock creaked.

Trinidad crouched and pressed his back against the wall beneath the loading dock, gaining only four feet of cover. His instinct told him to thrust upward and take out whoever lingered above with a single blow. But, familiar with the feeling, he argued instinct with logic. Probably a nurse or doc having a break.

The scent of cigarette smoke drifted down to him. How had a hospital worker gotten actual tobacco? Trade with the Midwest and South was infrequent at best, and it had been months since a caravan of luxury goods had even attempted Boulder. Businesses couldn't afford mercenary dray fees and many regulars had given up their routes. Life and limb weren't worth what the parishes paid to run trade. He frowned, considering. Only marshals were in a position to get such goods, taken as gate bribes. Or archwardens, who might trade for their silence.

The smoker took idle steps in his direction. Trinidad's hand crept toward the knife on his belt. If he had to go through a marshal to get to Father Troy, so be it.

Then he heard the door creak again and a question in a sharp female voice: "All right out here, Collins?"

The smoker coughed. "Yes, ma'am."

"Keep a close watch until the patrol comes around again." Sounds of footsteps carried her away.

"Ma'am." Collins muttered something under his breath.

Trinidad released a slow breath. *Keep a close watch.*

A cigarette fell over the edge of the platform, tumbling amid sparks, missing him by inches. Trinidad heard the rustle of paper as the marshal rolled another. He wasn't going anywhere, not until the patrol showed.

He chose his knife for silence, eased it from its sheath, and tipped his head up to listen for Collins pacing to fade back toward the building. As it did, he turned and hoisted himself up onto the chest-high platform, sizing up the broad-shouldered marshal clad in dark fatigues.

Roman's grappling hook scraped and jangled against the concrete. The marshal turned. Trinidad scrambled forward and tackled him at the knees. He threw himself on the man and stretched his knife up to press it to the marshal's jugular. The marshal reached for his pistol; Trinidad beat him to it with his other hand, keeping the knife snug against the man's throat.

"Quiet now." Trinidad was bigger, stronger. The man struggled again, and Trinidad wound his leg around the marshal's and used his weight as leverage. "The patrol. How long?"

"You're him, the Wiccan arch—"

Trinidad tightened the bite of the knife, strangling the words as his blade raised blood. "Focus. The patrol."

"A minute," the marshal said, sounding choked. "Maybe less."

Trinidad shifted up on Collin's body until their faces were very close. He angled his other forearm against the marshal's jugular, using his weight and his legs to hold him down. The marshal bucked and fought beneath him, knowing what was coming. Trinidad rode the struggle in silence. The knife slipped and sliced Collin's skin. Blood welled, slippery under Trinidad's bracer. Seconds ticked off like hours as the marshal weakened and finally slumped beneath him. More seconds passed. Trinidad gritted his teeth, knowing he should kill him. And then he thought of Castile in that cell. He was going to die at the hands of archwardens. He had to move before the marshal came to.

He quickly propped open the door to the storeroom. Let them think he went that way. He assembled his line and threw the hook upward. It fell back at him, clattering to the concrete. He had to jump aside to avoid getting knocked in the head. Two stories. That's all. He let out more line and threw again. It caught and he forced his sore body into the climb.

Old cigarette butts, trash, and broken cups scattered the ashy gravel on the flat rooftop. Filthy snow blanketed the corners where sun never hit. For a moment he just breathed.

Below, the door scraped the platform as someone shoved it open. A shout. Boots thudded on the pavement. Trinidad snaked the line upward, wondering if they saw it. He had to assume they did. Keeping low, he ran toward the center of the roof. He stashed his rope and hook in a pile of trash trapped by the raised stairwell in case he needed to climb back down. Then he tried the door. Locked, of course, but with a bolt and pin. He felt in his pocket for his torsion wrench and pick, old tricks from Roman. Within seconds, the lock clicked open. He left the bolt out and let the door rest on it.

He started down the silent stairwell, one hand wrapped around his gun, all the while wondering how he was supposed to find a man who wasn't supposed to be here, who wasn't even supposed to be alive. He had the room number where Roman had seen Father Troy, but what if they'd moved him?

He cut off that line of thought. Roman always said fatalism got you nowhere.

Trinidad stopped at a door leading from the stairwell and listened. When he heard nothing, he slipped out the door. The corridor, for the moment, was empty. Most of the doors were closed. He started down the hall and heard voices from around a corner. He turned and went the other direction. Two rooms back he found a custodian's closet and slipped inside. He pressed his back against the door, hand firm on the lever in case anyone tried it.

"All's quiet so far, lieutenant," a voice said, accompanying footsteps. "He might've given up and left."

"No," replied a female voice. "We've received official word. He's coming here. Carry on looking."

"Yes, ma'am."

Official word. Only Roman knew Trinidad would come here. He leaned his head back against the door, feeling sick. No, not Roman. He didn't know if he could stand the thought of another friend tortured.

Trinidad realized he was holding his breath and let the air ease from his chest. He felt around for a light switch and flipped it, hoping against hope they weren't in a blackout. It obediently brightened the room with a dim flicker. Of course the generators were more reliable at the hospital.

Shelves climbed to the ceiling, mostly empty. Mop buckets cluttered one corner. Someone had hung a small mirror between shelves. He peered at himself and grimaced. A bruise shadowed his cheekbone. Several cuts showed behind the clear glue Roman had applied and the edge of the cross peeked from between his drawn brows. He pulled down his hat and turned away to find something to wrap around his sword. A laundry bag made an odd-shaped bundle, and he buttoned his jacket over his armor.

An alarm crackled through speakers as he stepped back into the hall. Trinidad went cold at the rusty wail. Two nurses barely glanced at him as they trotted down the hall pushing a cart, and they disappeared through a doorway into the room next to Father Troy's. The door whooshed closed and latched, concealing them within, and Trinidad's shoulders dropped slightly in relief.

Trinidad tried Father Troy's door. Locked. He got out his tools again and reached for the door, but the female nurse reappeared with a clanking of door latches. He stepped back, palming his torsion wrench and watched her take in the bruises on his face.

"Can I help you?" she asked, her tone brusque.

"I'm just . . . no, thanks."

She gave him another look. "You all right? You look like you've been in a fight."

"With a set of stairs," Trinidad said, aiming for an embarrassed smile.

She gave him a tentative smile back. "Are you sure I can't help you?"

Trinidad decided he had to take the risk. He could neutralize her if it came to it. "Well, actually. I guess I'm a little lost. I'm looking for my dad. He's supposed to be next door and it won't open."

"It happens." She turned and peered at the scribbled chart next to the door. "The orders say no visitors."

"I just wanted to bring him his cane." He hefted the laundry bag, keeping the tattoo on the back of his hand twisted away from her. "And you know. Check on him. I won't stay long."

She looked him over again and sighed. "All right. If you wait here, I'll just finish inside and get the key for the room."

"Thanks," Trinidad said, but his heart thudded a vague alarm. Was she just buying time to call the marshals?

She disappeared back in the room next to Father Troy's, if he was still there. He looked up and down the empty hall and slapped his hands against his thighs. He pressed his ear against the door, but all the conversation inside seemed medical, ending with: "I'll be right back."

He stepped back as the door opened.

"Have we met? Around here, maybe?" she asked.

"I don't think so."

She gave a little shrug and turned to the write-pad. "Too bad."

It occurred to him she must be flirting with him. He gripped his sword hilt through the bag. She'd remember him. A problem. But she was opening Father Troy's door. "Is this your father?"

Father Troy lay on his back, eyes closed. When the door opened, he turned his head. He opened his mouth to speak and reached out.

"Dad, there you are." Trinidad turned back to the nurse, his relief genuine. "Thank you."

"Glad I could help."

Trinidad didn't move until the door had latched behind her. He quickly locked the door. Then he stepped forward, taking the priest's outstretched hand. "Thank God you're all right. They told me you were dead."

The priest's breathless voice held the same dry wit as ever. "Not just yet."

Tubes snaked from under Father Troy's blankets. His skin felt papery and cold, his fingers limp. Trinidad shifted his gaze to stare past the priest out the darkened windows. He caught a street comber's light below, flashing yellow.

Father Troy sighed and studied Trinidad's bruised face with his watery eyes. "What happened to you?"

Trinidad sank onto a stool, still holding Father Troy's hand. "Bishop Marius had Lord Hawk murdered. I got caught off guard when I found his body." He couldn't tell him all of it, couldn't tell him about Seth and Malachi. It would hurt the priest too badly. "I can't stay long, Father. They're looking for me."

"There's more. I can see it in your face."

Trinidad made himself meet Father Troy's eyes. "I killed Paul, Father. In the Barren. He attacked us and Castile wasn't armed . . ."

"Pray, my son. Christ will forgive you."

No. Not this time. He swallowed before forging ahead. "Marius has Castile. They tortured him."

Father Troy stirred, his hand squeezing Trinidad's. "He's stronger than he appears. Has he told you of prison?"

"A little. I know it was rough. I mean, it had to be—"

"Castile knew a man called Windigo there."

Trinidad felt cold. Something in the priest's tone. "An ecoterr?"

"No. A slaver."

Trinidad shook his head, but his stomach twisted. "I don't understand."

"Son, yes, you do." Father Troy shifted uncomfortably, a grimace parting his beard. "Windigo was powerful within the prison.

He found Castile in his first few days. He kept Castile alive, and also kept him as a slave. Do you take my meaning?"

Trinidad twitched a nod.

"I swore not to tell you. I am breaking that. I'm more than willing, because you are my son and Castile is very nearly like one."

Trinidad closed his eyes. "I thought he was dead. I wish I'd known he was there. I wish . . ."

Father Troy shook his hand slightly to get his attention and gave him a weak smile. "I thought it best that you not know. Adjusting to your life as a novitiate was difficult enough as it was. But for Castile, just the thought of you still alive and safe kept him going in prison. It was only recently he admitted to me that he needed you in his life. What you don't seem to realize is how badly you need him."

The door handle twisted, stopped by the lock. Trinidad heard the scrabbling of a key. He ducked into the bathroom, shut the door, and slipped behind the shower curtain. He reached for the cold steel of his pistol but reconsidered. Chambering a bullet would echo against the tile. Instead, he slid his sword from its sheath. The stink of body waste drifted up from the drain, mingling with his own sweat.

"How are things in here, Father Troy?" A friendly voice, female. Trinidad recognized it. Same voice that spoke to the guard on the delivery platform. His eyes narrowed. She called Father Troy by name, so she was in on the secret.

He's on painkillers, Trinidad thought. He could do anything, say anything. But Father Troy just said, "Fine, thank you. Resting."

"Oh, look, your pitcher is empty. I'll fill it for you."

"Not necessary, really—"

"Don't be silly, it'll only take a moment."

Trinidad held his sword across his body, muscles tensed to swing. The door to the bathroom opened, shedding a little light and silhouetting a vague shadow through the fabric. The tap spit air before water trickled out. The water pressure had been bad in this area for years, ever since an ecoterr bomb had taken out some water pipes. Trinidad held his breath, wondering how big a pitcher it was and how distracted she could get from watching water trickle into it. He watched her shadow carefully, but at last she shut off the tap and retreated.

"Here you are, Father."

"Thank you."

"Any visitors?" she asked.

Trinidad cocked his head, eyes narrowed.

"No," Father Troy said. "Trinidad is my son. He would never harm me."

"But the reports are ... disturbing." She sounded sympathetic. "Two archwardens are dead. And his Wiccan friend is a convicted terrorist." A beat. "I'll look in on you later, yes?"

"You're very kind, thank you."

Trinidad waited for the door latch to click and still counted to thirty before stepping into the room, gripping his sword at his side.

"Castile believes you are meant to stop the crusade," Father Troy said.

"Witches don't believe in fate." The words came out harsher than he meant.

"I put that badly, then. But he does believe in you. He knows you were supposed to die with your family."

A vice clamped down on Trinidad's chest. "Why are you bringing this up now?"

"Because, Trinidad, you walked away from an explosion that killed all those people. Castile understands how special you are. I'm trying to make you understand."

Trinidad gave the priest a close look and glanced at the clear bag hanging next to the bed, wondering what was in the drip. Father Troy's beard could no longer hide his gaunt cheeks, his pallid skin. White brows hung over his sunken, dilated eyes. He wasn't in his right mind.

*Christ, no. He's dying.*

Trinidad's gaze blurred with tears and he swiped at them with the back of his hand. He couldn't get into all this now, what the explosion was, and what it wasn't. "Father. You're wrong about me. Castile is wrong."

Father Troy arched an eyebrow at him. "Was Christ wrong to take you on as his soldier? Is He wrong about you?"

Trinidad ducked his head. He didn't have an answer to that. He'd failed Christ too many times to count, starting with the day his parents blew themselves up. It had felt wrong, all wrong, from the start. He'd stood there and done nothing.

"I should have gotten him out. Israel," he said, his voice breaking on the name.

"His death is not your fault. But his loss can make you a better man. A man of peace, not war. A man of Christ."

Father Troy held out his arms, barely raising them from the bed. Trinidad obediently bent over him and allowed himself a moment to lean on the old man's familiar chest. Countless times Father Troy had hugged him, even when he didn't want it, even when he pushed him away.

"I won't see you again, will I?" he whispered, drawing in the scents of antiseptic, of blood. Of death.

"Your parents made a mistake," the priest whispered. "But without it, I never would have known you."

It felt like shards of glass were working their way through his lungs.

Father Troy reached up and thumbed a cross over Trinidad's forehead with his quivering hand. "Go with God, my son. As you always have. I will see you again."

Trinidad couldn't think, couldn't answer.

He pulled free of the priest's weak embrace, crossed the room, and opened the door, fighting the urge to look back. If he did, he might not be able to walk away.

Seth and Malachi stood in the hall with bared steel and black cloaks emblazoned with the red crusader's cross.

# TWENTY-SEVEN

R eine d'Esprit huddled in her cloak, a hood concealing her
Indigo locks. A young man waited at the church gate, but he
didn't challenge her. He just bowed his head to her and called her
ma'am. The church grounds were deserted even in the middle of
the afternoon, emptied by the burgeoning army of crusaders gathering on a stretch of bare land inside the eastern wall. The church
building itself was empty and cold. A few torches flickered, reflecting against the polished wood stretching up to the ceiling and
the boarded-over colored glass windows. Beams arched into the
darkness. Unlit lanterns swung overhead, caught in cold drafts. She
crossed to a bench in the front and lowered herself to her knees,
like she heard Christians did. She'd stay a few moments to prove to
anyone who might appear that she had reason to be here, and then
she'd go find Paul.

She'd come inparish to start her own war, something to distract the bishop from her crusade, but she'd been suffering second
thoughts since she'd crossed the parish wall. That damn wall had
made her think about her own freehold walls.

Spearguards were working day and night laying traps of razor wire and trip lines around their freehold walls. Patrols roamed their county acreage, non-coms and children dug fighting ditches, and spies had been dispatched inparish. Two riders had raced out to seek help from other tribes. If they could bring in another size-able, well-equipped tribe or two, they'd have a decent chance of withstanding a siege. At least their mines and spears might dam-age the crusading army enough to give the children time to escape, though to where she didn't know. Hopefully the warning of the coming crusade was enough to firm up alliances. She didn't kid herself about winning any battles outright. It would be ugly. But worth it, so worth it, if they could fight off the Christians and if the tribe survived in some form. Even if they lost their freehold in the process.

Maybe Paul could help. Maybe he could stop the bishop.

She folded her hands on the back of the pew and stared at the grand table of wood raised up behind steps. It had a deep, beautiful sheen even by torchlight. Strange sculptures peered down at her from a glass case behind the table—a lion, an eagle, a queer-looking bull, and a man. She tried to relax, but the place was spooky.

Paul had been here, guarded his bishop here. She supposed he prayed here. He was a believer, willing to lay down his life for the Church. They rarely discussed religion. But he wore prayer beads around his neck and never hid the tattoos of his order, even when he snuck away to see her at her freehold. He bore scars from his duties as an archwarden.

She thought of the dream, his blood splattering the sand. Trinidad's sword had made a wound no man could survive.

But it wasn't real. It was just a dream.

A commotion behind her made her turn, her hand slipping to the knife inside her cloak. Four archwardens entered, carrying a litter between them. Cloth, white with a golden cross, draped the body head to toe. Sickness slithered through her gut. She got to her feet, glad she'd kept her locks hidden under her cloak hood. It was cold in here; it wouldn't be so strange.

"Don't feel as if you must go," one of the archwardens told her with a respectful nod. "The funeral isn't until evening. You've plenty of time."

She opened her mouth, made words come. "What is his name? I. I will pray for him."

They stared at her stoically, and she thought they were trying to see under the shadow of her cloak hood. One of them said at last, "He was called Paul."

She sank onto the bench behind her. They progressed down the aisle, carried Paul up the few steps, and laid him on the raised floor before the altar. They lit four candles and set them on the floor around the pallet.

One of them paused on their way back and glanced her way. "Are you all right, ma'am? I can stay if you're uncomfortable alone with him."

"No," she managed, sounding strangled, even to herself. "I'm fine."

The archwarden glanced back toward the altar. A frown rippled through the tattoo on his forehead. "He was a good man."

*I know. Fuckin I know.* She twitched a nod.

The archwardens strode toward the back of the church, their weapons and armor making little noises of war. The doors slammed behind them, echoing like explosions against the high ceilings. The flickering candles around Paul's body cast a glow against the pristine cloak shrouding the ugliness of his death.

Reine waited, hands gripping the railing in front of her, half-healed cuts stinging fingertips and palms. She got to her feet and walked to Paul's body. He smelled of rot and sweat. After a moment she lifted the cloak.

His face had puffed and bruised on one side. His lips hung slack, open, and one eyelid parted to reveal the white. Death had stained and stretched his face nearly beyond recognition.

She sank to her knees. Pain tore down her body as every muscle clenched in a spasm of grief. She squeezed the burial cloak in her fists, her forehead bowed against his chest, cold and still as a mountain cliff. It was real. Trinidad had killed Paul, had twisted his cursed sword through Paul's chest. Real blood. Real death.

A hand on her back, petting, soothing.

Reine raised her head.

Javelot didn't smile or taunt or speak, just offered her a hand. Reine stumbled blindly, pulled along by her sister. Jav opened the door to a side room—a closet, really—filled with crosses and cloths and they slipped inside, closing the door.

A door at the back of the church slammed. Footsteps pounded the stone, several people striding along the aisle. Rustling and muttering. Reine couldn't tell if it was male or a female. All that mattered to her was the silence surrounding Paul. Then another door opened, interior and closer to them, followed by quieter steps. Seconds passed in silence, finally broken by a hard voice.

"You told me Father Troy was dead. You lied."

Trinidad.

Reine started forward, a silent snarl on her lips, but Javelot gripped her arm in the darkness, holding her back.

# TWENTY-EIGHT

S eth and Malachi had Trinidad by the arms and forced him to his knees before the altar, though he would have knelt without protest. Seth climbed the steps to put Trinidad's confiscated sword in the archwarden armory. Malachi stayed behind Trinidad, his blade out. The point stung the back of Trinidad's neck.

The bishop stood on the steps leading to the choir loft in the sanctuary, gazing at the body, surrounded by candles. She passed a moment straightening the white drape over Paul before turning to Trinidad.

Trinidad bowed his head to the altar, crossed himself, and let Marius stare him down. He didn't attempt to look too contrite. She wouldn't have believed it anyway. Still, the effect of the sanctuary, the bishop in her robes, and the candles all reminded him of his well-honed sense of duty to her and to the Church. He thought of Paul ambushing him at the Barren, Castile in that bloody cell, of Hawk's brutalized body, of his priest dying alone.

"You told me Father Troy was dead," he said. "You lied."

"For his protection," Marius said.

"I would never harm him."

"How could I know that? After all, he came back with a bullet wound."

"It's gone septic, Your Grace," Seth said softly. "He's weak with infection and he's not long to live."

"Sadly, in the end, it doesn't matter after all," Marius said.

It mattered. It all mattered. But Trinidad's mind had calmed despite the injustice and grief. He'd had plenty of time to think in the stiff silence on the ride from the hospital to the church.

"You knew Roman would tell me Father was alive. Did you torture him?"

"Of course not. Roman is just trying to do what's best for you. He knows your proper home is with us."

Trinidad shook his head, unsure whether this was just another lie. "You never would have left Father Troy without guards unless you knew I wouldn't harm him. You used him as bait."

She exchanged glances with Seth. "Actually, I expected you to come to your Wiccan friend first."

"Leave Castile out of this." He cursed the tremble in his voice.

"Castile is already in it. He's an ecoterrorist. A murderer."

Trinidad lowered his gaze. "We've all done things."

"Like killing Roi d'Esprit? Like rebelling against the Church you swore your life to? Like helping an enemy of the parish? Those sorts of things?"

Trinidad shot Seth a wounded look. He must have told Marius about Roi. "Like crusading against innocent people," he shot back. "Like trying to bend God's will to yours."

She frowned and stepped closer. Seth grabbed Trinidad's arm to hold him in place, though he didn't move.

"It's not God's will I'm concerned with. It's yours. Oh, yes, I know what you are. You think I am blind to your wickedness?"

Trinidad looked at the faces of the archwardens but saw no shock. That could be their strict discipline, but he had a feeling this concept was not new to them. He suffered the inane urge to laugh. How many people had been accused of being both the Second Coming and the Antichrist within an hour?

"You give me too much credit," he said, realizing as he spoke that it was how she would clinch the parish's dedication to crusade. Trinidad made a good story to tell the parish. He had become the ribbon to tie around her neat package of lies: her scar, the angel demanding she crusade, and now Trinidad, the convenient Antichrist. His shoulders fell.

"They'll never believe you," he said. But his tone wouldn't have convinced himself. "The parishioners may be ignorant and hungry, but they aren't stupid."

"But we have the perfect witness," she said. "Castile is quite compliant now."

This time Trinidad lunged forward with a growl, but he barely touched the hem of her robes before the world tumbled end-over. His lungs screamed for air. He found himself on the stone floor, staring up at them through a fog, arms and legs limp. Malachi stood over him with a marshal's shock-bat. Seth stared down at him, some unreadable emotion on his face. Pity. Or loathing.

"Our efforts at reformation are wasted. Take him away," Marius said.

Hands rolled Trinidad over, stripped him of his armor, and bound his arms together behind his back. He couldn't raise the least fight in his limbs, the effects of the shockbat still numbing his body and mind. Their voices sounded like they came from a vacuum.

"Tell them," he mumbled. "Tell them where I killed Paul. Tell them about the Barren."

Or maybe he never spoke at all. No one responded to him. Apparitional voices mentioned the jail and other things, too, but fog thickened around him, obscuring the beamed ceiling of the sanctuary and the crosses overhead, banishing thought and protest.

# TWENTY-NINE

Reine sank to the floor as the bishop and her people left the sanctuary. Neither Javelot or she spoke or moved for several minutes. There was the low rumble of a dray, someone shouting orders. Then all fell quiet as a grave.

Javelot opened the door and peered out. The light from Paul's candles brushed a ghostly glow over robes, boxes and a large jeweled cross on a staff. She started to prowl around the small room where they'd hidden. "You all right?"

Reine didn't answer.

Javelot got her knife out and tried to pry one of the jewels from the cross.

"Leave it alone," Reine said. Her voice sounded empty, faint.

"Why? Superstitious? You a believer now?" She jammed the blade at the metal and twisted. The crimson bauble fell onto her palm.

Paul had believed. Reine let her forehead fall to her knees.

"Besides," Javelot added. "We need money for wherever we end up. Shit to trade and the like."

Reine's finger found the knife at her belt. It slid over the hilt, found the top of the sharp blade, and pressed hard and pulled. She tipped her head back and breathed, savoring the burn. It seared up her arm right to her brain. Hot blood dripped over the blade to the floor.

Javelot reached down and closed her hand over Reine's wrist. "Stop," she said softly. "Just stop."

"That thing's not worth the trouble. It's not real." She twisted from her sister's grip and knocked the big glass bauble from her hand. It skittered across the floor in pieces. "You disobeyed a direct order. You were supposed to stay at the freehold."

"Didn't think you'd have the stomach for the job."

Reine flared at the impertinence but forced the rigidity from her body. One thing at a time. Javelot's punishment could wait. She let her knife slide back into its sheath. "You're here. Make yourself useful then."

Outside they kept to the shadows, but Reine forced herself to walked with purpose, as if she belonged, making Javelot to trot to keep up with her longer stride. She could see the shaggy-haired shadow in the guard hut by the gate, but whoever it was never swiveled their way. That made sense. The guard would be watching for danger from outside the gates.

"How do you know where to go?" Javelot whispered.

"Papa had maps from old recon." Another thing Javelot didn't know.

The door to the other building was locked. Reine studied the windows. There were a few at ground level that appeared to lead to the basement. A few steps around a corner led to a perfect, quiet entry spot. She knelt and felt around the edges of a couple of windows, seeking one that wasn't latched. Unlikely, in this weather, but it was an old building . . . ah. The window frame gave under her hand, rusted metal flexing against the glass and creaking. She stopped and listened, but no one had noticed. She shoved the window open with her boot, cracking the glass, and slipped inside before anyone could see her. She landed in an awkward crouch on the ground, and Javelot followed.

The barest trace of light followed them from the window, fading fast. Reine's cut finger left a smear of blood on the glass. She turned to study the small room. Two narrow cots, rumpled covers. Clothes in neat folded stacks on a table. Archwarden quarters. Trinidad's?

The lever on the door rattled. Reine and Javelot sank back in the shadows, behind the swing of the door. Her back found cloaks and coats hanging from hooks on the wall. She reached back to feel for a weapon, eyes never leaving the door. Her fingers found a sword hanging in its scabbard from a hook as the door squealed open on its hinges. She closed both hands around the hilt and drew it, whisper quiet.

The archwarden was Mexican-dark like Trinidad, but rougher in the face, older. He reached for his sword in the same instant that his eyes fell on them. Reine swung before his blade escaped its scabbard.

She caught him in his bare throat, left open by a man not expecting violence to greet him in his own bedroom. He hit the concrete floor without catching himself, though he gaped up at her, gagging on his own blood. It had been a killing blow, but she stepped forward and ripped through his jugular again to make sure he'd stay dead. The scent of blood filled the room as she dragged his body to a far corner, leaving a wet trail of red to avoid on her way out the door.

Javelot stared at her, still pressed against the wall.

"What? No stomach for it?" Reine thrust herself through the door without a second glance back at the dead archwarden or her sister.

Wolf—teenaged and big but she'd recognize him anywhere—stood in the corridor, blinking at the bloody sword in Reine's hand. His hand went to the sword hilt at his belt, but she shook her head at him.

"Put it down," she said, gesturing with the tip of her blade to the floor.

He drew his sword, a double-edged blade, shorter than most archwardens used, though he had most of the height and breadth of an adult. He hesitated like he thought of challenging her with it. But he knelt and laid it down, kept his eyes rolled up under his shaggy bangs like he expected her to lop his head off.

"I guess John is . . . dead," he said, twitching his chin toward the door.

She nodded. The scent of blood already thickened the air. "Where is everyone?"

He blinked rapidly and his shoulders sank. "The jail." His voice broke. "And the crusade."

"Good. Just us, then. Very good." She bared her teeth in a grin. "Israel. Time to hunt."

He blinked at her, shook his head slightly. His expression slackened.

"You remember," she said.

His eyes blinked, once, slow.

She eased out a breath. The chemwiping cocktail and extensive priming had worked. His subcognitive was still solid, after all this time.

"You know where to go," she said.

He turned and walked down the hall, never turning his head right or left, taking even steps. Behind her, Javelot followed, a silent shadow. Reine left the bloody sword. She wouldn't be needing it any longer.

T he priest, Trinidad, and their Church had raised Israel into a strong near-man. Reine had to give them credit for that. After they broke into a shed at the graveyard and found a shovel, he dug with powerful, even strokes, tearing up the hard ground over the false grave without a word. But then, it was as Papa Roi had trained him to do, to work with silent determination, just as he'd laid a minefield of violence in his child-mind.

So far so good, she thought, glancing around at the empty graveyard, but she couldn't shake off the feeling of wrongness. The Flatirons loomed against the haze to the west. A tangle of skeletal tree branches made a barrier around the graveyard. No grave-robbers perused inparish cemeteries as they did in the county dead-fields. No marshals patrolled nearby; no vigilantes peered through the gates. Besides, every man and childless woman between twenty and fifty was at the crusade camp just inside the eastern wall, taking the cross. Israel had said so in his short chemwipe speak.

Still, she couldn't help the feeling this was all going wrong somehow.

*Thud.* Israel's shovel had found its goal. He stopped and blinked at her. Reine suffered a wild terror that he was coming back to himself. Next to her, Javelot caught her breath.

Reine muttered the cues at him again: "Israel. Time to hunt."

His expression relaxed, but he still didn't move.

"What are you waiting for?" Javelot said. "Open it."

Israel ducked down and went back to work, having to scrabble in the soil with his fingers to unlatch the box. Reine shifted from foot to foot and surveyed the area again. Raw dirt covered a fresh mass grave nearby. She sniffed at that. How many people lay here, souls disintegrating in lime-crusted pits? She could almost smell the rot. Indigo souls floated through the Ancestor's Veil on the wings of the body's ashes, purified by fire.

"At least we burn our dead."

Javelot ignored her.

Reine felt a hand on her boot and realized Israel had stopped messing with the box of explosives. He gazed up at her again with the expression of blank expectation that Papa Roi had trained him to with chemicals and harsh physical reinforcement.

"Move over. I can't see," Javelot said.

Israel moved.

Reine frowned. He'd been conditioned to take orders only from Reine and her father, unless . . . "Papa Roi set you as a prime."

Javelot shrugged. "Papa always took precautions."

But you never thought to tell me, did you, sister? Clear insubordination, requiring punishment. Not now, though. There wasn't time.

Reine leaned back to let the clouded skies shed a little light down into the hole. Javelot lay on her belly and sifted through the wires, starters, and explosive compounds. "It all looks good." She picked up a vest and held it out to Israel. "Put that on."

He obeyed, sparking another flare of anger in Reine. She bit down on it.

Packets of compound explosives were sewn into the fabric. The threads seemed stable, fine. The wires were good. He put it on. Where had the time gone? The vest had swallowed him as a child. But he was nearly a grown man who wore a sword on his hip. Soon, he would have earned the archwarden tattoos, she knew. He probably looked up to Trinidad, not even knowing they were real brothers. Javelot had looked up to her like that once.

He was probably dedicated to his Church, like Paul had been.

"Do you pray?" Reine asked him.

He just looked at her. It wasn't a question in his sublexicon.

"Stop talkin like that," Javelot muttered. "You're gonna distract him."

Reine squatted down next to her sister, her gaze still fixed on Israel's face. The shadows hid the burn scars, betraying how much he looked like his brother. Javelot might have been positioned as another prime, but she hadn't seen Israel when he'd first been brought to the freehold as a child, burned beyond recognition, screaming for his family when he wasn't passed out from the pain. She hadn't been the one to cradle the broken child when no one else could quiet him during long weeks of conditioning and chemwiping. Javelot hadn't lost herself to their father's schemes.

"What?" Javelot asked, not disguising her impatience.

"This won't work," Reine said. "Won't stop anything."

Javelot grunted. It was Reine's only warning of attack. Her sister leapt on her, punching, kicking, her hard, trained body produced killing blows. Reine fought back, but she knew deep inside that Javelot had been right in the end. She didn't have the stomach for it.

# THIRTY

A fter a planning session late in the afternoon, Bishop Marius felt confident. Scouts had reported back on the Indigo defensives, which seemed meager at best. Archwardens she trusted held the new army well in hand, though she missed Paul's steady hand on the tiller. They still hadn't found Castile's coven yet, or any others, but there was time for that. Doubtless the crusade would draw them out.

Seth gave a little knock and stepped inside Father Troy's office. Someone had been to clean it, and clear off the desk. The windows let in the last of the fading daylight. Seth's black cloak and armor drank it in, all but the crimson cross, turning him into a stern shadow. He pushed back his hood and let his hands rest on his weapons belt, fingers curled around the sweat-stained leather-wrapped hilt.

Seth had taken Trinidad in hand and managed his transfer to the jail. He'd been gentle, speaking quietly to Trinidad, who was docile and confused from the shockbat. It had made his ramblings about the Barren easy to write off to anyone who overheard.

"Well?" she asked, wondering how Seth felt about taking his brother-in-arms into custody. Badly, she assumed. Seth hadn't admitted as much as all that, and his face was set. Just as well, she didn't have time for hysterics. "Trinidad is more lucid now," he said. "He's admitted to killing Paul, Your Grace."

She frowned. Maybe he was just trying to protect Castile. "Details?"

Seth nodded. "He described the fight, knew the wound had taken a lung and heart. I'm inclined to believe him."

"Fine. Arrange for his execution at sundown."

"Your Grace, all respect, but despite his confession, the fight sounded like self-defense on Trinidad's part. And the order's charter requires a trial even in cases of confession. I can contact the mayor's office—"

"In times of war and severe unrest, regional laws decree the Church provides the justice system. I am the Church, am I not?"

Seth dropped his gaze. "Yes, Your Grace."

If it was up to her, she'd make Trinidad suffer. She'd hang the Wiccan first, let Trinidad watch his friend die. But she needed Castile to rove her. She wasn't about to take a chance with Trinidad roving her, though he'd proved he could by admitting he'd killed Paul. He was far too independent of a thinker.

Still. A simple hanging wouldn't satisfy the grief clawing at her belly like famine. But there wasn't time. Trinidad's revolt had to be put down today.

"And the Wiccan, Your Grace?"

She sighed, contemplating potential leverage against Castile. He couldn't outlast her forever. Maybe Trinidad's capture would help matters, a few hours of watching Trinidad scream. Something about the two of them . . . Trinidad had reacted so violently at the mere mention of Castile.

"His coven is at the root of Trinidad turning against us. We'll let him watch Trinidad hang, see if that doesn't persuade him to cooperate—"

She heard footsteps on the porch and the door swung open again. She rose to meet Malachi, who kissed her ring and provided her a proper, respectful space, retreating to stand next to Seth. "Your Grace, the civilians are starting to balk at the wait. We might see some of them slip away."

Not entirely unexpected, but she let a frown settle on her mouth. "Fine," she said. "We already outnumber the Indigos ten to one as it is. Do we have them mapped and scouted?"

Malachi's turn to frown. "The latest scouts report the Indigo freehold has banded with two more tribes. They've wagons set up on the outer fields, horse squads gathering, war tents and soldiers. They're digging trenches and laying razor wire."

This was new. He paused and she tipped her head at him, waiting.

"There are fires burning all the time inside the freehold. Forges."

She propped her chin on her hand, thinking. Indigo spear-guards were notoriously vicious fighters, no matter their weapons. Their spears were specially designed to pierce modern armor, made of scrap building metal with balanced shafts, and they practiced long hours at perfecting their throws. Every tribe had a stockpile of stolen guns and crossbows. They had defense down to a science, even schooling their young children in hand-to-hand with knives.

But none of that mattered. The army outnumbered three tribes of Indigos . . . they outnumbered ten tribes of Indigos for that matter. And she had troops who could take more injury than most, providing Castile was brought to heel, which gave her pause.

Perhaps letting him watch Trinidad die would be a mistake. If she led the Wiccan believe she'd let Trinidad live in exchange for his cooperation roving—

The boom of an explosion punctured her musings.

Marius leapt to her feet. Malachi spun, striding to the door. He swung it open and clattered down the cracked concrete steps, weapons jingling, sword in hand. Two more archwardens came running toward her but every other face turned toward downtown.

Seth took a moment to find binoculars and lift them to his eyes

"I can't see much, Your Grace," he said. "Smoke is rising. We should get you to a more secure location."

"Nonsense. Out of my way." She shoved past him. The evening took a breath before another explosion rumbled. A second plume of smoke rose over the city like a ghost.

"Not far. Center of town," Malachi muttered. "The church, maybe?"

"The courthouse has always been a target," Seth answered.

Or the jail. The Wiccans had come to free their imprisoned comrade.

# THIRTY-ONE

C astile woke with a jolt. The world rocked beneath him and he ducked his head under his arms as loose cement from the ceiling dusted his bare back. He registered: bomb. His training in the ecoterr movement, even after years away from it, banished panic. His brain took over, all calculating thought, processing the firepower in the explosion, sniffing for smoke to determine the chemicals used, listening for aftershocks and more bombs. Silence followed. Either the bomber had mistimed his explosives or he was out. Castile climbed to his feet and stumbled to his cell gate. Voices crescendoed in terror. He tried to pick out words amid the shouts and chaos. Lights flickered on and off in the corridor.

Another explosion made Castile duck back. Chunks of concrete stoned him from overhead. A massive crack split the ceiling and metal screamed as pressure twisted it. It ran down the wall toward his cell gate, nearly reaching the hinge. He thrust his cold, aching limbs into motion and rushed the gate, hoping to take advantage of the weakened wall before someone else took notice. The gate slipped free of its hinges but held fast, wedged against the warped frame. He slammed his palm against the metal in frustration.

Voices echoed in the hall, authoritative. On instinct, Castile dropped to the floor amid the heaviest rubble, closed his eyes, and fell still.

Someone paused outside. "Should we move him?"

"Probably. Bishop said to take special care with him."

The lock clunked open, though with more squeals of protest and a good deal of cursing from the guards. "Bomb killed the power," one of the marshals observed as he yanked the gate free with a violent clang. "Be hell to pay if we lose the important ones."

"Better grab Trinidad next." Feet drew near Castile. "Talk about hell to pay. The bishop will have our heads if he goes in this. I heard she wants a public execution."

Trin. Castile's battered body coiled. One of his legs sprang out at the nearest guard. He drove his bare foot into a groin and the guard dropped with a muffled curse. Castile leapt at the downed man, seeking a weapon, anything. His hands closed on a shock-bat and his thumb found the switch. It shocked the guard from the loop on his belt, sizzling through trousers where no armor protected him. The man stiffened and fell back, mouth wide in a silent scream.

He yanked the bat free of its loop as the other guard came at him with his own bat. It brushed Castile's free arm but momentum carried him forward. He thrust the shockbat up at the guard's throat. It landed awkwardly, but one touch made the man fall into a convulsive heap. Castile followed him down. His thumb jostled from the switch and the man moaned. Castile pressed the bat against his throat again and threw the switch, holding it until he smelled shit and piss. He repeated it with the first guard.

Neither guard was breathing when he finished, but Castile didn't care. He'd heard one of them raping the female prisoner in the cell next door the night before, recognized his husky voice. For all he knew, these guards had been part of his own torture. As he searched them for keys, shouts of terror rose all around the jail.

Wielding the bat and keys, he walked out into the hall and looked up and down. One end had been reduced to rubble and dust. Cold swept along the corridor in a stiff breeze, chilling his bare skin. Prisoners rattled their cages at him as he passed. He told himself he didn't have time, he couldn't free them all. Trinidad was here.

But prisoners reached for him and pleaded, rending something in his heart, opening him to the familiar Presence behind him, this time one of reasoned urgency.

"I thought you left me, Dark Horns," Castile muttered, and then he saw the Hunter's wisdom in shielding his escape with the other prisoners. "Ah. I won't make the mistake of doubting You again soon."

He unlocked cages as he went. Only one was too warped to open, but the prisoner inside didn't seem to mind: he bled from a head wound and he was covered in rubble. At first Castile warned off the prisoners with the shockbat, but they had only escape on their minds. The corridor filled with shouting people. Another explosion clouded them all in dust from shattered walls and shaken foundations. Castile was among the few who didn't scream. It threw him to his battered knees, but he scrambled up and staggered on.

He pushed past frightened prisoners to peer into each cell.

Hands and bodies pressed against his naked body. Terror rose up in him as the crowd carried him for a moment. A hallway bent to the left and Castile fought to move that way, if only to escape the terrified mass for a moment.

He heard a voice and stopped. It was deep and earnest. And he knew it; thank the Lady and her Lord, he knew it. He could taste relief on his tongue as surely as if he'd swallowed sweet wine. Castile crept closer, behind a guard standing in an open cell doorway.

"I swore my soul and blood to Saint Michael the Archangel, Lord Christ, and Holy God. I defend the helpless. I make my oath again, before you." A rattle of chains broke off the rough voice.

The guard took a step back. "I . . . I can't. Orders. I'm sorry. I just . . ."

Smoke billowed around Castile. A guard shouted out orders from down the corridor, cutting off the guard's excuses, and the tide of prisoners roared a protest, swelling down the short corridor. Castile pressed the bat to the back of the guard's neck and followed him to the stained concrete. Then he shoved his hair from his face, and grinned. He couldn't help it; he was that relieved to see Trinidad.

"Did you actually think he'd let you go because of that pretty little speech?"

The ghost of a grimace, a flash of white teeth. Dirt shadowed the cleft in Trinidad's chin and hollowed his cheekbones. His face was bruised and he hunched. His stare had a desperate edge. He rattled the chains holding his hands behind his back and securing him to the wall. "You going to just stand there looking at me all day?"

Castile patted the fallen guard and found the universal magnetic key they carried for shackles. "I think you meant to say,

'Thanks for freeing me from this disaster. I'm forever in your debt.' Are you all right?"

Trinidad winced as his bound hands came forward. When he was free, he laid a hand on Castile's bare chest as he peered past him into the chaotic hall. "Yes. You?"

"Still standing."

Trinidad stripped off his black wool tunic, wincing again, and shoved it at Castile. "Cover up that scar." He wore a tight synthetic under the tunic. It slipped up, revealing more dark bruising on his lean stomach.

"They worked you over, yeah?" Castile said, holding the shirt and staring at him.

Trinidad pulled it back down. It clung to his muscled chest and revealed the ridges of his pentacle if you knew to look for it. "Not as bad as you. Put that on."

The handmade shirt hung to mid-thigh on Castile, still warm from Trinidad's body. They'd surely beaten Trinidad, but he moved all right, not hesitating as they joined the throng of prisoners out in the corridor, shoving through inmates intent on freedom. The press of unwashed bodies, dust, smoke, and the acrid scent of human flesh cooking turned Castile's stomach.

Trinidad tripped over some rubble and a prisoner clutched at him, dragging him to his knees. Blood streamed from her chin as her lips formed the word like a prayer: archwarden. Castile shoved her away and hauled on Trinidad's arm.

Another explosion blasted some distance away. Maybe the courthouse or out on the street. Trinidad ducked as the crowd roared in fear, twitching free of Castile's grip. Another blast rocked the building, throwing them to their hands and knees. A gust of heat and then bitter cold swept over them. Dust and smoke clouded the air. Castile fumbled through the haze for Trinidad. He found him huddled against the wall, head ducked down. As the dust cleared, Castile pulled him to his feet. He shouted to be heard over the terrified voices around them, but Trinidad didn't even look at him. He dragged the archwarden along a few steps until they stumbled over a prone woman with blood running down one side of her face. Trinidad stopped and stared down at her, swaying like a reed in the heavy current of prisoners pushing past them.

"Do you want to stay here? Herne's balls, man, move."

Castile hauled Trinidad upstream past more panicked inmates, shouting to let them pass. One attacked Trinidad full on, screaming something incoherent. He tried to fight back, raining mismatched blows, until Castile stepped in and rammed the live shockbat under the man's chin. The inmate dropped without a sound.

Castile grabbed Trinidad and dragged him into another cell. Even against the wall, cold air, dust, and ash blew against them in a steady stream, stinging their eyes and airways.

Trinidad scrabbled at the wall, coughing.

"What a mess. I don't even know if—" Castile peered at him, teeth knocking, body shaking in the bitter, dirty air swarming around them. "What's wrong with you? You look like you're about to pass out."

"I saw Magpie."

A beat. Two. Castile shook his head. "No. No. She's at the hospital."

Trinidad drew in a breath, coughed again. "We'll get her out, Cas."

"Did you see that big hole back there? Bodies everyfuckingwhere."
Castile ran his hands down his chest and slapped his cold, bare
thighs. "Curse me, what if she's dead? I swore—"

"Castile!"

Castile blinked at him. Trinidad's eyes were wide. His body
visibly shook. Without a word Castile took his wrist and led him
back through the labyrinth of cellblocks, shoving past terrorized
inmates. Heart jack-hammering, pain stabbing ribs and bruised
knees, he pulled him deeper into the smoke, toward the bomb
crater. Smoke and dust wavered on the air, his eyes streamed tears,
revealing limbs and blood littering the floor. An almost whole
torso of a woman was still propped in a corner where the blast had
shoved her, her prison issue curiously clean except for blood staining the hem of her shirt. Below, everything blown away. Castile
shoved the images to the back of his head, burying them deep as
he hurried Trinidad past the damage and the dead.

Then a familiar face refused to be obscured by his will, fingers
in fighting claws, her cheek rent and gaping raw flesh from eye to
jaw. Magpie had been thrown against the bars of her cell and was
held at upright by rubble. Blood painted her torn face and body, a
graffiti of gore. Cold swept in from the broken ceiling, carrying the
putrid scent of her death with it.

Abrupt bullets pinged around them, scattering chunks of the
floor by Castile's bare feet. Fifty strides ahead, the rest of the building had fallen away, revealing smoky skies and a street teeming
with a desperate, screaming horde. Wailing sirens drowned out the
crowd noise and then faded. Castile felt Trinidad pulling his arm,
he stumbled alongside the archwarden without thought. He knew
there should be sounds of chaos, but he heard none of it.

They had to crawl through a ragged opening in the building, Trinidad shoving him through first. Castile glanced back and realized the jail and courthouse had been punctured like someone had sprayed it along the bottom with giant bullets. Shrapnel from the bomb, rusty nails, and bits of blackened metal scattered the ground. Somewhere deep, beyond his grief and shock, his mind processed the damage. The scavenged remains made the blast feel hurried or inexperienced. Homemade, amateurish, without precision. His mind whirred over what it all meant, but his body simply followed Trinidad.

Free of the direct blast zone, Trinidad seemed to revive. He led them west at a dead run, away from the damage. The dusk-shadowed streets teemed with people, some injured, prisoners running, marshals and parishioners coming toward the explosions. Trinidad glanced at the people running by and hesitated. But he didn't stop moving until Castile could barely breathe, his lungs stinging from smoke, his feet so cold and battered that every step was agony.

Trinidad led them down a long, quiet alley, slowed, and caught Castile's arm. He hardly sounded winded at all. "We have to keep moving."

Castile stared up at him, bewildered. Magpie's gory death reeled through his mind. "I swore, between Herne and me. Sealed with a circle. I couldn't handfast her, not with any honor, yeah, but I could damn well protect her."

"I'm sorry she died," Trinidad said. "But it doesn't change anything."

A caustic laugh escaped Castile at the archwarden's perfunctory sympathy. He leaned against a building and closed his eyes. Tried to breathe, but his throat closed. Magpie had been nude, battered.

Not just from the explosion. From torture. Rape. He'd refused the bishop, and Magpie had paid. "She died for me. Because of me."

"Sometimes a soldier's job is to die."

"No. She never should have been here at all. I never should have let her come. She only came inparish because she loved me—"

Trinidad caught Castile's head between his callused hands, fingers tangled in his hair. "Maybe she did love you. I don't know. But she came inparish because you and Lord Hawk ordered her to come. Roman always says commanders forfeit the luxury of grief." He kissed Castile's forehead, dry lips pressed against dusty skin, and released him. "Honor her for dying a soldier and forget the rest, Cas. She's at peace now."

It might have been the most words he'd ever heard Trinidad string in one go since they were little kids. Trinidad's breath on his face, his lips on his forehead. A quiver settled in his belly. Maybe it would never go away. "You do have a true heart, yeah?"

"Don't go all soft on me when I'm telling you to toughen up."

That made Castile smile, a little. "Sorry."

Trinidad turned away and started to walk. "I did want to run you through after I learned about Father Troy…." He shrugged and let the words die off.

If he kept Trinidad talking, he could avoid thoughts of Magpie, the blast, what it all meant. "Who is Roman?"

"My armsmaster. Who betrayed me today, I think." Trinidad's attention caught on someone lingering at the other end of the alley. Castile followed his gaze and felt the last his anger and hurt fall away in his surprise.

The scarred boy from the dreamscape staggered down the alley, leaning to one side. He had an odd shape about him, like he wore oddly bulky armor. The kid's scars looked different in true light, harsher, uglier. Or maybe it was his dull expression. Warning flared through him. Trinidad bolted forward to catch him by the shoulders. "Wolf. What are you doing here?"

Castile followed but stopped as he realized it wasn't armor that made the bulge around the boy's chest. Wires wrapped Wolf's torso, binding explosives to his back. "Trin. Let him go. Get back. Now."

"What?"

"Do it! Now!"

Trinidad released his brother and stepped back.

Wolf blinked at Trinidad. His scarred face stiffened, he balled his fists, and threw himself at Trinidad.

# THIRTY-TWO

Trinidad pulled Wolf forward into a choke-lock to suppress his struggles, but Wolf fought him, clawing at his chest. He reeked of smoke and another foreign acrid scent.

"Let him go, I said." Castile shoved between them. "You'll set him off!"

He caught Wolf's arm and pulled him away with a firm grip. As soon as Wolf's back was turned on Trinidad, his fight melted away. Castile led him a few steps. Wolf went docilely. He tucked his chin against his chest, huffing air through his snuffly nose.

"Set him off . . ." Trinidad stared. A bomb was strapped to his brother's back. He forced himself to take a deep breath, though it didn't dispel his panic. "Who did this?"

"Shut up," Castile said. "I'm thinking."

Trinidad obeyed, but his blood roared. He swallowed hard. The cold started to seep in, and he rubbed his hand over the faint ridges of the pentacle on his chest. Wolf had bruised him. They hadn't wrestled in a long time. He hadn't realized the strength in Wolf's growing body.

Castile sniffed, coughed, and sniffed again. He frowned at Wolf and lifted the boy's hand to his face. They were black with grime. Wolf didn't fight Castile's touch. "Yeah, smells like chemicals I worked with back in the glory days." He knelt to look at the vest from a different angle. "Easy, kiddo." But Wolf didn't move, just stared past them blankly.

"He must have been near the jail," Trinidad said. "But he should've been at school or . . ." What day was it? What time? He had no idea. "At the church. Why isn't he talking?"

"We have bigger problems," Castile said. "The vest is still armed. Can't see the trigger. Usually a suicide will just carry it. In his case, I think someone else has it." He cupped the boy's jaw and lifted his chin. "Who did this to you, buddy? Did they tell you anything? Like how much time you have? Or how to disarm the fucking thing?"

Spittle dripped from Wolf's loose lips. Castile wiped his face with his sleeve, gently. "Doesn't seem like he's in any condition to tell us. He's drugged or something."

The wind whipped up, whistling down the alleyway. A shiver racked him once, a violence that rattled his teeth. "Wolf doesn't do drugs."

Castile cast him a smirk. "Right. And I never played with bombs as a teenager." He looked up and down the alley. "I need tools—pliers, wire cutters, a blade. I have to get it off him."

Wolf glanced at Trinidad when Castile did and gave a drunken lunge in his direction. Castile caught his arm. "Whoa there, kid. I'll stay with him, Trin. You go."

Wolf focused vaguely on Castile and calmed.

Trinidad felt a burgeoning sickness rising in his gut. What was wrong with him? And what had Wolf done with his blackened fingers?

Castile's sharp voice cut through his anxiety. "Quick-like, yeah? Go!"

Trinidad ran down the alley a block, paused at the crossroad and checked for archwardens or marshals. He caught sight of black marshal uniforms, shields up against the chaos, directing traffic down the main streets. No one was looking away from the bomb site. He trotted down the next block, checking doors. One opened to a candle shop. Trinidad frowned at the mess of a storeroom and rummaged through shelves. He came up with a hammer. Great. But, convinced he was on the right track, he kept sifting through boxes of raw wax, balls of string, and other debris.

"What are you—oh!"

Trinidad spun. A slight girl with long blonde braids stood in the doorway between the storeroom and the shop. Her mouth hung open and she held a knife in one hand. For the first time he realized how he must look, covered in dust and soot, bootless. He supposed he was lucky to still have trousers on, unlike Castile. Her eyes flicked over him, taking in his tattoos.

Trinidad drew a breath and jerked his thumb over his shoulder. "I'm trying to help . . . with the bombing." True enough. "I need tools. Pliers. A knife, maybe, or a . . ."

His voice fell off as she walked to a shelf on his right and came up with pliers. He tried them. They were tough to open, nearly soldered shut with rust, but they would clamp on a wire well enough.

"Wire cutters?" he asked hopefully. She shook her head. He looked down at the knife in her hand.

"I . . . it's my papa's," she said. "He's out helping, checking on things."

"I'll make sure he gets it back," Trinidad said. "I wouldn't ask if it wasn't important."

She nodded and gave it to him, looking up at him. She stood very close to him, smelling good, soap and candlewax.

"What's going on out there?" she asked.

"I wish to God I knew," he answered, and paused. "Sorry. I must go. Things are . . . urgent."

She nodded again.

"You've been more help than you know. Christ's peace upon you." And he fled.

On the way back down the alley, he thought he should have warned her to stay indoors. Slavers operated better under cover of disorder. He could only hope the bombings would afford him the same opportunity against the crusade.

Wolf had sunk down to sit against the wall backing the alley. Castile lingered some distance away, his face white, his bare, muscled legs corded with tension under Trinidad's shirt, rubbing his hands together to keep them flexible in the cold, no doubt. He trotted over to greet Trinidad, took the knife and the pliers.

"How is he?" Trinidad said.

"You just stay well back," Castile answered as he approached Wolf. He started crooning, wordless. Wolf slumped over the vest, still enough Trinidad wondered if he was asleep.

"You going to disarm it?"

Castile grunted. "I cut this thing off him and we run like Dark Horns is on our tail."

"I thought you were an expert in explosives."

"I am," Castile said. "But this is some old-style rig—before my time. Get back, like so. Farther. And stay quiet so you don't rile him." He was already sawing through the wires and straps holding the explosives on Wolf's body. Wolf stayed slack, not protesting, but not helping either.

It might have only taken a minute or so, but in that time, Trinidad's joints locked and he swallowed down bile. Scenes from the prison bombarded him, body parts, terror, and blood, so much blood. The sound of the bomb kept ringing through his head. He trembled, thinking of the blasts rocking through him. He still smelled the tang of death and smoke on his skin. He lifted his hands to his nose and dropped them. He always smelled like death. Killing was dirty work and it didn't wash off. He still wished for his sword though.

He blinked. Castile was gently peeling the flattened, flexible explosive away from Wolf. A snarl of tangled wire lay by Castile's bare feet and he laid the explosives next to it. He whistled, low. "It's enough to level this building." He slipped the blade under a wire pressed into the explosive and yanked. It snapped.

Something caught Trinidad's eye. A female figure a half-block down, hooded with a blue scarf concealing her face. She slipped out of sight around a building.

"Come on," Trinidad said, turning away. "We have to go. Now."

"Don't have to tell me twice," Castile said, urging Wolf into a clumsy, lopsided run.

# THIRTY-THREE

Trinidad led them on a roundabout route, approaching the church grounds from the back. They'd been lucky so far in not getting spotted; the bombings had driven most parishioners indoors. But Castile kept thinking they couldn't expect it to last. Of course, maybe it seemed longer to him; he had charge of Wolf—no easy task since he kept wanting to stop and sit down.

Trinidad stopped in front of a tangle of razor-wire that barricaded a little house on the church grounds from the street. Just ahead, the church loomed, its blackened stone menacing in the daylight, its windows barred with rusting sheet metal and peeling wood. Castile wondered how Trinidad had ever found peace here, amid the asphalt and concrete, away from the hunt and the cave. The mountains could be unforgiving, but at least nature was a proper home.

"You come back here like a horse running into a burning barn." Castile had to force the words out between knocking teeth. He was so cold he felt like his balls were trying to crawl into his belly.

"We need weapons, armor, clothes." Trinidad seemed well-conditioned to ignore the cold, but shivers jarred him occasionally.

"What about the archwardens?"

"I'm more worried about the snipers on the belltower." Trinidad nodded toward the tower, but his attention was on the fence. "They have to be in exact position to see us here. We decided we didn't need to blockade this spot any further for security. Of course, they don't know what I know, and I couldn't tell without getting into a lot of trouble."

He reached through the fence, slow and careful to keep from snagging his skin on the rusted razors soldered to it. A couple of twists of wire, and the fence sprang open, plenty wide enough to admit a person.

Castile grinned. "You naughty boy. You cut a hole in your own fence."

"When I was too young to know better."

"Now, why, I wonder, would a young Trinidad do such a thing? Teenaged dalliance or two?"

Trinidad shot him a scowl, but he didn't have the same ruthless glare as usual.

They managed the back door all right and slipped inside. Father Troy's house smelled dusty and sour, like onions. It was dim inside, the windows covered with metal plating. Occasional cracks of light sliced through the gloom.

Trinidad led the way through the house and peered between curtains. The window by the door wasn't barricaded and it faced the church grounds. "The weapons and armor are in the sanctuary building."

That seemed odd. Wasn't that where they worshipped? "Why there?"

"Most secure for a standoff or siege," Trinidad said. All impatience from his voice was gone. "It's all stone with metal-plated windows."

Castile settled Wolf on the steps and joined Trinidad, who pointed at the tower, partially blocked by the red tiled roof of the church at this angle. Indeed, the building was thick stone. "Four snipers," he said. "They can see part of our path, just there, before we get under the cloister."

"The gate guard can see us from here, too," Castile said.

"That will be a novice, and he should be looking at the street." Trinidad let the curtains fall. "There's a door under the cloister on this end. It's usually unlocked this time of day. We won't have much time. Do you think you can get Wolf to go alone? Less of a target and they know him."

Castile gave Wolf an uncertain look. The boy slumped back against the stairs and stared at nothing. "I don't know. He's in deep trance, I think."

Trinidad sighed. "Come on. Let's get you clothes first."

Trinidad led him to a small room with a narrow window, a cot, and a tall, narrow dresser. A hammered metal cross hung over it.

A tingle ran down the back of Castile's neck. Despite the austerity, it felt of Trinidad. "Is this your room?"

"It used to be." Trinidad opened the bottom drawer of the dresser and tossed Castile a shirt and trousers. Then he reached under the cot and came up with a worn pair of boots. "Can I have my shirt back now?"

Castile peeled it off and tossed it at him. He rubbed his hands on his bare stomach and thighs where the wool had itched him before pulling Trinidad's old clothes on, smiling inwardly at Trinidad's appraising glance.

The trousers hung low on his slim hips and he had to roll them up a couple of times. He sat on the bed to pull on the boots, wincing. Still sore inside. The boots rubbed but would do. He liked going naked as much as the next guy, but he couldn't deny the relief in getting into warm clothes.

"You still have no boots yourself," he observed.

"I know. I'll just have to find some . . . somewhere." Trinidad turned to Wolf, who waited on his steps, staring unblinking into space. "You think we can we break him out of it? Wake him up?"

Castile considered. "A bad shock might bring him round, yeah, something that's so essential to this part of his consciousness that it draws him back out. We'll have to take him to Aspen. If a high priestess can't fetch him back, I'd wager no one can."

"Thanks for not arguing about bringing him."

"Wolf is better off with us anyway. I have a feeling about him." A bad, suspicious feeling, actually. He signed the Horns with his fist and pressed it to his shoulder, thinking of the oft-felt Presence at his back. He was more and more certain the gods had some purpose for Wolf and he was reasonably sure Trinidad wouldn't like it.

Trinidad turned his attention back to the problem at hand. "Just walk quickly, like you know where you're going. I'll send you first and I'll bring Wolf. He's given up fighting me, and from a distance, a marksman won't necessarily know it's me, just an archwarden with a novice."

"If he's not looking through his scope," Castile said.

"I'm hoping we'll move quicker than he can get a gun to his eye, and he has no reason to examine someone on church grounds."

No heads peeked around the battlements on the tower and the churchyard was empty but for a cold wind scuttling leaves and twigs across the labyrinth. Castile saw movement through the windows of the auxiliary building, and two guards shivered in the gate house, their backs to the churchyard. It made sense all the guards would be focused outside the church grounds, but he barely had dared to hope. He went out first, trying to move with purpose but feeling like a fleeing deer. Trinidad was right. The door was unlocked.

The blackened stone façade hadn't prepared him for the sheer beauty of the interior. Candles in lanterns lit the place, shedding their glow on grand wooden steps and a big table at the back wall. Quiet benches rested in rows and wide beams soared overhead, supporting a curved roofline with arched wooden beams. Stone pillars supported each beam, bigger around than two men could reach.

The steps beckoned. He climbed them and stared up. Over the altar, a cabinet of gleaming wood climbed to the bottom of a giant, round colored glass window covered on the outside with metal plating. Even in the gloom, Castile could see it would be stunning should sunlight be allowed to shine through it. It must be made of thousands of pieces of colored glass. On either side, upright metal pipes were suspended over more benches. Winged people perched on the tops of pillars. Crosses were carved into stone. Four white statues rested in alcoves over the carved table.

The door opened again, letting in a slice of daylight and snuffing it just as quick. Trinidad eased Wolf down to the steps, took a knee before the table, and bowed his head. When he lifted it, he signed something over his heart.

"He's gone," Trinidad said.

"Who?"

"Paul. His body. They took him away." For a moment, Castile thought he might say more, but he stood and walked to one of the walls on the side. He pressed his hand against a wall and a door hidden in the paneling opened toward him.

The tiny armory was dark as Castile's cave but Trinidad picked up a taper from the big, ornate table and lit it from a burning votive. Inside, he waved it around the windowless storage closet, revealing rifles hanging from pegs, shelves of short blades and old swords, buckets of ammunition, discarded pieces of armor. A complete armor harness hung neatly from hooks.

Castile's mouth opened and then he shut it, blinking.

"No clever comment this time, I see," Trinidad said. "Find some armor and suit up." He reached for the harness on the hooks and slipped the upper arm and shoulder protection over his head, settling it on his shoulders and buckling the straps over his chest. Next went his front and back plates.

Castile secured an old, scarred bracer on his left arm.

"I wore that when I was eighteen," Trinidad noted, picking up the other bracer and turning it over in his hands.

"All right, stop gloating about being bigger than me. I can still kick your ass," Castile said, holding out his other arm so he could snap it on. The bracers were heavier than they looked, laced with steel ribbing.

"It's old, but it'll stop a full-on sword strike," Trinidad said, fixing the bracer.

"Looks like it already did a few times."

"Indigos," Trinidad said. "When blades didn't work they got out their bows instead. That's why there's only one greave. Arrow broke the other."

"What happened to your leg underneath?" Castile said.

Trinidad shrugged and turned away to buckle on his sword, doubling the belt around his hips and putting on the rest of his armor. As he slipped bullets into a magazine, Castile peered around his shoulder. "Binaries?"

"No. Not inparish. Too many people."

Castile released a hissing breath. "So, you think we're stuck in the walls for a while."

"Getting out might be a challenge, especially with Wolf."

Castile clenched his bruised jaw, finished with the armor, and strapped a belt with knives sheathed on it around his middle.

*Herne*, he thought, *I will happily die should it be my day. But, be it Your failure or mine, I cannot go back to the Christian prison.* He felt a chill against the back of his neck, like the Horned One Himself had moved his hair aside and whispered against his skin.

Maybe he sensed Castile's tension or maybe it was for no reason at all, but Trinidad's fingers paused while loading the magazine and he looked up.

Castile spoke quickly, trying to hide his terror. He wasn't sure if he was talking to Trinidad or the Horned One, or both. "If this goes south, don't let them capture me. Swear you'll kill me instead."

"Castile, no. I can't do that. My vows—"

"Fuck your vows." Castile embraced the growing chill of certainty, of the sheer horror of his recent abuse. "Threefold Bane means I won't get out of this so easily and I'm only down two."

"What did you do?"

"I was convicted for ecoterr—"

"No." The word sounded like a gunshot in the close room. "What did you do?"

Castile swallowed. Maybe Trinidad was the third bane. "Stop trying to change the subject. Just swear you'll kill me if it gets close."

"I can't. I just . . . can't, Cas."

His terror tasted sour. It shamed him but he couldn't help himself. "You have to. I need to know I won't go back there. I can't go through that again."

Trinidad fell very still. His eyes glistened. At last he twitched a nod.

"Thank you." Castile took his hand, meaning to draw him close into an embrace. But the door of a dray slammed outside, muffled by the stone of the church.

Trinidad's grip tightened, making Castile painfully aware of the strength in the archwarden's sword hand. A frown deepened the cleft in Trinidad's chin and his gleaming eyes narrowed into his fighter's mask again. He blew out the taper and strode to the altar and blew those out too, leaving them in near darkness.

Castile thought with an inward chill what it felt to have that glare pointed at him. *I'm glad we're on the same side. Thank you, Herne. I think. I just hope we don't have to make good on our little hand-fasting right away.*

# THIRTY-FOUR

The crusader's camp was tense after the bombing and the coming night would make things worse. Malachi still hadn't reported in from scouting the bomb sites and Bishop Marius paced in the little house they'd confiscated, annoyed at the lack of word. James guarded her, unmoving by the door, but a commotion outside made them both turn.

He opened the door, hand on his hilt, steel glinting between crossguard and scabbard. Two marshals held an Indigo woman by the arms. She was wiry in the way so many Indigos were, betraying deep-set hunger, but she had the lopsidedly broad shoulders of a spearguard and archer. Each eyebrow had several notches plucked bare, giving her face a strangely mechanical look. A copper ring hung from her nasal septum and a couple of fine-linked chains had been woven into her locked braids.

"Have you disarmed her?" James asked, his bulk between the visitors and the bishop, so that Marius had peer around his shoulder. She fingered the bronze cross she wore over her armor.

A third guard held up two blades to show James she'd been searched.

The Indigo didn't struggle, just gave Marius a brazen smile. "You're gonna want to talk to me. About Trinidad. Tell him to fuckin leave off."

"She says her name is Javelot, Your Grace," the marshal said. "She's the second in command to Reine d'Esprit of the Indigo clan, out on Old Superior lands."

Marius nodded. "I'll hear what she has to say."

The marshals let her go. They'd bound her hands behind her back, but she was able to climb the steps with no trouble. James audibly drew his sword and hovered the point near the Indigo's kidneys. She didn't kneel, of course, but she twitched her head in a nod. Marius supposed that was about as formal as it got with county folk.

"What's this about Trinidad?" she asked.

"I saw him and Castile runnin from the jail. Half-naked, the two of them, but they looked sound enough."

Marius leaned forward. "How do you know Castile?"

"Fuckin who don't? He came the other night, wantin to savvy. Got us to catch Trinidad for him a few nights ago."

Marius turned her back on the Indigo and crossed to her map table, giving herself a moment to absorb that. Trinidad had lied— she'd known it, of course. But how deeply the lie had gone, she'd had no idea. "Do you know what Castile wanted with him?"

"Friends from way back. Trinidad was a Wiccan," Javelot answered promptly. "I asked around. Reine, she just takes the goods and goes off. She never sees the real payout. But I thought you might be interested, since it's different from what Reine knows."

Marius settled herself behind the map table and folded her hands. "Trinidad's heritage is well known in Christian circles, so you'll have to do better than that to keep my attention. Where did they go?"

"I won't say until we have a savvy," Javelot said. When Marius didn't answer right away, she added, "They did find that boy with the scars."

"Wolf."

"That's what they call him by. We call him somethin else."

Marius held off taking that bait for the moment. "Why should I care about any of this?"

"Trinidad had hardly any clothes. He was barefoot. Some bruises on him and dirt. No armor rig, no sword. I figure he was a prisoner at your jail."

Marius gave up her bluff. "I'll have archwardens see to their recapture, then, and thanks. James, would you escort Javelot to—"

"No! There's more." Javelot settled her shoulders and stood up straighter. "Can't go back home yet. Reine'll kill me."

Marius steepled her fingers beneath her chin. "That's why you're here, betraying your tribe? Because your queen kicked you out."

Javelot straightened. "Fuckin no. I'm takin queen now and I'm protectin my freehold."

"By giving your enemies information," Marius said.

"And I got more than just this, lady. But not till we got a savvy."

"You realize we could just torture you for information," Marius said.

Javelot grinned, baring stained, chipped teeth. "Why make an enemy when you can make a friend?"

"I assume you want us to stop the crusade."

"Lady, you can crusade all over the Western Territories for all I care. I'll even throw you Reine, if you want a quit from us. Fuckin I'll take a knee to you. I just want my freehold. I just want what's mine."

Ambition could be a dangerous tool, but a useful one. Marius settled back into her seat and crossed one leg over the other.

"Loyalty to the parish requires taxes. Crops from your lands. Tithes, they're called. To the Church. To do that, you'll need us to front seeds and animals, I'm sure. Reine does seem to worry about feeding your tribe, which tells me you've eaten your stores dry. It's a little more complicated than our accidentally strolling around your freehold instead of marching through it."

Javelot shrugged. "Figure we have to do some wicked to make it look honest, lady."

Marius bit back a laugh. If Javelot only knew. "I already have a perfectly serviceable alliance with your sister, who is still queen, if she yet lives?" She went on at Javelot's grudging nod. "Why would I throw that away for whatever information you might have?"

Javelot didn't miss a beat. "Because that savvy is over. She's gunnin for you now that Paul's dead. All broke up about it." An ugly smile as she observed Bishop Marius' lips press together. "You not know? Your archwarden Paul and Reine had a thing. I can't let her stay queen. She never was much good, but she lost it after she saw Paul dead at the church. Couldn't even set a bomb right."

Marius gave herself a moment to compose herself. The words still came out harder than she anticipated. "She set off the bombs?"

"Fuckin had Israel do it. You know, your kid they call Wolf? With all the burns. He's Trinidad's real brother, not just a fake one.

He was a sleeper who took out the jail for us. Was supposed to set himself off too. But fuckin Trinidad and Castile found him and carried him off. And there's more info where that came from, like where they went to hide. Now. Do we have savvy or what?"

Marius stared at the Indigo, with her broken teeth and scars, her notched eyebrows and piercings. She smelled of ash and sweat, of unwashed clothes, and unburied feces. Marius found her ignorant, ugly, and refreshingly honest.

"James, fetch a chair and something to eat. I'm sure the new Reine d'Esprit is hungry, and we've many things to discuss."

# THIRTY-FIVE

"T ake Wolf behind the altar," Trinidad said. Paul's funeral was supposed to be tonight, but the body was gone. It was reasonable to expect the funeral had been delayed and to hope no one would come into the sanctuary. He wasn't sure they could be so fortunate, but maybe hiding would buy them some time.

Castile guided Wolf behind the altar and sat down with him, shoulders pressed together. Trinidad felt a pang. He should be the one to comfort his brother. But he smothered the feeling and picked up a bucket filled with ammo and a belt.

He settled next to Castile, his back against the holy table. A thrill of dread stirred his stomach, which he cured by passing a moment gazing at the Gospel statues in niches overhead. When he'd been a kid, he'd help clean them. They were heavy, carved of solid oak, and rubbed smooth by decades of polishing. He'd always found comfort in their symbolism. Maybe, then, Christ was still with him.

They listened to the voices outside, and more doors slamming. Horses, stomping and blowing in the cold. Then the familiar rattle and engine whine of Seth's dray driving in and parking. Trinidad's throat closed. Seth bore his faith as a burden, his archwarden status and tattoos the only outward indication of his devotion to God. He attended services only when required, but Trinidad knew he took communion privately every morning. He had been like an older brother to Trinidad, a guide in the order, their highest-ranking member in the parish.

His order had hurt Castile. He could trust none of them. Not anymore. With a sigh, Trinidad pulled the ammo belt from the bucket and started loading bullets. His practiced fingers made almost no noise.

Castile shifted his leg until they rested thigh-to-thigh. "I think Wolf is asleep," he whispered.

"I'm not surprised."

"He's so heavy he's about to dislocate my shoulder."

"He's really grown . . ." Trinidad broke off to listen again and shook his head. "I just hope we can figure out what's wrong with him."

"You really care about him. It's not something I expected out of you."

"You think I'm some heartless bastard because I'm a Christian?"

"You kill because you're a Christian, yeah?"

"And you kill because you're a witch. An ecoterr."

Castile sighed. "I didn't know what to think before I met you again. I mean, the reports weren't exactly favorable, but I had some hope. And then when the Indigos killed your friend—"

"Daniel."

"Yeah. Daniel." Castile paused and his voice gentled. "When he died you seemed . . . destroyed, somehow. And then Paul . . ."

Their arms brushed as Trinidad continued loading bullets into the belt. The Wiccan's thigh still rested against Trinidad's with envious ease.

"You mean because of my parents," Trinidad said. "You think you know all about that, do you?"

Castile shifted next to him. "Hardly. We don't run in the same circles. It's hard to sort truth from fiction sometimes. People like to talk. Especially Indigos, and they know less parish gossip than anyone."

Trinidad dropped a bullet and it rolled between his legs. Castile slid his hand over Trinidad's thigh and captured the bullet. He put it on Trinidad's palm and closed his fingers around it. Castile's hand was cold.

"I know a little. My papa told me you were there." A pause. "That's why the explosions affected you like that in the jail earlier."

It wasn't a question. "Roman tried to train it out of me."

"Father Troy always said you didn't remember it."

"It was better he didn't know."

Castile gripped Trinidad's hand, fingers unyielding as the bullet dug into his palm. "I think you should tell me."

"Like you told me what you did to deserve Threefold Bane?"

"Please, Trin."

Trinidad leaned his head against the altar. He was talking almost before he knew it. "Israel and I got in a fight. Israel was crying—he was just being a kid, you know? But he was on my nerves. Papa was about as mad as I've ever seen him. He picked up Israel and he yelled at me and told me to—" Trinidad squeezed his eyes shut until he saw sparks.

"Wait outside," Castile whispered.

"He made me wait at the end of the parking lot under a tree. The shopkeepers used to give us candy, so I knew Israel was going to get some and I wasn't. Papa had a big bag over his shoulder. I didn't even think about it."

"You wouldn't have. You were just a kid."

"Papa was carrying Israel and giving me that mad look and the door closed on them. Mama didn't say anything. She didn't yell at us. She was looking at her list. She didn't even glance back at me. But they had testimony later. She knew. She was in on the whole thing."

Castile rested his cheek against Trinidad's shoulder. "They must have been relieved they could spare one of their children."

"No. They didn't think I was worthy enough to die with them."

Castile lifted his head. "That's some fucked up logic."

Trinidad tried to disengage his hand from Castile's grip, but Castile held on. "I didn't die with them. I couldn't die to save Father Troy. I couldn't even die trying—"

"Will you just stop, please?" Castile said. "Stop it. You think there's honor in martyrdom?"

Trinidad hadn't saved any of them. "There's honor in doing the right thing."

"Whatever that is. I killed half a dozen people before I turned sixteen. I was in prison at seventeen. You killed Roi d'Esprit because he threatened Father Troy. Reine carved that pentacle in you because you killed Roi. We're still no good to the world dead—"

The sharp noise of a slamming door broke through Castile's rising pitch. Trinidad slapped his hand over Castile's mouth to silence him.

Seconds drew on. Trinidad split in two, part of him listened for noise that meant impending discovery. The other half of him drew to the sensation of touching Castile, to the exact place where callused fingers met soft lips. He dropped his hand and closed the distance between their mouths.

The world fell away. Shock whipped up Trinidad's spine and corded him to Castile. The witch pulled him closer, fingers digging into the back of his neck—

A second slam broke through their kiss. Trinidad shoved Castile away, fingers fitting the belt into the rifle as quietly as he could, jaw clenched, lips burning, groin tight.

Someone lit torches. A faint glow filled the sanctuary as they crackled to life. Boot-falls hesitated on the stone floor, then moved closer. "Someone in here?"

Damn. Trinidad let the nose of his rifle show around the edge of the holy table. "Stop."

The footsteps died. "Trin?"

Trinidad's throat closed at the sound of the Seth's familiar voice. He swallowed. "Seth."

A beat. "What are you doing, bro?"

Quiet rustlings. He snuck a glance. Seth had edged up to the second row of pews and knelt between them. The black barrel of a pistol rested on the back of the pew. Trinidad pressed the back of his head against the holy table and clenched his jaw. Ornate carving dug into his skull.

He focused on a crucifix in his mind's eye. Christ, cruel crown of thorns pressing into a head slumped in acceptance.

Seth said, a little louder: "They're all over the grounds. Snipers are in position. I don't want you dead, but there are some trigger-happy folks out there. You come out with a weapon, any other way but in my custody, you'll get tapped half a dozen times, Trin."

Father Troy kept a crucifix in his office, an old thing that had been his mother's. He'd always indulged Trinidad's curiosity, had let him take it down and handle it.

"We know you've got Wolf and the Wiccan back there," Seth added. "We know you're together. We know about the bombs. We know you're doing magic. Going to that silver place. You trying to get them killed, too?"

Trinidad closed his eyes. Real, tiny nails held the plaster Christ to the wooden cross.

"—to me and I'll keep you alive," Seth was saying. "I got your back. I always got your back, brother."

It was tempting, to just surrender. He focused on Castile's weight against his side, Wolf's soft, sleeping pant. Castile gripped his bracer.

The bishop's lies had tempted him, too. He drew a breath, forced his panic into a knot under his heart. What did they have, what weapon did they have to keep them alive?

Castile murmured his name. A gentle prod. He met Castile's eyes, shadowed and black in the dim light. They'd tortured Castile, trying to get him to admit where the coven lived. He thought of the Barren; of killing Paul; of seeing Wolf as a kid, scared of that man; of landing in his own room inparish instead of the cave . . .

He had dismissed it when Castile suggested it. Now it wasn't so easy to set aside. Wolf gave a sleeping, snuffly sigh. His fingers twitched. Maybe he was dreaming. No. Roving. It was the only explanation for getting drawn to him, even if it made no sense.

"Get her in here. The bishop. Now," Trinidad said.

"She's still on her way from the camp," Seth answered.

"We'll wait."

The door slammed and Castile started talking, "They could just come in and—"

Trinidad interrupted with a hissed whisper. "You said something about Wolf. Before. You said he's a powerful dreamer. Do you think Wolf can rove to the Barren?"

Castile dug at his eye with the heel of his hand. "I think it's not going to matter in a few minutes."

"Castile. Focus."

"All right. Yeah, maybe. Why?"

Trinidad raised his hand and tipped his head, listening. Boots on the stairs, softly confident. The balcony, Trinidad thought. They're going to try to get a decent shot off from the balcony. Castile rolled his eyes upward and nodded that he heard it too.

"We only have one card left," Trinidad whispered.

"The Barren."

Trinidad trapped Castile's hand between his gauntlet and his thigh. "You meant what you said before. About my killing you."

Castile nodded, his gaze steady on Trinidad's face.

"Do you trust me?"

Another nod; not a shred of hesitation.

The doors opened again and fell shut. Trinidad nodded at Castile and released his hand.

A lengthy silence followed before Marius broke it. "You want to speak with me, archwarden, show me your face. Kneel to me as you're sworn to do."

Trinidad's knees involuntarily drew up at her voice. He closed his eyes and bit back an angry protest.

"I am sworn to Christ," he said. "Not you. Not anymore."

"You can't just undo your vows to the Church, archwarden. You don't get to pick and choose your loyalties. God holds you to them."

Trinidad ignored her. "There are three people alive who can rove to the Barren at will. One of them is me, and I'm holding the other two hostage."

Soft consulting out in the pews. Castile tapped his gauntlet. Trinidad ignored him.

"What do you want?" the bishop asked at last.

"This has more to do with what you want. You want the Barren. But you can't go there without us. We're the only people who know the way. It's advantageous for you if we live."

"I'm listening."

"We are going to walk out of here and you are going to let us. All of us, no shots fired, no threats."

"I can't guarantee that."

"You can and you will, because if one bullet flies, I will kill them both. And you will never see the Barren again."

"You would murder them in cold blood? Your brother? Your lover?"

He looked at Castile, who shrugged. "She's got some crazy ideas," he whispered.

"Not so crazy," Trinidad whispered back.

Castile bared his teeth in a savage grin. Trinidad clenched his fist and waited.

"How do you want to do this?" the bishop asked after another long pause

"Instruct your snipers to lay down their rifles. Tell the archwardens to gather in the graveyard, where I can see them, hands up.

I want Seth's dray on the street, already running. Nobody moves, nobody threatens us. One twitch, one sound, and I kill them both."

"We can try to capture you, and likely succeed," she pointed out.

"We will never rove for you," Castile called to her. "I think I've proved that. I'll die first."

"And this foolish plan is good for me how?" Marius asked.

"Letting us go is only half of it," Trinidad said. "I will take you to the Barren when you call off the crusade. When there is real peace."

Castile dropped his forehead to his knees. "You would say that."

"I accept your terms," the bishop said. "Not because I trust you, but because I don't."

"Likewise, bitch," Castile muttered.

"Clear the sanctuary," Trinidad said. "Everybody. Even the balcony and the narthex."

A soft curse and boots on the steps. Trinidad peeked around the table and saw shadows. Six men. Six she had up there, waiting for their opportunity to kill him. He leaned his head back against the table and sighed. Now he had to count on their not wanting to destroy the sanctuary with a firefight.

At the slam of the narthex door, Wolf stirred, yawned, and almost fell over. Castile caught his arm. "Whoa there, pup."

Wolf blinked at them from beneath his tangle of hair, his scars staining his skin red as blood. "This is going to sound really weird, but how did I get here?"

Trinidad chambered a bullet and pointed the gun at Wolf. "I trump your weird. You're our ticket out of here. I'll do my best to avoid killing you, but sorry in advance just in case."

Wolf scrambled back, lips parted in shock, eyes locked on the gun.

Castile shook his head. "Trin, give the kid a minute—"

"No, Castile. Don't. You the one who made me swear to kill you, before Christ."

Castile looked at Wolf, who had his hands vaguely raised as if he wasn't sure what to do with them.

"You really want them to capture him?" Trinidad demanded. "Do to him what they did to you? They'll torture him if he refuses to take them to the Barren."

"He can't withstand it," Castile admitted.

Wolf looked from one to the other. "Trinidad . . . ?"

"You've just become a hostage. Tie him up, Cas, hands behind his back."

Castile moved without hesitation. He jerked the altar cloth off sending cross and candles clattering to the floor. A quick cut with his knife and a rip provided him with a long cloth "rope." He bound Wolf. The boy struggled for a moment until the Wiccan cuffed him sharply on the back of his head. "Knock it off, kid. We're trying to save your life here."

"It doesn't seem like it." Plaintive, childlike.

Trinidad tested the knots without answering. They were tight enough the makeshift bonds would have to be cut to release him. "Give me your gun, Cas."

Castile complied and took hold of Wolf's arm to guide him.

A silent sob ran through Wolf. "Trin . . ."

"Shut up," Trinidad said, more desperate than harsh. He cleared his throat and straightened his voice into command mode. "Don't talk. Don't take a step without my say-so. Don't fight me. I mean it, Wolf. I'll kill you if I have to. If they catch you, they'll make you wish I had."

"But I don't understand."

"If the gods have mercy, you soon will," Castile said, rising to peek over the altar and then standing up all the way. He pulled Wolf to his feet by his arm. "If they don't, then it won't matter."

Trinidad pressed a pistol to the back of each of their skulls. "Go."

They walked down the center aisle, Trinidad staring down the rows of empty pews. Castile opened the door. The cold air of the dying day swept over them. Seth's dray rumbled in the street, doors left open, running rough. The gate was open, ready. Seth stood next to the guard tower, his pale face stern.

Twenty steps, give or take. Twenty steps to live.

Less than twenty steps to die.

Seven archwardens, Malachi and the bishop's men, had gathered into a loose knot in the graveyard, hands resting on their heads. They didn't look armed, but one could have a knife winging toward him in three seconds, a bullet in one. The bishop waited behind the archwardens—a compromise, Trinidad assumed, because her guards would have argued for her removal.

Seth cleared his throat and rolled his eyes upward. Trinidad didn't track his gaze. He knew snipers lingered overhead in the bell-tower, but he had no control over whether they would shoot him in the back or not. He was acting partly in good faith and partly on instinct, and it was too late to figure out whether they were, too, and well past time to do anything about it if they weren't.

"Seth can verify I've got my fingers on the triggers. They're depressed. If I'm shot, my hands will contract from the shock and I'll kill them both. If I sense a weapon about to be used against us, I will kill them. And myself." He sought the bishop's gaze through the steely faces of the archwardens. "And then you're left with nothing, your Grace."

She gave him a crisp nod. Her expression was bland, purposefully, he assumed.

Trinidad nudged Wolf and Castile along and they started walking. Trinidad kept his pistols pressed firmly against their heads. Depressing the triggers just the right amount took all his concentration, especially knowing one stumble could make him pull.

"What do you think you're fucking doing?" Seth asked lowly as they passed. "You don't even have boots on."

"He's trying to save the world," Castile answered.

Trinidad avoided Seth's gaze as they walked through the gate. It felt like a heavy yoke as they got in the dray, Castile first and Wolf between them. Castile slid awkwardly across the seat with his hands tied behind his back. Wolf moved in next to him, head turned, staring at Trinidad.

Trinidad kept his guns on them until he had to slide in behind the wheel. This was the most dangerous moment, when he had to set down one of the guns. But Seth's dray was armored and running and it leapt to life as he punched the pedal.

Trinidad stared straight ahead as he drove away, fast, trying not to anticipate a bullet chasing his head. Adrenaline burned in his veins and nausea pulled a string inside his stomach. It contracted painfully.

"I thought you were serious for a minute, about killing me," Wolf said.

"I was," Trinidad answered. "I am."

"Don't worry about it, kid. Not yet," Castile said.

Trinidad kept his gaze on the road, trying to focus on where to go next instead of his guilt over mistreating Wolf. No one was following. That he could see. Yet. "We need to ditch the dray," he said, pulling over.

"We go to ground, yeah," Castile agreed. "It's the only way we'll buy enough time get over the wall."

Trinidad had only gotten them as far as the prison, looming on its hill over the desecrated university grounds and the black-market shantytown that crouched in its shadow. Plenty of people wandered among the makeshift structures, but it wasn't a place of second glances or talking to marshals about what they saw.

Trinidad got out of the dray, cut Wolf's bonds with his knife, and drew his pistol. He wished he'd found some boots somewhere. Seth had made a good point about that.

His hands shook violently and he almost fumbled the gun.

"Give me that before you hurt yourself with it." Castile took Trinidad's pistol and tucked it in his waistband. The other he palmed against his thigh as he cast a wary glare at the cliff-like walls of the prison. Stained black from the ash-clogged air, streaks of red sandstone shone through like bloody scars.

"What now? What are we doing?" Wolf asked.

"Exactly as I say. Come with me," Trinidad answered.

"But—"

"Shut up, Wolf," Castile said.

Trinidad led them away from the prison down a street that backed to the south wall, weaving between tree stumps, broken concrete, and trash. The houses sat close together, boards and warning signs concealing windows. Protective symbols—Christian crosses, Wiccan horns, Indigo ghost glyphs—glared from doors. Dogs snarled behind metal gates, making this a formidable stretch of city wall.

Broken concrete and rocks scraped Trinidad's cold feet raw. A cat policed the fence across the street, setting half a dozen dogs to yapping. Castile stood still a moment, narrowed his eyes, and waded through trash to a sagging porch. He pressed his ear to the door. No sigils marked the doors. Metal plating covered the windows. "No dog," he said. "I think it's empty. Come on up."

Piles of blown rubbish mounded in the front yard and Trinidad had to watch his step closely. Edges of broken cans glinted like knives, papers, torn books, broken crockery, a shattering of glass, all covered in a fine mist of ash and snow. It was undisturbed. No one had crossed through but Castile in at least a couple of days. They had found a chink in the wall.

Trinidad nodded Wolf ahead. The teenager followed Castile, elbows jammed against his side. A pistol butt jutted from his waistband. Castile must have slipped it to him as they walked. Trinidad scanned the empty street for parishioners or patrolling marshals, but no one appeared. The bombings likely had everyone spooked or busy elsewhere. He picked his way through the trash toward the house.

After a quick glance around in the fading light, Castile backed up to the edge of the porch and leapt, kicking in the door. The kick broke the lock in the jam but it caught and scraped on something inside. Trinidad surveyed the street again, realizing how many of the houses looked deserted, windows boarded, doors askew or missing. Still, tension gripped him. If someone saw, if someone told the marshals . . .

Castile shoved at the door and beckoned them through. "A lot of these old houses aren't lived in at all," he said. "The cell used them for meets, like that old place on 4th."

Trinidad stared around at the shadowed, crate-filled room before Castile shut the door behind them. "We can go over the wall now."

"No. We sit tight until late, Hunter hold them from our gates," Castile said. He moved between boxes, then found and lit a lantern with matches left by it. The oil smoked, stinking. Soon it would be obvious to anyone outside someone was within. "You need off those feet. You're bleeding."

Trinidad had left bloody tracks. His feet were so cold he couldn't feel the cuts.

"Looks like some kind of storehouse," he observed.

Castile put his back to a water-stained bureau and pushed it up against the wall. Wolf jumped in to help.

"Good man," Castile said, giving Wolf a slap on the shoulder. "I'm glad we didn't have to kill you."

Wolf looked from Castile to Trinidad, eyes wide.

Trinidad sighed. Where to begin? They didn't have time to hash it all out. "You can rove and the Bishop wants you."

Wolf shook his head, bewildered. "Rove. I don't know what that is."

"Roving," Castile said. "Dreamwalking. Don't pretend you can't. We know. All those weird dreams you have—they're real. You're going into other people's heads."

"All three of us can do it," Trinidad said. "Marius already tortured Castile. I can't let her have you, Wolfie. She wants us to take her to the . . ." He paused. Wolf had no idea about the Barren. "She wants to use us. In the crusade."

"But we're with the army," Wolf said, giving Castile an uncertain glance.

"Not any more, we aren't," Trinidad said.

Wolf blinked at him. He drew himself up and shoved his hair back from his face. "Let me go out and get you boots and some coats. I'll go to the trade shop."

"With what? We have no money. And they'll catch you." Or you'll turn yourself in. He could hardly blame Wolf if he did. The Church was familiar, home.

Wolf lowered his brows. "No, they won't. I'm better than that. Best in my class."

Castile glanced around at the boxes. "And we have stuff to trade. Good stuff, maybe."

Part of archwarden training included going to ground, avoiding those seeking them, in case they had to transport a priest inparish in adverse situations. But Trinidad didn't like the idea of Wolf going out alone. It was stupid to split up.

Trinidad ran his hand over his face, trying to scrub away his exhaustion. "This must be the most poorly run escape in the history of mankind." He shook his head at his companions. "And these things aren't ours to trade."

Castile gave an exasperated sigh. "Today's been a busy day. Wolf blew up some buildings. We broke out of jail. You abducted us at gunpoint. I think your god will forgive you a little theft, yeah?"

Trinidad noticed he left out Magpie's death. On the backburner, then. He had no doubt it would come back to haunt them.

"I . . . what?" Wolf looked from one to the other of them.

Trinidad tore into a box. "Don't worry about it, Wolf."

Cans of vegetables, shipped in from the West Coast. Trinidad pondered a can while his stomach growled, wondering if he could cut into it with his knife. Would ruin the blade, he reckoned, and tore open another box. Machine-made dresses, plain and loose. The Eastern Seaboard still had some manufacturing but few of its goods reached so far West. Castile hunted through two more boxes and came up with socks. He tossed several pair to Trinidad and to Wolf as well. "Something I learned in the field, kid. Never turn down fresh socks."

"Roman always says that," Wolf said.

Trinidad sat to pull on the socks and realized just how badly cut up his feet were. He'd been too busy watching his surroundings to avoid the glass in his path.

Castile knelt before him and grasped one of his feet, tipping it upward. He gently picked at a shard of glass—an inch-long bloody dagger—and pressed a sock to it to stem the flow. "Not good, my friend."

"I'll be fine," Trinidad said, steeling himself against the sting. He stripped his gauntlets off, rubbed his hands together, and pulled the socks on. His feet had been too cold to even feel it, but blood flow and warmth sent needles of pain shooting up his legs.

His armor constricted his chest and sweat chilled him in the cold air of the dusty house. Ache settled into his bones and head. The drain of adrenaline dragged his eyelids down.

Wolf disappeared around the corner into the kitchen. Trinidad heard the tap come on, the sputter of air, the groan of empty pipes. Then a splash and gulping noises.

Castile laid his palm over Trinidad's forehead. "You're pale and hot."

"Just tired."

"What's on your mind? Something."

"When this is all over . . ." Trinidad shook his head. "Never mind."

"This is hard on all of us. But hardest of all on you."

"How can you say that after what they did to you?"

Castile just gave him a tired, wry smile, his eyes locked on Trinidad's.

"Don't," Trinidad said. "Not with me. After all this . . . if we're even still alive, I . . ." The words faded. He wasn't even sure what he was trying to say. He'd spent so much time focused on the moment, this was his first chance to consider the future.

"We'll stay together," Castile said. "You and me and the kid, yeah?"

Too tired to argue or even consider what that really meant, Trinidad relented with a nod.

"Then it'll be all right." Castile flashed him another grin and tore into another box. "Oh—here. This'll do nicely for a trade."

He held up a box of small batteries. Trinidad rose, forgetting his bleeding feet in his shock. "Where did they get those?"

"Must be an Indigo storehouse," Castile said, shrugging. "Raided or traded off a caravan."

"Indigos wouldn't set up here, inside the parish. Not like this," Trinidad said. He rubbed his hand over his mouth. Who owned this stuff? Not the Church.

"Stranger things have happened," Castile said. "Real recent like, yeah?"

"Indigos come inparish sometimes. But this . . ." Trinidad looked around the boxes half-spilled from their exploration.

"Is it so shocking? The Church is so busy tramping all over the county lands that you ignored your own yard. Divide and conquer, the right hand doesn't watch the left, pick your euphemism. Reine d'Esprit is ignorant and mean, but she's not stupid."

Sensitive subject. "Why do you bring her up?"

"Like her or not, she runs the biggest tribe in the county—"

A creak outside on the front porch made them both look up.

Trinidad eased his sword from its sheath. Castile drew his gun, though he didn't risk the noise of chambering a bullet. They slipped back into the kitchen and put their backs on either side of the doorway. Wolf appeared in the doorway of the room off the kitchen, and Trinidad gestured him back. But large eye bolts screwed into the floor caught his eye.

It all clicked into place. He hadn't thought to look in there yet, and obviously Wolf hadn't realized the eye bolts were for shackles. This wasn't an Indigo warehouse. He gestured to the bolts and mouthed to Castile: *slavers.*

Castile nodded grimly, his jaw set.

The front door edged open and hit the bureau in front of it. "Maldición. Someone broke this lock."

Another voice answered, low and gruff, "Move it, shithead." Shuffles echoed on the hollow front porch. Soft clinks and a muffled sob. The latter sounded female. "The fuck with the door? We got to get inside." Someone slammed against the door and the bureau shoved forward a couple inches.

Trinidad whispered, "How many?"

Castile shrugged and shook his head. Then he mimed his wrists tied together and shook his head again. No idea how many armed slavers, nor slaves.

Trinidad scanned their surroundings again. The back door,

cracks seamed with ice, was barred. The only thing left in the kitchen was the sink in a metal cabinet. Dirt and grime blackened the corners. The faucet dripped, plunking against the metal, echoing. It left an ugly rust stain on the steel.

Castile chambered a bullet, trying to time it with the scrape of the bureau on the floor as the slavers shoved the door open wide enough for them to get through.

"You hear that?" one of the slavers said.

Noise of a shove and a muffled cry, and a succession of chambered bullets—at least four, Trinidad reckoned.

"Sí. Visitantes."

# THIRTY-SIX

F lying snow stung Reine d'Esprit's wind-burned face, but she pulled down her scarf to smile grimly at the tents stretching across her freehold's sallow winter fields. Fires burned in the snow and smoke hung over the encampments like a dense fog. If she looked close enough, she could see person-shaped shadows moving in the smoke where it was thickest, right over the fires. The tribal war parties from outcounty had brought their Ancestors along with them.

An outcounty scout challenged her, an arrow to her string. Fresh shafts bristled from a quiver on her back. She had a gun on one hip, probably passed along with scouting duty. Her armor and scarf were clean, fierce paint obscured her face, and rows of braids capped her helmetless head. As the scout looked her over, Reine thought of her own locks, grown more from necessity than style, and the dirt ground into the cuts on her fingers.

"Reine d'Esprit," she introduced herself, and winced. Talking made her head hurt.

The guard gave her the dip of a knee due a spirit queen before moving along, and it wasn't until Reine reached the gates that she realized the guard hadn't said a word.

She didn't have the energy to wonder at that for long. Her head was a raging mess of pain, centered on the bruises Javelot had left on her face. Fury still broiled in her gut. Her own guards recognized her and swung the gates open. She straightened her back as best she could and walked through. They slammed shut, gears not making the usual rusted sounds. Someone had been at them with cooking grease, and when she glanced over her shoulder she saw they'd been reinforced with additional metal crossbeams.

Tents crouched pole-to-pole between houses, cook fires burned, and children scrambled in the dirt, bound in little cloaks, playing at war with sticks and string bows. Treating it like a party. Of course, the outcounty tribe would have only sent their warrior families, and war was a party to them. She turned toward her house. Their last party, no doubt.

Cur intercepted her and pointed at the common house. "Captains're waiting on you."

Of course they were. She sighed and changed direction without answering.

Cur trotted along at her heels. "How'd it go inparish, if you don't mind my asking, Reine?"

"I mind," Reine said, mounting the steps to the common house and shutting the door in Cur's face.

They'd cleared things out for the evening and a fire burned in the hearth. Just the two: the bowcaptain and the guncaptain. Javelot, the spearcaptain, was missing, of course. The bowcaptain, Darleen, tended a couple of small animals on the spit, showing this was a private meeting, no kin or help. Darleen rose from the fire and faced her, pressed her hands together, touched her fingers to her chin and bowed. "Namaste, my queen."

Reine repeated the gesture tiredly, more out of respect for Dar's ability with the bow than agreeing with her faith. She pulled down her scarf. "Peace to you, too, Dar."

"You look like shit, Reine," Hugh said.

Hugh had run the riflemen under Reine's father and knew her from diaper days, so he'd earned the right to skip formalities. He was ancient now, near sixty-five, and still a dead shot. When there were bullets.

Reine let them look her over hard, touched the back of her head ruefully, and sat. "Fuckin Javelot knocked me out and left me inparish. Coulda been caught or worse." She glanced around, feeling like Javelot might pop out from a corner. "Thought she'd come running back here so I could fix that problem."

Dar shook her head and sighed. She was young, younger than Reine, but she had four kids already and it made her act old. She grabbed rags and took down one of the spits, laid stringy bits of meat on a tray. Groundhog, looked to be.

"How'd the Israel gig go?" Hugh asked.

"You heard the bombs out here, you must've."

Hugh shook his head. "Wind carryin from the east tonight. Nothing comin from the valley but crusader scouts."

"Not even them tonight," Reine said. "They're all inparish, cleanin up. Seems quiet, at least from as close as I got, which wasn't very. Still. Won't take long for the bishop to march."

"Make a new savvy with the bishop, then. We convert or whatever they want."

Reine would have laughed if she hadn't been so depressed and tired. "Fuckin convert? Marius doesn't want us to convert."

"Surrender the hold. We pay her taxes then."

"She wants us dead, Hugh." Spirits, she was tired. "She won't stop until we're dead."

Hugh broke the silence by asking the question hanging between them. "Where's Javelot now, then? What exactly happened between you?"

Reine sat and leaned her elbows on the table. "Shit went south and fuckin Javelot took over. I was gonna stop the bombing. Not why Javelot thought, not because I was scared, but because it felt wrong."

Dar asked slow and careful, "Wrong how?"

"Fuckin I could've kept the savvy, I think, before Jav . . ." She swallowed hard as Darleen put a plate of food between her elbows on the table. The smell nearly made her lose her guts. "We dragged the other tribes into this fuck-all, and we're all still going die here. Can't fit them all in the freehold and the crusaders'll just burn us out if we did. But I didn't know. Javelot didn't tell me . . . Well." She met both their eyes, knowing she sounded as disjointed as she felt. "I didn't know until I got back the other tribes would be here now, so soon."

She pushed the plate away. Her head hurt too much to eat. Every joint ached, down to her fingers, thawing out from her hike. Prickles sparked under her skin with the heat and she had to kill a moan. She looked down at her fingerless gloves and frowned at the blood running on her fingertip, staining the fingernail, the knife in her other hand. She hadn't even realized she'd cut herself.

Hugh and Dar blinked at each other. "Javelot didn't tell you?" Dar asked. "We knew they were comin two days ago."

The air sucked from her lungs like someone had stuck a bellows down her throat. Reine stared at them, waiting until she had a voice, and then waiting more until she could use it without shouting. The captains shifted on their bench. The meat, stringy but smelling enough to keep her stomach twisting, lay untouched between them. Reine got to her feet.

"Roi always said 'live a fool, die a fool.' No more. You ever see Javelot again, fuckin bring her to me. Dead."

The others accepted her orders without comment. Hugh pointed outward, swept his arm, indicating the tribes. "What about them? What do we tell them?"

Reine turned to go. "Tell them to fight. Dead Day is comin early this year."

# THIRTY-SEVEN

T rinidad was a mere shadow in the dim lantern light, his back pressed against the wall next to the doorway leading into the front room with the boxes. He held his sword point downward. Castile wasn't fooled by the low guard; he'd seen how quickly the archwarden could move his blade.

Cautious steps and stumbling. Someone hissed a string of curses, coupled with a muffled moan. Castile concentrated on his lungs, breathing steadily, softly, filling his lungs with near-silent air and releasing it. His heart maintained a steady rhythm through sheer willpower.

"A raid, you think?" Another voice, low.

"Shut up," the other said. Then, louder: "Amigos, ¿Dónde están?" the slaver sing-songed. "Come out to play."

Castile rolled his eyes in a twitch of nervous disdain. Trinidad stared at him, still as stone. Smoking lantern oil filled Castile's lungs with every silent breath.

Another length of silence, interrupted by the brush of cloth and soft movements. "Shit. You and your nerves. There's no one here."

"Someone's been here. I heard them. And look at this mess—" A wet cough broke through the words. He sounded of ashrot, though the availability of medical services in Mexico usually prevented it. But he spoke with a thin accent, peppering his English with Spanish rather than the other way around. A local trafficker trying to adapt to his Mexican bosses, maybe.

The answer came in Spanish, which Castile understood enough of to get the gist: "You didn't hear shit you paranoid son of a bitch."

More confident, heavier footfalls drew near, and again, the patter of bare soles stumbling and a low cry from a female. The noises paused. A thousand questions pounded Castile's brain, leaving an ache of uncertainty: how many? How were they armed? Did they wear Flextek or cheap mesh? How could they take them out without killing the captives? Then a snarl and a body fell through the doorway.

A woman, more a girl, really. She fell to her knees near their hiding place, lost balance, and landed on her shoulder. The impact forced a muffled cry from her. Someone had wound a scarf around her face, creased tight between her teeth. Her arms were bound behind her. Violent shivers racked her narrow frame. Blond hair hung in tattered braids. She wore only a short shift and bruises. The back of one thigh oozed blood from a crimson, raw spot. Castile felt anger surge through him. They'd branded her with a slaver sigil.

She looked up at Trinidad holding bared steel and gasped through her gag. He hunched down but drew his blade high, neatly bypassing the cowering girl as he moved through the doorway. A bullet stung the air near his head. Castile spun into the doorway next to him and took a half-second's worth of their foes' measure before firing.

Two men by the door. One took a bullet and shouted in surprise, Castile cursed and fired again, but the slavers ducked down behind boxes. A third slaver held another woman as a shield. Trinidad went after him as Castile registered the slaver's gun, bladestop mail shirt, and tattoos of wings on his pitted cheeks. Wings fired, but the round just blew out a chunk of wall as he ducked Trinidad's sword and simultaneously shoved the woman at him. Trinidad halted mid-strike and cut to the left, shearing the air over the woman's head and finding flesh. Wings' shoulder spouted blood. He screamed in pain and rage but the cut wasn't deep enough to take him down. Yet.

Convinced Trinidad could take the wounded slaver, Castile turned his attention to the other two. He plugged the first, injured target and the man fell against the bureau.

Castile spotted a gun barrel snaking around the side of a box. He shot the box.

Castile's first victim scrabbled at his gun, trying to get it up on his thigh and shoot. *Herne's balls, I thought you were dead,* Castile thought as he put two bullets in the man's brain. He slumped over, leaving blood and gore dripping from the bureau.

Another gun barked and the woman spared by Trinidad's sword fell in a cascade of blood. Castile blew through nearly all his rounds, shredding the crate the slaver hid behind. Trinidad kept after Wings, who took aim at the archwarden with his Savage, a vicious snarl on his face.

"—blocking my shot!" Castile bawled too late amid the fire.

Trinidad fell hard. His sword skittered away. Bullets coursed the air over his prone body, forcing Castile back behind the kitchen wall. The sawed-off Savage made quick work of the doorframe and cracked plaster protecting Castile, fogging the air with dust.

Trinidad was down.

It was all Castile knew, even with bullets blowing cavern-sized chunks from the wall. A beat passed. Two.

Trin.

They had killed him. He didn't have more than a few steps to back up. He turned his pistol on the doorway, full auto.

Click.

Fuck.

A slaver rounded the corner with a sadistic grin. He wasted no time leaning into his shot, reaping bald-faced terror from deep inside Castile.

# THIRTY-EIGHT

T rinidad tried to scramble to his feet but another shot made him duck. A bullet painted a crimson streak through the slaver going after Castile in the kitchen doorway, spraying flesh and shards of bone across the boxes. The dead man toppled back in a bloody heap. Trinidad twisted toward the door, scrambling to get upright, the shot ringing through his head. His stomach and chest hurt with a constricting ache. Someone carried on screaming, but Trinidad could barely hear it behind the echo of the shots.

Wolf crouched in the doorway just off the kitchen, cupping his pistol in both hands, coursing its sight over the room. He kept low, as he'd been taught. His aim danced from forehead to forehead as he backed into the kitchen. The slave girl in the kitchen scrambled back from him and her screams died off as she likely wondered what fresh hell he was about to wrought. It hit Trinidad then. He knew her, or her face, at least.

"Clear," Trinidad husked out, or tried to; he could barely hear himself speak. The echo of the shots persisted, scarred on his ears. He forced the word again: "Clear."

Wolf lowered his gun. *Castile?* he mouthed. Or spoke. Trinidad couldn't be sure with the shots ringing in his ears. He climbed to his feet, wondering if he'd read Wolf's lips right. He felt like he was underwater. He stumbled across the gory leavings of the gun fight, slipping. Blood soaked his socks, warm and tacky.

Castile lay in the kitchen, flat on his back, face tilted away. His pistol had fallen from his grasp. Even the echoes fell silent. Trinidad dropped to his knees by the witch's side. Wolf made a vague word-shaped noise behind him, but it sounded like it came through two panes of glass. Trinidad bent closer to probe Castile's scalp for bruising and his throat for a pulse. In that moment, he saw the blood staining the witch's armor.

Castile opened his eyes and the isolating bubble popped. Whimpers from the slave girl, huddling in the corner. The clogging reek of fresh blood and released bowels. Wolf's voice behind him, asking if Castile was all right, what had happened, who were these men. The thud of his own heart.

Castile reached up and rubbed the side of Trinidad's head, quick, gentle. He breathed heavily. "Not dead yet I see."

Trinidad sat back. "Stay still. You're bleeding." He gestured to Castile's opposite arm.

Castile looked at the hole in his armor releasing a steady stream of blood. He pushed himself up with some difficulty. "Trin. It's just a scratch. I'm okay." But the words came out chopped into hoarse little bits.

"You're damned lucky," Wolf said, and Trinidad shot him a frown.

"Well, he is," Wolf said.

Castile gave a tired grin as Trinidad helped him sit up. "Good thing we brought you, pup."

"I guess. What happened? Who were those guys? And . . . uh." He didn't seem to know where to put his gaze between all the horribly dead bodies and the barely clad girl cowering in the corner. "Her."

"Slavers," Trinidad said, getting to his feet.

Castile slid back to lean against the cabinet, face pale. The wound hurt worse than he let on. Trinidad picked his way through the gore to find the box of socks. He pressed one to Castile's arm, making the witch wince.

"Bad mojo around here." Castile gave Trinidad a once over. "Looks like I need to rewrap your feet. Goddess knows what nasty you caught from walking in their sludge."

"Let's take care of your wound first."

"Skimmed me, that's all. I'm fine."

"Get your armor off so I can bind it."

"I'll get you some boots, Trin," Wolf said. He gestured with his pistol, still held in a white-knuckle grip. "He looks about your size." He knelt and reached out to fumble with the ties on the dead man's boots. Wolf was waxy with sweat and his hands shook, but he wasn't running to puke like the first time Trinidad had seen people torn apart by bullets.

The electricity chose that moment to roll on. Somewhere in the house a fan whirred and the light overhead crackled to life. Castile and Trinidad looked away from the bodies as the blood came into sharp relief. Wolf swallowed hard. Behind them, the slave girl slunk out of sight around a corner. Trinidad ignored her for the moment.

"You really all right?" he asked Castile in a low voice as he helped the Wiccan off with his bracers.

He nodded. "Just a shitstorm of a headache."

Trinidad grasped Castile's jaw, tipped his face toward the light shed from the dusty bulb overhead and thumbed his eyebrows to examine the Wiccan's pupils. They narrowed as the light shone in them. He released a sigh of relief. "How did we come through that without worse?"

"We're just that good." Castile shook loose of his grip and spoke louder. "Come on out, girl. We're not going to hurt you."

Wolf stopped messing with the boots and watched as the girl cautiously appeared in the doorway. Then she was on her knees before Trinidad, clinging to his armored knees and crying again. He stared down at her and felt his heart sink into his stomach. The girl from the candle shop, who had given him the knife. It seemed days ago rather than hours. He gently pried her off and pulled her to her feet. "You remember me? You're all right now."

"I . . . I don't know," she stuttered through sobs. "I don't . . . know . . ." She collapsed again, trying to pull the short shift down over the tops of her thighs. She was shivering, freezing. He pulled her to her feet and she huddled against him.

He held her as best he could with his armor on. "Your name?"

"I don't know. I should know. But I don't—"

"You remember giving me that knife? Remember me at all?"

She shook her head, chin quivering.

"Chemwipe. I'd put a gallon of fresh cow milk on it," Castile said.

Wolf looked at her, his scars creased with horror.

Whoever had done this to her had it down to a science. They hadn't erased her language or social knowledge, just the things that made her an individual. He looked at Castile. "She can still talk well enough, at least. Targeted synapse blockers. This wasn't some random job." It was slavers, funded by rich, fertile Mexico.

"She's a pretty thing, yeah?" Castile answered. He gestured toward the dead with a fist, thumb tucked between his forefinger and middle finger. "Must have been headed for someone who wanted more than spread legs in a stall."

They took a moment to absorb what that meant. If she'd been carefully prepared for someone, they might want her back. Trinidad ground his teeth together over silent curses. And worse, what was he to do with her? The last thing they needed was a tagalong, and the thought of staying inparish . . .

"We have to take her somewhere," Wolf said, his dirty face creased with worry. He'd been watching Trinidad. "Get her help."

Trinidad exchanged a glance with Castile.

Castile bent over to get a better look at the fresh brand marring the freckled skin of her thigh. He spat a long, colorful string of curses and finished with, "It's liable to get infected if we don't get her treated. Like your feet."

"And your arm," Trinidad shot back.

"We'll bring her to the coven. They'll take her in, keep her until all this blows over."

"Why not leave her here for the marshals to find?" Trinidad said. "She'll be safer inparish, right?"

Wolf shook his head. "Nothing's safe. Not anymore." He yanked a boot from the foot of the dead man, whose head made a wet squishing sound as it slid across the rough floor.

"Wolfie, come on. This is one girl. The marshals won't harm her—"

"We're going to the coven anyway," Castile said. "It's the only place that's safe for us right now. When things settle, we'll get her back inparish."

"I don't see how she'll ever make it. We have a long hike—"

Wolf broke in, quiet and earnest. "Father Troy would never let her go. Father would have taken her in and seen her safe. She's one of God's people, like you said about him." He jabbed a finger toward Castile. "Remember? That's what you said. Even though he's Wiccan, you said you're sworn to protect them, too."

Castile lifted his gaze to Trinidad's face, eyebrows raised. Trinidad felt his cheeks heat.

"You can't leave her here," Wolf added. "She'll always be different. No one understands."

Castile nodded, still eyeing Trinidad. He said soothingly, "Yeah. Yeah, pup. Of course we'll take her."

Trinidad knew when he was beaten. He turned away to peel the gory socks from his feet and slip on fresh ones and the boots, still warm and sweaty from their previous owner. His feet still bled, but the sooner they got out of here, the better.

They scrounged clothes for the girl from the boxes and weaponed up from the dead slavers. Castile waved his horn-tattooed fist around at the gory scene before they left and muttered an inaudible prayer. Trinidad could guess well enough what he was saying. Herne guide us, see us safe. He mentally added: *If it should be my day to greet Cernunnos, protect mine.* And shrugged off a chill. Had he just prayed to Herne instead of God?

They pried open the rear door, ruining the barrel of a rifle doing it, and slipped through the back yard, toward the final fence that marked the boundary of the parish. All of them took great gulps of the cleaner air outside, but Trinidad knew from long experience that he couldn't escape the cloying reek of death so easily. He glanced to the west, wishing for full darkness. But they couldn't wait any longer.

Castile and then Trinidad scaled the back fence. Wolf stayed on the inside, helping lift the girl to Trinidad, who hung over the fence. Silent, limp shock seemed to be setting into her. They heard a shout. Trinidad glanced up to see a light flashing against the houses from out in the street. It spun, blinking over each surface. "They're here."

Wolf glanced behind him as he cupped his hands to give the girl a leg up. But she dropped to her knees at the noise.

"Come on," he said. "Grab Trin's hand."

"Get up here," Trinidad commanded.

He hung over the fence, a grunting Castile holding most of his armored weight from the county side. The girl just cowered lower, wilting in Wolf's arms. Someone rattled the gate and boots thumped on the front porch. Dogs barked. Voices and flashlights cut through the gathering dusk.

Trinidad suppressed a curse and willed himself calm. "Come on, sweetheart," he said to the girl. "You can do this."

"Trin, we have to go," Castile said.

Trinidad ignored him, focused on the girl. Wolf coaxed her, but she started to fight him. Trinidad tried to catch her by the arms and pull her over the metal bars, but he couldn't reach her.

He heard voices and steps coming from the side of the house and setting off a fresh cacophony of dogs barking.

"Wolf!" Trinidad yelled. "Get up here now."

Wolf looked up at him from where he crouched by the girl. "It's no use. She won't come. I'll stay. I'll hold them off."

"What? No. Get up here—"

"I'll hold them off."

"No." A command belied by a desperate wave of his arm to catch Wolf by the arm, the hair, anything. "You can't stay here. You have to come with us. They'll—"

"Come on!" Castile pulled on Trinidad's legs, trying to yank him down on the other side of the wall.

The back door slammed open. A light coursed through the murky area and snagged on Wolf, who stepped away from the fence, well out of Trinidad's reach.

"No! Wolf, come on, now!"

"Go." Wolf straightened his shoulders and spread his arms, readying for arrest.

Or bullets.

"Wolf, no! Get up here!"

Castile yanked Trinidad down as he tried to scramble back over the fence toward his brother. They tumbled in a heap of hard armored bodies and limbs. His knee jammed with a blinding burst of pain. Castile pulled him to his feet, dragging him into the no-man's-land between the wall and the dim buildings of Martin Acres beyond. Trinidad could hear the struggle on the other side of the fence, marshals shouting, the girl screaming. He looked back. Lights flashed through the fence slats, silhouetting a mad scramble of bodies. Ahead, the last of the sunlight slipped behind the mountains.

He spat out, "Wolf, he's—"

Castile hissed for silence, a sound so fierce Trinidad obeyed without thought. Bullets scuffed the dirt at their heels. They kept running and let the shadows swallow them.

# THIRTY-NINE

They drugged Wolf and laid him on a cot, his wrist bound to Marius' so he couldn't escape while he roved. It didn't take the bishop long to fall asleep, despite being tied by lengths of rope to Wolf and two more archwardens. Exhaustion was an ever-present shadow on the cusp of her crusade.

After succumbing to the sedative, Wolf had first roved to his own room in the barracks. He spent what seemed hours there, ignoring Marius. She was willing to wait. He was hers now, whether he realized it or not. But by the time he roved to the sanctuary, looking for Trinidad, her patience gave way. He quickly realized he could rove nowhere without Marius in tow. So he refused to move from the church, staring past her. Candlelight gleamed off his scarred cheek and neck, the slick burn looking crimson and alien against his unmarred skin.

And yet Marius reflected, the boy had a certain appeal. The unburned side showed promising signs of adult handsomeness. But it went deeper than looks. He had a quiet charisma. Familiar, and highly annoying.

"Why are you following me?" he said, casting a glance at the shadows dancing against the corners of his dreamscape, where her archwardens waited. His good eyelid twitched.

"To make certain you don't do anything else wrong."

"I-I haven't." He paused, blinking in confusion.

"You went to the jail and freed Trinidad and the Wiccan," she said.

His brow furrowed. "You mean Castile?"

"Castile," she agreed. "You freed them. I have a witness who saw you with them."

"I did?" he said. "I don't remember."

She drifted closer. "You don't remember a lot of things. Convenient, that."

He opened his mouth but closed it.

"But there is something," she said. "You remember how to rove."

His arm, bound to hers, involuntarily twitched. "I thought I was dreaming. I didn't know this . . . rove."

"Don't you want to help your brother?" she asked.

His gaze flicked to her face. "You put him in jail."

"To keep him safe," she said, and knelt by him. "I'm trying to protect our people, as Trinidad does."

"Trin protects all the people. Not just Christians."

That made her stumble, but she recovered quickly. "Yes. And that's why I want him back. We need more men like him with us, to show us the way. He's very godly, our Trinidad."

Wolf blinked, considered.

"Will you take me to him?" she asked.

"I tried . . . I can't find him."

"He's not asleep yet," she said. "But he must be tired. He'll rest soon. Where will they go?"

"They won't want me to say," Wolf said, straightening his back. He knew, then, more than he was letting on. A clear signal to find out what the boy was made of.

"Do you know what happens," she said, drawing the sword at her side and turning it between them so the candlelight flickered along its edge. "When we kill in dreams?"

Wolf nodded, dark eyes fixed on the blade.

"But it doesn't have to be that way," she said. "You saw Trinidad's scars, didn't you? The silver. It heals. It's holy, a gift from God. We need the sand to help our people. Trinidad and Castile know the way there. They claim you do, too."

He opened his mouth to protest, shook his head. "I don't."

She laid the flat of her blade on his shoulder. "Then perhaps you're not as much use to me as I thought."

He tried to lean away. She let her blade nick the side of his neck.

He swallowed hard. She pressed it deeper, watched blood well over the razor edge. He blinked hard. "Don't. Please."

She sighed and slowly slipped the sword an inch, making the slice in his skin longer. He cringed away; the blade followed.

"I have no time or patience left for those who do not serve God. I know what you did. I know about the bombs—"

"That wasn't my fault. That was . . ." he faltered.

"It was what?"

He shook his head. "I don't know. I don't know what happened. Trin . . ." he stopped, looked up at her. His throat moved against her blade as he swallowed.

"Trinidad put a gun to your head."

A sorrowful nod. "He said he was taking me hostage and that he might have to kill me."

"Hmm. That doesn't much sound like a man protecting his brother."

"He was! He …" His voice was barely audible. "He said he was."

Marius wondered what he was thinking, what he was remembering. But she really only needed the answer to one question. "Where is Trinidad?"

Wolf lowered his chin. He held himself stiffly, trembling against the blade. "The cave. Castile's coven. But I don't know where it is."

She pulled the blade away as a reward. "You can find it."

He pressed his fingers to his cut. They came away smeared with a good deal of blood. "I can't."

"You can. You've been there. You just don't remember since it was from your former life."

"I don't know what you mean—"

"You had another life. You even have another name. I know you don't remember. Would you like to know what it is?"

He blinked rapidly.

"Israel." She whispered it, softly, as Javelot had instructed her to do. Toying with a trance subject's keyword was dangerous.

For a moment he looked blank, erased, as if a trance was taking hold. But his lips parted and he shook his head. "You're lying."

"Those burns are from your parents' explosion," she said. "Trinidad's parents as well. You're truly brothers, not just adopted."

He placed a hand on his scarred cheek, still shaking his head.

"I can fix that for you. I'll take you to Denver Parish. We'll bring in the best doctor we can find, see that you're healed, that new skin is grown to replace the damaged," she said. "But first, we have somewhere to go, don't we?"

"Kill me," he whispered. His lips quivered, but he stared her in the eyes. "I won't ever take you to Trinidad. So kill me."

She smiled and pulled the sword back. Flicking the blade

toward him drew a violent flinch. Her smile broadened. "A noble plea, but I doubt you're willing to die so soon. And I do need you. We need each other, as it turns out. I can't kill you."

She gestured behind herself with the sword and Wolf stared past her at the slave girl. She huddled between the archwardens, head down, sniveling.

"I can, however, kill her," Marius said.

"No!" Wolf lunged for her, but Marius yanked the rope, throwing him off balance. He fell to his knees. "She didn't do anything!"

An archwarden drew his sword blade, awaiting instructions.

Wolf clung to their rope and stared up at Marius. "You won't hurt her?"

"As long as you do as I ask."

He swallowed hard and the shadows morphed into craggy walls. Sleeping sounds, a cough, sounding small in the cavern. Her vision adjusted and she saw the Wiccan graffiti on the walls of the cave, sigils and drawings, pentacles, quartered circles, and rough-drawn Celtic knots. The archwardens drew their blades. She looked around with interest. Whose head were they in?

"Find Trinidad and Castile. Kill anyone who gets in your way," she said.

"No!" Wolf pulled back. He fumbled at the knot, trying to free himself.

The archwarden who stayed at her side yanked viciously back on the rope, jerking Wolf to his knees.

"Don't kill them," Wolf said, tears rolling down his scarred cheek.

"You rove well. Good instincts. Come along now."

She turned and walked through the cave, forcing him to

stumble to his feet. He walked along behind her at the end of the rope, crying softly. In the unknown mind he'd roved into, the cave was quiet and sleeping. Curious. She'd only ever been in the Barren before, though Hawk had explained dreamscapes to her.

The archwardens met her amid several rough buildings that leaned against craggy cavern walls. They dragged a young male Wiccan between them. He was around twenty, his bare chest marked with pagan signs and scars. By his broad shoulders and the way he fought them, he was a warrior. His sandy hair hung in his eyes, and he snarled Wiccan curses at them, invoking his gods, twisting in their grip. They forced him to his knees before her.

"We could only find the dreamer," one of the archwardens said. "He claims he hasn't seen the Wiccan or Trinidad."

She shrugged. "Then the crusade starts here, now."

"NO!" Wolf shouted, but it was too late. The archwarden stabbed his sword into the Wiccan's back, found his heart, and wrenched it back out. The wound spurted blood. The Wiccan gasped and fell forward, dead before his face hit the ground. The world dimmed, all the details faded, until they were back in Wolf's mind again, in his room.

"You ... you ... God will condemn you for what you have done," Wolf said, his voice shaking.

Marius reached out and smoothed back his hair. "God has already forsaken me. Now. Take me to the next dreamer."

"No. You're going to kill them. I won't dream for you again. You can't make me." He pulled back, but she jerked the rope. Wolf's nostrils flared and he stared her in the eye, even as he sank to his knees.

She looked down at him. "You're willing to let her die for these heathens, Israel? You stayed behind to protect that girl, and now you're going to let her die? An innocent Christian girl?"

Tears gleamed on the boy's scars as he closed his eyes and carried them to the next dreamscape.

# FORTY

Martin Acres lay quiet. Too quiet. Barely a flicker of light from the cracks in boarded windows. No one walked the streets. Trinidad didn't look east as he limped along next to Castile. He didn't want to see the glow of the crusaders' campfires east of the old neighborhood.

"He'll be all right, Trin," he said. "They'll probably consider him our victim."

"No. They'll make him rove. I told Marius he can. It's my fault. I didn't think it through."

"It was a good ploy. It got us free at the church, didn't it?" Castile held out his arm to halt him in the shadows before they attempted the open space that lay ahead. Moonlight glinted off the snow, making eerie shadows of stumps and rocks.

Trinidad caught Castile's arm, trying to capture his attention. "Don't you see? She'll make him find us, maybe make him take her to the Barren."

Castile nodded and pointed at a shed. "I know, Trin. But look. Horses."

He broke into the shed and bridled the horses with barely a jingle. They looked at the humans with curiosity and snuffled low. He handed the Appaloosa's reins to Trinidad. "Sorry. They didn't have a white one."

"Cas—"

"I know, I know. We'll get Wolf back. But it can't happen tonight and they'll still come after us in the flesh."

Castile was right. Trinidad nodded reluctantly and threw himself onto the back of the horse. He urged the animal into a lope. It seemed sound enough but he had no idea how long the animals could last. Castile led them due south, but Trinidad knew they'd have to cut across Old 93 at some point to get to the canyon that led to his coven's cave. Trinidad guarded their rear, gripping the slaver's Savage. It flaked dried blood. To the south lay the graveyard of the windfarm, old propellers thrusting giant ghostly spades against the dark skies. Finally, they slowed the panting horses to a walk.

"They're not coming. They have Wolf," Trinidad said. "They don't need us anymore."

Castile didn't look back at him but he slowed, too. "We'd better cross now before we get any closer to Golden. Keep uphill."

After long, cold hours they emerged from the cover of a rock outcropping near Dragonspine, walked south along the road, and then turned westward into Clear Creek Canyon. High rocky cliffs rose up on either side of them, centered on a river frothy with snow along its banks. A bit of water ran between the ice-laced boulders. Cold wind swept down the gorge, whistling between rocks and rustling dead grasses like an animal on the scent of prey. Castile led them to the south, through the river shallows, the horses balking at the ice and then breaking through it as their riders forced them on. They walked deep down the natural trail toward the cave. All was quiet. Still, he drew his sword and halted his horse almost without realizing it. He scented the air, letting instincts take hold. Something else besides ash. A faint, foul sweetness.

Blood.

He opened his mouth to warn Castile, but he'd already jumped to the ground. Trinidad urged his horse closer, squinting in the darkness. Castile ran ahead and knelt by someone huddled inside the opening of the cave.

"Spring," Castile said, his voice choked. "He's dead."

Trinidad dropped to the ground and strode over to study the prone figure. The witch sprawled just outside the narrow cave opening, his face slack. Blood trickled between his lips and leaked from under his unscathed armor, blooming against the dirt floor of the canyon.

"It happened fast," Trinidad whispered. But how? The man's armor was whole.

He tipped his head back and scanned the high stone walls, dark but for tiny sparks where starlight filtered through the shifting smog and clouds. He listened hard, heard nothing but Castile's muttered prayers. If this was a broad assault, the attackers were already inside.

He gripped the Savage under one arm, his finger holding the white scope-light on, as they stepped inside. It flashed like lightning across the mica embedded in the craggy stone walls of the grotto. Castile's breath brushed the back of his neck. Their feet scuffed the floor.

The grotto was empty but for the Wiccan altar, dark and cold.

Trinidad stopped and listened. He exchanged glances with Castile, who shook his head.

"I don't know," he said. "There should be more guards."

They passed from the grotto into the narrow inner corridor, moving with near silence over the stony path, and almost tripped over another body. Castile barely paused but bolted ahead into the next cave, Trinidad a step behind.

"My lady?" Castile swung the curtain to Aspen's house aside. He took a step forward and stopped.

Something made a tiny mew, like a kitten.

For a moment, Trinidad couldn't make sense of what he saw. Two low lumps indicated sleepers on low pallets. Aspen curled around her child, crying, pleading in wordless noises. The other pallet was covered in splotchy black shadows. Blood rode the air, thick and sweet, and Trinidad realized the awful truth in those shadows.

Castile stumbled forward with a hiss and knelt. Trinidad followed, shone his light close.

"Aspen!" Castile said, sharp. She twitched violently. The baby's tiny eyelids moved and blinked. Mewling turned to a full-on, yelping cry.

Aspen clutched her child, still laying on her side. "They're killing us," she whispered.

"It's a dream. It's all a dream." Castile knelt low, his arms around her.

She pushed herself up and spoke over the crying baby. "We're under attack."

Trinidad knelt by the other sleeper. Only she wasn't sleeping. Not anymore.

"Castile," Trinidad said, lifting the bloody covers to show him. Castile turned and stared.

The Wiccan woman's head hung from her body at an odd, wrong angle. Her face froze in a grimace, eyes staring forward like she'd just woken from a horrible nightmare. A bloody grin crossed her throat, deep enough to have easily severed her windpipe. A warrior, Trinidad registered. She had a knife nearby but hadn't woken in time to use it . . . but what use would it have been against a sword anyway. An ugly chill climbed his spine, as if there were eyes on him.

A sword. She was still covered but the sword blade hadn't sliced the blankets. No killer, no archwarden, would stop to cover someone they'd just murdered in their sleep. And they had, indeed, just murdered this witch in her sleep.

"Wake them all," Trinidad said, his voice hard, quick. "Cas, move. We have to wake them."

Aspen stared at them both, clutching her crying infant.

Trinidad gripped Castile's arm and hauled him to his feet. "They're in their dreamscapes, killing them. Move."

Castile tore away from him and out into the cave, launching into high-pitched coyote war cries. The cave stirred, made noises, some of which erupted into screams. Trinidad followed, gripping his sword futilely. An older woman dragged a warrior out by his limp arms, bloodied with a wound amid the protective sigils inked over his ribs. Torches flared all around as the coven woke to their nightmare.

Trinidad muttered a prayer through his clenched teeth. Someone touched his back. He spun, his hand on his blade, but it was only Aspen. She stood with a blanket over her shoulders, cradling her baby, who had stopped crying. "They need me, not you," she said, and held out the infant. "Put away your weapons and take her."

His hands did her bidding without consulting his mind. He stripped his gauntlets off and took the child. She nestled against his armored chest, soft and wrong in his arms. He patted her curved back, feeling brutish. Aspen strode away, calling out to her people. He followed slowly and found Castile kneeling with his arm over the curved back of a crying gray-bearded man, warriors arrayed around them like the petals of a gruesome flower. Everywhere cries were echoing thick against the walls.

The baby stirred in Trinidad's arms and he realized the racket of keening would upset her. He couldn't take her to Aspen's house where the bloody warrior lay. Instead he walked deeper into the cave, staring forward, his arms locked around the coven's newest member. On the way he grabbed a torch, remembering how dark Castile's cave was.

Once there, he lay the baby on the pallet and pulled the rumpled covers up around her. She protested at the insult of the cold bed.

He hushed her, softly. She squawked louder.

"I don't even know your name," he said helplessly. "I'm sorry."

Talking to her didn't work, either. It was cold, so he turned to setting a fire. Castile kept a neat stack of starters and kindling nearby, and it caught quickly. He picked the baby up and moved closer to the hearth, holding her so she could see the flames. "See?" he said. "You'll be warm in a little while."

She settled against him, snuffling and insulted, staring at the play of flames against the blackened firewell.

"They warned me that calling on you would only bring us harm. I never should have brought you here."

Trinidad turned. Castile stood in the doorway, feet apart, his face graven with shock.

Trinidad rose and laid the baby down again. "I'm sorry, Castile."

"Goddess curse you, sorry means nothing. You're one of them."

Trinidad had to pause to catch his breath. The accusation—or maybe it was the truth of it—gutted him. The baby started crying again.

"Not anymore, Cas." Trinidad moved toward Castile, toward the cloth-draped doorway of the cave, away from the crying baby. "You're making her cry."

"Fuck you! We could have killed the bishop. You refused because of your stupid fucking vows to your false god!"

Trinidad's muscles tensed, his well-honed instinct warning of attack. Castile still got a shot in before Trinidad could throw up his arms to defend himself, a hard knock to his temple that made everything go pitch black for a moment. Momentum crashed them to the rocky ground in a tangle of limbs and bruising armor. Gravel and dirt ground into the back of Trinidad's head as the witch did his best to knock his teeth loose. Every blow sent sparks ricocheting through his skull.

Trinidad managed to block two strikes in a row and heave himself on top of Castile. He straddled the witch and pinned his flailing arms to the ground with his knees. Castile snarled beneath him like a writhing cat. The baby wailed from the bed.

"Stop it," Trinidad said, spitting blood to one side and leaning his weight on the smaller man until he gasped for air. "This solves nothing. Damn it, Castile. Stop."

Castile fell limp abruptly, chest straining, making strangled gasps, his face slick and shining with tears.

Trinidad put his face down close to Castile's. "I'll swear to anything you want, by all the saints and Holy God, by my vows, my life. Don't you see? They made Wolf rove—" his voice broke.

Neither of them moved for a long moment. Trinidad didn't breathe. The baby's crying punctuated the silence between them.

Castile stared past Trinidad with oily eyes, black with pain. "Get off me."

Trinidad rolled off Castile, sitting on the hard ground for a moment to get his bearings. His head hurt again. The cave walls seemed to be closing in. The baby wailed some more. He squeezed his eyes shut, gathered the shreds of his balance. *My God, Wolf, what did they make you do?*

Castile crawled to the baby and cradled her in his arms. He sat with his knees up, staring at the fire. He didn't move until she stopped crying. Anguish washed all the liveliness from his features. Trinidad crawled closer to the fire and held his hands out to warm them. The light flickered on Castile's silvered wrists and over his silvered nailbeds. This close, he noticed Castile was trembling.

He moved slowly, like he would with a skittish animal, and pulled the blanket up around Castile's shoulders. "How many?" he asked softly.

"Twelve."

Trinidad bowed his head. He couldn't drag a prayer into his mind. He crossed himself instead.

Castile wouldn't look at him. "I need to know you're with me."

He had nowhere else to go, no one else. "I am."

"And I need to know you'll carve your name in the body of whoever did this. For real this time."

The air went out of Trinidad. He gave a stiff nod and thumbed another cross on his forehead. "Right next to yours."

C astile slept soon after. Trinidad was exhausted but sleeping made him wary. He doubted the bishop would come after them until daylight. He pressed a knife into Castile's limp hand, watched him for a moment, and then took the baby back to Aspen. She asked him to help remove the bodies.

He carried them out one by one, recognizing some of their slack faces with detachment, and walked each up the main canyon toward two witches building a pyre. No one spoke, though they gave him curious glances.

When he got back to the cavern, he found Aspen preparing the altar to honor the dead. She adjusted a candle and turned to him. "They died together; they will be honored together. It's the best I can do."

"Father Troy said our best is all that is expected of us." He bowed his head to her. "You will honor them and I will pray for them.

She studied him a moment. "Did the priest die when you took him back?"

He glanced away. His lips twitched. "He was going to die anyway. Cancer."

"Castile brought him here, caused him injury," she said.

Trinidad thought of the witch huddling in the silver sand, escaping his torture in the Barren for a few, futile moments. "Castile has atoned. Don't ask any more of him, my lady."

Her eyes narrowed. "I would not have his deeds reap evil against us."

"The bishop took him captive, they hurt him—" His voice caught. He cleared his throat. "The wrongs are balanced." *It won't happen again*, he thought. *I won't let it.*

Except, it could be happening to Wolf in this moment.

She studied him for long moments. He held perfectly still, face and neck hot under the attention. At last she nodded. "You may stay for the ceremony if you wish. But you must clean yourself first."

"I remember." He turned away, knowing he'd never feel clean again.

# FORTY-ONE

C astile roved. He knew he shouldn't but he couldn't help it. At last he found the bishop. Her dreamscape was austere. A room with no windows, four gray walls. Castile realized he had a knife in his hand. He rushed for her but before he could reach her, he tumbled out . . . into Wolf's dreamscape. The boy was in Roi d'Esprit's room again, his back to Castile. He stared out a dark window, holding himself stiffly.

"Wolf," Castile said. "It's all right. It's not your fault."

"I didn't know what else to do. They killed Wiccans. They were going to kill the slave girl right in front of me." He paused. "I don't even know her name."

"We'll get you out, yeah? Trinidad won't rest until you're free."

"No. Tell him not to come for me. It's too late."

"Wolf—"

"That's not my name."

"I know. Trinidad told me about the chemwiping. About the amnesia. But you remember this place, yeah? So maybe you remember something else."

"I do remember." He turned. The scars were gone; his face clear, skin a flushed tan, expression as hard as Castile had seen on Trinidad a thousand times. "I am Israel."

Wolf's roving. The dreamscape. The scars. The bomb. Roi d'Esprit and Reine. Shattered pieces fell into place. "I'll tell Trin. He'll get you out."

"Don't tell him. Please. He can't come here. Don't tell him."

"I have to! Israel—" The dreamscape swept out from under Castile. He woke sitting up, clutching a knife in one shaking hand, his blanket in the other. He smelled of blood, of sweat, of fear.

"Goddess curse you, Reine. Fucking Indigos. Curse you." She knew; she had to have known. He thrust to his feet and paced, letting his mind fall in with the motion.

Not telling Trinidad . . . it was the smartest thing. Trinidad would go back inparish, he would find Wolf . . . Israel . . . and with him, Bishop Marius. Trin wouldn't survive that, and Castile . . . he bowed his head, succumbing to his stinging eyes and shuddering middle.

But only for a moment. "Gods. Just admit it, at least to yourself," he muttered, swiping his arm angrily across his eyes. He couldn't make himself hurt Trinidad like that, and he couldn't bear to lose him again.

C astile went through the motions of worship woodenly, though the Circle drew the Powers, and with Them, he gained some respite from his roiling emotions. Aspen allowed Trinidad to stay in the grotto. He watched from the shadows. Castile mostly avoided him, but his gaze snagged on him a few times without his meaning to. He felt the others' eyes on his naked back, on his scar. He said nothing of it. To him, the scar had become just another sigil of war.

Afterward, he resolved to shove this business with Israel aside and left Trinidad to himself. He didn't want to talk to him just now. Israel was who he was; telling Trinidad now would only hurt him.

People moved about, speaking in low tones and cleaning bloodstains from the stone floor, grimly getting on with the business of life. No one spoke to him as he strode through the cavern. Maybe they guessed what he was going to do. Maybe they didn't want to know.

After taking refuge in his own home again, he painted the customary protective sigils on the armor Trinidad had given him, horns over a pentacle across his breast plate, the Eye and a Cup on the backplate, triskeles on the forearm bracers. Then he re-dressed and slung his cloak over his shoulders. Before snuffing the torch, he looked around his home.

It might be sealed up as a tomb for all the chance he had of coming back here.

He found Trinidad in the gathering area of the main cavern, sharpening his sword. It hissed against the strap and gleamed in the firelight. His armor was also scrubbed clean; someone else had done it because they had painted horns atop a cross over his heart. Aspen sat nearby nursing her daughter and crooning an old lullaby. Others were busy readying weapons for war.

Castile wondered what Trinidad was thinking. Was he worrying over Wolf . . . Israel? The truth rose like bile. He swallowed and tried to sound normal, easy.

"You look better," he said to Trinidad. "Cleaner."

"Lady Aspen told me to wash," Trinidad said, gesturing toward the priestess. He sounded a little plaintive.

Castile nodded. He knelt on one knee before Aspen and drew

in the thick, sweet scent of mother's milk, wondering if it could erase the reek of his coven's spilled blood.

"I danced with my parents as a child in dense woods," Aspen said, watching her baby feed. "A young man played Herne and he frightened me, but my papa just laughed and told me it was our friend Will, taken with the Lord's spirit that day. I was looking forward to someday seeing you dance among the trees instead of in this cave."

"Maybe someday you can find trees again," Castile said. "Maybe you should take the coven and look now."

"Not yet." Aspen looked up at Castile as if noticing his armor and cloak for the first time. "You're leaving."

"I'm going to the Indigos," he said. "I need to warn them about the bishop roving." That wasn't the half of it, but he didn't need to burden Aspen further.

Trinidad stopped sharpening his sword and ran it across the leg of his boot, cleaning dust from the blade. He slipped it into the sheath, caught up his cloak in one hand, and walked closer.

Aspen tucked a stray lock of hair behind her ear and cleared her throat. "Hawk made a mistake, one that cost him his life, and those of his coven."

Castile released a slow breath. "My lady, I—"

"Let her speak," Trinidad said.

Castile fell silent.

"He wouldn't tell me where he roved when he slept, and I didn't press him. I think I didn't want to know. But after you went inparish, after the baby came, Hawk told me how the bishop nearly killed you in the Barren. How the sand healed you and you gave her that cut on her forehead." She glanced up at Trinidad. "And how you killed Paul."

The corner of Trinidad's mouth twitched. "Paul was a traitor to the Church and our order."

"Hawk said Paul was a good man," Aspen said.

"Like Hawk would know."

Aspen's voice sharpened. "Hawk thought if he could bring the factions together, show them magic and the Powers, he could make peace. He didn't understand the bishop and the lengths she would take to protect Christianity."

"No. He didn't understand at all." Trinidad's gaze rested on Castile instead of Aspen.

Castile clenched his jaw. Oh, I understand, though. I understand plenty, archwarden.

"Hawk also said Reine and Paul were in love. Paul must have thought he could keep Reine safe by bringing her into the savvy with the bishop. Paul trusted Marius."

"He knew her best," Trinidad said thoughtfully, and fell quiet.

No one said anything for a long moment. Castile reflected how any silence with Trinidad in it was hard, unyielding. "There was never going to be peace between us. Why would Hawk take her to the Barren, my lady? It doesn't make sense."

"Because you go to the Barren using magic, Hawk thought—" She glanced at Trinidad.

"He thought Christianity is false," he said. "He thought roving and the Barren proved it."

Aspen nodded. "I'm afraid so. Hawk meant well, but power is still power by any other name."

"Hawk was no worse than the bishop in that," Trinidad said.

Castile shook his head and sighed loudly but they ignored him.

Aspen lifted her chin. "He made mistakes, but in good faith. I wonder if that isn't Bishop Marius' way as well."

Castile had to physically bite his lip against retorting. Aspen lowered her head, as if she couldn't stand to see the truth in his face, and he was glad he didn't speak, glad she didn't know first-hand the violence that had killed her husband. She looked worn, exhausted, like she'd aged years. Hawk's mop of black curls, flat-tened by sleep sweat, capped her infant's head. Castile realized he didn't even know her name, that there'd been no chance to wel-come her properly. He felt a pang. Aspen was sad because Castile only knew worship within the grotto. What if her daughter only knew a world of war?

Trinidad turned and paced a few steps away. "If the Indigo queen trusted Paul, if they were together . . ." He turned to look at them. "There are rumors about the bishop and her archwardens. Paul, especially, was her favorite. Some say he shared her bed as well."

The torchlight revealed his reddened cheeks. Castile concealed his amusement at the archwarden's embarrassment. "You're saying a love triangle caused the crusade?"

But Aspen shook her head. "No, but maybe it's enough to destroy the savvy between Reine and the bishop."

"Right," Castile said. "I'll find out if the alliance between Reine and Marius is dead."

"Yes," Aspen replied. "If there's no hope for peace, then we will run, as you say. But just in case, if only to honor Hawk's efforts, I want friendship between their tribe and our coven, as near as you can get it."

Castile shook his head. "My lady, we can't. She's not trustworthy. She wants to kill Trin—"

"Trinidad is welcome to stay here."

"No," Trinidad said. "I go where Castile goes."

# FORTY-TWO

The rising sun cast the tribal tent city into long shadows and pierced Trinidad's eyes as they rode east toward it. He squinted and pulled his hood up. Indigo warriors had gathered to bow to the east. He could hardly blame them. No wonder they had gone back to worshipping the sun, fire, and their ancestors when Christians were so fickle and Wiccans so few and private. Fire and sunlight were precious commodities in hard times, and it was difficult to think of death as the end when it lingered around every corner.

Scouts patrolled in the distance, small groups stopping to watch them without approaching.

"Why haven't they challenged us?" Trinidad asked.

"They're outcounty tribes. This isn't their land so they're leaving us to the locals to deal with." The cold wind threatened snow, pulling strands of Castile's hair from the strap he'd tied around his head. "The Indigo envoy. Let me take the lead on this."

Two Indigos carried banners on their spears, riding ahead of six warriors centered on Reine, all mounted on horses in no better shape than the tired, hungry animals Castile and Trinidad rode. Everyone slowed their horses and Castile raised his hand.

"Peace to you," he said. "I come to savvy."

Reine d'Esprit stared at him. Dirty blond dreadlocks, woven through with bits of wire and chains that glinted in the sun, haloed her head. She wore her scarf high, covering her face to just below her eyes. It hung over a painted metal breastplate, hammered by a decent smithy. It seemed surreal to Trinidad that she was the one who had cut him, tortured him. She looked the same, but something about her felt different. Gone was the hatred, replaced with exhaustion. That was it. She looked as if she hadn't slept since she'd hurt Trinidad. He knew how she felt.

Every spearguard in the small company aimed their weapons at Castile and Trinidad. The poles were salvaged pipe, well-balanced with heads of forged steel sharp enough to slice leather. Indigos killed elk and deer with those spears. Trinidad had seen what they could do if thrown by someone who knew what he was doing: run a body through, cracking armor and ripping flesh. They could certainly kill an armored man within fifteen paces.

Reine narrowed her eyes, but she said, "You say words to hold my spears."

Castile laid his hand on his chest and bowed his head. "I come with information, in good faith."

"And you want what for it?"

"The same from you, and maybe a real savvy this time."

"Who's that?" Reine gestured toward Trinidad with her spear.

Trinidad pressed his lips together and drew back his hood. The Indigos grunted and he involuntarily stiffened, glad for his armor.

"You bring this man who kills my kin to my freehold?" Reine said. The skin creased around her pursed lips and narrowed eyes.

"I go where Castile goes," Trinidad said.

Reine looked at Castile, brows raised. "You got this archwarden on heel?"

Castile nodded. "Consider us blood. Kin."

Reine studied them again as the wind whipped its promised shards of ice in their faces. "Who sent you? Your lord is dead."

*Steady*, Trinidad thought as Castile shifted on his horse and a few spears twitched in response.

"My lady sends me," Castile said.

"And you, archwarden? You gonna speak for the parish?"

Trinidad urged his horse a step closer, so that he stood next to Castile, their legs almost touching. "I speak for no one."

"Still got the marks. You still one of them."

"I bear the marks of Christ and my order," Trinidad admitted.

"And a pentacle."

Trinidad just looked at her. It would take more than that to rattle him. He was cold and exhausted and in no mood to die on the end of one of those spears.

"I think his debt to you is paid, yeah?" Castile said.

Reine held for a long moment before giving them a curt nod.

"You won't like what we have to say," Castile said. "But we're here to help."

She raked them with her hard stare again and turned her horse, indicating with an offhand wave for them to join her. Her spearguards encircled them.

The path through the gates was rutted with recent tire tracks and hoof prints. Their horses slipped slightly in the iced mud. People and tents packed every inch inside the freehold walls. She led them to a graveled paddock filled with warhorses with different brands on their flanks. After they dismounted, a couple of wide-eyed Indigo teenagers took their horses away, staring daggers at Trinidad.

Reine whistled, low. Abruptly, the guards turned on them, grabbing Castile. Trinidad caught the motion out of the corner of his eye. Adrenaline scouring his veins, he drew his sword and swung a wide arc, making the Indigos leap back.

The Indigo guard holding Castile tightened his arm around his throat. Castile clawed at the brawny arm, but it didn't make a difference. The Indigo gave Trinidad a savage grin. "Do it. I'll choke the backsass right out of him."

"Castile is my blood," Trinidad said. "Spill his and I spill yours."

"Enough," Reine said. "Put them in the cell 'til we sort this."

They dragged Castile down to the trampled mud and searched him for weapons. He writhed and fought in their grip, cursing, and Trinidad had a sudden image of what it what it must have been for him to have been violated in prison and then in jail. Fury erupted inside him. Two spearguards blocked his way when he lifted his sword into high guard. They drew their spears back.

"Put it down," Reine said to him.

"We came here to help you," Trinidad said. "Not to fight."

"Archwardens only know how to fight," Reine said. "And that Wiccan's been nothin but trouble."

"If Trinidad wanted to fight you, you'd already be dead," Castile said, sounding strained under the weight of the Indigo on his chest.

Trinidad shifted his sword toward a spearguard edging toward him. "Let him up."

"We're here to help!" Castile yelped as someone kicked him. It couldn't have hurt too badly with his armor but Trinidad stiffened from his jaw to his toes, rubbed raw from the dead slaver's boots.

"Got me enough help from Wiccans and Christians at the moment," Reine said. "Put that sword down before we stick him."

"You can't harm him," Trinidad said. "He's here to savvy. He said the words."

"I'm figurin out why you're here before takin what you say as dead true. Even savvy talk. Fuckin put it down."

Trinidad held for another couple of seconds, considering options and coming up empty. Jaw clenched, he laid the sword down. Spearguards instantly surrounded him, though they didn't throw him to the ground as they had Castile. Their fingers found all his weapons, the knives hidden in his bracers and his boot, his pistol and the Savage slung over his shoulder. One of the Indigos held up the Savage. "Blood on this, queen."

"Slaver blood," Castile muttered as they hauled him to his feet. "Friends of yours, yeah?" One of the Indigos backhanded him across the face, nearly knocking him down again. Trinidad struggled against the hands gripping him, but they held him firm.

"Into the cell," Reine said.

Under the eyes of curious Indigos, spearguards marched Trinidad and Castile to a low reclaimed cinderblock building with shuttered windows. They shoved them in and Castile tripped to his knees on the rough dirt floor. He shrugged off Trinidad's offer of help as the door slammed shut behind them.

"How quaint," the witch said, frost lacing his breath as he glanced around. "It's the old West all over again."

Two windows with ill-fitted metal shutters bolted over them. A patched metal door hinged on the outside, last century by the looks of the rust, but secure enough to require tools to break through.

Trinidad sat against a wall, laid his forearms on his knees, and looked at Castile. "When the Bishop doesn't find any more witches awake, she'll come here next."

"I'm aware. At least it's morning. They're bound to all be up for a while yet." He shook his head. "This is your fault. You had to insist on coming with me, didn't you?"

"You're the one who made me promise to kill you if you got caught again," Trinidad said. "Well, you're caught. You want me to break your neck or strangle you?"

Castile rewarded him with a sour grin and slapped his hands against his thighs. "Cold in here."

"Come sit," Trinidad said, but Castile paced across the little building to press his eye against a crack in a shutter. Light knifed through the dusty gloom when he drew back.

"I don't see Reine," he said.

"She's going to sweat us for a while. It's what I'd do." Trinidad leaned his head back and closed his eyes. He thought of his sword in the hands of some Indigo, then pushed it from his mind. His face felt cold but his cloak and armor kept the rest of him at a bearable temperature. He couldn't deny the relief of getting off his feet. The ill-fitting slaver's boots were protection against further cuts, but not making those he already had feel any better. He started to feel the dragging that warned of sleep until Castile's voice broke through.

"You're fucking napping?"

Trinidad sighed. "She's going to let us cool it here for at least a couple of hours. Might as well get some rest."

"Maybe they're just planning on how to best kill us."

"Castile, relax. We gave her enough hints to make her curious."

"One of us should stay on guard," Castile said. "The bishop and her men could be roving. I can wake you if they attack."

"Suit yourself," Trinidad said, letting his eyes fall shut again.

T he sanctuary took shape around him, candles flickering crimson in their little red glass cups, dark beams quiet overhead. Trinidad knelt in the aisle and bent his forehead to his knee. No words of prayer came. He felt empty without Father Troy to guide him. He swiped at his stinging eyes and climbed the steps to the altar. But when he tried to touch it, his hand passed through.

Someone else's dreamscape.

"Wolfie?" he asked into the silence.

A shout answered, faint as if it passed through an ocean of water or sifted through sand. Alarm prickled Trinidad's back and he fled for the Barren.

In the little valley where he always first arrived, surrounded by silent tombs, Malachi, Seth, and Bishop Marius stood in a circle. Wolf stood a short distance away, as if to respect a private conversation. Trinidad couldn't quiet him in time.

"Trin!"

They all turned, hands reaching for hilts. Malachi drew first.

Trinidad leapt toward him. He ducked inside his guard and jammed his right palm upward. Malachi's nose gave way with a nauseating crack and blood spouted. He gave a strangled, wet cry.

With his left hand, Trinidad grasped Malachi's sword by the blade and wrenched it free of his grip. The honed steel bit deeply into his fingers, sliced them to the bone. He darted away as quickly as he'd attacked, switched grips to hold the sword up in an effective defensive position, and thrust his wounded hand deep into the sand. He grunted in pain as the silver cauterized his wound.

Malachi struggled up from his hands and knees, a hand to his bloody face.

Marius shrieked, "This is your chance! Kill him!"

Wolf started to move, to grab for a sword from Seth. The archwarden swung it easily away, smacking Wolf with the flat and knocking him to the sand. Seeing Wolf fall was almost Trinidad's undoing. Then Seth was on him. Barely ducking the attack and unable to fully regain his balance, he returned an awkward slash, one that would have only blocked Seth's blade with luck. But his sword found only empty air.

"Wolf?" he shouted, spinning. "Wolf!"

Not so much as an echo answered in the dead, empty world. He sank to his knees and let the blade of the sword sink into the sand between his thighs. It had all happened bewilderingly fast. Wolf had seen it start to go wrong for Trinidad and roved them away before they could do him harm.

Trinidad had no doubt Marius would make Wolf pay dearly for his disobedience.

He leaned his forehead against the cold steel hilt and whispered, "Wolf. What have you done?"

"Wake up, Trin."

He blinked as a draught of cold air swept his face. He flexed his empty hand and examined his fingers, slashed through with silver.

The sword had stayed behind in the Barren as he'd been dragged back.

Castile knelt on one knee next to him. Beyond, four hard-faced Indigo spearguards with notched brows and hairlines waited in the open doorway, faces covered to their cheekbones with blue scarves.

# FORTY-THREE

Reine noted how stiffly Trinidad moved as he entered her house, like he was hurt. When Castile sat at her invitation, Trinidad took up position behind the Wiccan, one hand hooked on his weaponless belt, the other hidden under his cloak. They both wore scoured armor, freshly painted with Wiccan sigils. They were clean down to their fingernails. Wiccans were always fussy about that anyway. Castile laid his hands on the table. She caught sight of silver fingernails before he curled them into fists.

"We start with truth," Reine said. "Tell us, Castile, about payin me to bring Trinidad to you."

Trinidad's soulless stare didn't flicker from her face. "This isn't about that," he said. "The crusade is begun."

She realized she'd never really heard him speak calmly before. His natural voice was soft and gentle. It didn't match the strong lines of his face or the harsh black cross tattooed on his rigid brow or the things he'd done.

"Look," Castile said, lifting a hand and straightening his fingers. "We know it all. We know you savvied with the bishop. We know about you and Paul—"

She stared at Castile's raised hand until he lowered it back to the table. "Fuckin Trinidad killed him."

"Good. We're not lying to each other anymore." Castile glanced up at his archwarden, forehead creased in a frown. Trinidad didn't talk, so he went on. "We had to blow out of the parish yesterday. Got to the cave last night to find the coven under attack."

Her brows dropped. "They found the cave? How?"

"No. Archwardens roved through their dreamscapes and killed a dozen witches," Trinidad said. "They would've killed more if we hadn't woken the rest of them."

Castile sat still as death, gray eyes glittering like the silver embedded in his fingernails. "You get what we're saying? They killed them from inside their heads. From inside their dreams."

Reine found her hands were gripping her thighs. She spread her fingers on the table in the universal savvy posture. "Who roved them? Not Lord Hawk."

"They got a new rover," Castile said, flinty. "You know the kid called Wolf? Apparently, he's a witch, too. Of course, he's forgotten he was. He was chemwiped at some point. But the ability to rove stuck."

Reine held her face perfectly still, riding dual waves of shock. Roving mojo should have been chemwiped from the kid along with everything else that had made him Israel. If he could rove into witches' heads and to the Barren, he had powerful magic, Israel did. Maybe that meant Trinidad did, too, if such ran in families. But she didn't like talking about Israel. Too many issues around him, starting with the chemwiping and ending with the bombs.

She swallowed to dampen her dry throat. "We'll sleep with spears—"

Castile barked a pained laugh. Trinidad moved and made her

spearguards shift their weapons to a battle-ready two-handed grip. But he just shifted closer to Castile.

"You think we don't sleep with weapons? They ghost right inside your heads," Castile said. "And, even if they don't manage to kill you right off, Indigos don't have magic. You can't rove away. You can't escape them or chase them down. How long can you ask your warriors to go without sleep? How will you keep all these people, your children—" he swept an arm "—awake? By sundown they'll start picking you off."

So, it had come to this. "We'll have to run, then."

"Roving knows no boundaries," Trinidad said.

Castile nodded. "Distance means nothing. They're not going to stop until they get to you. You've been to the Barren. That makes you a liability to Marius. Don't pretend to be stupid now that we're finally being honest with each other."

She thrust herself up from the table to pace. "What, then? You bring us a dray full of problems and no fix."

Trinidad edged back from Castile and turned to the window. He stared out at a couple of kids playing in the mud. Their giggles penetrated the silence. "There is a way. We take the battle to them."

Castile twisted around to look at the archwarden. "So we can all die sooner rather than later? Brilliant plan, Trin."

"Not all of us will fight. Just me." He turned. His cloak made a quiet swish around his boots. "I'll challenge Bishop Marius to single-handed combat."

Castile leapt to his feet so fast the bench tumbled back. "No."

Trinidad stepped forward and righted the bench without answering.

"She's old," Reine said. "You can take her."

"No. She can still fight. Even so, she'll choose a stand-in. Probably one of her archwardens."

Castile stepped up, pushed his face close to Trinidad's. "Even in the off-chance Marius agrees to it, you could still lose."

"I'm good. I have a shot. But in the end, I don't think it'll matter."

"Why are you so fucking determined to die?" Castile smacked his fist against Trinidad's armored chest. Trinidad didn't flinch.

"Nothing means more to archwardens than our vows. We fight to defend our Church, but we swore ourselves first to Christ. To peace. A challenge like this might be enough to make some archwardens remember their vows to Him. At least some of them might lay down the cross. If they do, parishioners will follow."

Castile shook his head. "You stupid, stupid fuck. This will never work."

Trinidad lowered his voice. "We can't fight that army and win. We have to destroy the crusade from the inside. It's a small chance, but it's the only one we have."

The two men stood as if there were no one else in the room: eyes locked, close without touching.

"It was never going to work anyway." Trinidad gripped Castile's shoulder. "You have a life. A home. I don't. I lost mine a long time ago."

Castile shrugged free of Trinidad's hand. He paced away, flexing his hands and drawing a deep breath before turning back to Trinidad.

"Wolf is Israel," he said.

# FORTY-FOUR

The only sound in the Indigo's house was the jingling of the chains in Reine's locks as she turned to look at Castile. Everything faded into the roar starting in Trinidad's head. His cheeks flushed hot. Israel is dead. He didn't even know if he spoke the words aloud, but Castile raised a hand as if he had.

"It's true," he said. "It was an Indigo store your folks blew up, yeah? Israel survived. Indigos found him, took him from the wreckage, brought him to the freehold. He was barely alive."

Reine flicked a hand and the spearguards filed from the room. She crossed to a shelf, uncorked a stoneware bottle, and drank. The harsh sting of alcohol filled the air. She offered Trinidad the bottle; he didn't take it.

"No," he said. "No one survived."

Castile spread his hands. "You survived it, Trin."

"They left me outside. But Israel—they took him in."

"He made it," Castile said. "The Indigos took him. Roi d'Esprit chemwiped him. Think it through. His burns, his amnesia." He glanced at Reine. "The bombs. Tell him, Reine."

Trinidad could only stare at Castile. He realized they were waiting for him to speak. He turned his head toward Reine. "Did you
chemwipe Wolf?"

Reine eyes flicked between them. Her lips twitched. "Papa Roi
did."

Trinidad spun and drove his fist into the wall. The house shuddered. Pain split through his knuckles, leapt up through his wrist.
He shook his head, shook all over. The Indigo queen and Castile
watched him warily, giving him wide berth.

"Inparish tribers found him," Reine said. "Would've given him
back, too, till we learned Wiccans did the bomb. They knew he was
a Wiccan kid. He had a pentacle pendant."

Trinidad had dropped his own under his family's marker,
burying the craft along with them all.

He'd forgotten to breathe. He sucked in sour, dirty air.

"He was burned bad." Reine touched her own cheek and let
her hand fall back to her side. "I tended him while Papa was havin
talks, findin stuff out. You were inparish by then, but Papa sorted
out who he was—Israel."

The world started a slow spin, the throbbing in Trinidad's fingers and wrist keeping time with his racing heart. Israel, his baby
brother, the son of murderers, left at the mercy of Indigos. My god,
Wolfie . . .

"Roi turned the kid into a sleeper," Castile said. When Reine
didn't speak right away, he growled, "Tell him."

She bit her lip, flicked her gaze from one to the other. "Revenge
mojo got to Papa. Fuckin always settlin scores, that one. Couple of
ours died that day in the bomb and Papa, he's gonna make someone pay. Trouble is, we had no idea where Cave Coven is. Then

Israel wakes up not knowin who he is. Half the job is done already, so Papa chems the kid. Teaches him to make bombs in a trance. By the time he's ready, Trinidad is gone Christian, and Papa thinks he can do one better than revenge. He can pull the trigger when we need it, head off a wicked big attack. Like a crusade." Reine seemed to come back to herself. Her voice sharpened. "Worked like gold, too. We sent him inparish and the Church took him in."

Of course. Father Troy. Always collecting strays. Trinidad's knees felt watery. He locked them to stay upright.

"We didn't know if we got the chemwipe to stick inside Israel until Javelot . . . she was the one. I went soft on the whole idea." Reine sounded ashamed. Trinidad couldn't tell if it was for using Israel or for going soft. "But she kicked my ass and she took Israel, made him do it."

Trinidad could barely get air behind the words. "Do what?"

"Blow up the jail. He was supposed to go to the church and blow that, too. Never made it. I don't know why."

Castile cleared his throat. "He didn't make it to the church because we stopped him."

Reine blinked at him, chapped eyelids over bloodshot eyes. "You knew all along?"

He glanced at Trinidad. "His nightmare we roved into? I recognized Roi d'Esprit. And he asked for you, remember? I thought it was strange, but you told me he was chemwiped. But still. He could remember. I thought I'd get something on you to hold over Reine in the savvy. So this morning I roved. I found Wolf and he told me."

"How did he find out?" Trinidad asked.

"I don't know." He shook his head. "Really, I don't."

Trinidad looked at Reine, at her hard, lined face, her

dreadlocked braids haphazard around her face, her fingers cut and bleeding. Her thumb pressed against the blade of her knife. She put it away under his stare.

"Did you tell him?" he asked.

She twitched her head no. "Javelot. My sister. She's missin. Maybe they caught her and made her tell."

Trinidad tightened. The bishop would use this against him, just like Castile was trying to do.

Castile flinched, but his next words came hard and angry. Defensive. Like he'd had reasons to lie, good reasons that trumped their friendship and loyalty. "I couldn't tell you. He asked me not to. And he was right. You would have gotten yourself killed, Trin, like you keep trying to do. But you have family now. Great Horns, Wolf—Israel is your brother. He needs you. You can't die on him now."

Trinidad just looked at him. Wolf had always been his brother.

"You see how trying to make up for what your folks did isn't working? You can't undo what they did any better than I—" He swallowed whatever he was going to say. "I know you're angry with me for not telling. I know I fucked it all between us. But Israel needs you."

Trinidad shook his head. What had any of this to do with his parents? He was just trying to live up to his vows. The bishop would use Wolf against him. The sooner he could fight, and maybe die, the less opportunity she'd have to do that.

"Let Trinidad decide," Reine said.

Castile laughed, caustic against the tension in the room. "That's fucking rich, after you carve him up and dump him for dead at my feet. Now you want him to fight for you?"

"You're the one askin for him in the first place," Reine said.

Trinidad couldn't think. It all was coming too fast, colliding and smashing like bullets into bodies. "Stop. Just—stop talking."

He turned away from them. His armor constricted his breath, his mouth tasted like iron, his skin slicked with cold sweat. Israel . . . Wolf. Wolfie. He closed his eyes, throat held in the vice grip of unshed grief.

And Castile had lied to him, betrayed him.

A stiff silence enshrouded them. He felt Castile's anxiety rippling through it.

"Get out," Trinidad whispered to Reine.

Reine tread across the floor softly, latched the door behind her with the barest of clicks.

"I'm sorry. I should have told you." Castile stepped closer, arms wrapped around his own body. Sometimes he seemed a strong, controlled man. Other times he was a cornered, frightened animal, like in the Barren when Trinidad realized they were raping him back at the jail. That desperation was back, tenfold. "I know you're angry. But you can't do this. Don't do this, Trin."

Trinidad's anger evaporated. The lies seemed like a small thing in the face of war. He could almost understand why Castile had done it, even why the Indigos had hurt his brother. But everything had been taken from him in his life, and he didn't know how to make Castile see that he only had one thing left to trust. "Christ died for me. The least I can do is return the favor. I know it means nothing to you, but it means everything to me."

"Christ was just a man, Trin."

"I am just a man."

Castile ran both hands through his hair, shoving it back from his face. "And Israel?"

The thought of losing his brother again stung deeply, but he forced himself to continue. "Wolf is a Christian. He wants to be an archwarden. He understands my vows. What kind of example would I be to him if I failed to act when I could?"

He couldn't tell Castile he didn't want to die, couldn't say that he'd only started to feel alive again, that if anyone could make him turn his back on his vows, and gladly, it was Castile. He couldn't explain, couldn't make his lips shape the words in time before Castile spun away to reach for the door latch.

"Do you know how dead your eyes get when you fight?" His voice shook. "Then you say something, you look at me, and you're back like you were never gone. I don't fucking know what I'm going to get from one second to the next with you. But I do know this. You're not leaving me again."

Castile slammed the door open and burst through it. A cold wind of dancing snow and silence swept in.

He watched Castile throw himself on his horse and gallop through the gates. No one stopped him. Reine turned her head toward Trinidad. She stood motionless a long time, staring at him.

Pain raked him. Violence welled up and he clenched his fists against it. Christ's peace. He'd sworn himself to it. But why can't You grant it to me?

"Eli Eli, lama sebachtani," he whispered.

God did not answer.

# FORTY-FIVE

C astile slowed his horse to a trot on the way out to the dirt road that crossed from the Indigo freehold to Highway 93. With every step he felt the distance between him and Trinidad stretch into true severance. He blamed his stinging eyes on the cold wind and tried to concentrate on the Indigo army as he rode past them. They were already gathering into tribal regiments, fifty warriors there, two hundred here. Smoke wisped away from fires. Banners caught in the cold breeze, moving like painted spirits overhead. There were more Indigos than he'd ever hoped for.

There wasn't anything like enough.

No one challenged him, and he was glad. A dull roar thudded through his skull. He felt dried up and worn out, like he'd ravaged himself with cheap drink. Yet he felt nervy, too, hands trembling, heart thudding. Trinidad was going to die soon, the fucking fool. A sword blade would carve the life from his body. He'd end up in the Barren, meaningless, dead, and there wasn't a damn thing Castile could do about it.

He found the road, kicked his horse to a gallop, and let his hood fall back. Faint snow stung his cheeks, the wind whipped up the turmoil and fury in his heart, and he rode hard and fast, away from Trinidad and his death.

A dull glow lit the distance, well upriver from the cave. Someone had lit pyres to send the warrior-witches to the Summerlands. Castile wished he could have worked the pyres. He should have stayed to care for their dead, for all the use he was to the living. Instead, he turned to the path toward their cave, treading through the creek. It bubbled through the ice and snow. His horse snorted and shook its head, prancing and slipping over icy rocks.

Once inside, he waited for Aspen to speak, shifting from foot to foot after making his report on what had happened at the Indigo freehold. She took the news of Trinidad's challenging the bishop to singlehand without comment as she scrubbed her guard's blood away from the stone floor with stringy rags. Her baby daughter slept near the fire.

He finally couldn't stand her silence anymore. "We have to run, my lady. We need to get out of the county as fast as possible. Deeper into the mountains."

Her scrubbing didn't miss a beat. "In winter? With the children?"

"I can put them in the dray. You can ride with the baby, I'll drive. The adults will have to come behind. We have a couple of horses for the old ones. I've heard there's a herding settlement at the old quarry. It's easily defensible but they could probably use more fighters."

"How did you hear that?"

Castile cleared his throat, glanced away. "In prison."

"I'm to take the coven through mountain passes in the dead of winter on the word of murderers?"

Once a convict, always a convict. "I'm a murderer, so yeah."

The rag finally stilled under her hand. "That's not what I meant, and you know it."

Castile ran a hand over his face and squatted on his heels. Talking to Aspen's back while she bent to her gruesome task was getting to him. "If we don't appear, if we don't fight . . . I think they'll leave us alone. After Trinidad dies . . ." He let the word fall away. Just thinking it was bad enough. "Afterward. It's going to be a fucking massacre. The Christians are going to torture the Indigos into telling everything they know about us. Somehow, they'll find the cave. We'd best not be here."

"They'll still hunt us in our dreams, like before, if they want us dead that badly," Aspen asked.

It was an unarguable point. "I'll kill Wolf. Israel. The one who roves them. The next time I see him I'll kill him."

The rag started scratching at the bloody stone again. "Maybe it's just you they want, Castile."

He realized she was leading him, maybe trying to trip him up, and he was glad her back was turned. Lying to a priestess's face was bad mojo. "She wants Trinidad." He stopped to breathe. Just saying the name gutted him. "She thinks she can manipulate him with religion, get him to rove her. She hates me for allying with him, for protecting him. Shit lot of good it did either one of us."

Aspen dropped the rag in her bucket of brackish water and turned around. "Why did you come back to the coven, Castile?"

"To warn you. To get you all out."

"Not tonight," she said. "I mean after prison."

He shook his head, bewildered. "This is my home."

"I think we both know it isn't," she said. "You chose a path away from the coven, away from the craft, a long time ago. You chose to fight and to use magic to do violence, and that was well before prison took you from us."

Understanding thundered through him. "You mean the eco-terr war."

"I love you, Castile, but I will never understand you. I don't know how you could choose death and violence over life and love. It isn't our way." He opened his mouth to protest but she squeezed his hand. "No. Hear me out. You changed after Trinidad left. You were a child, so it was to be expected. But the old Castile never came back. Then you fell in with the ecoterrs—"

"It was a worthy cause."

"Was it? People died."

"It was war. I fought for the world, the craft. I was fighting for my people." His voice faded. He sounded like Trinidad.

"I don't think you were fighting for anything. I think you fought against the parish, punishing the Christians for taking Trinidad from you."

"That's ridiculous. I didn't even do all my work inparish."

"I know."

"What?"

She smiled, but tears glittered in her eyes. "You're not the only one with prison informants. I know how you managed to come out of prison with barely a scratch. You gave yourself to Windigo to protect you—"

Castile stared at her, cold and stiff.

"You can fight well. You could have taken him, maybe not killed him, but gotten him to leave you alone. So, we figured he had something on you. When you came out, Hawk did some digging. He paid off some prison guards to get to him directly. Windigo said your bombs destroyed that Denver church, the one where Marius was priest, and her home."

A weight grew on his back, like someone, or something, was pushing him forward. Chills climbed his spine at the touch. Herne. Shoving him toward the truth. No escaping, not this time. "He'll tell," he whispered. If he hadn't already . . .

"No. Hawk killed Windigo."

Castile stared at her, stunned. Windigo . . . dead. Only Lady Aspen knew the truth now. He thought he could trust her. She was telling him, not telling other people. He wanted to trust her. "My lady—"

"Whatever Hawk did wrong," she said, "and whatever you did wrong, he was prepared to take care of you, Cas, as one of us. As family. You're my family, too."

She fell quiet, waiting. His voice sounded dead, even to him. "I thought her house was empty. We were trying to scare her, that's all. You know she's been talking crusade since she was a young priest. I didn't know . . ." He swallowed and thought of Father Troy's little house pressed up against the church in Boulder Parish.

"And that has to do with the environment, how?"

"You know as well as I do its Christian rule that destroyed the Earth. They don't care about here, now. All they care about is their precious Heaven." He shook his head. "They got worse than they bargained for with the Barren."

"As did we all."

He leaned toward her and took her hand. It was wet and chilled from the bloody water. "Marius doesn't know it was me. I'd be dead if she did. It's not why she came after us. She came after us because I can rove. Because Trinidad can."

"Odd. The way I understand it, you went after Trinidad first."

He swallowed and thought of fighting Marius in the Barren, of the slash across her forehead and the one across his back. He looked down at his hand holding hers and pulled it away, tucking his silvered fingernails out of sight. "I thought he was roving them. I was scared he would use the Barren against us."

"You fear the Barren?"

"Don't you?" he asked.

"Funny thing about fear. It has an odd way of turning into hatred. Marius knows an ecoterr bomb killed her family, and she knows you're an ecoterr. You are close enough to the real thing, even if she didn't know you're actually the man who killed her family. That she doesn't know explains why you're still alive. It also explains why she tortured you, why they raped you."

The word fell like a bomb between them, obliterating Castile's ability to speak. His armor constricted his breathing, he unsnapped his breastplate and dropped it at his side. "Trin told you."

"This whole time, I hated Marius," Aspen said. "I feared her and I hated her for using her personal loss to fuel a crusade. I hated her for killing Hawk. Then I hated her for hurting you and killing our people. But now I can understand her, just a little." She glanced at her daughter. "I would kill without blinking to protect my child."

"You won't have to, my lady. I'll take of you. I'll do what Hawk couldn't—"

Hawk, who allied with the enemy.

Hawk, who knew what Castile had done and let him back in the coven anyway.

Aspen was watching him carefully and nodded. "Hawk made mistakes, Cas. But when you went inparish with Trin and didn't come back, he was frantic with worry."

"Because of Magpie," Castile whispered.

"Not just her," she said. "I think Hawk was just realizing how he misjudged the bishop and their savvy, how badly we needed your help. Honestly, when he went inparish, I think he wanted to get close enough to the bishop to kill her. He cared about this coven, all of us. When you came back from prison and asked to rejoin us, he was the first to speak on your behalf. I worried over how it would work out, we all did. But Hawk wanted to trust you. He even let you bring Trinidad here."

Hawk had fought Trinidad and Castile a thousand ways since they were kids. Trinidad had only really fought back once, had attacked him like a rabid animal, scarring his face.

He shook his head. "How could he have allied with the bishop? He had to have known what she might do. I can't believe I ever trusted him."

"He couldn't trust you fully either. You refused to talk about your past. Then you brought Trinidad here, so injured. Hawk realized something happened that day to make the Indigos choose revenge over food when they were starving. I think you lied to them, Cas, said something to get them to act. I'm guessing it went south." She sighed. "With all you've done, all the secrets you've kept, it makes me wonder what else you've lied about."

Trinidad had been so bloody, so hurt. A tear traced a hot path down Castile's cold cheek. He heard his voice, though he hadn't meant to talk. But candles burned, the Dagger and Cup lay nearby, and Aspen gripped his hands. This was as sacred a Circle as any.

"Trin killed Roi d'Esprit. I guessed where Trin would hide him, and I was right. I found the body but I didn't have proof Trin killed him. Just rumors. Reine's too smart to take revenge without proof. So I carved a cross on the body."

Aspen hissed a breath. "Does Trinidad know?"

He shook his head. Cold seeped in and carved rivers of grief in his bones.

"You lied even to him." Another sad smile. "It destroyed Trinidad to know they hurt you. I could see it in his face, the way he talked about you. He loves you, Cas. I know it doesn't seem like it. He's different than us, because of how he was raised. He's a soldier. And he's damaged. But he loves you."

Castile slumped, bitterness thickening his voice. "He only loves his precious vows."

Aspen slapped him, leaving a stinging heat on his wet cheek. The baby stirred at the echoing crack. "You're so blind! When I asked you to go to the Indigos to savvy, Trin was dead set on going with you, even when I offered to keep him here safe, even after what the Indigos did to him, even if they might kill him." Aspen lowered her voice. "By all we hold sacred, you will regret it to the end of your days if you let Trinidad die alone, Castile. Go to him. Go to him now, before it's too late."

Castile's heart lurched in his chest, urging battle, fight—Herne, pumping through his veins, shoving him into action. Lady Aspen was his priestess, and she had given him a task. Before he had a chance to think through what he was doing, he dipped his chin to her and got to his feet.

# FORTY-SIX

R eine moved her hands over her horse uneasily as they prepared to ride out. "You're not going after Castile?"

"I told you I wouldn't," Trinidad answered.

"Why are you doing it?"

He shook his head wearily. There was no way to make her
understand his vows and obligations—or his debts. Mutual debts,
now, with the Indigos. He'd killed Roi d'Esprit, who had destroyed
Israel. "It's the only way to end this."

At least she wasn't trying to apologize for Israel, or for marking
Trinidad with the pentacle.

Trinidad had heard of the spirit tribes' war paint, but he'd
never seen it up close. It was nothing like the slavers simple stripes.
Everywhere he looked grimaces leered at him, crimson streaked
from eyes as if they cried tears of blood, lines crisscrossed their
cheeks like scars. Some had intricate teeth painted on their lips,
fashioned into false grins. One woman's face was painted stark
white with black circles around the eyes and nose, a living skull
staring back at him.

The Indigos and other tribes insisted on escorting him. He had the idea they still thought they could take on the Christian army and win. He didn't have it in him to argue.

Reine d'Esprit gave Trinidad a decent horse to ride. "Marius won't take your challenge seriously if you turn up on that old nag," she said.

He nodded his thanks as he mounted, avoiding her gaze.

Reine opened her mouth as if to speak again but just shook her head, jingling the chains woven through her locks. She mounted, calling to her spearguards and the rest of her ranks to follow suit.

The wind kicked up, snapping the banners that fronted each tribe. First came the cavalry, led by the elders of other tribes, and Reine d'Esprit and Trinidad. He judged himself to be the youngest among the riders. They weren't very many; horses tended to perish in lean winters. Behind walked the spears, bows, swords, and guns. Even the children followed their parents to war. It was a chattering, clinking army, armored in salvaged metal refashioned into breastplates and greaves. Women laughed roughly; men boasted. But the undercurrent of nerves sounded louder to Trinidad, the shuffling feet, the crying babies, the anxious mutterings. He stared at the children, a sea of them armed with slings and small bows. Inparish, Christian children huddled in their beds, if they had them. His breastplate felt tight again, compressing his chest. He realized his breathing had quickened to a hard pant. He readjusted the latches on his armor and turned to Reine. She'd been watching him, but war paint masked her thoughts.

"They should keep their distance from the army until we know what the bishop will do. It might take some time."

"Come on, to the front," she said, and they cantered up to take the lead.

They kept a good clip, letting the others fall behind. Trinidad focused outward, tasting his environment with all his senses. Ahead, scouts ranged by foot and horse, calling faintly to one another and signaling with faintly luminescent flags. A flatbed dray rumbled and rattled behind them, overloaded with replacement munitions. The world smelled cold and dirty, like frozen smoke. Grit coated his airways. A dirty headwind stung his eyes. It deadened the sounds of the army behind them.

He wiped his eyes with his sleeve and coughed, harsh enough to hurt his chest. His horse sidestepped beneath him. Trinidad reached down to pat its neck, half expecting his hand to pass through the animal like in a dreamscape. He chided himself when it didn't. You are doing this. This is real. He smoothed his mind into a blank canvas, letting his fear rush away as far as the tombs went in the Barren. He wished he were there now, sitting in the quiet peace.

The branches of dead trees beckoned like crooked fingers, clawing at the sky as they shadowed the graveyard of rotting houses in Old Superior. The town had died before his time as water ran out and various tribes stole the last of the town's rights. The once prosperous neighborhood climbed the hill to a road that led to Old 93, where Castile surely rode. He would warn his people about what Trinidad was going to do and that the crusade would likely begin in earnest in the next twenty-four hours.

*Let him make it. Let them get to safety*, Trinidad prayed fiercely. But he didn't believe they could. Part of him still couldn't believe Castile had left him to do this alone. He half expected him to reappear and make a bad joke, reassure him with a glance.

He shoved his mind away from Castile and the Wiccans, left them behind as well.

They climbed over the final ridge before the valley, slowly now as the horses picked their way over dirt and past chunks of broken roadway. Ahead, the silhouette of a skittering horse topped the hill, lit by the light of early dawn. The Indigo scout. She turned her horse and trotted back to meet them.

"Their camp's awake," she called out when she was barely close enough to talk. "A big camp is set outside the gates, Queen."

Denver Parish must have arrived with its army. "There's too many of them to gather inparish by now," Trinidad said. "The officers and archwardens will be inside."

Reine reined in when the scout got close enough to speak with some amount of privacy. "Are they marchin?"

"No," the scout answered. "It's like they're waitin for us."

"That's because they are," Trinidad said.

Reine looked at him. "What now?"

"It doesn't change anything," he said. "You still think you should come?"

She gave him a nod.

He pursed his lips. But he couldn't command her to go her back. "Leave the bulk of your people here, with scouts on watch. Give them a half a chance at running if it goes wrong."

Reine sighed and stared up at the sky. "Pass the word," she directed the scout. The scout bowed her head to Reine and passed them at a trot, back to the army stretching out behind them.

The wind still whipped away the noises of their motley assortment of troops. Over their heads, weak fingers of watery sunlight clawed at the hazy eastern horizon. In the valley below, hundreds of torches and campfires lit the fields outside gates of the parish. The ground glowed more than the dawn. Marius' army had the space and used it. Thirty thousand. He'd heard that figure thrown around. But he'd never imagined how big an army of thirty thousand could be. His stomach yawned wide, clawing at itself. She would never accept his challenge. If she was smart, she'd shoot him on the spot.

"They're comin," Reine said.

A small, ghostly party emerged from the field of fires. Trinidad couldn't make out the red crosses on the black cloaks in the shadow of the hill leading down to the valley. He didn't need to. He almost felt his own order approaching.

"Get your guards and the other tribe leaders," Trinidad said. "We should ride to meet them. I'll talk." His mouth tasted bitter and dry. His hands sweated inside his gauntlets.

He scanned the faces of the Christian contingent as they closed in. Some he didn't know; marshals who acted as advisors, he supposed. Malachi was there, wearing a surly frown. Seth granted him a slight lift of his chin in greeting. Two other archwardens flanked Marius, swords bared. It was a formality, he knew. He didn't reach for his. To her credit, if Marius felt any shock at seeing him there, she didn't show it.

He let his chin fall as was customary. "Your Grace."

"I hope you brought them to surrender," she answered. "For their sakes."

"No, Your Grace," he said. "But I didn't bring them to fight, either. I come to challenge you to singlehand on their behalf."

She must have stiffened; her horse shifted nervously under her. Her cloak fluttered as she calmed it with a hand on its neck.

"If I win, you'll surrender?"

"If you win, I'll be dead," Trinidad said.

Her eyebrows rose. "What good are you to me dead?"

"I can yield then, if you wish. In exchange, Reine d'Esprit and the other outcounty tribes will keep their freehold in exchange for taxes, freedom to worship as they will, and a guarantee of no harm. You will own the rest of the county, all the lands, with no harm to your army. I'll, of course, need your sworn word."

"And you'll rove for me?"

"Not to kill," he answered.

"Of course," she said dryly. "And if you win?"

"Everyone goes home without harm. Both armies will disband under peace treaties."

"What of the Barren then?"

He turned his head away to stare out over the parish, gated and quiet. That was it, the crux of the whole thing. "I wish to Holy God that Castile had never found it."

"You realize we can crush you," Marius said. "There is no earthly reason why I should take your challenge."

Reine hissed. The others around them moved and muttered among themselves. The sun climbed behind Trinidad and lit the scar on Marius' forehead.

"I know, Your Grace. No earthly reason. But there is the godly one."

# FORTY-SEVEN

M arius admitted Seth into her council room. He waited, chin
up, the heel of his hand resting on the hilt of his sword.

The house had been a pretty home once, windows framing
a fine view of the mountains. Wind whistled around boards and
mumbled against the few windows with glass left. Tumbleweeds
and chunks of broken concrete marked the hole in the ground
where a pool had once been. Beyond lay her army. She could hear
the low rumble of voices day and night.

"They believe Christ binds them to war," she said softly. She
turned to look at the tall, pale archwarden. His white hair and
brows frosted his glacial expression. "Do you?"

Seth bowed. "I swore myself to Him, Your Grace. Christ binds
me to you in His stead. I am bound."

She wanted to slap his face red, get some color in those pale
cheeks. "What have you come to tell me?"

"Your Grace, news of Trinidad's challenge has spread through
the troops. They don't understand why he would do such a thing.
But he is known to them, Your Grace. They could turn against you

in this, especially since crusade is not the glory they dreamed it to be."

"An indirect way of telling me the locals hope he'll win."

"He has given them an escape from the war, Your Grace. An opportunity to turn away from the hardship of crusade. They're miserable out in that camp, and bored, and it's only been a few days."

"I'm feeding them, at least."

"True. Hunger binds them far more securely than Christ at the moment. And confusion and sadness, in these dark times. Many of them have lost much."

*I've lost much.* "You think I should accept this challenge and send the army home."

"With a champion in your stead, of course."

"I can fight." She did fight him. *And I won. I think.*

Seth colored slightly, spots of color harsh against his white skin. "You're the bishop, Your Grace. You cannot fight him. It would be as if Trinidad is fighting Christ Himself."

"I don't give myself that much credit, and you shouldn't either," she said, hating that he was right. She paced away a few steps and turned on him. "Why did you take the vows of your order? Why did you take the cross?"

"To serve Christ."

"It must be an insult to serve me."

The barest hesitation. "My order follows your commands."

"My God, man, you probably don't even like me or respect me." Especially not after what she had done to Castile. She should have killed the filthy Wiccan when she had the chance. No doubt he'd put Trinidad up to this challenge. "Tell me why you're in the order. And don't quote your vows to me."

His lips parted to speak, but he hesitated again. Pretty lips. Curled just so, but too pale. Her own mouth suddenly ached for a kiss, a throb that sank past her belly. She waved a hand, trying to dismiss the feeling. "Never mind—"

"Faith that God can work miracles for our tired world." He paused. "Even through the likes of you."

"You think I should stop the crusade? Before it's even begun?"

"I think, Your Grace, that you should let God decide."

# FORTY-EIGHT

The day stayed cold. An Indigo built a fire to ward off the chill, and Reine and Trinidad huddled close to it watching the mass of crusading humanity milling downhill from them. As morning dragged into afternoon, Reine's anxiety grew. She shifted, tapped her fingers, sharpened her knife. Trinidad felt detached, distanced from all of it, from the strangers he now led, from the idea of dying. He ate the small amount that was offered without tasting it. He closed his eyes and dozed, falling into a calm trance where his heart beat out the slow passage of time and he was alone.

A contingent of leaders from the other tribes had gone inparish several hours ago but had yet to return with word. Reine had sent a boy named Cur in her stead. Trinidad wasn't sure why she didn't go himself. Maybe she didn't trust Trinidad to stay and do as he said he would.

"How can you just sit there?" Reine demanded, getting up and walking around, slapping her palms against her thighs.

Trinidad opened his eyes and sighed. "Whatever the bishop decides, I'll fight today." And likely die. The only difference was whether he'd be doing it alone. His mind strayed to Castile's absence; he forced the thought to retreat.

The colorful contingent tread the rocky no-man's-land between the Christians and the Indigos' temporary camp. "They're coming back," he said.

She spun and stared hard at the group of mounted spirit kings and queens. Cur urged his horse ahead of the others and threw himself to the ground before them, so intent on Trinidad he nearly stumbled into the coals.

Trinidad laid his forearms on his knees and looked up at him.

"She agreed." A broad smile broke out on Cur's red face. "She agreed! As soon as you can get there! You're fightin a champion, of course—"

Exhaustion and resolve settled in him. "Who?"

Cur shook his head. "She didn't say. They were arguin it out and she stopped it until we left. She said he'd be ready—whoever it was—as soon as you could get there."

"Where?"

"Folsom."

The prison.

Cur's smile faltered at Trinidad's hard stare. "She said it was private. That's all she said."

"Thanks, Cur," Reine said. Cur turned away. Reine waited until he was out of earshot to speak. "It's a trap. You're never going to get out of Folsom alive, no matter what happens."

Trinidad got to his feet, stiff from his cold vigil. "I always had two fights. Her, and then the others. The important thing is that you all will escape, safe." The retreat back toward the freehold had already started. "Go back now. Get clear of this."

"I'm comin with you."

"Send someone else. Your people need you."

"You don't trust Marius?"

"I'll trust her more if I win."

He watched her absorb that. The bishop wouldn't be dead, but the fight and terms would be known. He could make sure of it. But if he wasn't around to enforce it, the bishop could say anything at all, discredit him.

"I'm comin," she said. "It's no small thing, Trinidad. You savvied your life for us, fuckin I don't know why. But you're doin it, and we're comin."

"I killed your father," he said, incredulous.

"I got business inparish and you're my ticket inside."

That made more sense. Who was he to tell her what to do? He nodded.

They mounted in short order, Trinidad reflecting he had little to pack. He'd need little enough when he was dead or made a prisoner and only his sword and armor between now and then. The tribal leaders, each with a guard, kept close and quiet. As they rode, a sour ache started in his belly. He tried to focus on what he was about to do. Not the fight—that would play out as it would—but the prison, the labyrinth of cells where concessions and viewing boxes had once been, makeshift cages built into the stands. Marius had played her hand well. It would be easy for her to make him disappear in there without a real fight. But he somehow knew it wouldn't happen like that. Marius had something to prove; she had ever since she'd first seen him. He didn't understand it, though he knew it was true. But he didn't want to go in there, didn't want to think of the times he'd been there with Father Troy, not ever realizing Father Troy knew Castile.

Castile. The ache sharpened.

He urged his horse up to Reine. "You don't owe me anything. I have no right to ask you for anything. But Cas—" His voice broke. The city gates were already open, Folsom Prison looming beyond, waiting to swallow him. They were approaching the Christian army camp and Trinidad realized he dreaded passing through it more than he dreaded going into the prison. He tried to coax a little moisture into his dry mouth. "He'll never understand why I'm doing this. But I never forgot him, not before and not now. Can you tell him?"

"Yeah." A pause. "They're gonna kill you today."

"I said I'd yield if it comes to it. It will. She'll get someone good to fight me." Seth, probably. He'd thumped Seth before in sparring. *Not this day,* he thought. The words sparked the unhappy memory of Father Troy.

Reine shook her head, jingling the chains in her locks. "I still can't reckon why you're doing this. You're one of them, not one of us."

"No. I'm neither," he said.

Their horses slogged through mud-strewn snow of the ramshackle war camp. Indiscriminate fires burned hot against the gloom. Recruits lingered around the flames, warming cold hands and clutching blankets over their shoulders. Most weren't armed beyond knives more suited to eating than killing. No archwardens clad in black armor; no marshals with worn fatigues and well-fingered weapons. The parishioners looked like migrant poor rather than an army. The weight of their collective stare felt a physical thing, crawling under his armor and over his skin, taking in his Christian tattoos and his armor marked with Wiccan protection sigils. Even out of sight, the silver pentacle carved in his chest felt like ice.

Many crossed themselves at his passing, and a few chins dipped in acknowledgment. He did his best to stare straight ahead, telling himself most of them likely had no idea what this was about or who he was. I'm doing this for you, he wanted to tell them. So you don't have to. But he wasn't sure if it was the truth.

He wondered if Marius would display his body if he pushed the fight that far. The pentacle on his chest bared for all to see, his skin sliced, throat cut—for that was surely the blow that would kill him—maybe his head severed. It all felt unreal. He wasn't frightened or angry or any of it. His mind kept straying to mechanical problems and solutions. The reach of his sword. His knee he favored. Various faults in different archwardens he'd sparred against. Roman's training had paid off after all.

Reine shook her head. "This is what we're scared of?"

"They outnumber the Indigos by at least five times, maybe ten," Trinidad answered. "And she would have armed and trained them, given time."

"If she'd done, you wouldn't have got the chance to stop her," Reine said.

T rinidad had been inside the prison a half-dozen times over the years and he'd always been glad to come back out. The prisoners were kept in inhumane conditions, shivering when the winter laced the air with ice, sweating when summer seared its way through Boulder Valley. They never were fed enough and the most dangerous were kept meek with shock collars, tiny cages, and regular beatings. Gang warfare ruled with a deadly hand. Priests and others had sometimes brought them little bits of food, whatever the parish could manage. Prisoners bowing their heads with Father Troy in prayer always seemed a mystery to Trinidad. Why pray when your life is a ruin?

Trinidad had been fullsworn only a month when Troy first brought him to the prison as one of his guards. Trinidad had guessed at the nature of the prison bartering system, but that day he saw it firsthand: younger men and women pleasuring stronger, usually older prisoners in plain view. The priest had ignored it, walked by as if it weren't happening. But Trinidad, shocked, had protested the abuse. He started a fight that took ten guards and a forty-eight-hour lockdown to contain.

Later, back at the church in the candlelit chapel, the priest took Trinidad's hand. "I know. It's frustrating. But you can only do what you can do. It will make a difference. You'll see."

Trinidad had jerked away. He was an archwarden, trained from childhood to defend Christendom with his skills and his body. All he'd been able to do was earn a few bruises and cause a riot. "When does that happen, Father? When do we actually make a difference?"

The old priest had given him a gentle smile. "Someday, son. Not this day, but someday."

He should have known the memory would sneak back up, coming here. Trinidad blinked it away and looked around the little room where he'd been put to wait for the fight, an interrogation chamber replete with chains and bloodstains. He'd sent Reine and her fellow spirit kings off, not wanting their anxiety to nerve him up. They'd gone without protest to wherever the archwardens said they could watch from.

He sank down at the table and let his forehead fall to his clasped hands. He couldn't remember the last time he'd prayed aloud, prayed more than a few fleeting hopes amid all that had happened in the past days.

"I don't know if I deserve to live, or even if You want me to. But I give myself to Your will."

Paltry, but all he had to offer. The only answer was his own heartbeat. He traced a cross over his breastplate and noticed the Horns Castile had painted there. He supposed he ought to be having a crisis of faith, but he believed in Christ even if He wasn't making Himself known.

He'd seen magic, he couldn't deny roving was real. But what he felt in church and with Father Troy was just as real. Christianity had its own brand of magic. His archwarden vows bound him like a living thing, not something he could forsake. Even though all this, even when Indigos and others looked upon his marked head and hands with revulsion, he'd never felt a moment's regret.

Except for one thing, one person. He closed his eyes and let his forehead rest against his palms.

He heard a sound, scrubbed at his eyes, and raised his head. Seth opened the door, face and hair white against the black of his armor and cloak. He was clean, his cloak freshly brushed. "They're ready."

Could he really have forgotten just how enormous Seth was? "Are you fighting me?"

"No."

It must be one of the bishop's personal guards then. Not entirely unexpected. Trinidad pulled on his gauntlets, rested his naked sword on his armored shoulder in the traditional battle-ready gesture, and followed Seth into the hall. He'd passed some time warming up his muscles for the fight; his every motion cut the still air like a knife. Honed. Contained. Ready.

A dull roar started in Trinidad's ears, clogging off the sound of his heart, dragging his steps. Not until he had trekked halfway across the field did he realize the roar was hundreds of voices. Prisoners rattled cages, guards and marshals clanged weapons. The place stank of sewage, smoke, sweat, and blood.

*The Barren smells like nothing,* he thought.

He might be there soon, his scoured bones joining the rest of humanity's. He wondered what gods had built the tombs. If their work was finished or if they made more. He wondered if his tomb would be engraved with a cross, a pentacle, or nothing. He wondered if his dying would make the slightest difference. If it would change a damn thing.

Someday, son. Someday. But not this day.

Except this was his last day.

Marius stood near one of the rusted chain-link cages where prisoners took their air. Someone had cleared the snow and smoothed the ground inside for them, readying the dirt for spilled blood. There were fewer immediate witnesses than he expected, the bishop amid four cloaked archwardens. Reine d'Esprit and the other spirit kings hung to the shadows.

Marius wore armor. Her scar glowered at him, bright as a star against the grim sky. She held two helmets in her arms and one of them was his. He recognized the scratches.

He jerked his chin toward the spirit tribe leaders. "Will you give them safe passage back to their people no matter what happens?"

Marius lifted her chin. "I agreed to the terms, did I not?"

She held out his helmet and he took it, surprised he didn't fumble it with his stiff fingers. Her gaze flickered downward to the horns painted over his breast and back up to his forehead, inscribed with Christ's cross. He wanted to tell her he knew it was wrong, he knew he should choose. But how could he choose between the remnants of faiths culled from a broken life? Never mind. The time for sorting it all out was over. Trinidad swallowed hard and blinked at Marius' boots, looked up as he heard footsteps in the slushy mud of the prison field.

Roman, armored and cloaked. His strong legs carried him with ease and grace. He rested his bared sword blade against his armored shoulder, signaling he was ready to fight.

Trinidad shook his head. "You can't—"

"I can. I am."

Trinidad looked from the bishop to Roman. "This is crazy. This isn't his fight."

"Never has been, boy. Didn't stop me from making a living off you fools before and it's not going to stop me now." Roman gestured toward the open gate of the cage. "After you."

She'd paid him off then. Gold for Trinidad's life.

Roman could win. He could beat Trinidad. He was the only one who could, for certain, kill him in an evenly matched fight. Roman had an ambidextrous grip; he liked to surprise his opponents with his left. Roman's reach outdistanced his own. Cutting inside the bigger man's guard was damned near impossible, and Roman had years more fighting experience.

But Roman had trouble defending below the knee because of an old back injury, his left shoulder had a bullet wound that stiffened in the cold, and he left his right flank open on certain forms.

Trinidad knew how to slip his point where Roman's back-plate gaped from the old-style skirting over his hip during a backswing. He'd done it before, a few times, catching his armsmaster off-guard in practice.

He knew all Roman's strengths and flaws, just as Roman knew Trinidad's. This fight would be less a contest of strength than a contest of perfection. Roman had never given an inch, even in practice. Trinidad's first mistake would be answered with blood. Marius had chosen her champion well.

Tension knit his spine into a knot. He squared his shoulders and settled his helmet over his head, dampening the jeers of the prisoners, and led Roman into the cage.

# FORTY-NINE

The dark prison tunnel swallowed Castile, digesting his counterfeit bravado. He was in a passageway used to bring illicit goods inside. Every prisoner knew it. The guards let it go on as long they were paid off. About once a year someone used it to escape. They were inevitably captured and brought back as an example. Castile shuddered. Any hopes of escape had been destroyed by the sight of his first "example" hanging by his wrists, screaming as his guts spilled from a deep slash in his belly. Not long after, Windigo had spoken of what he knew of Castile's past, and Castile had belonged to him thereafter.

It wasn't long before he realized maybe he'd chosen the worse of the two options.

*Windigo is dead*, he reminded himself. Killed by Hawk. Also dead.

The reek of his sweat drifted from under the armor constricting his chest. Sewage fumes permeated the air—prisoners were forever working on the ancient, faulty plumbing. Herne knew he'd done his time in the bowels of the prison. At least no one down there had rape or murder on their minds, or anything other than getting out as fast as possible.

"Great fucking balls of Herne," he muttered, annoyed with his nerves. "Never thought I'd be breaking *into* the damn prison."

He instantly regretted speaking and stopped to listen. A whistle of air and the press of stale cold dogged his steps. He'd brought some Alteration to buy his passage inside, but found the gate unmanned. He puzzled over that for a second before realizing the prisoners were on lockdown for Trinidad's fight. No need for a gate guard.

Good old Trin, causing a stir wherever you go.

He drew the knife from his belt, felt the comforting weight of a coven rifle across his back. Before, he'd had only his wits and fists as weapons. Now it was different.

They'd be down on the field in one of the run-pens. Castile trotted hard, trying to breathe evenly, circling the arena at ground level in a back corridor left quiet and dark from lockdown. At some point, he'd have to pass through cells to get out to the field. He'd have to face the metallic stink of the bars and the taunting of the prisoners inside.

He'd forgotten how loud the prison was, even in lockdown, the never-ending voices of thousands of prisoners and their guards. But a sudden dull roar, like a bomb going off a few blocks away, stopped him short. It had begun. He ran harder. He had no illusions it would last long. This wasn't a spectacle for show, it was a fight to the death, meant to stop a war. An assassin's double-tap. He thought of how Trin looked when he lifted his sword, no hatred, no emotion, only death in his eyes, movements mechanical, strategic. At one point he'd hated and feared it. Now it was his only source for hope.

He skidded to a stop. Most of the entrances to the field had been closed off and blocked by cells as prison population grew; there were four with actual doors that led to the field below, all lined with cells. They were privileged areas, cleaner, brighter, open to the daylight but more protected from the weather. Deep inside there were no windows, and out on the stands the prisoners were at the mercy of the heat and cold in makeshift cages. He'd spent his first months deep inside, living with the rats down there, until Windigo...

He stared down the passageway, his passageway, to his and Windigo's cell. He stayed in the shadows and held his breath. No guards, as usual. The guards used to leave Windigo pretty much alone and seemed to have kept the habit for this block.

Still, felons stirred in their cages, ears pricked. They knew he was there, felt the foreign presence like he felt their own familiarity. They would jeer at him, shiv him if he got close. Nothing lifers hated worse than the guy who got out.

He didn't want to go down that hall. He didn't want to see the cell he'd shared with Windigo, who had paid off guards to get Castile moved. He thought of those rough fingers wound in his hair, pinning him to a demanding body...

He blinked at the patch of dreary daylight at the other end of the stained concrete. Coughs rattled, so rampant in winter. Chapped hands gripped the bars. Probably trying to get a glimpse of what was going on. They wouldn't have been told, but the tide of rumors would have swept the truth of it through the prison population. They knew about the fight.

Without his realizing it, his feet were carrying him down that hall, toward the gray light. Toward Trinidad. His heart pattered out a rhythm. Don't die. Don't die. Don't die.

A low whistle. "If it isn't Windigo's bitch, come back from the living."

"Fuck are you here, Cas?"

Castile kept his stare straight ahead.

"Cassie."

Castile startled and spun, yanking his knife from its sheath. No one called him that. Not Trin. Not anyone. Only one person, and he was—

"Dead," he whispered. Aspen had said Windigo was dead.

The inmates fell quiet. This was a better show than a couple of fool archwardens trying to die on each other's swords.

Same crooked, fist-flattened nose between small eyes. One meaty hand emerged to grip one of the bars of his cage. Castile couldn't help staring at that hand.

"Ain't dead, Cassie. I ain't dead, baby. And here you come to get me, like you say you would before you got out."

Castile opened his mouth and closed it.

Someone hissed low, behind him, and Castile moved forward quick, instinctive. Get close to the bars and someone could kill him. But not too far forward. Not within Windigo's reach.

Windigo smiled, a slash of red tongue against fleshy lips. "Ain't you nervy? No one's gonna jump you with me here, Cassie."

Windigo had broken the neck of the last guy who'd tried to kill Castile, four months after he'd taken Castile into his bed. After Windigo had choked the attacker to the death, Castile had felt a vicious gladness that he was dead.

"What is it?" a sleepy voice muttered from the shadows of the cell. Rustling. Someone shifting on the hard lump of mattress Windigo called a bed. Better than a lot of inmates had.

Windigo turned his pocked face away from Castile. "Don't concern you, bitch."

"You got another one—" Castile bit down on the words, hating the way he sounded.

Early days he used to whine when Windigo fucked anybody else. It was all fear back then, terror that he'd been discarded. Windigo used to slap him around for the whining. Not hard. He liked Castile pretty on the outside.

Windigo pressed his face between the bars. Deep lines creased the skin around his small eyes. A new red scar slashed his pocked cheek.

"Got to keep warm at night, Cassie. Ain't like you, though. I missed you, baby. You look good, baby. Beautifuler than ever."

A knife twisted in Castile's belly. When he crooned like that, he used to hold Castile, pet him until he fell asleep. It was almost nice. But Castile never knew what he was waking up to.

Windigo smiled, baring jagged teeth. "You brought us a weapon, huh? We gonna do a little damage on our way out?"

Another collective shout roiled from the field below.

"I'm not here for you." And then, because he wasn't sure he'd said it loud enough, or really said it at all: "I'm not here for you."

Windigo's face hardened. The speed at which Windigo could move from gentle to cruel was the source of every nightmare Castile ever had.

"What did you say to me, bitch?"

Castile stepped back, signed the horns at Windigo. Hunter, help me. "You heard me. You can fucking rot."

A hiss down the hall, dull laughter turned into a cough.

Windigo stared at him with eyes flat and deadly as a snake's. "You better hope I never fucking get out of here. You'll pay in blood. I'll flay your fucking skin off your bones and stuff your cock down your throat. You hear me? You're gonna—"

*Click*. Castile slid his rifle under his arm and chambered a bullet. His hands were shaking, but he was able to meet that hateful stare with level eyes. "You're the one in the cage, asshole, and I'm the one with the rifle. So just keep talking shit to me."

Silence. Windigo stared at him, speechless for once.

Castile blinked, steadied the gun, aimed it at Windigo's chest.

The sound outside burst to a deafening level, like snowmelt crashing through a canyon. He turned his head. Trinidad. What was it Trin had told him? You can only do what you can do. Yeah, well, he could do better than this. Trin was out there, maybe dying, and Castile was in here wrangling with the past. He had better people to put bullets into than Windigo.

He turned and walked away, Windigo screaming after him. "I'll tell them, Cassie, I'll tell them what you done, what they don't know. You'll be back inside by the end of the year and I'll cut you into pieces, have us a barbeque . . ."

It almost stopped him—the threat Windigo had held over him, had whispered to him whenever Castile got uppity. But he could see the chain-link cage outside where two men in black circled each other.

Trinidad was still in it, still standing. Still alive.

Castile released a slow breath. Someone shifted in the shadows, cast long by the meager sun and distorting the familiar silhouette of Reine's dreadlocks. More shadows appeared as his eyes adjusted to the light: the other tribal leaders. He yanked his cloak hood up, hid the rifle under the folds of fabric over his shoulders, and walked out into the daylight. With luck he'd look like an Indigo.

"Good thing I'm not aiming to kill you just now," he muttered to Reine.

"You fool. Fuckin kill you if they find you here." She didn't take her eyes off the fight.

Both men in the cage were covered head to toe in impassive black armor, but Castile knew Trin the second he saw him, the calculated way he moved, the measure of his steps. The other guy was bigger. "Who's he fighting?"

"Roman, they said. He trains them inparish."

Roman looked strong as a bull, outstripping Trinidad's strikes with crashing blows. Trinidad feinted with his sword and swung a gauntleted fist at Roman's head. Roman slapped his arm down easily. They both backed off a few steps.

Fuck. The armsmaster. Trin had talked about the guy like he was a warrior aspect. "So is Trin—"

It happened so fast he almost missed it. Roman slammed his sword at Trinidad's shoulder, Trinidad barely got his bracer up in time. Roman's blade skipped off his arm and smacked Trinidad's helmet. Trinidad staggered back. Roman pressed him, crashing two more blows on him, forcing Trinidad to block with his sword— probably notching that precious blade of his—and step back. He was only a stride away from the fence, a stride away from getting pinned.

Trinidad shook his head as if trying to clear it. Roman struck another blow and Trinidad killed its momentum by catching it mid-swing. They locked together, too close for blade-work. Roman elbowed Trinidad in the head; Trinidad wheeled away, still near the fence, but out of reach. He realigned his grip on his sword and limped backwards, his cadence off.

Roman stalked Trinidad, measuring his strides, taking his time, waiting for the opportunity to strike a killing blow.

Trinidad abruptly spun away, right boot out. His toe hit the fence and caught just enough to give him a leg up. He shoved off and came down twisting in the air and crashed onto Roman, sword first. It was an awkward hit. They tumbled to the ground, wrestling, slamming each other with elbows and fists. Trinidad's helmet fell off and rolled. Thinking for a split second it was his head, Castile unconsciously took a few steps forward; Reine stopped him with a firm hand on his wrist. The group around them shifted and muttered uneasily and hands went for weapons.

They rolled in the mud, splattering and grunting, wordless shouts. Castile realized Trin had his grip on his sword wrong; underhand. It was useless in this melee of fists anyway. Trinidad forced his weight on top of Roman and smashed the grip of his sword into Roman's face. Helmet or no, Castile heard the blow where he stood. Roman's head jerked to the side.

"Yield," Trinidad said. The harsh word carried across the yard.

Castile had no breath to speak. *Fuck, this is no time for that, Trin—*

Roman swung at Trinidad, Trin easily knocked his arm down. He grabbed Roman's sword and threw it out of reach. "Yield."

To anyone else, Trinidad might look impassive, but the way his lips moved, his jaw tight . . . Castile could see agony in every line of his body.

*He can't do it. He can't kill him. He won't.*

Trinidad drew back and hit Roman with the hilt of his sword

gripped underhand in his fist, a full-on strike of blunt steel against his metal helmet. The armsmaster fell limp under him. Chest heaving, Trinidad got to his feet. Castile saw how he favored his left leg, smeared with bright blood. For a moment Trinidad looked down at Roman. Then he turned and looked at the other side of the cage where the bishop and her knot of archwardens were watching. All of them, even the bishop, had their hands on weapons. Trinidad was a sitting duck in the cage, trapped. They could spray him with one burst of bullets and end it.

Castile broke free of Reine's grip and strode forward, leaned on the fence with one hand, found the trigger of his rifle with the other. Trinidad might have won, but with a bunch of trigger-happy archwardens staring death at him, Castile wasn't taking any chances.

Trinidad pulled off his helmet. "Is this good enough?" he asked, his voice soft, deadly. "Or do I have to murder an unconscious man?"

Roman rolled onto his side, silent, and reached for his sword.

"Trin!"

In that second, Roman rolled toward Trinidad and threw a wild punch at the side of Trinidad's injured leg. Trinidad stumbled and spun at the same time, his sword coming up in a defensive sweep. The edge of it caught Roman under his raised chin. Blood spurted. He fell back, writhing, grappling at the wound.

Trinidad flipped his sword to underhand. For a breath he held, stone-like, and then stabbed down with his blade, unerringly ripping through Roman's exposed throat. He pulled the sword back, staggered back, and fell to his hands and knees. Blood ran red against his armored thigh.

The prison field erupted. What few prisoners could see the fight shouted their approval for bloodshed and brutality. Guards shouted back at them. The archwardens shifted in unison, organized, running for the gate to the cage. Castile stuck his rifle barrel through the fence and sprayed the archwardens, some bullets pinging uselessly, others finding marks in the black-cloaked melee. Four of the five fell; one kept running. His cloak hood slipped back to reveal mottled scarring. Wolf. Fuck. He could have killed the kid.

The bishop ran the opposite direction from them, bared steel in her hands. Alone, she moved quicker. She fumbled with the latch on the gate and threw it open to rush Trinidad from behind. Castile shouted wordlessly and fired at her. The bullet missed, pinging off-course through the chain-link. Castile swore and took aim again. The trigger locked under his finger. Fuck! Jammed. Castile beat the rifle against the fence and tried it again. Nothing.

Wolf bolted after her into the cage and fell on Marius, trying to drag her back. She shoved him off, spun, and stabbed her sword into his unarmored chest. It sank half-way in and she yanked it back. Wolf gaped at her as blood jetted from him. She shoved him off her blade with her other hand and he crumpled.

Castile ran around the fence toward the opening, slamming the useless rifle against the fence again. The trigger still jammed.

Marius reached Trinidad, sword raised in both hands, point aimed for his throat. He twisted, trying to get his blade up to deflect her blow. Her point skipped off his breastplate and caught in the narrow join where it met his shoulder armor. She shoved, hard, throwing her body into it. Trinidad's mouth opened in a soundless scream. Or maybe it was lost in the commotion, in the *whup* of a bowstring near Castile's ear and a muttered curse. The bishop slumped against Trinidad with a sharp cry, a feathered shaft jutting from one side of her back, in the mesh-protected joint by her arm.

Next to him, Reine had her bowstring to her cheek, another arrow already nocked. "Go get him."

Castile ran to Trinidad, falling to his knees and shoving the limp bishop off him.

"Cas . . ." Blood bubbled crimson on Trinidad's lips.

"Shh, don't talk. Don't talk." Castile laid his fingers under Trinidad's jaw, found his skittering pulse. He bent low and kissed Trinidad's cold lips, tasted blood.

Trinidad didn't kiss him back, he just gasped a raspy breath.

"You're okay. We'll get you out." Moving him would only make the blood flow faster. No time. No place to go. No help—

The *putt-putt-putt* of a weapon made him press low over Trinidad, who moaned.

"Castile."

Castile looked up, dazed. Reine had walked around the fence with her bow. Several prison guards scattered the outside of the fence, stuck with arrows. More black-cloaked archwardens sprawled in the churned mud like fallen bats. Castile's eye fell on one who had taken his turn at torturing him in prison. Malachi. How did he remember that name? Reine's fellow tribal leaders were holding back more prison guards with a few well-placed shots.

"Looks bad." Reine nocked another arrow. "Want me to put him out of his misery?"

"No! Fuck, no." Castile grabbed the pentacle hanging from his neck, rubbing it compulsively. "We have to get out of here."

"Fuckin pick him up then."

He heaved Trinidad up. Trinidad was unconscious and limp now; he made no sound as Castile and Reine maneuvered him onto Castile's shoulder. Castile didn't speak, could barely draw breath under Trinidad's dead weight. He just ran, stumbling and bent, back the way he'd come. The Indigos covered them; the guards had recovered enough to snipe a few bullets their way. It was half-hearted, though.

They cut behind the cover of some solid-walled cages and the bullets stopped. Reine was breathing hard. "Why aren't the guards chasing us?"

"We're above their paygrade," Castile said, staggering under Trinidad's weight.

"They'll be calling in marshals," Cur said, huffing behind them. Catcalls started up down the hall.

Castile stopped in front Windigo's cage. "Where can we hide? Somewhere they won't go."

Windigo just chuckled and shook his head.

"Friend of yours?" Reine asked.

Castile shook his head, shifted to better distribute Trinidad's weight. He needed Windigo's help, gods help him, Castile needed him again. And he'd alienated the son of a bitch, let his temper get to him. If he'd lied, if he'd been able to stomach a little more pretending . . .

Reine raised her bow. "You got three seconds."

"You point that thing at me you best shoot—"

Castile jolted at the twang of the bowstring, almost dropped Trinidad on the concrete floor. Cur stepped forward to grab some of the archwarden's weight.

Windigo fell in a shower of blood and gore, two feathered shafts jutting from his chest. His new bitch screamed from the darkness behind him.

Reine yanked another arrow free of her quiver and laid it on the string. "Start talking. Three. Two—"

"Fuckin no one goin down pipes today! We're on lockdown!"

Reine peered into the darkness. "You're Indigo?"

Windigo's boy swallowed audibly and crawled out into the dim light. "No. Amber." He cowered by the bars, edging away from Windigo's body. "Please don't kill me."

Castile swallowed and averted his eyes. His knees started to give way under the weight of the unconscious Trinidad.

"Castile, right?" From behind him. Castile turned his head to look. The big pale archwarden, cross glaring against his white forehead, walked toward them. His blade was out but he slid it back into its scabbard. "Let me take him," he said.

"No."

"I'm not going to hurt him."

Castile didn't like letting go of Trinidad but he couldn't hold him much longer. He transferred him with a grunt and eyed the archwarden. Reine, though, was still interested in the Amber.

"He's right," Castile said. "No one's going to the pipes today."

"Can't leave him sitting in all that gore—" Reine began. "He's just a kid. Why are you in, kid?"

"Stealing."

A beat. Two. Castile's eyes stung, his throat closed. *Please. Lord and Lady, hear me.* Trinidad hung, bleeding and broken between the two men. Was he even breathing? *Hunter, please make him breathe. Keep him breathing.*

"Trin doesn't have time for this." He started walking. He knew a nearby pipe room.

"Fuckin don't deserve to be someone's bitch, not for stealing," Reine called. "He ain't like you, Castile."

The inmates jeered at the comment.

Castile turned to stare at her, heart pounding. "No. He's not like me."

Reine cast a glare around the hallway, at the inmates watching with interest. She nudged the chest of a slim Indigo with brown skin and a hard face. "You make sure it's clear but keep low. Get the kid out. Anyone chases us to the pipes, fuckin clean house in this hallway. You got me?"

"Sure, Queen." The Indigo nodded and ran down the hallway, fleet and silent as a deer.

The sewer room was lit by a battery-powered light; Castile found it in the dark. Sewage stench rose up like ghosts in the basement room. They found a bare spot to lay Trinidad down, as far away from the open hole that led to the main line as they could find. All the Indigos pulled their scarves up and glanced around at the tangle of pipes. How many times had Castile found that light, dropped down into one of those tunnels with a shovel to dig out the bowels of the prison? No time to think of it now. He pulled at Trinidad's armor, shifting him to strip it off him, baring his wounds. More blood flowed. Trinidad's pulse was weak, his body cold—

Castile turned to Reine. "Give me his sword."

Reine looked down at the sword in her hand like she'd forgotten it. She handed it over, awkwardly. The leather wrap on the hilt was damp with sweat. Dried blood crusted the blade.

"Now. Hit me."

"You fool—"

She wasn't going to do it. He could see it in her face. She'd soft-ened toward him. "It's his only chance. Knock me the fuck out, right fucking now. Do the right thing, for once in your miserable—"

Reine crashed her fist into Castile's head just as he reached for Trinidad. All the colors of the world shattered into silver. Castile leapt to his feet, sinking into the sand, feeling the warm, dead air on his skin, and spun, staring around frantically, the sword a foreign weight in his hand. He screamed Trinidad's name into the silence, over and over. But for nothing. Trinidad wasn't here.

# FIFTY

**T**rinidad had one thing on his mind. He'd seen the bishop coming, seen her slash through Wolf's throat, knocking him down. He'd seen all the blood, so much blood, and he knew it was too late. He burst toward Marius with the last of his energy, the rove solid and sure.

He stood in the labyrinth in the churchyard, bathed in sunlight. A warm day, warm enough he instinctively wanted to take his shirt off, feel the sun on his skin. Cas always burned in the sun but Trinidad loved the feel of it, the prickling flush of color. He looked down to see if the sun had colored him brown yet, like his papa had always said.

His shirt was bloody with a growing crimson stain. He pulled the shirt off, found the deep gash right where two points of the silver pentacle met. He knew the sort of wound it was. He felt the edge with his fingers. More hot blood. He drew a deep breath, testing, and coughed. Tasted blood in his mouth. No pain though. It all came back to him. Roman. He thought of his armsmaster, the giant gouge he'd left in his neck. They'd been fighting, but he hadn't wanted to do it.

The memory got fuzzy after that—until Castile kissed him. Then the world, and pain, had swept over him, stealing his breath. He shuddered, wishing for Cas now. But that was just a dream. Castile couldn't come inparish. They'd tried that once and look how it had turned out.

The churchyard was quiet. He wanted to sit down. He was sleepy and warm in the sun.

"Trinidad."

Trinidad turned, hating the voice but unable to fight obeying it.

Bishop Marius sat on the low stone wall around the laby-rinth, bent crookedly. Blood stained her robes under her arm and dripped from the hem.

"Your Grace," he said cautiously, nodding his head to her.

Her eyes widened as they lit on his scar. She gestured faintly with her sword, which she then laid across her thighs with a gri-mace. "Polite to the death, eh? Sit."

Trinidad's knees buckled. He sank down to the stones of the labyrinth. A voice deep inside, buried there by training, protested: *Up, archwarden. You go down now, you're staying down.* Something Roman had always said.

"I didn't want to kill him." He loved him as a brother, as a sol-dier, as a friend.

"I know."

He bowed his head. It was quiet here. He could stretch out on the sun-warmed stones and sleep for days. How long had it been since he'd really slept?

"I would have taken you in, you know," Marius said. She ran her finger along the sword blade that lay across her lap. The edge was stained with blood. "Groomed you. You were the best fighter in the order. You could have been its leader, taken Paul's place."

He shook his head. "You're lying."

"Not about this."

He tried again. "I only meant to protect Father Troy."

"And you failed."

The truth tightened its noose around his heart. Father Troy was gone. He hadn't been able to protect him.

"You're going to stop the crusade?" he asked.

She shrugged. "Look at me. Am I in any condition to wage war? No doubt they'll condemn me and martyr you and it will all fall apart." She sighed. "It could end Church rule, you know."

Trinidad thought of the Barren, wished he had the strength left to rove himself there. He'd like to feel the warm sand on his feet again, just once, and listen to the tiny bells and the silence. "Perhaps." Was that a bad thing? He didn't have the energy to think it through.

"I suppose you think your Wiccan friends are the ones who should rule."

Trinidad shook his head slowly. *None of us should. Or all of us.* He wasn't certain which. "I don't think Castile would say that."

Castile . . . the noose cinched tighter. He looked down. Blood flowed in a red river through the silver valleys Reine had scored in his skin. He closed his eyes and only pried them open at Marius' voice.

"And yet you wear their mark," she said. "It's blasphemy."

He'd been born a witch, had felt Herne's breath just before the blast that had killed his parents. It had made him step further away, had spared him injury from shrapnel. He felt a similar thing now, to be honest, a warning caressing his skin. He knew in his heart the Lord and Lady had never forsaken him.

And yet who was he to refute the Church who had taken him in, who had raised him and loved him as their own? He owed Christ his life. Christ had not forsaken him.

It was he who had forsaken all of them.

"Why do you hate the Wiccans so much?" he asked. "Why do you hate Castile?"

She tried to stand but stumbled to the ground, landing on her hands and knees. Her sword clattered against the stone pavers in the silence. She grappled for it with a clumsy, futile gesture, knuckles white. She must feel as sluggish as he did. Only hatred and fury were keeping her here, alive and talking. He looked around at the edges of the labyrinth, tried to stare past it at the walls of the church, sought his parents' tombstone, but found only fuzzy edges and a mere suggestion of the necropolis. His blood dripped onto the stones of the labyrinth, filled the edges of the name on the brick beneath him.

"Israel," he whispered.

But it was in the wrong place. She recalled Israel's brick in the wrong place, in the middle of the labyrinth rather than to the side. Her dreamscape, not his.

He settled onto his side and laid his cheek on his arm, but his mind lit on the thing he'd been avoiding. "You killed him. Israel."

"Yes. You and I have that much in common." She sounded very far away.

*I don't understand.* The edges of the dreamscape darkened to deep, black shadows, oblivion closing in. He squinted at Marius, saw her form waver. The air around her looked steamy, like heat rising off a tar roof on a summer day. He was going to die here and no one would ever know the truth of it. He couldn't summon the energy to care. There was peace in the confusion.

"Christ has abandoned you, just as He abandoned me," she said. "The blasphemy on your chest proves it."

No. It had been Reine d'Esprit, because he killed her father, who had threatened Troy and, he knew now, destroyed Israel. He worked to keep his eyes open, watching the flow of his blood stain the pavers.

"And what does the Barren prove, you bitch?"

Trinidad twisted his head. The motion almost cost him his consciousness. "Cas—"

It was barely a whisper, but Castile heard him. He knelt by Trinidad and laid his hand on his arm. He gripped Trinidad's sword in his other hand. Silver grains clung to the blade where there had been bloodstains. He watched them gleam in the dull dreamscape.

"You were supposed to come with me," Castile said. "Not here."

Trinidad saw a blur of movement and Marius was there, on her knees by Castile, raising her sword. He wondered vaguely how she could do it, how she could move so fast when she was dying.

But maybe she wasn't dying. He tried to cry out, to warn Castile as her bloody sword lifted behind him. Castile bent low over him, trying to catch his gaze. All Trinidad could do was look past him at Marius. She had all the power to kill him here, in her dreamscape, to make him die alongside them. He wanted to warn Castile, to tell him all these things, but sleep was dragging him down. He opened his mouth, shoved out a sound vaguely like *Marius*.

Castile lowered his brows at Trinidad, the bishop's sword behind him in a sure, steady descent. He blinked, then spun on his heels and swung Trinidad's sword, awkward, low. It cut through Marius like a match through a flame. She distorted, her mouth opened too long and wide in a silent scream, and the whole world winked out. Trinidad felt himself slipping, sliding from consciousness. Castile screamed. Trinidad clung to his voice, but it faded until he wasn't sure if it was echo or memory. The abyss dragged him down. He felt a flash of pain, like a knife twisting near his heart, and then nothing.

# FIFTY-ONE

A hot poker seared Trinidad deep in his lung. He couldn't
breathe. When he opened his mouth, he tasted the dry
metallic flavor of the silver sand. He coughed out a mouthful and
thrashed against it, seeking escape. His lungs screamed to breathe.
The searing didn't let up, only got worse.

A spray of sand caught him across the back, stinging his bruised
skin. The chiming sand penetrated the pain and made him look
up, shove up on one arm. Castile had Trinidad's sword raised over
his head, clumsily. The bishop, her robes bloody but moving as if
she were healed, swung. Castile stumbled back, fell over Trinidad.
They collapsed in a tangle as the bishop advanced.

Trinidad grabbed for his sword hilt, pried it from Castile's fingers. He shoved the witch away and rolled, wincing in pain as the
bishop's blade split the sand between them.

Flat on his back, Trinidad clenched his abdominal muscles and
half-flipped to his feet. Agony clutched at his chest and the silver
world tarnished almost to black. He swung, wildly, to one side.

Castile screamed: "No! Me! I'm the one you want!"

Marius turned her head toward Castile. Trinidad's blade hit her with the wet, certain thud of blade parting flesh. She screamed horribly.

Under the scream, Castile cried out, "No! I'm the one who killed him. I should die, not you."

Trinidad fell to his knees, pain blasting anew through his chest. The silver sand reached up to seize him.

A rms encircled Trinidad. He felt the warm beat of a heart under his cheek. "Cas." His mouth was dry, his voice scratchy.

"Easy. You lost a lot of blood. You weren't ready to do all that."

He sighed and unraveled himself from Castile's arms, moving slow, gingerly. No real pain. The pentacle still glowed in his chest, but his new wound was gone.

"Her blade went right through the silver." The witch's voice was rough, choked. "I guess you're fine."

Trinidad frowned. That didn't seem right. He'd felt death snag him, he'd been . . . dead.

"Don't look so disappointed," Castile said.

"What's wrong? You sound sick."

Castile rubbed the back of his neck under his tangle of hair. "Nothing. Nothing. Marius is dead. You're alive. The crusade is over, I think. You did good, yeah?"

Trinidad looked around, avoiding Castile's eyes. He saw a lump on the sand nearby and tipped his head at Castile.

There were tear tracks in the grime on Castile's cheeks. "I just grabbed you and roved the fuck out. I wasn't quick enough. She got hold of me."

Trinidad pushed to his feet and walked over to look at her.

Marius sprawled against the sand, still clutching her sword. Her cheeks were gaunt, hollowed. She looked smaller, lying there on the sand amid the tombs and gravestones. It was hard to think of her as the person who'd started a whole war.

"She meant to kill you," Trinidad said softly. "I tried to warn you but I couldn't talk."

"You did warn me."

"I could barely roll my eyes."

"You did what you could do. This time, it was enough."

Trinidad nodded and looked away. He wished he hadn't gotten up so fast. He liked sitting in the quiet. He wasn't sure how to ask Castile to hold him again, or if he even should. So, he kept looking down at Marius' body.

"Their baby was only nine months old," Castile whispered.

*We've all done something*, Trinidad thought. *We've all murdered.* "You were what? Fifteen, sixteen?"

"I should be dead or sitting in Windigo's cell. I don't deserve any better."

Trinidad eased himself to his knees and gripped Castile by the shoulders. "I knew, I mean, I'd heard you were an ecoterr. Father Troy told me you died." He swallowed. More lies. "Every time I went to the prison, I used to thank Christ you weren't in there."

Castile shied away and bolted from him.

He was quick, but in a flat-out race, Trinidad had the advantage of longer legs. Still, it took some doing, trailing Castile as he weaved between tombs and battered statues, deep sand dragging at every step. At last Trinidad caught his arm. They hit the sand hard, a confusion of limbs and knees, silver chiming beneath their bodies as they tumbled into the statue of a leafless tree. Castile fought him, but Trinidad threw his weight on top and trapped him between the statue and his body.

Trinidad held Castile. His fight finally deteriorated into sobs, the sound scoring Trinidad to the soul. Castile slowly relaxed and Trinidad eased his grip. After a long while, they separated by mutual, silent agreement. They sat up and brushed the sand from themselves, not meeting each other's eyes.

"Don't blame Father Troy." Castile snuffled and rubbed his red nose with the back of his hand, swiped at his eyes.

Trinidad nodded.

Castile scooped up a handful of sand and let it fall. "Are you all right?"

"I miss Wolf." Trinidad couldn't say the rest, not with the agonizing cocktail of hatred and regret and sadness roiling in his gut. He suffocated it. The Indigos had stolen Israel from him and Marius had stolen Wolf, but there would be plenty of chance to mourn him. For real. But not this day.

"I'm sorry, Trin. You don't know how sorry."

Trinidad had to wait on his voice to answer. "I'm glad he didn't see me like this, after all I've done."

"Like your parents couldn't stand the thought of you seeing them after? Is that why you think they killed themselves?"

"They were cowards." The words spat forth like someone had slapped them from him. "And worse, they left me trapped inparish, away from everything I ever knew. Away from you."

Castile reached out and took his hand, rubbed his thumb along Trinidad's callused palm, and let his hand go. "I don't think they tried to trap you, Trin. I think they tried to set you free."

# FIFTY-TWO

Trinidad cut off the conversation, claiming the need to go on back and resolve things at the prison. "The situation needs to be secured."

Castile could almost smell the grief on him while they were in the Barren, acidic and raw. But when he woke up, back cold and stiff against the filthy pipe room floor, Trin sat up next to him and stretched like it was all just a day in the life of an archwarden. His dark eyes were veiled again, face carved into his perpetual frown. He rose and put his armor back on while the others watched him move without a trace of pain or injury.

"Back from the dead, huh." Reine d'Esprit stopped pacing around them like she was casting a Circle and offered them water.

For his part, Castile felt like he'd downed a jug of her home-still liquor and gone five rounds with a brick wall. His bones felt splintery inside his skin. He gulped at the water.

"Something like that," he said, pushing to his feet with a wince. "How are things here?"

"Enough noise, but none came." Reine jerked her chin toward the door where her men stood listening, rifles in hand.

"I need to go out and see to Marius' body," Trinidad said.

"Trin," Castile said. "Let someone else—"

"I have to claim her body to claim her power."

Castile blinked. "And just when I worried you'd put aside your last vestiges of heartless bastardy."

The Indigos exchanged nervous glances. But Trinidad just bent down to retrieve his sword, spent a moment scrubbing it against his armored thigh before putting it away. Silver grains chimed against the concrete. Then he stripped off his gauntlet, turned to Reine, and stuck out his hand.

She stared at his hand, marked with the sword of his order. His face was streaked with sweat-caked dirt, dulling the tattoo on his forehead. Blood had dried in a sickening stream down his side.

"We're enemies," she said. "Killed each other's people."

"Yeah." He kept his hand out.

"We're not going to be friends, even in savvy."

"But we don't have to make a point of killing each other."

Castile couldn't help but grin at that, a little.

"Fuckin isn't gonna fix anythin," she agreed, gripping Trinidad's hand.

The corner of his mouth quirked, breaking through his steely facade. Two prison guards stood at the entrance to Castile's old hallway. They glowered at Castile with recognition.

"Is there a problem?" Trinidad asked, icily polite.

Castile watched them weigh the odds, taking in the archwarden's bloodied armor, his hand on his sword hilt, his strong stance. The Indigos hung back, gripping their weapons.

"No, sir. Just securing the quad. There was a murder here earlier—"

"Where is the bishop's body? And the others?"

"Taken to the church."

"Thank you. Christ keep you in peace," Trinidad said, nodding to them. They mumbled some reply. He turned and continued down the hallway, heading back toward the field. Evening tinged the square of sky visible through the open doorway.

Castile's feet slowed at Windigo's cell. The body was gone, the door hung open. He took a step inside and stared down at all the blood, at the dirty mattress he'd called a bed for so many years.

"It's over now," Trinidad said. "Come. We need to see the warden."

Castile could count on one hand the number of times he'd seen the prison warden during his incarceration. He was a smallish man with whiskery ears and stubby fingers. He met them in the field and led the way to his office. He stared guardedly at Castile, maybe trying to place his face, but was all too happy to provide transportation to the church and rid himself of the people who had disrupted his little empire. He reddened as Trinidad politely blessed him before climbing into the back of the prison dray. The Indigos climbed in after, giving them wide berth, eyes darting as the warden shut them into the dray. No lock secured them in, though; Castile was listening.

Still, he didn't relax until the prison gates closed behind them. Then he bent over, hiding his expression by fixing his boot, cursing his sour stomach and stiff muscles.

"What's wrong?" Trinidad said.

"The last couple of times I went to the church I walked out at gunpoint."

"But you did get out," Trinidad said.

"You're enjoying this, aren't you?" Castile said.

They dipped into a pothole and the Indigos shifted uncomfortably. Trinidad shook his head, sat back, and fixed his gaze in the middle distance. "No. It's not over yet."

T he tall archwarden who had helped carry Trinidad in the prison was pale as one of the Indigo's Ancestral ghosts. "I ought to arrest you," he said to Trinidad. "But frankly I'm too glad you made it."

Trinidad looked past him. Several draped bodies lay at the front of the sanctuary. A bank of small candles burned nearby. A woman knelt in front of the big wooden table at the front of the church, hands clasped, head bowed.

Trinidad strode down the center aisle toward the bodies. Before he reached them, he took a knee, drew his sword, kissed the blade and laid it on the floor. Then he climbed the four steps to where the bodies lay. The Indigos hung back, staring around with wide eyes. Of course, they'd probably never seen a church before.

The pale archwarden frowned deeply and started to follow. Castile caught his arm. "Don't take it personally. There's no reasoning with him. Let me."

Castile paused behind Trinidad as he knelt by one and pulled back the shroud. Israel's burned face had relaxed in death. Someone had cleaned away the blood and wound cloth around his throat to hide the gash that had taken his life.

"He shouldn't be here," Castile said. "Laying next to the person who murdered him."

"We all end up together in the sand, anyway."

Castile nodded. He dug in his pocket and came up with a collection of mismatched coins, held out two to Trinidad.

"They're Christian, Castile. They don't believe in the ferryman. You don't either, by the way."

Castile pressed the coins into Trinidad's gauntleted hand. He knelt and gently laid coins on the indentations that marked the bishop's shrouded eyes. "I'm not sure belief really matters anymore," he said, moving to a body wrapped in an archwarden's cloak, the crusader's cross glaring red against the black wool. "Or it might mean everything. Either way, I'm not taking any chances."

Castile laid coins on the cold, still face, and another, until they all had their fare. By the time he finished, Trinidad had laid the coins on Israel's eyes. He replaced the sheeting gently, laid his hand on his brother's chest, and bowed his head. But when he lifted it, no tears stained his face.

# FIFTY-THREE

Trinidad stood quietly, his arms crossed over his chest. He wanted Seth. Father Troy. Anyone else to take charge. But they kept coming in and asking him questions as if he had answers.

Castile paced in the chilly house the bishop had claimed as headquarters. The air was frosty, impossible to keep warm with people stepping in and out for the past few hours. "What now?"

Trinidad sighed. "I didn't know when that captain from Denver asked me and I didn't know a few minutes ago when Seth asked me."

"I thought you were buying time to think."

He gave Castile a look. "I'm an archwarden. I take orders, not give them."

Another knock. Trinidad sighed and strode to the door. Reine. He backed a step to admit her.

"They want to see you," she said. Beyond he could hear the rumble of voices.

"I just wanted people to stop killing each other." Trinidad looked from one to the other. "What am I supposed to tell them?"

Reine narrowed her eyes and rubbed her cut up fingers across her lips. "Papa Roi was a bastard, but he knew how to draw a short line between him and what he wanted. That's what you need to do. Take the short path."

Trinidad thought for a moment and came up empty. But then, maybe thinking wasn't the answer. He hadn't spent much time thinking in the past few days and somehow they'd persevered and ended up on the other side. His stomach clenched. If he'd thought things through better, would Israel be alive? Would Father Troy?

He pushed past Reine and walked outside.

Seth stood in the shelter of a tent with the bishop's archwardens, the two left who hadn't died in the skirmish at Folsom, and several army captains. Seth nodded to him. The archwardens and the army captains stared.

"I don't know what to say."

"Just tell them it's over." Seth said, and instructed the army captains to speak to their troops. The captains dispersed and the archwardens followed Trinidad as he climbed the rough steps up the wall.

The sugary scent of Alteration and acrid wood smoke rode the air. The boots of the army churned the snow to icy mud. The rumble of voices slowed and faltered when he appeared, stumbling to a slow skid of coughs and wet shuffling. Trinidad thought the army, Denver Parish in particular, would not simply disband on his command, not after weeks of Marius' rallying, recruiting, and organizing. They'd been promised war against the heathens, and they still craved blood. He was glad they'd sent the spirit tribes' army back to the Indigo freehold. A fight might have broken out.

"You shouldn't be here," he told Castile lowly.

"I go where you go, yeah?" Castile forced a smile, teeth chattering from the cold wind. "But for fuck's sake, be careful."

Trinidad bowed his head. He wondered if they thought he was praying. Maybe he was in a way, hoping God would give him words. He certainly didn't know where else they would come from.

He lifted his head. Many of them were easing closer to the wall, trying to get a better look at him.

He swallowed, cleared his throat, his cheeks flushed and hot, his belly churning.

"When Bishop Marius came to Boulder Parish and preached crusade, I wanted to believe in angels. I wanted to believe in the Church. But I knew her claims were lies." He paused and scanned the crowd. Chatter filtered up from the ranks and died. He realized their captains and commanders were walking among them, quieting them.

"I should have spoken then. I should have trusted God to see it right. I did not and people died for it."

Trinidad hesitated, and then started to undo his armor. Castile moved to help him, pulled the plates from his back and chest, collected his cloak and bracers and weapons until Trinidad stood only in his shirt and trousers. Cold swept through the wool. His stomach knotted. But they had to see it. They had to know the truth.

"When I was young, my parents killed Christians and Indigos. If you asked them, they'd say the Earth is sick and people are her disease. But killing is no answer."

He stripped off his shirt and stood in the cold, waited for the gasps and shouts to die down.

"Reine d'Esprit carved this pentacle in my chest. Not an angel. Reine d'Esprit, here next to me. She sought revenge because I killed her father. He threatened my priest, and I thought I had the right to kill him for it. My parents thought they had the right to kill Christians for harming the Earth. Bishop Marius thought she had the right to crusade against those who don't believe in Christ. Like I thought I had the right to kill her for crusading and lying." His voice sharpened. "But none of us have the right and none of it amounts to any kind of faith I've ever heard of."

The crowd shifted below him, still quiet but for a few coughs. Even those who had to be too far off to hear him kept still and quiet. Too quiet, as if a whirlwind of fury was about to rise up from the ground.

"I can't tell you what to do. I have killed. I have sinned. I have turned my back on gods and Christ, and people have died for it. I certainly can't tell you where to find faith." He swallowed, his throat tight. "Maybe you'll find it at home. Maybe you should try there first."

Seconds crawled by. Trinidad stared out at them and they stared back, boots in the snow and mud, gripping their makeshift weapons and wearing only the crimson crosses on their shoulders for armor.

He pulled his shirt on and turned away. The crowd erupted and surged forward with a rush of thousands of voices, of rallying cries, of pleading and questions and cheers and anger. Trinidad didn't look back as he climbed down off the wall, making his way quickly down the ladder.

Castile hurried after him, still loaded with the armor and cloak. "You're just walking away?"

Trinidad shook his head wearily and kept walking, his long strides forcing Castile into a trot to keep up. "I don't have any answers for them."

"But—"

"What do I tell them? Do we start roving people to the Barren? How long until war starts up again, once they learn what the sand can do? Or should I lie to them? Like Marius? Like you? Like ..." He cut himself off with a sharp breath and kept walking.

Castile trotted after Trinidad, quiet now. They passed through the city gates under the stares of the marshals. Trinidad climbed into the prison dray that had taken them first to the church and then the command house. He didn't to know where to put his hands. Hard trembles coursed through him. He clenched his fists to try to hide it.

"Trin. It's all right."

"It's not," Trinidad said. "It's not enough."

Castile dumped the armor and cloak in a heap on the floor. The words came out with a knife's edge. "It has to be. It will be."

Trinidad shook his head and eased down onto the metal bench inside the dray.

Castile sank to one knee in front of Trinidad. His hair was tangled, his face smudged. They both reeked of blood and sweat. He reached up to wipe the dirt away from Trinidad's tattoo with his thumb, let his fingers trail over his temple and cheek. Trinidad shuddered under Castile's touch. He had to struggle not to pull away.

Crowd noises grew outside, but Castile kept his voice soft. "You stopped the war. It's enough for today at least, yeah?"

Trinidad swallowed, hard. From one angle, Castile was right. From another, the world needed more amends than one man could make.

Castile steadied himself with his hands on Trinidad's knees, leaned in, and kissed him.

The world roared around them, a harsh mix of voices, hard and argumentative, low and tired, jubilant. Trinidad tasted salty tears, sweat and dirt and blood. His hands came up to curl around the back of Castile's neck, locking them together, mouths hungry, teeth bumping, beards scraping. The dray rattled to life. Trinidad yielded to the primal comfort of desire.

At last they parted, gasping. Trinidad's heart pounded in his throat. His lips stung from Castile's unshaven face.

Castile slid away and heaved himself onto the bench next Trinidad. A noisy swell of humanity surrounded the dray. It bumped along slowly.

"What now?" he asked.

"A nap. A long one," Trinidad said.

Castile chuckled.

They had family and friends and enemies to bury. "And I was thinking your chimney needed work. The smoke didn't draw correctly last I was there."

Castile leaned forward, forearms on thighs, and turned his head to look at him. "You're a witch again? Just like that?"

The cave was quiet. The Barren was quieter. "No. I'm not just a witch."

Castile gave a slow nod. He didn't answer for so long Trinidad wondered if he'd refuse or argue. But Trinidad couldn't see another way. Reine was right. The shortest path was best, and the road ran straightest between the parish and the coven.

At last the dray stopped in front of the church gate. Trinidad started to pull his armor on and then stopped, left it on the muddy floor. He needed a break from its constraint.

Castile studied the floor as if answers were scuffed into the dirt there. "Your new priest will need your help keeping the peace, yeah?"

Trinidad eased a breath. "Your help, too, Cas."

He offered Castile his hand and the witch let him pull him to his feet.